SKALLAGRIM

IN THE VALES OF PAGARNA

BOOK ONE

STEPHEN R. BABB

Skallagrim – In the Vales Of Pagarna
© 2022 by Stephen R. Babb

www.stephenrbabb.com
www.soundresources.net
www.glasshammer.com
Facebook: fb.me/stephenrbabb
Twitter: @GlassHammerProg
Youtube: www.youtube.com/user/ghprog
Instagram: @stevebabb_glasshammer

Published by:
Hidden Crown Press
Sound Resources Publishing

ISBN: 9798755141307 (paperback)
ISBN: 9798761052024 (hardcover)
First Printing

Cover Art by: Waking Of Sky Tree
© Cover design: Franziska Stern - www.coverdungeon.com -
Instagram: @coverdungeonrabbit
Map Illustration by: Sayan Mukherjee
Skallagrim Illustration by: Luke Eidenschink
Typesetting by Crystal Peake Type

SKALLAGRIM

IN THE VALES OF PAGARNA

For Glass Hammer fans. Thank you for years of support!

"Why must there be evil men
Strike them down, they come again
Think they're dead but then my friend
That's the way of this world
This wicked world must surely pass away

But that's the world wherein I found
A sea where sorrows could be drowned
There I heard the distant sound
Of trumpets blown in the morning
Carried on a breeze from unknown shores"

The Watchmen On The Walls (excerpt) – Stephen R. Babb

CHAPTER ONE

Two things happened nearly at once, both of them bad. First was the horrifying sensation of watching a cruelly curved knife plunging toward his left eye. He managed to jerk his head back in time to save the orb, but the thrust became a slash, and the knife made sickening contact with his cheek. No pain yet, though he knew he had been cut as warm blood cascaded down his face. Second, the lightning strike of a well-aimed cudgel as it smashed into the base of his skull. Instant pain this time, perhaps made worse, for when dodging the dagger, he had thrown his head back into the oncoming cudgel.

Stunned, Skallagrim staggered, then crumpled to his knees, involuntarily dropping his short sword. His frantic hands swept sweat-drenched brown locks from his face, then searched the wound below his eye. Just as he realized the curious, blood-slick flap dangling from his face was, in fact, the shredded remains of his left cheek, he swooned and crashed to the ground, nearly landing on his own blade.

Before that, everything had been a blur, frightful images of an angry mob crowding a cold, damp, torchlit courtyard formed by the convergence of two alleys. There was an extraordinary, otherworldly light carried by a man in dark robes to a waiting wagon. Then there was no light at all, just a girl, heartbreakingly beautiful, held captive while Skallagrim watched helplessly, too busy fighting for his life to save her. Her eyes had darted pleadingly toward him as she was forced into the back of the wagon, but he could not do anything.

Then there was the face—the glaring, mocking, arrogant visage, contrasting with the tragic beauty of the girl over which it leered.

A man, yes, but with the faintest hint of red flames flickering in his eyes. Not the reflected glow of torchlight, more like an inner heat suggesting a demonic, sinister intelligence lurking within.

A conjuror, surely, he thought.

Skallagrim had no idea how he knew, but every instinct warned him of the malevolent spirit inhabiting the man with the arrogant face. The flame-flecked eyes, the menacing demeanor, even the flamboyant robes that billowed and writhed in the chilling gusts that snaked down the alleys—all were signs alerting Skallagrim's reeling mind to the presence of the supernatural, the sorcerous, and likely, the insane. This was a man to be feared, a man who inspired hatred.

The ringing in his ears and the merciless pounding in his head slowly forced Skallagrim back to consciousness. He tried to rise, but the attempt was feeble and hindered by a sudden wave of nausea that swept over him. He tasted thick, salty blood on his tongue. Then came the pain, as if a red-hot poker had lanced his face.

A stench, a foul effluvium, assaulted his senses—the blended aromas of alleyway refuse and stale alcohol. Greasy smoke rose from pit fires wherein meats of questionable origin were spitted and smoked for the clamoring throngs that packed nearby gambling establishments and taverns. It was overwhelming, overpowering his senses. He heaved as if to vomit but could not, the effort causing his head to erupt with fresh agony.

He collapsed for the second time. Rolling onto his back, he looked up to see the squalid edifices of Archon looming overhead. Archon! How had he come to this decadent, corrupt city, the most dangerous in all of Andorath? Archon! A pitiless agglomeration wherein abominable statues and monoliths rose to challenge dreaded towers of sorcery. Archon!

He lay there bleeding in that nightmare city of degenerates where depraved masses worshiped deranged gods in cathedrals dedicated to madness. With its leering sculptures, broken spires, haunted tombs, and decrepit mansions, this was the city where hope came to die, a disordered, overcrowded dreamscape reveling in its own ruin. A city of the damned.

Yet there lay Skallagrim, his head pulsing with pain and his heart weighted with despair. His vision was going in and out of focus, but he swept his gaze past the horrid slums and the menacing towers that teetered alarmingly over the alley to the night sky directly overhead. A single star shone down through an unlikely gap in the racing clouds, which boiled ominous and black, for a storm was brewing.

As if to confirm this impression, lightning arced across the sky, followed by a thunderclap that resounded through the city's maze of streets and alleys. It had the effect of scattering the mob of which Skallagrim was still dimly aware. For a moment the alley grew quiet, though he could hear a commotion coming from the direction of the wagon. The girl's whimpering and her struggle with her captor were unceasing.

It had been a mistake to come to the city, and for the life of him, Skallagrim could not recall his reason for being there, let alone for bringing the girl along. There were no dreams there for him, only a living nightmare. Yet the same was true for all who came.

Gamblers, thieves, and smugglers all plied their trade in Archon, or the Dreaming City, as it was oft called by those who had the good sense to avoid it. The city stole dreams, or thus was the prevailing belief among many. It was the price of entry, they said.

"The city dreams," the saying went, "but go there, and you will not."

Yet fools came with their dreams anyway, seeking fortunes amidst Archon's haunted palaces and towers. Fools came, and fools died.

Thieves were drawn there like moths to a flame, their visions of treasure-filled tombs soon exchanged for the reality of sudden death in rat-infested pits or deep holes down which no light had ever shone, the depths of which the wise dared not calculate.

None of this mattered to Skallagrim, who felt himself just one in a long line of fools who had come to no good end in that cursed place. His head pounded from front to back, and he wished the yelling, screeching, and yammering of the retreating mob would cease. Yet on and on it went unmercifully.

I've got to get up!

That thought cut through the throbbing pain in his head and the burning sting from the slice to his face. He had to get up, and quickly. They were taking the girl, and led by the red-eyed fiend, they would surely finish him off before they fled.

The girl! The girl! His lover, his lady! She was the most important, most precious part of his life, yet he could not remember her name. The pounding in his head, the ringing in the ears, it was all confusion and overwhelming panic.

Some things he could recall, though only with great effort. "Thief," they had called him. So that was it! He had come like so many others to rob the tombs of Archon and had stumbled onto something. However, like the girl's name, he could not pin down precisely what it was.

Something old, something terrible—a thing buried and undreamt of—unless by minds twisted and broken from sorcery. What was it? Ah, too horrid to fathom. Too appalling to have been real. The world could not birth such a thing—would reject it if it did. It should be cast into oblivion where it might die if such a thing was even alive to begin with.

For a torturous second, his mind's eye glimpsed the abomination again, though, mercifully, the thought fled him fast like the clouds that raced overhead, where the hopeful star hung, fixed and shining, the storm swirling around it like some mad, feral dancer in a lunatic ballet.

The girl, his life, these were his immediate concerns. He could not save her if he continued to lie bleeding in the gutter. Skallagrim had to get up, to reclaim his sword, to kill his assailants.

Kill them?

The thought caused his heart to pound as a wave of panic swept over him. The blade had only been for protection. He had never imagined he would use it to take another's life. Killing was not a skill he could claim. Skallagrim was no slayer of men, not yet. Of course, that was about to change, as reluctantly, he took up the sword.

The vociferous mob was returning as he struggled to his knees, then rose to his full height. Wobbly, yes. Head swimming, yes. But the nausea had passed, and the panic was ebbing, replaced by a searing anger as he took stock of himself.

His buckskin pants were ripped at the knee and smeared with dark blood. His black tunic was torn, soaked with the effluent foulness of the street. Despite his predicament, this last infuriated him to no end. The tunic was new and wonderfully embroidered. He groaned at the ridiculousness of this futile, petty frustration, then shook his head to clear it. Random thoughts flew at him like noisy crows from the thick fog of his confused mind.

Taking a step backward, he nearly tripped over his travel-stained cloak. But he steadied himself with his free hand while sweeping his matted, blood-soaked hair out of his eyes with the other.

The noisome throng was crowding the alley, and any approach to the wagon and its captive was impossible without cutting his way through flesh first. Strange. They were all dressed in the same faded red houppelandes, their long sleeves and high collars worn and tattered. Daggers hung from each belt, though from all appearances, most of the blades were merely ceremonial. However, six of the mob carried spears and were making some effort to guard the wagon against the rest.

There were others of a different sort present though, and Skallagrim's eye quickly took in the situation. There were five men, all of them brutes, much larger than Skallagrim, and all dressed as soldiers or fighters. Sellswords perhaps, as they did not wear the uniforms of Archon's Watch or the City Guard. They might be a personal bodyguard for the robed and leering villain in the wagon whose attention had just turned Skallagrim's way.

Three of the five—short thrusting swords in hand—were also scrutinizing him from a few yards away. The other two were much closer and turning to face him as well. One, a greasy-haired man with slits for eyes, carried a cruel-looking cudgel. The other was clutching a wicked knife—the same wicked knife that had just ruined Skallagrim's face. It had the unpleasant look of a surgical blade rather than a weapon, but dripping with Skallagrim's blood as it was, such distinctions were unnecessary. Its wielder was dressed better than the rest, with a sheathed saber hanging at his side and a wolfish look to his face and lean body.

Smiling wickedly, he pointed the bloody blade at Skallagrim. "Look there, Olog!" he shouted over the noise of the mob. "You need to give that one another knock on the head. He doesn't seem to know when to stay down."

"Look at 'is face, boss!" the greasy-haired man jeered as he thumped his cudgel against his thigh. "You carved him up pretty good."

The man with the wicked knife laughed. "I was going for the eye! But I like the effect." His voice sounded like the growl of a feral dog guarding a rotten carcass. He eyed Skallagrim with a predatory gaze. "Something he can remember me by. Now hit him again."

"You can hit 'im if you want," the greasy-haired fighter with the cudgel retorted. "And you can slice the other side of his pretty face too while you're at it. But the boss said to cut off that sword arm."

"Well, that'd be blade work!" one of the other swordsmen bellowed, all of them creeping toward Skallagrim. "Get 'im on the ground, and let me do the hacking."

"There will be no hacking!" the wolfish-looking man with the dagger said. "It's to be precision work for the arm." He fingered his curved knife, turning it in his hand. "Best to tie him up and take him with us. Just beat him senseless or cut him till he gives up or goes down. I'll take care of the arm later."

Skallagrim was appalled and humiliated, for they spoke of him as if he were nothing more than a beast to be slaughtered or a slab of meat to be carved for dinner. Worse, these sadists found the situation humorous.

There was nowhere to run, and he dared not make off without trying to get to the girl. Hopeless as the situation was, he gripped his sword, ready to strike at whoever attacked first.

Sensing his misery, the wolfish man laughed. "The boss would prefer we take you alive. But as I understand his instructions, it's not entirely necessary."

Skallagrim, though untried in battle, held his weapon at the ready. He loathed the idea of having to use it to stab, hack, or cut one of these men, but he feared the touch of their blades even more. He was trembling, and his face was flushed. *I've got no chance!* His sense of awareness was heightened, as sharp as a dagger.

Skallagrim, his eyes wide as saucers, sought out the face of the girl and saw anew her beauty. A crushing sense of sadness was his reward.

He could recall very little, but their love had been as warm as sunshine in summer. Now the bitterness of winter flowed between them, an acknowledgment of hopelessness and loss, as if the spirit of death stood betwixt them, ripping one from the other with fierceness and finality. He tried to say with his eyes, *If I'm to die, I wish you could be the last thing I see.* Then he tore his gaze from hers and faced the approaching men. *This is how it ends!*

CHAPTER TWO

Skallagrim's mind raced for some way to postpone the inevitable. "Why does your boss want my sword arm?" he shouted above the clamor. It was a ridiculous question, and he was a fool to let them see his lip quivering as he asked it. The last thing he needed was to look weak or fearful, but it was more pain than fright working against him now, making his body tremble.

"I've peeled off half your face, you know," the wolfish man taunted, gloating over the savage cut. His voice was smug, with the refined inflections of a cultured gentleman, but the sound of it was deep—too deep—and his piercing eyes radiated the cruelty of a mindless beast that toyed with frightened prey. "What harm will it do to take an arm? You're a freak now. A monster, if I may speak honestly. Ugly as a ghoul, isn't he boys?"

The other men laughed cruelly. Skallagrim searched the wound on his face with his free hand, which only caused him more pain. Spitting blood onto the filthy street, he eyed his abuser with fear.

"Well, I'll tell you this, freak," the wolfish one continued, apparently the leader of this group. "Something is about to happen, something big, and you need to be less one arm before it does. But bloody hell," he said, shrugging, "what do I know of the affairs of sorcerers?" He looked over his shoulder toward the wagon and the cloaked, red-eyed man, then back at Skallagrim. "You have gotten the attention of Forneus Druogorim, my friend, and if he says to take your sword arm, then trust me, take it I shall."

He motioned to one of the swordsmen, who closed with Skallagrim and lunged, aiming his thrust not at Skallagrim's arms but his abdomen.

Skallagrim dodged aside, but the broadsword came at him again. "I'll gut him first, then you take the arm!" the swordsmen bellowed.

"Easy, ladies!" the leader shouted. "There's more coin in taking him alive." But the swordsman on Skallagrim ignored him, making yet another jab at the thief that, if successful, would be fatal.

"Balor's Bones!" The leader was cursing now, angry for having had to hire the dregs of Archon's thugs and hoodlums. This affair was sure to be botched.

Skallagrim parried the second thrust, sweeping the blade aside with his sword. His squeamishness over the use of a sword was forgotten in the moment, swept away like dead leaves in a winter gust.

In desperation, he swung his blade with all his might toward his assailant's helmeted head. The blow landed flat on the helmet, sending a shock up Skallagrim's arm. By chance the blade slid downward to slice his foe's unprotected ear. Rattled and wincing from the blow yet more angry than injured, the swordsman stepped backward, then, astonishingly, tried the same thrusting attack a third time. Skallagrim was ready this time and in position to sweep right with his blade. He managed to parry the thrust and make a ghastly cut to the attacker's sword hand that sent his blade flying. It hit Olog squarely in the face, blade end first. Ignoring the curses of both men, Skallagrim thrust hard into his foe's abdomen and was surprised at the resistance of the leather armor he wore. Throwing the weight of his entire body behind the thrust did the trick though, and the blade sank in. His attacker howled then, surprised by the sudden turn of events.

However, the fight had not gone out of him yet, and he threw several punches at Skallagrim's face with his uninjured left hand, desperate blows raining down on his face. To his dismay, Skallagrim found that his blade would not come free of the man's stomach. Then he remembered something about twisting a sword to remove it from such a wound. So, twist he did, all the while taking brutal hits to his head. With another hard turn of the blade in the opposite direction, the punching ceased. Mortally wounded, the assailant screamed and doubled over in pain, making it all the harder for Skallagrim to withdraw his sword. Still tugging and twisting for all he was worth, Skallagrim finally kicked the man, driving him backward into Olog.

At last the blade came free, and his attacker fell to the ground. Skallagrim stared at the writhing body in its death throes, sickened by the violence. He had not asked for this spilling of blood, this savagery. But these lowlifes, regardless of their leader's orders, were out to murder him. He was determined to return like for like if he must, no matter the cost to his psyche. It was that or die.

Blood was streaming from his face. Fearing the bitter finality of his impending death, his resolve grew. He would resist the thrusting blades and the painful cudgel, and he would kill them all.

Letting out a stream of curses, Olog dropped his cudgel to clutch his wounded face. But things were not going Skallagrim's way just yet. He still had two large swordsmen to deal with, Wolf Face and one other, and saw several more fighters heading his way from the wagon carrying wicked-looking spears and round shields. Wolf Face switched hands with the knife, drew his saber with the other, and made to close with Skallagrim.

Skallagrim had but a split second to decide—run or fight? He hesitated, his thoughts bent upon the terrified girl. He could not abandon her. Running was simply not an option. The two swordsmen shoved Olog aside and were on Skallagrim in an instant, giving him no time to ponder alternatives.

The wolfish leader came in low and swung the flat of his sword at Skallagrim's side. Skallagrim jerked his body away just in time, and the saber, rather than bruising a rib, hit his leather belt instead, blunting the blow. There was no time to launch a riposte as the next swordsman stepped in and, with the flat of his sword, landed a hit directly on Skallagrim's unprotected head. He saw stars, crashed to his knees, then gasped as a blade sank into his left arm. Searing, jagged pain!

For a moment he could see nothing. But he could hear Wolf Face laughing at him. He forced himself to stand, swinging his sword wildly in self-defense. The desperate response made him feel ashamed and convinced him he was about to die a terrible death, deprived of dignity. But then his blade knocked another away.

He swung again, and this time he connected with flesh. His vision cleared in time to see a swordsman backing away, clutching his neck. Blood spurted through the man's fingers as he crumpled to the ground, dying in choking horror.

The leader was unhurt, but had taken a step back. He truly had the look of a wolf: long black hair with streaks of grey, the hungry smile of a killer, and cunning eyes that bore into Skallagrim's own. He took his time, sizing Skallagrim up, planning his next attack.

Skallagrim lunged, thrusting his sword toward the man's stomach, then at the last second lifted his blade just enough to jab at the man's unprotected throat. His attack was easily parried, and the wolfish one laughed again while retreating another step. He was in no hurry, reserving his strength while calculating whether to strike or to let others do the work. Meanwhile, the spearmen were forcing their way through the mob, closing the gap. They would be in the fight in minutes.

The situation seemed hopeless. Skallagrim was bleeding from his face and arm, bruised and scraped from falling to the ground, his head was swimming from several hard blows, and try as he might, he could not catch his breath. With little fight left in him, he stood as tall as he could and looked once more at the girl in the wagon.

What is your name? Why can't I remember?

She looked back at him beseechingly as tears streamed down her face. Then her eyes darted to the cloaked villain who stood over her, glaring. His red-tinged eyes burned with madness as he watched Skallagrim.

"Why is he still standing?" the sorcerer shouted. "Kill him!" His tone was full of confidence yet ghastly, sepulchral—a trumpet of doom more than a voice. He tilted his head back to observe the growing storm swirling above Archon. "Straker! We will find another sacrifice. Just kill him! Take his arm! Get it off him at once!" The funereal voice was different now, tinged with a hint of fear.

Straker. Ah, the wolfish man had a name, and Skallagrim would not forget it.

Straker winced at his master's remonstrance but stood aside to allow the spearmen to do their work. He had orders from another master, one far more powerful than Forneus Druogorim. And *that* master required a different outcome altogether.

Hell's teeth. Why did I agree to such a thing? He had to delay the slaying of the thief somehow, without Forneus catching on. But how? Skallagrim's short sword would be no match for six-foot-long spears. *Damn them both! Damn all sorcerers!*

His instincts bid him stand back and let the spearmen kill the thief. Then he would gladly cut the arm away and the head too for good measure. But no, he had to drag this out. Straker's eyes darted to the sky, then back to Skallagrim. *How long now?*

The spearmen were nearly through the crowd, only a few yards distant and closing. Skallagrim despaired as he watched events unfold, knowing death was but a few agonizing moments away.

"Help me," Skallagrim said, though to whom he spoke, even he did not know.

Fear was boiling inside him, and he cringed away from it—from the death of those lying at his feet and the death that was coming for him.

"Help me!" This time louder, this time a genuine plea, spoken to someone. He could not remember who it was, only that there was someone once, someone powerful, someone who was holding him to a promise, someone who had judged him and cast a great doom upon him yet loved him still. No name, just the knowledge of something or someone, both terrible and glorious. "I'm crying out to you!" he shouted. "Help me, or I'll die here and now!"

All at once, lightning flashed, and a thunderclap boomed in a deafening explosion. The spearmen, now only feet from Skallagrim, stopped in their tracks. Straker leaped back from Skallagrim, nearly tripping over his own feet. The crowd ducked, but as the sound of thunder died away, volleys of slashing rain came blowing sideways with a fierce wind, and many began to flee the alley. Those who remained rose slowly and turned to stare in awe at Skallagrim. No one moved, all eyes on him.

Whether it was the lightning's flash or some effect on his mind from the blows to his head, Skallagrim could not tell, but something was different. Though the wind caught at his hair, the rain swirled past him. There was light all around Skallagrim, only him, but he was so filled with dread that he failed to perceive what others around him were sensing. A tremendous fear settled in over them all as they stood mesmerized, soaked, and shivering. It was as if a great and terrible judgment was about to be pronounced from above. No one's face showed it more than that of the arrogant, evil Forneus Druogorim, who slowly tore his gaze from Skallagrim to stare fearfully at the sky above, shielding his eyes as he did.

A shadow of foreboding had hung over doom-haunted Archon since early that morning. The sun had risen a sickly red that cast only a dismal half-light over the city. Folk had looked around them, whispering to one another of sky demons and black magic foolishly taken to profane extremes. "Something is coming," they surmised. "They've roused some doom. Damned necromancers will be the death of us all!" At this they would glance anxiously at Archon's most ancient spire wherein dwelt the sorcerer Griog'xa. "He would know what sort of calamity this is," some posited. But no one in living memory had lain eyes on the fabled Griog'xa in person, and all thought it best to keep well away from his tower. Its shadow stretched long over the city, too long for its apparent size and never quite in sync with the sun. Furthermore, it seemed to be the epicenter of curious rumblings that shook the old buildings of Archon now and then, and odd lights flashed and flickered from its topmost rooms on the darkest of nights. Men feared it and its master, and thus, merely shaking their heads, they went their way, cursing the evil day that had befallen them.

Shops closed early, and even the taverns saw little trade as evening approached. The old ones just shook their heads. No one had listened to them when, a month earlier, the strange, pulsing star appeared over the city. They had complained of "the creeping dread" even then.

Cold Star, some named it. Black Star, others said. But all agreed that nothing good would come of it. Very bright it was, even in the day. Yet sometimes it radiated a blackness that even the most learned astrologers could not explain, and folk huddled close as unnaturally frigid winds sprang up and blasted through Archon's haunted streets.

Cold Star. Black Star.

The eldest of them all kept his opinions close, only hinting that it was something other than a star hanging over their city. "My father's father saw it happen during the War of the Great Rebellion when the forces of Andorath invaded the south." At this the young folk scoffed. No one believed him, and no one believed in the great war he frequently reminded them of. "There's no south," they mocked. "Nothing but a wall of mist."

The elder would shake his fists. "It's all true, I say. That is no star—black, cold, or otherwise. You'll see soon enough." The youngsters hurled their insults, and the old man lurched away, keeping further baleful tidings to himself.

But now a storm raged around the star, and a sudden squall sprang up, bitter as the winds from the North of North, whence few men traveled and even fewer returned. Lighting flashed again and again as thunderclaps boomed. Between flashes, everything was dark, except for the sanguine, solitary beam of light from above that lit up Skallagrim. Thief Skallagrim. Dying Skallagrim. Hopeless and doomed Skallagrim. His eyes followed that of the sorcerer as he regarded the night sky, peering into the raging storm and beyond to see a sight most astonishing—and terrifying.

The star was growing, pulsing white light and then hellish black.

Skallagrim wrenched his gaze back from the storm-wracked sky as he heard the ghoulish voice of Forneus Druogorim rise to challenge the throbbing light.

"Terminus Rex!" he shouted. "Bugog ch'nak'yarnak kadishtu Terminus Rex vulglagin!" He flung his hands at the sky, and for but a moment, the growing light seemed to diminish. However, whatever blasphemy he had uttered, whatever spell he had intoned, it was all for naught. Lighting lanced from the light itself this time, striking so close to the red-eyed Forneus that he was nearly thrown from the wagon. The horses strained at their traces, threatening to bolt.

Still, the mysterious starlight grew.

No, it was not growing; it was falling, its one beam remaining piercingly bright and centered exactly on Skallagrim. Then he heard it. They all heard it. The star was screaming.

It plunged, and its scream rent the night. The mob fell to the ground clutching their ears and hiding their faces. The storm howled, but the star screamed all the louder. None who heard it and lived would ever forget it; such was the awfulness of that horrific shriek.

It fell quickly, past the storm clouds, and then hurtled downward in a wailing, flame-flickering fury. It was clear to all now that it was no star.

It passed the topmost turret of the haunted Spire of Griog'xa, screaming like all the banshees of Craghide Mountain had been loosed. Only when it was level with the crumbling tower that crouched over the alley where Skallagrim stood gaping did its calamitous descent begin to slow.

The screaming ceased, as did the storm. As the plunge of the curious light slowed in a path that brought it directly over Skallagrim, the chilling winds retreated, and the once threatening clouds dissipated, leaving only the stygian night sky with but a few dim stars and a bloated moon.

Everything grew still.

Skallagrim stood watching, his head craning backward, his mouth ajar. The light continued to descend, slowing as it neared the beleaguered thief.

As wary as a wolf, Straker watched too as he silently placed more distance between himself and Skallagrim. The spearmen, now close to the thief, were back on their feet but made no threatening move as they and the mob around them watched the light and waited. The girl in the wagon and vile Forneus were watching too. He seemed frozen in awe, or perhaps fear, though he lost none of the malevolent threat that his stare radiated.

The brilliance of the object began to fade, though not completely. It came to a final stop just above Skallagrim and just within his reach. To everyone who looked on, it became glaringly apparent exactly what this thing was.

A sword. A killer's sword. Hilt down, blade shining, and baneful edge glittering. A blade both beautiful and dreadful to behold.

Skallagrim could never adequately explain his next move, though few ever dared ask him to. Whether he was driven by the desperation of the doomed or compelled by the curiosity and opportunistic nature of a simple thief, he dropped his bloody short sword and, reaching up, grabbed the hilt of the alien blade.

Then all hell broke loose.

CHAPTER THREE

The horses reared and screamed in terror. Fell Forneus bounded into the driver's seat. "Into the fray, you cowards!" he cried out in his ghastly voice. "Destroy him! Kill him!" A second later, he was whipping the horses into a frenzy, sending the cart bolting down the alley, presumably with its bound captive still in the back.

Everything was bedlam. Skallagrim still faced what remained of his original foes and the approaching spearmen, but now the raucous throng was rushing back toward him as well, daggers out and full of fury.

Unexplainably, Skallagrim's fear melted away, the pain of his wounds going with it. A madness came over him as he gripped the sword's hilt in his fist. He held pure, unconquerable will in his hands, dazzling white-hot steel, blinding glory, but there was no time to stop and take note of this sharp-edged gift from on high.

Skallagrim saw with different eyes. The impossible became possible, even though the spearmen were once again moving toward him. A battle song was screaming in his head, a keening sound that sang of glory and of slaying and death. He held the sword like a veteran fighter as he grasped the hilt with both hands and let the blade rest upon his right shoulder. The first spearman stepped in, having the advantage of reach on Skallagrim with his six-foot weapon, and held his shield high to ward off a longsword's blow should it come.

Skallagrim sidestepped the spear thrust. With a downward stroke, he cleaved the wooden shield, sending splinters flying. The momentum swept the deadly blade through his opponent's shoulder and half the length of his torso. A quick twist of Skallagrim's wrists, and the dead man fell free of his sword.

The second spearmen had no time to consider the severity of the strike upon his cohort. He jabbed his weapon toward Skallagrim's right side. Skallagrim dodged left, then swung his sword in a downward arc toward the spearman's unprotected neck, nearly severing the man's head from his shoulders. His lifeless corpse, head lolling unnaturally to one side, took two staggering steps backward, then fell with a crash in front of the remaining spearmen. These two hesitated, seeing the bloody devastation that had been wrought upon their fellows. Skallagrim, however, did not hesitate.

He went in low this time, getting beyond the spear point of the closest spearman. With a sweep of his blade, he took a leg from the unfortunate man, who fell with an agonizing scream. This left only one spearman who lifted his weapon high to strike Skallagrim, then thought better of it and turned and ran back toward the encroaching mob. Crazed, cult-like sycophants of the malefic Forneus Druogorim, they surged over the remaining yards toward Skallagrim like a frothing tide, their faces wild with bloodlust.

The lupine-faced Straker stood his distance, smiling sardonically at Skallagrim's blood-spattered face whilst testing the edge of his saber with a cautionary finger. This was not going to play out the way he wanted. He had been promised a straightforward job, but there was nothing straightforward about this so-called thief who had grabbed a screaming sword from the sky. He felt betrayed, caught in a battle of wits between two rival sorcerers, for Straker served two masters—Forneus Druogorim and the mysterious Griog'xa. He little understood the motives of either, but he feared them both.

Of course, the evening's mayhem and slaughter, even the bungled abduction, all were likely factored into the plans of the smarter of the pair. *Take him alive. No. Kill him instead. Kidnap the thief. No. Just take his arm.* This nonsensical grab bag of contradictory instructions came from Forneus Druogorim. Griog'xa had stated the job clearly: *Drag out the encounter with the thief until the star falls.* He could obey both easily enough, but sorcerers be damned! He would finish this dangerous, wearisome job, but he was having strong doubts it could be done tonight.

Straker refocused on Skallagrim. "Freak!" he shouted over the clamor. "Monster! When they're done with you, I'll still be coming for that arm!" Sneering, he stepped aside to make room for the rushing throng.

Olog staggered to his feet, cudgel still in hand. Like Straker, he leapt out of the way as the crowd closed with the lone thief.

Skallagrim held his sword at the ready. Out of the darkness, a spear was thrown at him. He swept it aside with his light-pulsing blade. Another was flung, but he ducked as the spear scythed overhead, thudding into the wall behind him.

Leaping over the bodies of the fallen, two babbling, dagger-wielding fiends were the first to reach striking distance. Skallagrim whirled his sword, meeting little resistance as it sliced through both of them at once. Another cultist, this one a real brute, dove in next and took a brutal sword thrust to his groin when he slipped in the blood of his predecessors. Others approached, slower now due to the growing pile of bodies in front of their unyielding target.

Still, too many foes!

He knew he would shortly be overwhelmed as the mob pressed upon the fighters at the fore, threatening to trample them while they strove to close with the sword-wielding focus of their wrath.

Skallagrim held his sword in front of him, ready to slice either way. The uproar was maddening, and he was growing tired again and suddenly so very thirsty. With the last of his newfound strength ebbing, he retreated a few steps to place his back against the rain-slick wall of one of Archon's shabbier gambling houses.

What's this?

His right foot had bumped into something oddly yielding. A man was sitting bound and gagged at his feet, completely unnoticed until just then. Dressed in the finery of a wealthy merchant, the man glanced up at Skallagrim, his eyes wide and oddly pale. He shrugged as if to say, *What now?*

Something was off about the man. But Skallagrim, bewildered sufficiently by all that was happening around him, had little time to consider this latest piece in the puzzle. The girl was gone, the love of his life lost, and the jackals, brandishing a variety of weapons, were closing on him. His mind raced. *What have I done to these people? This makes no sense.*

The sword pulsed with light as it had in its plunge from the sky above Archon. A scream rent the night, a terrifying wail as from some enraged, cornered beast from forgotten antiquity. This stopped the surging horde dead in their tracks, some even turning back into the press while covering their ears to block out the pernicious shriek. It was the sword, screaming again as it had during its descent. Skallagrim watched as dozens of his assailants stampeded back the way they had come, their attack now a route in all directions. Those who remained were cowering, seemingly frozen with fear. Even Straker was dismayed by the shrill screech of the sword and backed farther away from Skallagrim.

Olog was still standing, his legs shaking but his cudgel held firmly in his grasp. With a grunt, he made to throw the short club at Skallagrim but was dramatically and fatally interrupted. Another object had come screeching down from the sky, stopping with an abrupt, unwholesome squelching sound about two inches inside of his head. The missile came loose from his skull when he slammed to the ground, dead. It bounced away with a clatter, coming to rest at Skallagrim's feet.

The scattering mob veered left to escape down a narrow alley as a new threat emerged from the broader alley to their right. Soldiers were coming, members of Archon's Watch. Black robes, red-plumed helmets, dull-grey breastplates, and wickedly curved scimitars marked them as such.

A full company of the Watch swarmed the crossroads, using the flats of their blades to beat at the crowd, herding them toward the center, while a half-company marched down the narrow alley, closing off the escape route. An officer rode amongst them on a huge destrier, shouting orders and marshaling his sergeants to greater exertions. Concentrating on the mob, they had yet to notice Skallagrim, Straker, or the bound man at Skallagrim's feet. The latter began struggling with his bonds while a stream of muffled words, clearly pleas for assistance, poured out of his gagged mouth.

Skallagrim, his face bloody and in tatters and his mysterious blade pulsing an alien light, shifted his gaze back toward Straker, who stood glaring just yards away, poised to run. He smiled grimly. "You're not sticking around for this?"

The question was rhetorical, and Skallagrim put it forward only as a parting shot. He would distance himself from this alley and the sudden military threat as fast as he could. But where to run? The full weight of the situation was settling in on him. The pain was returning, and with it came the confusion brought on by the trauma to his head. He knew his face was a wreck, and he was growing weaker by the minute. *If I live at all, I'll be a monster,* he told himself. But he stood strong, his shoulders slumped only slightly from exhaustion, his chest heaving from the worst brawl of his life.

For a moment Straker thought he might be staring at a demon, so fearful did Skallagrim appear amidst the carnage of the alley. He suppressed a shiver, then shook his head in disgust. He should have remained in his home country of Yod, far to the north, and finished his business there. *Revenge and conquest!* Well, that would have to wait. As he had predicted, this entire affair was botched. Still, there were contingencies in place and assurances that wherever Forneus Druogorim went, the thief would follow. Straker might fail to take down the demon with the screaming sword tonight, but he would have another chance on a dark stretch of road in the near future. Unless, of course, he received a new set of nonsensical orders, which he considered likely.

"No, I'll not be staying," he said, smirking as he backed away. "But I'm certain to see your hideous face again. A few nights hence and we'll have another go, you and I. You'll see."

With that, Straker turned and loped away, vanishing amidst the eerie shadows that loomed over Archon's latest back-alley battlefield.

Skallagrim edged farther into the shadows, hoping to avoid the soldier's attention. The bound man at his feet was still trying to get his attention, to no avail, for all was chaos in the alley as the Archon Watch struggled with the screaming, protesting horde.

A thousand thoughts chased one another through Skallagrim's weary mind.

The girl is gone. That knowledge and the brief glimpse he had of her hauntingly beautiful face caused a sudden jolt of heartache, piercing, and all consuming.

I brought her here. Then came guilt.

I have killed these men. A sharp pain came with the admission— unfamiliar, alien. Only minutes before he had been a lowly thief. Now he was a killer as well. A premonition of doom, as dark as a sepulcher, stole over his heart as if he were sinking into grey, oozing mud, the stench of which he would never wash away.

The sword. He stared down at it as blood and gore dripped from its nearly three-foot blade. For a second he caught his reflection in its metal and recoiled from what he saw. *I'm a monster. She'll never love me again.* The realization came as a sickening gut punch. Whatever had been before could never be again.

Damnation! A ruinous destiny had befallen him. Why him? Why now? Skallagrim had called for help, and help had come, yet somehow he knew he was inexorably tied to the freakish sword, its monstrous nature further proof of his own.

He knew something about the thing he held in his hands because it was vibrating and humming with unnatural life. *Revenge, immortal hate, rage at the world, rage against the dark—an insatiable thirst for the blood of the wicked.* Alien thoughts were pouring into his mind from the sword. He tried feebly to drop it, to shake loose of it, but it was as if the thing were melded to him.

So be it.

CHAPTER FOUR

That brief battle of wills left him completely exhausted. He glanced back at the alley in time to see one of the soldiers look his way, then run toward the commander, shouting and pointing at Skallagrim.

"Phew!" This from the richly dressed prisoner at Skallagrim's feet as he rid himself of his gag. He appeared to be a man of perhaps fifty years, though he could have been younger or older. His face seemed devoid of color and lacking eyebrows. His long icy-white hair was arranged in a top knot that spilled down his back. He wore a blue velvet frock coat with lace protruding from the sleeves, yellow doeskin pants, and a fine pair of riding boots. A bejeweled ring glistened on the index finger of his left hand.

"You want to help me untie this?" he beseeched Skallagrim, holding up his rope-bound arms. His request had the entitled tone of the wealthy addressing the lower class, like one of the aristos who held court at the more extravagant parlors near the city's decadent center. *Probably a cutthroat merchant, grown rich on the backs of smugglers,* Skallagrim thought, *or maybe just an honest man in need of help?* It mattered little at the moment. He seemed an unlikely ally, but Skallagrim, good-natured at his core, saw no reason to withhold his assistance.

He knelt with a grunt to undo the loose bindings, the effort making him dizzy. Then they both went at the ropes that hobbled the man's ankles.

"Help me up!" the man demanded, then frowned. "Actually, never mind. You look a sight worse than me." He got to his feet, then pointed at a cellar door that jutted into the alley. "In there. Quick now, or we will be swept away with the rest of this rabble!"

"But I've done nothing wrong!" Skallagrim protested as he

glanced over his shoulder at the chaos in the alley. "Why not just tell the soldiers I was attacked by the sorcerer and his men? Hell, he just kidnapped a girl! He has to be stopped!"

Skallagrim rose and turned his back on the man, torn as to what to do.

"I don't know about the girl, but come with me, or they'll have you in irons. You'll be tossed in a dungeon to rot!" There was a hint of panic in his otherwise haughty voice. "If you wish to help this girl, you need to trust me!"

The commander of the Watch was looking their way but was clearly distracted by the mayhem that swirled around him. Any moment he might decide to investigate Skallagrim's role in the night's madness. Skallagrim turned back to his would-be companion, who waited wild-eyed and ready to flee. With nothing else to go on, he opted to gamble on the man and make his getaway.

"Alright, lead on."

"Wait!" the man called, then gestured nervously at the object lying on the ground that had recently come free of Olog's skull. "You'll want that. I'll lay good odds that it and your sword are a matched set, what?"

At their feet lay an extraordinary red-leather scabbard, intricately etched with arcane symbols, some quite wondrous and others weirdly ominous. Finely worked silver adorned both ends at the throat and the chape, the latter of which was smeared with blood.

The man made no move to retrieve the scabbard himself; he even seemed fearful of it, so Skallagrim reached for it, wincing at the pain the motion caused him. Blood dripped from his face and spattered on the paving stones, but he shook off the queasiness it inspired.

"There you go. Now follow me!" With that the man hastened to the cellar doors. Flinging them open, he disappeared into the gloom. He had every earmark of a wealthy man, but there was something off about him, an uneasy wariness that betrayed itself in every word he said and every move he made. But considering the circumstances, Skallagrim supposed this was to be expected. Reluctantly, he followed him inside, stopping only to pull the wooden doors shut behind him. Hopefully, the soldier had not seen them make their exit.

"We need to put some distance between ourselves and Rum Alley." The peculiar man was struggling with match and tinder, and with a bit of effort, had a lantern lit in a few seconds. Setting it on the floor, he went straight to a pile of rags in one corner and searched through them until he found one that met with his approval. Rising, he looked at Skallagrim's face and grunted, unable to hide his concern.

"My face is ruined. True?" The words came hard, and Skallagrim could taste blood.

"I have seen worse, though the man was dead." He held the rag up to Skallagrim's face. "This is not clean by any stretch of the imagination, but it will have to do for now." Saying this, he bid Skallagrim hold still while he tied the rag around his head to hold his wounded left cheek in place. "It's not bleeding so badly, but we have a hike ahead of us, and we cannot have you losing half of your face along the way." He produced a half-full vial of glowing blue liquid and, opening it, held it to Skallagrim's mouth. "Don't ask; just drink."

Too dazed to protest, Skallagrim did as he was told and was immediately refreshed, his mind clearer and his pain reduced. Strength flowed back into his limbs, enough at least to remain standing upright.

Though the light from the lantern was dim, Skallagrim made out a few scattered crates and discarded remnants of broken lumber lying about. Against one wall was the remains of an ancient bookcase. Setting the lantern down, the man approached the bookcase, put his shoulder to one side of it, and pushed it sideways along the wall to reveal the entrance to a tunnel.

"Through here! I can get you some help." He grabbed the lantern and motioned Skallagrim forward.

Skallagrim followed, sword in one hand and scabbard in the other. The weapon was no longer pulsing with strange light, and even the vibrating hum had subsided. Now it seemed like an ordinary, if not exceptionally light, splendidly made longsword.

With the bookcase back in place behind them, the pair made their way down a rickety staircase, then turned right and proceeded down one gloomy corridor after another. The lantern bobbing in the man's hand as he went forward cast unwholesome shadows on the damp brick walls. Vermin scattered beneath their feet, though some merely continued gnawing at whatever morsel they had dragged into the passageways.

"Smugglers use these tunnels under the city," the man whispered over his shoulder. "Convenient for us and confusing for any who might follow."

So, perhaps the man was a smuggler. But there was a nervousness about him that forced Skallagrim to wonder about the nature of his business. The relief at having been aided in his narrow escape was greatly diminished for no tangible reason he could produce. Yet, the longer he followed the man, the warier he became. It must have been the way the man muttered nervously to himself as he sloshed along the flooded passages, leading them first down one tight corridor, then another. There were random turns at odd angles, iron doors that led to corridors full of more iron doors, and rooms where the gaping darkness was so old and complete that the lantern sputtered, its light nearly extinguished.

On the whole, the odd fellow remained quiet, though, at times he would make a seemingly normal comment or salient observation about some peculiar feature of the subterranean maze he seemed to know so well. Mostly, this was directed over his shoulder at Skallagrim, though at other times it was as if the man was addressing some unseen companion. At every turn he would whisper to himself in a language that Skallagrim could not identify. In one particularly dark, tomblike chamber, his eyes darted to and fro as if something were amiss. He seemed to calm after an awkward moment, then laughed to himself for no apparent reason.

He glanced at Skallagrim with something akin to suspicion, then shrugged and motioned the thief into the next passage. "Never mind me," he called back. "It's the job that keeps me on edge. You understand, right?"

Skallagrim did not understand. Still, he stumbled and staggered on as best as he could, fearing to lose sight of the lantern. He did his utmost to remain conscious, all the while pondering his peculiar companion.

There was something curious about those pale eyes, as if they saw simultaneously in this world and another. Could the man be commandeering an escape from the recent alley fight while also engaging in some hidden, titanic struggle of which Skallagrim was unaware? Something supernatural, perhaps? What sort of dealings or enterprise would weigh so heavily upon a man as to cause his very comportment to suggest otherworldliness?

Still, there was something else about him, even beyond his pallid face. When Skallagrim had seen him in the light, though not a tall man, he seemed very fit for his age. In addition to the stamina implied in his physique, his aquiline nose, and his intelligent eyes, there was something formidable about him that gave the impression of a barely repressed vigor. Despite his oddities, this was a man to be reckoned with.

After a time, Skallagrim gave up worrying about it. The man was an enigma, a contradiction, just plain peculiar.

"Where are you taking me?" Skallagrim asked, his voice echoing in the gloom. They had traversed the catacomb for the better part of an hour, and it was high time he asked the obvious question.

"Shhh! Talk quietly if you must. There are more than rats hiding in this labyrinth. But if you must know, there's a hidden room beneath a tavern at the edge of the city, near the walls. There's a passage not much farther up that will take us directly to it."

Skallagrim was so exhausted he could barely keep up the pace. The blue potion was keeping him going, but his many wounds still pained him, and he needed water badly. But on they went, coming at last to a set of stone steps that led up to a stout wooden door.

The man rapped on it, paused, then knocked again.

They heard shuffling on the other side and then the door cracked open, spilling yellow light into the corridor.

"It's me and one other," the man whispered. "He's the one I told you about—Skallagrim. Now let us in, then go fetch Old Tuva. My friend here is in a bit of a state, what?"

The door opened wide, and they were ushered in by a colossal ogre of a man, wearing soldier's gear, a broadsword hanging from his belt. The room was a little larger than the original cellar they had entered but richly appointed with a table, chairs, shelves, a desk, and a small bed in one corner. A brick fireplace smoldered on the far wall, and light flowed from lanterns ensconced on each of the four stone walls. On the table sat a neat stack of leather-bound books. A pen and quill sat upon the desk along with a mess of papers.

"Skallagrim, meet Hartbert. Hartbert, meet Skallagrim."

Hartbert gave a grunt of acknowledgement as he bolted the door behind them, then made his way to another door near the fireplace.

"Oh, and Hartbert, have them send down some refreshments from upstairs. A jug of wine and whatever they can scrape up from the kitchen would be appreciated."

"Food and wine, no problem. But I'll not go down *there* to fetch Old Tuva," Hartbert grunted. "I'll send Gam. He's too dense to recognize the danger." With that, the giant left, leaving the two men alone.

The room appeared to be a normal basement fitted out as a study or office, a room of deep, musty shadows that no mere lamp or hearth could dissipate. Tapestries adorned two of the walls, one with scenes depicting ships in what might have been Archon's harbor. The other was more of a panorama, detailing a battle of odd goblin-shaped combatants. In the center of these scenarios, taking up most of the tapestry, was a picture of the Spire of Griog'xa towering over a smoldering city.

Skallagrim laid the sword and scabbard upon the table, careful not to disturb the books, then reached up to touch the improvised bandage on his face. A sharp, jagged pain was his reward.

"You have me at a disadvantage, sir," Skallagrim remarked.

"Whatever do you mean?"

Skallagrim eyed the tapestries again, fixating on the panorama with the sorcerous theme, then cast a weary look at his host. "You know my name, but I don't know yours. Who are you?"

The man frowned in disbelief, then bowed with a flourish. "Why, I'm none other than Griog'xa," he proclaimed as he stood upright. "Griog'xa the cunning though much-maligned Sorcerer of Archon."

Skallagrim eyed him suspiciously, saying nothing.

"You know, the evil chap in the haunted tower who 'no living man hath seen'? I think that's how the saying goes. I saw you admiring my tapestry there."

Skallagrim's face remained quizzical.

"Wait just a minute, you really have no idea who I am, do you?"

"You mock me, sir," Skallagrim replied. "I've never seen you before. If you are this conjuror, as you say, I want nothing to do with you."

"Well, it was merely a joke, of course. What's the matter with you?"

Skallagrim leaned heavily on the table, steadying himself. It was that or fall over, for the room was tilting this way and that. "I thank you for your help. If I might have just a drink of water, I'll be on my way. Though, of course, I have no idea where you've led me."

"Skallagrim, it's me. Your friend, Erling."

Skallagrim shook his head again and shrugged.

"Erling Hizzard? I was only joking about Griog'xa, you know." The man chuckled. "Imagine me, a sorcerer of his caliber. Though 'Hizzard the Wizard' has a nice ring to it, what?"

Erling smiled at his own jest, then, tilting his head, gave Skallagrim an inquiring look. "You really did take a hit to the head. Sit down or lie down if you will on the bed yonder. Old Tuva will come and patch you up. She's not gentle, nor is she easy on the eyes, if you take my meaning, but she's damn good with a needle, and her potions are of the highest quality. Just the thing you need."

Still dizzy, Skallagrim obeyed Erling and sat on the cot, though a little harder than he intended. The movement caused his head to throb and his world to go spinning again.

"She lives down deep in this maze of tunnels that run beneath the city. Only a few know where to find her, and even fewer dare to go there. But in a pinch, she's the best surgeon we're likely to find tonight." Erling leaned close to Skallagrim. "So, you're telling me that you truly don't recognize me? True enough, in my trade, I have been known by other names, but to you I am and remain Erling Hizzard. Either way, my face is the same. You don't remember me?"

"No. Though much of tonight is strange to me. I remember very little of anything at all," Skallagrim admitted.

"You know your name though, right?"

"Indeed. If my memory of it holds true."

"Oh, it does, my friend. You are Skallagrim, of that there is no doubt. Skallagrim Quickhands, to be exact, though the last bit's just a nickname. What else?"

"I'm unsure," Skallagrim replied, shaking his head. The movement brought fresh pain that pounded his skull like a hammer, and the nausea threatened to return. Cold sweat began to bead upon his forehead, and he feebly swiped it away. "Why should I tell you? I mean, no offense intended. I untied you, and you helped me escape. Beyond that I truly don't know why I should trust you."

"Well," Erling said, "I didn't see anyone else offering to help you. We're in the same boat, so to speak. But I would not have been in Rum Alley at all were it not for you."

"Why so?"

"Skallagrim, we're friends. We have a history of, well, dealings, shall we say?" Erling grabbed one of the chairs from the table and seated himself next to the thief. "You wrote to me a month ago. Told me I should meet you there. Said you had something important to show me. Whether that was an artifact like you have brought to me in the past or just information, I don't know. The letter was vague."

"Okay, I don't remember that. But I suppose I'll have to take your word on it for now. Did I mention the girl? Do you know who she is or why that sorcerer and his men attacked me?"

"As a matter of fact, your letter did mention a girl. As to Forneus Druogorim, I have connections, people I can ask. Whatever else you do, you will need to rest the night here. I'll send out some feelers, see what I can find out."

"I have to find her, you know," Skallagrim fretted. "It's my fault she was caught up in this. You saw her trussed up in the sorcerer's wagon, right?"

"Skallagrim, I was bound myself and on the ground. I could just discern Forneus over the heads of that mob of his. I'm sorry, but I saw no girl."

"And I'm sorry I got you involved in this with my letter. But she was there, and now he has her. Do what you can to find out why and where he might have taken her."

Erling nodded. "You know her name?"

"I remember her face, but her name eludes me, and I don't know why." Skallagrim locked eyes with Erling. "She was so scared. Whatever happens to her, it's my fault. I have to find her. Do you understand? I have to find the girl."

Sometime later, Hartbert returned with an old woman who had a decidedly hag-like countenance. Skallagrim shivered when he saw her, for as the door opened, and she was revealed in the uncertain light, a chill crept into the basement room. It was an unnatural coolness that spoke of an outré darkness, of the loneliness of wraith-haunted crypts crumbling in the frigid night of winters long past.

Due to his ogre-like size, Hartbert would normally inspire fear in some men and hesitation in even the most stalwart, but he seemed suddenly of no consequence in the proximity of the hag. He merely carried a tray of food, a jug of wine, and two glasses.

The old woman, however, just by her mere presence commanded the room's attention, and this while bent over with the weight of two satchels, one hanging from each shoulder. She was dressed in filthy rags that were adorned with scraps of fur. Her hair was white and oily grey, hanging mostly in thin, wispy strands. The rest was matted and wound in such a way that it seemed to writhe about her head in a most unappealing manner. A sinister-looking necklace of talismans and jagged, metal charms hung loosely about her neck. Otherwise, she was unornamented.

On the table the sword and scabbard began to vibrate and radiate a dim light of warning that Skallagrim felt more than he saw. The hag went wide around the table to avoid the blade, scowling at it as she passed.

As she crossed the room, almost gliding, an unwholesome fume, not unlike burnt hair, filled the chilly space, assailing Skallagrim's nostrils. When she laid eyes on him, she smiled wickedly and quickened her pace. "Old Tuva is a coming fer ye again!" she shrieked with terrifying glee.

Almost in a flash, she was upon him. Her long, spidery fingers probed and tugged at the bloody rag tied about his face. Her breath was foetid, and her face was a twitching horror of scabs, squamous growths, and ulcerating cankers. Skallagrim jerked his head back involuntarily and thrust out his hands to push her away. What met his fingers was not the expected coarseness of old rags but rather a yielding, undulating fleshiness that caused him to recoil, though not before one strand of mangy fur hanging from the crone's fleshy garments struck out and bit him on the hand, growling with a singular ferocity. This caused the old woman to cackle.

"Calm down, boys," she said, scolding the wriggling rags of her filthy raiment and the twitching bits of fur that gibbered and snarled, full of menace, at Skallagrim. "Don't you worry none 'bout dem and dey bad attitude," she croaked at Skallagrim, who sat frozen, mouth agape. "Dey just smells dat fresh blood on dem pretty hands of you."

She laughed again, blasting Skallagrim once more with her rancid breath. He stared into the cavern of her maw, saw her grotesque tongue writhing amid the jagged gravestones of her yellow fangs— saw and could not look away. Saw and new fresh terror. The fear of violent death that had assailed him, threatening to consume him only an hour before in the thick of the fight, was forgotten now, replaced by a preternatural horror, an unavoidable consequence of the nearness of evil.

Someone shoved a glass of wine into his hand.

"I have to leave this place," Skallagrim said, "find the girl. Do you understand? I need to get out of here now." If anyone answered him, he did not understand them. The sound of voices seemed slow and unreal. Nothing made sense in the swirling miasma that assailed his senses. His head was swimming, his heart was pounding, and his ears were ringing with pressure. He needed to get out of that room. He felt like its walls were closing in on him, and he wished for a window or any opening that might bring in fresh air from outside. But he was underground, though how far underground he did not know.

Panic set upon him like a ravenous wolf. He tried to rise, feeling the need to run, to be anywhere but in that tiny room with its three odd occupants. But he was far too weak to get up, and so he just sat there, gulping the foetid air.

"Drink up," a voice said, and he obeyed. "There you go." Everything was going dark. "Lie back now and let her work." Hands, not Old Tuva's, gently pushed him back onto the bed. Blackness was overtaking him, and he had no strength to fight it.

"The girl, the girl," he moaned over and over as waves of sickness and regret washed over him.

"Hold dat boy still," the hag said. The gentle hands gripped him firmly about the shoulders while two more held his legs. "I can't make dat face pretty like it was, but I'll make something workable out of it." More insane laughter as a new blast of cold air full of foulness and rot swept through the room. The chill of the tomb and the stink of open graves was all too much for Skallagrim, who finally surrendered to the darkness, letting his mind slip into that merciful realm where only dreams dared go.

But Skallagrim was in the Dreaming City, and all that he might have dreamed had already been stolen.

CHAPTER FIVE

One minute there was the hag, the fear, and the throbbing pain of his wounds. The next minute he was slipping into the blackness of a bottomless pit. It swallowed him up, and he was gone. A moment passed, maybe a thousand moments. Pain ebbed, and strange sounds swirled through his mind: voices, concerned voices. Someone spoke, and he heard their words as if through a tunnel. *His face will break more mirrors than hearts, I fear. Such a shame, for he's so young.* Then laughter, maniacal laughter. The clink of glasses and then a door slammed, and a lock clicked shut.

A sudden and unwelcome wakefulness slammed into him with the force of a war hammer to the head, yanking him from the darkness and flinging him back to the world of the living. It hurt, and it angered him, this sudden return to consciousness.

"What time is it?" he growled to no one in particular.

"Ah. There you are."

Propping himself up on one arm, Skallagrim saw Hartbert sitting at the far end of the table, a glass of wine in one hand and a smoldering pipe in the other. His sword and scabbard lay where he first set them, but between the two was a platter of food. The effort to rise set Skallagrim's head to spinning, but he fought through it, admitting he felt somewhat better than he had.

"It's eleven o'clock tomorrow morning, or at least it is to you. It's eleven o'clock today to me."

Skallagrim laid back down and probed the wound on his face, which had been stitched. It was tender and sore, causing him to wince.

Hartbert slid his chair back from the table and stood. "Mister Hizzard says you're to rest but that I'm to fetch him should you wake. And wake you have."

"Hartbert, there was a girl with me last night. She was taken prisoner. Did Erling mention her? Did he find out anything?"

"He has been out all night, he and his spies, trying to find out anything they can about what happened and why. I'm sure he will tell you all."

"Am I a prisoner here? I need to leave as soon as possible to find her, you see?"

"Nope, not a prisoner at all. But troops are scouring the streets for you. The city is buzzing about the events of last night, and the stranger with the screaming sword is being blamed for the lot." Hartbert sipped his wine, drops of which glistened in his beard. "The bloodbath in the alley is only part of it. When they were running from the soldiers, several of the mob trampled three well-to-do tavern goers who had just come out to see what the fuss was about. Then a few of them ran willy-nilly into another establishment, knocked over a cooking brazier, and set the place on fire. It was chaos, and the powers-that-be of Archon are not happy about it. No, if you leave now, you won't get far before you're apprehended. But Mister Hizzard has his ways. He'll smuggle you out of here first chance. Then you can find your lady."

It hurt to think about the girl, her eyes pleading with him. The heartache came in waves that threatened to drown him. But if his sorrow was a sea, then what was that unwelcome thing that was bobbing about trying to breach the surface? *Ahhh . . . .the hag.*

"That woman, Old Tuva, what is she? A witch? What has she done to me?" It hurt his face to talk, but he had to know.

"Mister Hizzard might have warned you better, should have prepared you for that at least. Tuva, well, I can't say exactly what she is. A witch? Probably. Maybe something a little less than human though, if you believe in such things."

"Well, if I didn't, I do now."

"Mind you, she's no friend of mine, that hag. But we could not call a physician for you, not with half the City Guard out hunting for a man with a jagged cut to his face. She demands her price, mind you, but there it is. Mister Hizzard paid it. Paid her to mend you and put you back on your feet, so he did. I've seen men with wounds like yours laid up for a month, but the hag's magic is powerful."

Skallagrim touched his stitches but then withdrew his hand in reaction to sharp pain. "Is there a mirror in here? I'd like to see." He instantly regretted the request, certain that seeing his face would send him plunging into fresh despair.

Hartbert blew a smoke ring, watched it dissipate, then shook his head. "Let's hold off on the mirror. Plenty of time for that later. Just be glad you're alive, lad."

Skallagrim shuddered. "I confess, I thought I was a dead man. There was so much blood."

"You're a mess, to be sure, but you're stitched up now, and you won't bleed out at least. She gave you something for the pain too and said it should keep it at bay for a while."

"I'm thankful for that. There was a terrible fight, but for the life of me, I don't know why. It was like ... there was nothing at all, just darkness. Then I woke up in the middle of a fight. I don't know how the girl and I came to be there."

Hartbert rounded the table and approached the bed, where he towered over Skallagrim. The thief gave him an appraising look. Hartbert's face was rough though kindly in its way. A black beard, streaked with grey, spilled down his barrel chest. A bushy mustache nearly covered his mouth but failed to conceal the smile that hid within. Skallagrim thought it might be the first genuinely decent thing he had seen in some time, that smile. Such a simple thing. It was a cheerful expression that came from deep inside the huge man and seemed to spread to every part of him, even giving his eyes a good-natured twinkle. Hartbert appeared younger than Erling, maybe forty? Forty-five? One bandaged bear paw of a hand rested on the hilt of the sword that hung from his belt. The other scratched his beard as he considered Skallagrim.

"They, meaning Old Tuva and Mister Hizzard, say you got

addled. You have a knot on the back of your head from a cudgel strike. That would have been enough."

"Enough for what?"

"Enough to addle you, of course. You've lost your memory, or at least a good deal of it. It happens. Either that blow to the head or, well, some other sort of trauma might have caused it."

Skallagrim put a hand behind his head to feel for the lump. It was at the base of his skull and about the size of a walnut.

"While you were out, you were muttering some fairly strange things, if you don't mind my saying so, Mister Skallagrim."

"Like what?"

"Well, no one was around but me, and I'll keep it between us, you see. I wasn't taking notes, mind you, but something may have happened before the fight. So, you have the big knot on your head, which was enough to kill you, by my reckoning. But I think you saw something too, something that might have caused a . . . well . . . a shock to your mind, if you will."

Skallagrim propped himself up again, then managed to sit upright on the bed. "Just come out with it. What did I say?"

"Monster! That's what you said. Kept saying it over and over. Monster! Monster! Monster! And then there was a good deal about something that eats minds. You went on about having looked into a deep void too."

Had he been raving about himself being a monster due to his loathsome wounds? The tragic girl in the alley would never see him the same way again. He shrugged inwardly, for self-pity would get him no answers. He strove to concentrate, hoping to recall something beyond his own condition that might shed light on recent events. Surely something awful had caused his wretched predicament. "I do remember something else, something terrible, as you say. But whatever it was, it's gone now. I just can't think of what that would be. A thing that eats minds, you say?"

"That was it, though what that could mean, I dare not think." Hartbert leaned in close. "What you do with Mister Hizzard is your own business," he whispered. "I know him to be a smuggler, and there's no knowing what other sort of enterprise he's involved in. He pays well enough. I bang heads for him now and then, you see, or act as his guard if we go into the darker corners of Archon, which we frequently do. But he tells me you're one of his best collectors, as he calls them. And we both know that means thief, right?"

Skallagrim acknowledged the point with a nod.

"If you went poking around the tombs and dungeons of Archon, there's no telling what you saw, or even worse, what saw you. You take my meaning?"

"Enlighten me."

"No time now." Hartbert puffed away on his pipe, filling the room with a dense, aromatic cloud. "You think on it, but rest up first. I'm bound to fetch Mister Hizzard, and so I shall. You and he will have much to talk about, and he was anxious to see you as soon as you woke." He turned to leave, then turned back to Skallagrim. "If you have a pipe, I can fill it. And if you don't, I have an extra."

"Thanks, but no. I don't smoke." Skallagrim was just barely suppressing a cough as it was. *Who needs a pipe in this cloud?*

"Suit yourself." With heavy footsteps that threatened to break the floorboards, Hartbert made for the door. "That food there is for you. Eat up."

With that, Hartbert took his leave.

Parched and famished, Skallagrim emptied a half-pitcher of ale, wolfed down the better part of a roasted chicken, a large platter's worth of sharp yellow cheese, and several biscuits, then sat back at the table and admired the sword that lay there, motionless but menacing.

It was a thing of lethal beauty, perilous in its eldritch implications. It roused within him a thousand unanswerable questions, a cautious curiosity that caused him to both admire and fear the sky-born weapon. Perfectly balanced, it could be used either two-handed or one-handed. The edge was razor sharp, honed to deadly perfection. The shallow-grooved fuller, running the length of the blade, was inlaid with silver, intricately engraved with wondrous patterns and symbols that reached to the base of the ricasso. There the blade flared outward in twin edges. These were like barbs or hooks, extraordinarily clever in their design, lending the blade a more dramatic and more murderous appearance than any longsword Skallagrim had ever seen. The guard featured an unusual carving, a monstrous face with jaws agape, its eyes glittering with two tiny jewels. The pommel, no less exquisitely etched, was capped off with mysterious runes and the figures of two dueling serpents.

This was a hero's sword, a king's sword. But even as he admired it, dread flowed from it in waves. In the fight, he had perceived a singular rage throbbing from its hilt and radiating along the length of its blade. *Rage, yes. A murderous rage!*

It had a will of its own, this thing of magic and iron, an unconquerable, unshakable will. And while Skallagrim had wielded it, he had shared its mind and its power, a power that bespoke of dark glories, unending wars, and an insatiable fury of a kind that no human mind was meant to bear.

The sword's powerful will strove with his own. Even as he contemplated it, perplexed by its mystery but attuned to its contumacious sentiment, its brooding sentiency was ascendant. What terrible thing had he done to himself when grabbing this thing? For now he was bound to it and it to him until the doom at the end of the age.

Strange, intoxicating thoughts flooded his mind with epic visions of apocalyptic significance. Doom! The rise and fall of principalities and powers. A final day of judgment and red wrath.

These musings were not the product of his mind. It was the sword, the poetry of its sinuous shape and design, that inspired these grandiose ideas of war and of alliances seldom considered, partnerships between men and the iron they wielded rather than the treacherous coalitions of tribes and nations.

Man and brutal iron. Bright steel and the killing stroke. This was what mattered most. No revenge could be exacted, no frail mortal girl rescued and reclaimed, no honor redeemed, and no destiny of blood and glory realized if not for the iron.

No, these were not Skallagrim's thoughts. He tore his eyes away from the blade, breaking the spell.

What a curious thing to have fallen from the sky exactly when he needed it. Well, not exactly when he needed it, he mused. A little earlier, and he might have needed fewer stitches and suffered fewer bruises. There was no doubt it had saved his life though. It had lent him strength, granted him its own sense of purpose and indomitable will. Or, at the very least, it had helped him to find his own will to live, to survive the violence inflicted on him by a sorcerer and his gang of killers and cultists.

Doom be damned. He had lived, and that was all that mattered. Skallagrim would take this gift, wield this meteoric, screaming monstrosity of a sword if that would help him find the girl and kill the red-eyed fiend who had taken her from him.

Skallagrim checked himself, then stopped to listen. It was as if strange words were hanging in the air before him. Was the shrieking sword now speaking? What was it saying to him, this oddly hypnotizing, freakishly exotic creation?

The door through which Hartbert had exited opened once more, and the ethereal words were lost, the peculiar whispers drifting away like gossamer on a twilight breeze. The moment had passed.

In strode Erling with Hartbert's huge bulk following close behind. Little did Skallagrim realize, he was about to hear the worst of news.

CHAPTER SIX

Erling had a look of deep concern on his face as he took a seat opposite Skallagrim, careful to avoid touching the sword, which lay between them. As Skallagrim made to speak, Erling waved his hand to stop him.

"I know you have questions, and I'll get to them by and by. If you allow me to speak first, many of them may be answered in what I have to say."

Skallagrim nodded his assent. "By all means."

"Good." Erling poured himself a glass of wine and took a precautionary sniff of its bouquet. Seemingly satisfied, he continued. "Well, it's hard to know where to begin, but there are several things you need to know. First, your face." Erling lowered one hairless brow and grimaced as he eyed Skallagrim's stitches. "It looks worse now than it will later. You are very swollen about the face, and the bruising is quite severe. This, Tuva tells me—and frankly, my own experience says the same, limited as that may be—will eventually subside. A significant scar will be left, of course, and mayhap it will be to the liking of the ladies. You'll look like a rugged warrior; that's for certain." Erling laughed at this, but neither Skallagrim nor Hartbert joined in, and the moment became awkward.

"Another half inch, and you'd be Skallagrim One Eye instead of Skallagrim Quickhands, what?" This observation also failed to get a rise from either Skallagrim or the giant, though Hartbert sighed deeply with disapproval. "Well, there are stitches in the back of your head, too, and a few in your left arm. You have a black eye there, your right one," Erling said, pointing. "The rest are just scrapes and bruises. Leave the stitches alone for a few weeks, and do your best to keep the wounds clean. Any physician you can find will be able to remove the stitches then. Hell, I could do it in a pinch."

"Thank you for having me stitched up. Frankly, I don't know what I would have done without you." Skallagrim looked at the empty plate. "And thanks for the food as well."

"Not to worry. You would have done the same for me."

Skallagrim was not ready to concede this point and remained wary of this forgotten ally. "You say that, sir, but I swear I don't know you."

"But you do," Erling retorted. "I assure you that you do. You have a nasty lump on the back of your head, and sometimes a wound like that can cause memory loss."

"Yes, so I've been told," Skallagrim said, looking at Hartbert.

"Maybe your memory will return. Maybe quickly. Maybe not at all. One cannot be sure of such things. Time will tell, Skallagrim. Time will tell. Beyond all of that, how do you feel?"

"Better. Last night was tough. There was a great deal of pain, but most of it is gone. I feel a good deal stronger too."

"Good, good. You'll need your strength."

"What of the girl? Any word on where the sorcerer took her? I feel like I have lain here long enough and should be out searching for her now. So, I truly hope you've heard something."

Erling shrugged. "I have my theories."

"Theories?"

"No one saw her, and you don't even know her name. I mean, that's the crux of it, right? We don't even know who we're talking about." Erling took a sip of wine, then drained half the glass in one gulp.

"True," Skallagrim replied, "but she's real. You said I wrote to you about her. Someone must know something."

Erling was growing frustrated. "Forneus Druogorim. He would know if anyone, of course. I dare say we cannot ask him though."

Chastened, Skallagrim nodded for Erling to continue.

Erling took a deep breath. "Forneus made his escape just before the Watch arrived. So, asking them, even bribing them for information, is worthless. The only others present besides you and me were the men you slew and the mindless rabble—the cultists. They are crazed and dangerous. They cannot be bribed, nor can they be believed."

Skallagrim began to ask a question, then stopped himself as Erling continued.

"Who are they? That particular mob was a sect of the Enlightened of Balor. They are a cult. Of course, they would not dream of acknowledging that fact, but there it is. Now, I have not the time to explain them further except to say they are fiercely loyal to Forneus. He holds sway over them and has been gaining influence with the many cultists of Archon for some time now. Suffice it to say, they are but pawns in the great game he is playing. That's where you come in, and perhaps your mysterious damsel in distress as well."

Erling leaned in close, lowering his voice. "The girl, how old would you say she is?"

"I don't know. I don't even know how old I am," Skallagrim admitted, embarrassed.

"You, if my own memory holds, are twenty-two. Take a guess about the girl."

"From the look of her, maybe seventeen? Twenty? I can't be sure, but with only the vaguest recollections on the matter to go by, I'd say she's younger than me."

"You have no solid memory of her, yet you are sure somehow that you know her?"

Skallagrim thought for a moment and took a deep breath, letting out a slow sigh. It was overwhelming, all of it. The fight, the death, the wounds, the storm, the sword, the escape, then the horrible, horrible hag—the entire affair was staggering to take in. But thinking about the girl was as painful as the bruises on his face, as shocking to his system as Old Tuva's spidery touch. Thoughts of the helpless captive, her innocent face, and her fear-filled eyes were like fresh wounds, deeper than sword cuts.

"Everything I got from her when she looked at me, it roused these . . . feelings. Not specific memories, but, well, it's almost as if my mind is keeping secrets about her, and now and then, it lets things slip. I know I brought her to the city, and I know she came because she trusted me. There are moments when I feel as if I can glimpse a past with her, but I can't make sense of it. Not yet at least."

Erling nodded. "Any other impressions?"

Skallagrim thought for a moment. When his eyes had met the girl's, it was like sudden heartbreak, more wonderful than the beauty of spring's first flowers but more painful than the sudden slash of a knife.

"Seeing her, well, it was like catching a fragment of a song from a distance. Say, a cherished song from childhood. But the sound is snatched away on the wind, and you are only left with a hint of it, not even the melody, just the knowledge that you heard it and once knew it well."

"Feelings and songs," Erling replied. "What can we do with those? I say, Skallagrim, you sound as poignant as a poet today and not at all like the thief I know you to be."

Hartbert grunted from his station at the door. "There you go, Mister Hizzard. You pry the man with personal questions, then insult him when he gives you an honest answer."

Erling turned to face the seven-foot-tall mammoth and pointed a finger at him. "You are paid well for guarding my person and for the occasional act of violence that guarding might require, not your opinion. You would do well to remember that."

Hartbert sighed and said no more while Erling directed his attention back to Skallagrim. "Hartbert thinks I lack empathy. Truly, it's not that at all. I am, I assure you, interested in helping you find your girl if indeed she exists."

Skallagrim grimaced and grew tense. Though he did not realize it, he had clenched his fists. "He's right, Hartbert. I'm a thief; you said so yourself. And after last night, apparently, I'm a swordsman and a killer too. Though when I think about her, all that goes away. It's a helpless feeling, but it's so intense that I know she exists. I cannot have imagined her." Erling and Hartbert both stared at Skallagrim, impressed by his conviction. "Frankly, whether I know her or not is irrelevant," he continued. "That devil trussed up an innocent girl and has made off with her. I mean to find him and kill him for it. I mean to rescue the girl too, whether you believe in her or not."

"No, no, no." Erling held up a warding hand. "I believe you. It's just that we have so little to go by, and I'm considering how best to aid you. It's likely to require a dangerous journey to find your phantom lover, my friend. I have a thought, you see, but my proposal is extremely dangerous. I'll get to it momentarily."

Skallagrim forced himself to relax and slumped in his chair, resigned to hear everything Erling had to say.

"Considering her age and her youth, do you suppose she is—well, not to be impolite—a virgin? Or were you lovers?"

The question seemed off, entirely too personal, but Skallagrim was determined to hear out his strange ally, so he merely shrugged. "I don't know. I want to think we were lovers more than I know that we were. I suppose she could be a virgin." He remained silent for a moment, contemplating. "Again, it's just a feeling, but I think she probably is. I don't know why, but that's the best I can come up with. Does it matter?"

"It may matter, and it may not." Erling's brows furrowed, and for a moment, he seemed deep in thought. "If one were to postulate that you stole something from Forneus, then revenge might be a motive. You did come here for something, that much I know. So perhaps you were caught and then pursued to the alleyway where he attempted to abduct you and your friend or lover, whichever she is. But revenge is not his way. I cannot see him resorting to that extreme. He's smarter than that, and he has other more clever ways to achieve vengeance, should he seek it. Forneus would have risked too much in this action, and it clearly resulted in him having to bolt from Archon."

Skallagrim nodded.

"Then, there is the matter of your sword. He was certainly afraid of it. That much I could see written on his face in the alley. I could not see your lady, but I could see his haughty face bobbing above the crowd, and he was worried. He instructed his men to cut off your sword arm, though just killing you would have made more sense. Of course, just about the time the sword fell, he changed his mind and ordered you killed. That entire exchange is a mystery to me."

Skallagrim shifted uncomfortably in his chair but remained silent.

"Women and girls are kidnapped from Archon and sold into slavery. That is a fact. It happens more often than most folk know, but Forneus has no traffic with slavers. He's not a carnal man, given to lasciviousness, so he did not want her for himself. So, then why did he take her?"

Skallagrim shrugged. "I don't know. His face was arrogant and full of hate. And fear! You're correct there. I saw the taint of it in those demonic eyes of his."

Erling slammed a fist on the table, causing the sword and scabbard to rattle and startling Skallagrim and Hartbert. "Right! Fear! Anger and fear! And therein hide the clues we need to explain the reason."

"Go on." Skallagrim was on the edge of his seat now.

"I could not make sense of it, you see, none of it. He has so much to lose by the actions he took last night. But then I remembered the date, and fortunately for you, I know a thing or two about sorcery and its practitioners."

"Yes, and . . . ?"

Erling took a deep breath. "This is Tuesday. The Night of Mog Ruith is nearly upon us. That will be Friday evening. It's an anniversary of great significance in sorcerous circles." He paused, then locked eyes with Skallagrim. "If I'm correct, in just four nights at the midnight hour, Forneus Druogorim will sacrifice your young lady."

"What?" Skallagrim rose from his chair. Erling also pushed back his chair and stood, seeming to grow in stature and potency.

"Oh yes, on a stone altar stained with the blood of innocents. Virgins." He spoke with authority, waving his hands in an animated display of conviction. Skallagrim and Hartbert stepped back to give Erling space as he stalked the room like an actor on a stage. Even the shadows in the stifling room seemed to grow more ominous, like black clouds before a storm.

"The stars will align! The portents are ripe! The screaming sword is surely a sign, don't you see?" Erling pointed a trembling finger at the blade on the table.

"No, Erling, I don't see!" Skallagrim tensed up, staring at Erling as if he had come unhinged.

"Forneus serves darker forces than his own mind, abhorrent though it may be. It's the bargain he made for the power he wields. That's what he fears, for these forces are beyond him. He has promised much to these masters and the unnamable horror that they, in turn, serve. I am, you see, a connoisseur of such abominations. I study them. Worse yet, I've seen them!" Erling's pale eyes grew wide with this revelation, and he laughed as only the mad can laugh.

The tension in the room became palpable. Skallagrim suppressed a shudder as the lanterns sputtered, and the shadows lengthened and danced frightfully.

Hartbert left his post at the door, rushing to Erling's side. "Get hold of yourself, Mister Hizzard! This won't do!" He knew his master's many moods, had weathered many spiteful outbursts and more than one "nervous fit," as he called them. He placed an enormous hand upon Erling's shoulders to calm him, but Erling shook it off.

"What have you seen? What has that sword to do with it?" Skallagrim shouted.

Erling wrung his hands, and his voice quivered when he continued, speaking rapidly and with tremendous conviction. "Forneus is, by my reckoning at least, a minor sorcerer, his techniques unrefined, his access to lore limited, and his understanding of certain essential grimoires outmoded. He's no petty caster of spells, of course, and he's still dangerous. But he wants more power. It's my belief he will go to extreme measures to raise himself in the ranks of the great sorcerers of Andorath."

Erling was distraught, struggling for the words but clearly building to something. "There are rumors about him, but they come from reliable sources that I cannot ignore. They tell me he has disturbed something, something from deep down below and beyond." His eyes grew wide as he fixed his gaze on Skallagrim. "Something old and dreadful beyond your comprehension!"

Erling flinched as if an unseen hand had taken a swipe at him. Then a maniacal grin stretched across his face that unnerved Skallagrim. His head was reeling with these revelations, these theories. The implications were vast, and he was filled with uneasiness and doubt. What sort of madness must he unravel to find the lost girl? He listened with growing frustration as Erling continued.

"He thinks he will attain power, enough to rule Archon, perhaps. But he's an arrogant fool. The monstrous force he has awakened is beyond him. It will devour him!"

Skallagrim glared at Erling, pointed a trembling finger at him. "I care nothing for sorcerers or the demons they serve. I care nothing for the spells he weaves or the power he craves. If I can find him, I'll kill him before his demons can!" He paced the floor like a caged lion. "What have I done? Why did I bring her here? Why did a sword come shrieking out of the storm? None of this makes sense!"

"Oh, I can't explain it all. There's no time." Erling slumped into his chair. "I'm sorry; please forgive my outburst. Hartbert can tell you, I tend to be high-strung. I have spent too many years studying these . . ." He twirled his hands in the air as if trying to conjure the right words. "These affairs of darkness. I have, perhaps, learned and even seen too much. I seldom speak of it to anyone, and when I do, I get swept away by it all. I suppose it has preyed on my mind." He leaned back in his chair, finished the last of his wine, then motioned to Hartbert to pour him some more. "You must think me insane, but these are not the musings of a disordered mind! I'll tell you what I can, though much of it's just me playing at a guessing game." He motioned at the sword, still careful not to touch it. "Skallagrim, if you would please, put the blade into its scabbard."

Skallagrim did as Erling bid him, pausing only to take in the elegant beauty of the red-leather scabbard.

"We can get you a baldric or a back harness for your weapon," Erling said. He appeared calmer now, though perhaps it was merely exhaustion. "Either will do, of course. Though if you prefer the baldric, you will have to wear it rather high." He glanced at Hartbert, who returned his stare with a knowing look. "Go ahead, Hartbert, show Skallagrim your hand. Tell him what happened."

The giant held up his bandaged right hand and undid the wrapping to reveal a deep red burn on his palm. "I tried to pick that sword up after you passed out last night, just to make room for the food and wine, mind you. It was like touching a hot iron." He held his hand close, so Skallagrim could examine it.

Skallagrim shrugged. "I don't know what to say."

"It did not burn you just now," Hartbert observed.

Skallagrim shook his head. "What does it mean?"

Erling motioned for Skallagrim to sit. "Hartbert doesn't know. Nor do I, really. Again, just theories. And yet . . ." He scratched his chin. "It's highly probable that only you can hold that sword. Or maybe it's truer to say your sword arm is the only arm that can wield it, which is why Forneus wants that arm." Erling shook his head, frustrated at his own line of reasoning. "See, it's all preposterous. But then, Forneus is probably insane by now. Try making sense of the schemes of the mad, and you will go mad yourself." He shifted in his chair and sighed. "Skallagrim, there is no time to sort out the sorcerer's motives or to give you a history lesson or a lecture on star charts and dates or instruction on matters demoniac." He shook his head in exasperation. "You want to kill Forneus, and I, for my own reasons, wish him dead too. You want to find the girl, and she must be where he is. I think I know where they are. If you can get there by midnight, four nights from tonight, you will arrive in time to save her."

Skallagrim made to speak, but Erling stifled him with a wave of his hand. "I think. It's not a promise, mind you. But I think it can be done."

"Then tell me where to go, and I'll go now."

"The Archon Watch is out looking for you. Half the city is in an uproar over last night's storm and that shrieking meteor of a blade that plunged out of it. Luckily, they have no idea who you are. But any stranger with a fresh gash on his face like yours who also happens to be wearing an exotic-looking weapon like that one will be arrested and interrogated."

He stood up and walked to one of the shelves, where he tugged free a rolled parchment that was lodged between two large tomes. "If that happens, we cannot help you. We will have to wait until dark, and you need to rest more anyway. Tonight Hartbert and I will guide you out of Archon. Not by the gate, mind you, but through another smuggler's tunnel that I know." He unrolled the parchment on the table, using three books and a candle to hold down the corners, revealing a highly detailed map. "From there we must bid you farewell for a bit."

"So, where do I go from there?" Skallagrim asked.

"Oh. Well, that's the rub." Erling pointed at the map and chuckled. Looking across the table at Skallagrim, he shook his head. "The sane won't go where you will be going, my friend. No indeed! Only a desperate man would take the path down to Pagarna and beyond!"

CHAPTER SEVEN

A long day passed in which Skallagrim ate his fill of meat pies, cheese, nuts, and bread. He found his strength slowly returning, and along with it, his ever-inquisitive mind seemed to clear. His panic and fear dissipated, but many questions remained.

He considered his memory loss to be the most distressing facet of his predicament, but he also pondered the mystery of the screaming sword, the trustworthiness of his new allies, and, of course, the girl.

Her eyes were devastating, their beauty unmarred by the fear that resided within. In the midst of the fight, Skallagrim caught fleeting glimpses of her face, but those glimpses were crushing, heartbreaking. Such was the curve of her cheeks, the fullness of her lips, and the way her golden curls swept down about her face as sunlight might shine through morning mist to fall upon a fair lake at the coming of dawn.

What else? He strove to recall, though it was hard to think of anything beyond those eyes, so piercingly blue and bright that he could see the glimmer of them as they flashed in the gloom of the alley. Of course, she was small of frame too and delicate, far too delicate to be handled so roughly and with such abuse. There it was again, the obsession. He could not see her beauty in his mind without also seeing the ugliness of what had happened and the arrogant face of the devil-haunted man who caused it all.

Night was approaching, or so he was told. Hartbert had been away much of the day, doing whatever it was Hartbert did. However, he returned at last with a knapsack stuffed with supplies for Skallagrim's journey. Erling had been in and out as well but had spent a good deal of time between his comings and goings pouring over maps with Skallagrim, advising him of the best route from Archon to the tower of Forneus Druogorim. The ancient stronghold, Fort Vigilance by name, was reputed to perch vulture-like on a bluff overlooking the Pagarna River, a watercourse that itself was known as a place of danger and dread. Memory or no, even Skallagrim recalled a feeling about it, like a half-remembered nightmare from childhood.

The Vales of Pagarna were, as far as anyone in Archon knew, virtually uninhabited. Ancient, crumbling towers were strewn among the forested ridges and craggy mountains on either side of the river, squatting empty and lightless, watching over the sad ruins of villages and towns that had been abandoned for hundreds of years. All but one, Fort Vigilance.

Whatever people once toiled there in the perpetual twilight of the Vales, whatever knights and barons once lorded over them, all were long gone.

Explorers and trappers might venture along the 500-mile length of Pagarna from time to time, but often as not, such brave souls failed to return.

One who did return told tales of a lost city populated by a mysterious race in the tangle of mountains at the northern end of the Vales. Another spoke of savage mountain folk. They were reputed to be a wild, backward group, fiercely independent, who kept to themselves and hid on the mountaintops, farming the steep slopes, hunting the hollows, brewing fiery moonshine, and singing strange songs around their fires by night.

A few claimed the empty forts along the river were reoccupied by sorcerers, that Forneus was handing out keys to any of his nefarious order who would acknowledge him as leader. But there was no solid, trustworthy news from the wild region, no report that could be verified.

It was just the sort of ruined land that a madman like Forneus Druogorim would be drawn to, a place where dark magick could be practiced in seclusion and where age-old blasphemies might yet lurk to assist. The old folk shuddered and warned that ghouls roamed the vine-choked forests to pillage ancient burial mounds, mouldering and lost amid the Vales. Some whispered of tentacled monsters that slimed about near the riverbanks amid patches of quicksand and stagnant pools, where ichorous black mud bubbled and squelched. If rumors were to be believed, even nightgaunts were hibernating within the inky depths of cliffside caverns, quiescent but ready to take nightmarish flight upon leathery black wings should a careless traveler disturb their slumber.

"Do not forget the Old Man o' the River," Harbert interjected during Erling's litany of the potential horrors that Skallagrim might encounter.

"Who's that?" Skallagrim inquired. A shiver ran through him at the mention of the potential threat.

"Not who but what," Erling said, his tone taking on the aspect of a lecturer. He paused to sip his wine before continuing. "It is, or was, an Undulant. Probably no threat, as one of them has not been seen in many centuries."

"But I thought it haunted the river. I've heard that for years," Hartbert countered.

"The river, my oversized friend, is five hundred miles long. It could be anywhere." Erling spread his hands wide. "There were only ever three undulates, if the tales are to be believed. One was reputed to haunt a deep lake in some vague wilderness far to the northwest. Another is buried in ice over the sunken city of Zagzagel in Hyperborea—has been for centuries. And that much-fabled ruin lies far beyond the border to the North of North."

"There's many a rumor about Zagzagel," Hartbert interrupted. "They say its gates only open once in a century!" He scratched his beard and cocked an eyebrow. "Or was it every thousand years?"

Erling scowled. "Yes, but—"

"And a terrible demon sleeps down in its dungeons!"

"Ahem!" Erling silenced Hartbert with a devastating glare. "As for the Old Man o' the River, well, if the thing still lives, which I doubt, it could be anywhere along the length of the Pagarna. As far as the Vales go, you stand a greater chance of tripping over a root and breaking your neck than being devoured by that thing."

"Well, that's a small comfort," Skallagrim commented.

Erling took a dainty sip of wine and smiled. "Or you might sink in a festering mire and drown, what?"

"Ah," Skallagrim said with a sigh, "such encouragement."

"The whole dratted wilderness is problematic. I wish it were not necessary for you to go there, but I see no other way."

If this was the trackless waste where Skallagrim must go to find the girl and kill the fiend, so be it. He cared not for rumors or even the safeguarding of his sanity. He might have forgotten most of his past and, therefore, had no way to gauge a possible future, no steady ground upon which to make a claim. He might be a thief and now was most assuredly a killer. He was wounded, scarred, and disfigured, but none of it mattered. To find the girl, to kill the man who took her, that was all.

Adrift on a sea of madness, Skallagrim would have been rudderless if not for this one pursuit with dual aims: rescue and justice. Find the girl, kill the man. Nothing about any of it made sense, the violent events of the previous night or the bizarre mission set before him. And he had no way to test the information given to him by Erling and Hartbert except to follow them to the city's edge and then plunge further into the nightmare.

He had only the barest memory of his own identity, let alone the horrid world in which he found himself—Andorath. Shadowy phantoms, the product of questionable retentiveness, flitted around his mind, taunting him to recall what he could not. Impressions rushed at him, wraithlike and vague, hinting of a cursed land, of decadent cities ruled by despotic sorcerer-kings, of frontiers and vast wildernesses ruined by war and haunted by things far worse. He could lock on to none of it except the merest glimpses of solid fact. Archon was a city, damned and corrupt. How much worse could the Vales of Pagarna be?

Find the girl, kill the man.

It did not matter—the greater picture, the landscape on which his irrelevant, pain-haunted life had suddenly appeared. He was but a tiny figure, the merest dot on the outlandish canvas on which he had been painted. Whoever the artist was, he had a pitiless, monstrous mind to have employed his creativity thus, to have painted in such broad strokes of bloody red over turbid, nightmarish landscapes in ghastly, terrible detail, only to have inadvertently splashed the misshapen drop of paint that was Skallagrim into the midst of it. It mattered not.

Find the girl, kill the man.

As the time for departure neared, Skallagrim began to pace, anxious to leave the stifling basement room where he had been kept for so long.

"Time is not on my side."

"It's not the worst possible news," Erling said. "The crisis moment is still four nights away; you have time to find her. Thanks to me, you know where she is, most likely. You have rough terrain to navigate but only forty miles of it. And you, my dear friend Skallagrim, are in possession of two stalwart allies: the troll by the door there," he motioned at Hartbert, who grunted at the insult but then nodded at the truth of it, "and me. I'm wise and full of guile." Grinning, he performed a mock bow.

Skallagrim stopped pacing and looked at them both. He started to speak but was interrupted by Erling once more.

"And don't forget, you have a power of your own to wield."

"What do you mean?"

"Why, that iron monster hanging at your side, of course." Erling indicated Skallagrim's sword. He and Hartbert had fitted Skallagrim with a wide red-leather baldric that came close to matching the scabbard in color. It was an expensive gift, with engraved metal trappings, tiny pockets, and even a small affixed satchel where items like blade oil and cleaning rags could be stored.

"Forneus fears the sword as much as he fears any undead god or devil he made his unkeepable oaths to." Erling jabbed a finger at the sword. "That, my friend, is Terminus. You, dear Skallagrim, for reasons we may never know, have been gifted a blessing and a doom. You are Shield Shaker! Foe Breaker! Wielder of Terminus Rex!"

"So you say. But you don't know that for certain, do you?"

"If you were listening to the spell Forneus attempted in Rum Alley, you as much as know. He called to it by name." He held his hands high in a hammy imitation of the spell caster. "Terminus Rex. Bugog, blah blah blah. Terminus Rex. It was some gobbledygook like that."

"Yes, I heard him, but what of it? What is Terminus? A sword, yes, but you say it's a blessing and a doom?" Skallagrim hoisted his knapsack into place while Hartbert helped him adjust the leather straps.

"Most of what I have heard are old legends. Still . . ." He jabbed a finger at the sword. "It screams! In fact, it screams in precisely the same manner as the Terminus Sword in the legends. We both saw the effect of that deafening shriek on the mob and Forneus. It exhibits a miraculous, terrifying nature that granted you power when you needed it most and put fear into the hearts of your enemies."

"And the doom?"

"I have read of such things," Erling replied, raising an eyebrow. "Swords seldom fall from the sky shooting lightning bolts on the way down, what? You cannot simply reach up and grab something like that out of the air. At least not without expecting there to be a price to pay, you see?" He paused, started to say something, then seemed to think better of it. Sighing, he continued. "But mystical weapons and other oddities have appeared in Andorath over the years, and they always seem to have a complicated destiny." He gave a skeptical laugh, then continued. "Admittedly, it sounds like fairy-tale rubbish, but there it is. Either this weapon chose you, or someone with a power far greater than Forneus Druogorim sent it to you. No knowing for certain what any of it means just yet. I think, my friend, you will just have to live with it for a while before you find out more."

"I suppose," Skallagrim said, nodding thoughtfully.

Hope. That was the blessing. He had been emptied of it in the alley, then the sword fell, and hope came with it—an angry, jagged hope but hope just the same. Or maybe it was some shred of hope that remained in him that caused him to call out the way he had.

Crying out to the unnamed, ineffable, mysterious someone he could not quite recall. That was hope, right? Or was it despair? Did it matter? To Skallagrim, yes, it did. But he would have time to sort all of that out later. *Find the girl, kill the man. Just stay focused.*

"And while I'm tramping through haunted forests and fending off ghouls, you two will be where again?"

"I have business to attend to," Erling explained. "Still, I think we may be able to help. Hartbert and I will be traveling the same route your sorcerer took."

Skallagrim frowned in confusion. "Please, elaborate."

"Very well. There's a road that goes a long way around the Vales. About sixty miles from here, it hooks back toward the mountains that line the Pagarna River on the western side. I showed you on the map." He drew a finger along the parchment where the road, dubiously named Devil's Race Highway, was plainly marked, leading northwest from Archon. "The road will be crawling with patrols, some looking for you, no doubt. But there's a war brewing farther up near the city of Ophyr, and that will mean additional traffic of the sort you will want to avoid. Regardless, Forneus was seen leaving Archon and heading up Devil's Race in his wagon with a handful of his guard following on horseback. We assume he had your girl in the back, perhaps hidden under a tarp or some hay. But right here, have a look." His finger landed on the map where the highway swung back in the direction of the river.

Skallagrim peered over Erling's shoulder and saw two jaggedly drawn mountains marked "The Smokestacks." A narrow river snaked eastward between them to join the larger Pagarna River about ten miles from the highway. This backcountry area bore the name "Bald River Gorge."

Erling frowned over a torn corner of his map. "What you don't see is the unmarked road running along that river there. It will bear a wagon straight into the mountains toward your sorcerer's hideout, an ancient track that long ago would have serviced the forts and towers that guarded the Vales and the river. It leads right to his doorstep." Erling tapped a spot on the map, pleased with his revelation. "He could easily have made the first sixty-mile leg by now. No one would have stopped him. Avoiding the patrols would be simple as they are looking for you, not him. Devil's Race Highway is a wide-open road, you see?"

Skallagrim nodded.

"That will be our road too," Hartbert interjected. "If for some reason he did not take the old Gorge Road, we can continue up Devil's Race toward Ophyr and track him down." He puffed up his chest and crossed his meaty arms. "I have done my share of hunting men over the last few years. I'll know if he stopped along the way, took the Gorge Road, or kept going north."

"We shall see about that," Erling said. "Other wagons will be on the road making tracks, you know."

Hartbert frowned, conceding the point.

Skallagrim scratched his chin. "I can't just travel with you?"

Erling held out his hands to explain. "Unlike Forneus, I have no wagon in which to hide a passenger. Besides, I would not dare. Troop movements mean the highway will be closed to any who don't have a pass. Since I often do business for Archon and its military, Hartbert and I can get through. But there will be checkpoints, and trust me, they will be checking."

Skallagrim's head drooped. He did not relish the idea of a wilderness trek, alone and unguided.

Erling rapped the table to get Skallagrim's attention. "Pay heed. If you are with us, and we're stopped by soldiers, well, I don't fancy spending time in the Watch's dungeon." He rolled the map up and placed it back on the shelf. "You are not officially an outlaw, of course, but there would be questions if you are spotted, and we will all be held while they sort it out. They will want your sword, but you will refuse. They will fight you to take it and torch themselves when they lay hands on it." Seeming impressed with his line of reasoning, Erling continued. "Then they will know you are the man at the center of last night's chaos, the very chaos that left the gutters running red with blood." Erling dropped his hands back to his sides and smiled. "You see, it could all get nasty and terribly complicated really quick."

"I could wear a hood," Skallagrim rebutted. "We could travel by night, or if that doesn't work for you, I could go alone. If Devil's Race Highway is the fastest way, it seems worth the risk."

"I would say you were correct except for two things. One, our route leads to a bridge that must be crossed directly beneath the fort. Cross it, and you will be seen. Two, your sorcerer has magically locked the front door to Fort Vigilance. No one can enter unless he wills it. Going by the road will still not get you in."

"Well, dammit then! What am I to do?"

"You'll have to use your skills as a thief, Skallagrim," Erling said matter-of-factly.

"What? Like climb the tower or dig a hole underneath and chisel through the floor? Maybe take a pickaxe and just pound away till I knock a hole in the wall?"

"No! No! There's a hidden backdoor somewhere along the southern ridge where the fort sits. It's doubtful Forneus knows about it. In fact, I'm certain he doesn't. That will be your way in." Erling smoothed the end of his ponytail with one hand. "I wish I had more details for you, but," he shrugged, "I don't. You'll just have to search until you find it."

Skallagrim absently ran his fingers through his hair. "I see," he answered doubtfully.

"Trust me, Skallagrim, go the wilderness route and simply follow the river till you come to the ruins of an old city. You'll see Fort Vigilance perched on the opposite ridge. It's the first such tower you'll come across. There's no missing it."

"It's not ideal, but I get it," Skallagrim replied. He paused and took a deep breath, trying to rein in his frustration. "Thank you, both of you, for getting involved." He yawned, then hissed with pain as the motion pulled at the stitches in his left cheek. But the yawn was contagious, and Hartbert followed suit. Not one of the three men had slept adequately the night before.

"Let me be clear," Erling admonished, stifling a yawn of his own. "I'm already far more involved than I wish to be. I must attend to some unpleasant 'business' north of here. I have no wish to get too close to your sorcerer, but a short detour is not out of the question. If I'm right, and he's headed to Fort Vigilance to perform some diabolical ritual involving your virtuous young lady, then we'll follow him from a safe distance. If so, and you can affect a rescue, we will be nearby. Look for us where the two rivers converge, or just wait by the banks, and we'll find you."

"Easy enough."

"Easy? Not really." Erling raised a brow. "Nothing about this is easy. There's no getting around the fort or the cliffs it sits upon, for you or for us. You'll have to find the back door, and then you'll have to exit out the front."

"I thought the front door was locked by a spell."

"Correct. You cannot get in that way, but leaving is another matter entirely." Erling smiled as if something had just occurred to him. "Oh yes, think of this." His eyes gleamed, and he snapped his fingers. "If you kill the sorcerer, be sure to take his key. All the magic is wrapped up in that. If you get the key, you will be the new master of Fort Vigilance."

"I have no need of a fort, but . . . point taken. I just want to find the girl."

"Of course. What's left of his guards may well kill you, or Forneus himself might melt you into a noxious puddle of goo with some infernal spell. It's what sorcerers do, you know?" Erling laughed, causing Skallagrim to throw his arms up in exasperation, but he ignored him as he continued. "If such is the case, Hartbert and I will make our exit from the scene, ever so quietly, I assure you." He grabbed a satchel and his cloak as if preparing to leave. "There is, of course, the slightest chance I'm wrong about it all, and he has continued onward to Ophyr, in which case, so shall we."

"Then what? How will I find you?"

"If you find the tower empty and no sign of him there, make your way out to the Devil's Race Highway and cross it. Head northwest across the countryside. Stay in the shadows, and avoid the troops. In about five miles, you will come to a country lane that leads to a town called Stiff Knee Gap. Remember? You saw it on the map?"

"Vaguely, yes. It's about fifty miles from the fort, right?"

Erling snapped his fingers. "That's the one! I'm owed many favors by the folk of that town, and you will be safe there. Look for us, or at least leave word at a tavern called the Down and Out. We will do our best to check in there now and then."

"Got it. Again, my thanks to you both." Skallagrim watched as Erling and Hartbert, each wearing swords now, checked their gear and water flasks. *Finally, they're preparing to leave.* However, he had reservations now that he had thrown in completely with Erling and his plans. His excitement at finally being able to leave that place, to head into the wilderness and find his girl, was diminished in some way, though he could not define the premonitory chill that gripped him.

"Oh, and Skallagrim." Erling stopped in his preparations and stared him in the eye. "You are a very good friend to me. That's the only reason I'm doing this, any of it. If it all turns out well, I hope you will remember this favor one day." It was more of a statement than a request.

"Absolutely." Skallagrim fidgeted nervously with his gear, apprehensive about his ally and anxious to be on his way.

Erling nodded and then finished off a second glass of wine that remained on the table. "I mean it, young man. My plans last night did not include being tied up in a back-alley hell while you played at sword fighting." He dabbed at his mouth with a linen napkin and smiled at Skallagrim. "But then, what sort of friend would I be if I abandoned you now? You would help me if I were in a pinch, right?"

"Of course," Skallagrim replied. "If you need me in the future, you have but to ask." He meant it, though with reservations.

"Then, gentlemen, I think it's time we departed Archon. Shall we?"

Erling indicated the door that led back the way they had come the night before. Hartbert opened it and ducked into the passage. Erling motioned for Skallagrim to go next, and so he did, plunging once more into the stygian black of Archon's labyrinthine underworld.

CHAPTER EIGHT

"Where were we anyway?" Skallagrim queried as they approached the end of the drainage tunnel that would lead them beyond the walls of Archon. Much of his physical strength had returned, but with only a few hours of sleep the night before, he was mentally exhausted. "I mean, you never said the name of the tavern we were under."

"No harm in telling him," Hartbert muttered. The giant man had been forced to squeeze through too many tight spaces on the way out, bumping his head more than once on rocks that protruded from the low ceiling. He was in a sour mood and had not said much during their subterranean trek.

"Of course not. He used to know anyway," Erling noted. "It's aptly named, the Alibi." He had a flicker of pride in his voice. "I own it."

A pale light was coming from just ahead, and Hartbert, who was in the lead, motioned for the others to lower their voices as they splashed forward.

"Last night's affairs will be forgotten in a month," Erling whispered. "Something worse will happen. It always does. If things go sideways at the fort, and we can't find one another, head back to the tavern after the dust settles. The manager knows your name, and you will be taken care of."

Skallagrim glanced back over his shoulder at Erling. "Sure! If I'm able!" *Find the girl, kill the man.* He had no idea where he would land after the matter before him was settled, assuming he came out of it alive.

"Littlegate Street near the north wall," Erling added. "That's where you'll find the Alibi. Though, as I said, the Down And Out is where we'll check in should we lose you. Got that?"

"At Stiff Knee Gap. I can find it."

"Good. But hopefully, we shall meet at the fort, what? Ah. Here we are!"

The three emerged from the tunnel and were rewarded by a fresh but chilly breeze, the first clean air Skallagrim had felt in many days. It was early spring, and daylight, when it came, would reveal the green of the new year. But the nights were anything but warm, and Skallagrim pulled his cloak tight about him to ward off the chill.

It was early evening, and the nearly full moon was gleaming upon a little creek formed by drainage from the tunnel. Looking back, Skallagrim could see they had exited from a low, tree-covered mound, much farther from the city walls than he had expected.

"The fools of the Watch know nothing about this tunnel," Erling whispered. "The farmers who live outside the walls think this grove of trees is haunted. They never come here. No one knows about it, so mind you keep it secret."

Skallagrim nodded and took a deep breath of the clean, refreshing air. The sounds and smells of the city were far behind them. Archon was still visible though, perhaps a half mile away, the walls looming black and the oddly shaped towers crowding unnaturally close. A greenish haze swirled around their turrets, and baleful lights flickered from within them. Yet from the tallest tower of all, the ominous Spire of Griog'xa, no light shone.

Perhaps the sorcerer, "whom no living man hath seen," was slumbering. Skallagrim suppressed a chill when he looked at that ill-reputed tower, refusing to dwell on the legendary necromancer who haunted its halls. He forced himself to look away from the spire and back to the city over which it loomed.

When seen at night from a distance, Archon was an evil-looking place, like an overcrowded graveyard of weirdly leaning mausoleums and crumbling tombstones slanted this way and that. And for all that it reeked of death, it seemed alive and sentient. It felt like Archon was watching him, leering at him, plotting revenge for his escape.

Be damned for the pain you have caused me! Whatever evil lies at your heart, I'll find it one day and cut it out of you! Skallagrim vowed as he gripped the hilt of Terminus and turned away from the city. He would not see it again for some time.

They were standing in a grove of tall pines upon a thick bed of needles, still damp from the storm of the previous night. Hartbert bid his companions keep their heads down and remain quiet, then crept to the edge of the grove where he crouched and listened.

Skallagrim hunched low and looked back toward Erling's shadowy form. "You want Forneus dead too. Why?"

"I have my reasons."

"As you will." Skallagrim dropped to one knee and continued to watch Hartbert for any sign of trouble. Erling sighed and knelt beside him.

"I'm a collector of many exotic things, Skallagrim. I'm also a habitual compiler of records and accounts. It comes with the trade."

Skallagrim glanced sideways at Erling and nodded. "Your point?"

"I compile lists too."

"Yes, and . . . ?"

"This goes no further!"

"Alright, no further." Skallagrim sat down, leaning against a tree.

"I have an exhaustive list," Erling whispered, "of nearly every sorcerer from Hyperborea to the Southern Void. Better yet, I know where most of them are and what they're planning."

Skallagrim's eyes grew wide at the implications. Even he recalled the secretive nature of sorcery and its practitioners, and he knew such a list would be nearly impossible to come by. True, some of these fiendish spellcasters were open about what they did, many of them even ruling over cities, as was the case of Griog'xa and Archon, but they were secretive to a fault regarding their purposes. Many of them kept their name, their lair, and in some cases, their existence a secret.

"Forneus is not the only sorcerer whose sanctum is hidden in a savage, trackless wilderness. There are others." Even in the dark,

Skallagrim could see the flash of a wicked smile on Erling's face. "Some are hiding in dungeons beneath the great cities, working on diabolical schemes for mad princes and kings. Some are joined in loose cabals, plotting coups and wars, concealing their lairs in deep caverns or heavily guarded forts and castles. Others are hiding in plain sight!"

He leaned in close to Skallagrim, lowering his voice. "They are murderers; pitiless, arrogant, and assuredly insane, their minds blasted by the blasphemous things they have conjured and seen. They don't deserve the power they have gathered." Erling paused, considering his next words. "One by one, I would see them all dead, Skallagrim. Do you understand?"

Skallagrim pulled back from Erling, noting the peculiar gleam in his eye. "So, my killing Forneus has become part of an ongoing crusade of yours?" he asked, hearing Hartbert making his way back to the pair.

"Sure, Skallagrim. We'll call it a crusade. I like that." The wicked smile evaporated as if Erling regretted the unsettling way in which he had answered, but he recovered quickly. "Oh! Speaking of sorcery, I nearly forgot!"

He rummaged about in his jacket pocket, at last producing a small vial containing an oddly glowing blue substance, much like the one he had given Skallagrim the night before. "Here's a bit of sorcery you may need."

"What is it?"

"Well, actually, it's more wizardry than sorcery, and there is a difference, mind you! It's Caeruleum—very rare! I gave you a dose when we first escaped, remember? It kept you alive till Old Tuva could sew you up." Erling unfastened one of the small pockets on Skallagrim's baldric and secured the vial inside. "Frankly, my friend, in your condition, you should not be up and walking about. Tuva did more than stitch you up, but then you know that. When her magic wears off—and it will—or should you find yourself terribly injured again or up against some foe you feel is beyond you or your terrifying sword there—and you may—drink this potion. Caeruleum will grant you a burst of strength and might just see you through."

Skallagrim's eyes narrowed. "Does this come from Old Tuva?"

Erling waved away his concern. "No, no. It's from my own stock, another gift from me to you. And Skallagrim, you know I spoke of returning the favor one day?"

"Yes, I'm indebted to you. I don't deny it."

Erling's voice dropped to a conspiratorial whisper. "I should like a peek inside Fort Vigilance. I mean, if all goes well, and you manage to kill Forneus, I would like to search the place."

"I'll kill the fiend," Skallagrim growled, displaying more confidence than he felt. "When that's done, I'll give you a guided tour of the place."

"Get the key, Skallagrim, and the favor will be paid." Erling smiled and began to say more, but the conversation ended as Hartbert returned, his giant shape rearing like a dark pillar over the two crouching men.

"We're good," he said. "There's nothing out there. Let's go."

He led them to the edge of the pine grove, where they crossed a shallow stream by way of a wooden plank bridge. They found themselves in a grassy meadow, the ground soggy and rutted from the passage of wagon wheels. Ahead was rolling pastureland bordered by shadowy hedgerows. It was all easily visible in the moonlight, and Skallagrim grew wary, preferring the concealment of the trees if soldiers were indeed searching for him. But he had a knack for sneaking about in the dark, or so he guessed. If he had to cross these fields, he would simply stick to the hedgerows.

Far to the right, a mile or so distant, the lights of a village were visible. The smell of cooking fires wafted now and then on the breeze, and Skallagrim thought jealously of the families who might be sitting down for dinner there. *Wouldn't that be nice: a wife, a couple of fine, strong sons, dinner, and a warm bed!*

No, it was not to be, not for many years at least. Maybe never at all if the dread doom of the sword was real. He had sensed something from the beginning, amidst the fight, an uncanny attachment to the blade and a feeling of supernatural woe. Erling had mentioned it too—doom.

"This is where we take our leave," Erling stated. "Hartbert and I have horses waiting for us at a stable not far from here. That is out of your way though. Best we part here."

Skallagrim was jarred from his gloomy thoughts. "Point the way, sir, and I'll be off."

Erling indicated the village lights. "Head north, that way, but keep the village on your right. About a mile past, the land begins to slope toward the river valley. You'll cross a country lane, and just beyond, you'll see a forest. There's an old timber road you can take for another mile or so, and then that will run out. From there on it will be downhill to the river. There's a trail with several switchbacks, and I'm not sure you can see it in the dark. If you can't, the descent will be very steep." He paused and nodded to Hartbert to fill in the rest.

The giant cocked an ear to listen. Dogs were barking in the distance, and a whippoorwill had begun its evening ritual, calling to its mate. Satisfied that nothing was amiss, he picked up the thread. "We're on a plateau, so to speak, Mister Skallagrim. Down at the bottom, you'll come upon the Pagarna River. There is, or was, an old stone bridge to the other side, and you'd do well to take it, as there won't be another till you get to Fort Vigilance, and it's sure to be guarded. If you can't find the trail down to the river, just try to remember the bridge is on a straight line with the timber road. Once across, there's an old roadbed, flooded in places but passable. It will eventually run you right to the fort." He held out his hands and shrugged. "Beyond that, I can't tell you much. Neither of us has been farther than the bridge, and that was a few years back." He paused for a moment as if struggling with a memory. "Something happened down yonder. Seems like we got into a terrible row with—heck, I can't remember. You recollect, Mister Hizzard?"

Erling shifted uneasily. "Vaguely."

"I know I lost something down that way, but . . . oh well. It doesn't matter." Hartbert looked at Skallagrim. "I wish I knew more that could help you."

The whippoorwill had shifted its base of operations to a tree in the nearby pine grove, and the three turned to stare back the way they had come, annoyed by its insistent call. The dogs were barking still, closer now, but they paid them no mind.

"Forty miles?"

Hartbert nodded. "You saw the map, Skallagrim. It's forty miles of rough going."

"Four nights?" Skallagrim directed his question to Erling.

"It's Tuesday, or what's left of it," Erling affirmed. "The rites of Mog Ruith will be performed on Friday at midnight. Your lady may be safe till then. You have time, but you best get moving."

"Shhh!" Hartbert motioned the two to silence and, turning to his right, cocked his head, listening. The dogs were howling, and the racket had grown alarmingly close. The howling was soon joined by the sounds of horses and shouting men. Skallagrim, Hartbert, and Erling froze where they stood.

"There!" The giant pointed into the night, but there was no need, for they could all clearly see the shapes of riders heading toward them. Several torch-bearing figures on foot veered away from the main group toward the village. Hartbert motioned for his companions to duck. Keeping low, they made their way back into the tree line where they were less exposed.

"Balor's bones!" Erling cursed under his breath, grabbing Hartbert's muscled arm. "What now? Do we break and run, split up, or what?"

"Could be hunters," Hartbert answered. "But the riders are heading our way. Like as not, they're looking for Skallagrim." The horsemen were two hundred yards distant and closing fast. The dogs, snarling now, would be even closer, running ahead of their masters, though the animals remained unseen in the darkness.

Skallagrim gripped his sword hilt but resisted the urge to draw his blade. "They couldn't have tracked me underground. We just emerged from the tunnel."

"No, but they've got your scent now." Hartbert pulled the two close. "My job is to guard you, Mister Hizzard." He gave Erling a hard look. "You and I can run for it and probably get to our horses. Skallagrim, make for the river. It's now or never!"

"On foot?" Skallagrim pointed toward the approaching riders. "I'll never make it!"

"Correct," Erling confirmed. "They're too close. The matter is decided," he said, gathering his resolve to face the inevitable confrontation. "Draw swords, my friends." He rose and, turning to his companions, bade them do the same. "Besides, in my dealings with sorcerers, I have learned a few tricks that might help." Not waiting on the others, he drew his sword and then stepped into the open as six horsemen and a pack of growling hounds bore down on him.

The horseman closest to Erling reined in. "There!" He pointed at Erling and then kicked his mount into action, drawing a curved scimitar. The remaining four drew their swords and charged as well, two of them dropping torches onto the wet ground. Hartbert drew his blade and lumbered forward to join his master while Skallagrim leapt to Erling's right, his blade already drawn. Terminus glowed brightly in the night but withheld its uncanny shriek.

The dogs were mere feet from Erling when he held up his left hand and shouted something incomprehensible at the charging beasts. The jeweled ring on his hand flared red. There was a flash of searing light and a sudden boom in the air, a heart-stopping thud that hit Skallagrim square in the chest. The moonlit night went blacker than black for a second while a thunderous voice, not Erling's, bellowed a dreadful shout, a word of command full of dread and fury.

Chaos erupted. Two large hounds skidded to a stop at Erling's feet and then keeled over, dead. The rest of the pack veered away and fled back the way they had come, yelping. All six of the horses reared, kicking and screaming in terror as their riders struggled to regain control. Four of the riders were thrown and landed with sickening thuds as their mounts bolted into the night. The remaining two horses crashed into each other, their riders cursing. One of the beasts dropped to its knees and then fell to the ground, dead, its rider kicking free of the stirrups and jumping clear at the last second. The remaining rider managed to regain control of his horse and charged Erling to ride him down.

Hartbert jumped in between his master and the horse, its eyes wild with terror. The giant's size and strength were such that, for the beast, it was like hitting a stone wall. Hartbert struggled to reach around the right side of the animal to grab its rider but stumbled backward into Erling to avoid the rider's scimitar as it came sweeping toward his head. Skallagrim, keeping one eye on the other riders struggling to stand, jumped to the horse's right side and skewered its rider with Terminus. The horseman screamed and, dropping his scimitar, grabbed futilely at the gaping wound in his stomach, unable to stop the gushing flow from the mortal wound. His eyes were wide with shock and surprise as he slumped, then fell from the saddle.

He was not of Archon's Watch. None of the riders were. There were no black robes nor red-plumed helmets. These were Straker's sellswords, cutthroat mercenaries hired to do the bidding of Forneus Druogorim.

Skallagrim was alarmed by the suddenness of his own response, sickened by the feel of his blade penetrating flesh and the soul-churning remorse that came from killing a man, even if it was in defense of another. Chaotic emotions surged around him like twisting vines, threatening to paralyze him into inactivity.

He was caught off guard by the suddenness of the attack, battered and sleep-deprived from the previous night's events. But he was still a man, still knew he must force himself to move and to fight. The sword was humming, vibrating in his hand, goading him to action. He acquiesced to Terminus and, allowing its will to embolden his own, stepped free from the mire of self-doubt.

First things first. He reached out with his free hand and steadied Erling, who was staggering to his feet after his collision with Hartbert.

"I knew that ring would come in handy one day." Erling dodged the horse, who was lashing out with its hooves. "But that is the limit of my supernatural contributions for tonight. Now it's sword work for us all!" Saying this, Erling charged the remaining riders. They were stunned and scrambling to regain their feet but had already drawn their blades.

Skallagrim freed himself of his knapsack and then dashed forward to join Erling, who was already trading blows with a swordsman. Terminus flashed in the moonlight as Skallagrim swung the blade at the largest of the group, but his foe brought his own blade up, and the two swords rang like anvils. The clash sent a jolt through Skallagrim's arm, but he slashed sideways, raking his sword across his opponent's neck. The sellsword dropped his blade, clutched at the savage cut to his neck, crashed to the ground, groaning.

Skallagrim stalked toward another swordsman while Hartbert, not to be outdone, stomped into the fight and rammed into one of the foes, knocking him to the ground. The giant placed a heavy foot on the fallen man, pinning him to the dirt, then parried a sword thrust from the remaining swordsman.

Skallagrim's opponent swung wildly with his scimitar, then retreated beyond his reach, having missed him by a foot. "This one's got the damned sword!" he cried out to his mates.

Even if he could not see the swordsman well in the dark, Skallagrim could hear the fear in his voice and smell the dread coming off him like billowing smoke, for his senses were heightened, his body electric. He was no longer the battered thief who only hours before had fought alone for his life in the alley. He had allies fighting at his side now. Unease and self-doubt were vanquished as Terminus came alive in his hand, eager for blood and sharing its savage power with him. He could feel it transforming him, snatching up the darker parts of him and molding them into a weapon.

Now Skallagrim *was* the weapon, forged of hatred for all things vile and an unquenchable desire for revenge against the immortal dark. He circled his foe, careful to find firm footing on the wet grass. "Yes, I have the sword." He was glaring now, and if his foe could have seen the stitched and bruised horror that was Skallagrim's face and the seething fury of his eyes, he would have turned and run. "Is that what you've come for?"

Why? Why now? Why again? He wished only to be moving, striding away to unknown Pagarna and to hell with its monsters and ghouls! Yes, on to the Vales of Pagarna, to cross the wild river, find his way into the sorcerer's fortress, and reclaim his love. Yet a fool with a scimitar stood blocking him, keeping him from the blue-eyed girl—the tragically, beautiful, blue-eyed girl—who would be murdered if he did not find her in time.

He stamped forward, lunging with Terminus, but the man parried, then backed away again, unsure whether to fight or to flee.

Erling's opponent, gasping for breath, called out to his companions. "Straker says to kill him!"

When Skallagrim heard the name, he remembered the laughing wolf-faced fighter who had cut his face so viciously. He would not forget Straker, and he hoped he would have a chance to meet him in combat again one day. But for now his current opponent was scurrying away, his sword held nervously in front of him to ward off Skallagrim's attacks.

"Well, Straker ain't here, is he?" The man shrugged at Skallagrim, dropping his guard and backing off another step. "Look here, I got no real fight with you, mister. Let's just call it a day, hey? I only want to get back to my family."

While the fight raged around them, Skallagrim's opponent dropped his hands to his sides, his sword pointing toward the ground. Skallagrim relaxed his guard for a second as he considered the man's words. But he was missing nothing; he knew this was merely a ruse, and he was ready for the man's next move.

The soldier's sword came up, and he leapt through the air, closing the distance between himself and Skallagrim in a flash. Skallagrim dropped to one knee that sank into the damp earth. He steadied himself, holding his sword straight out and locking his arm. The soldier was in midair, realizing his mistake but unable to alter his attack. He shrieked as his body's momentum drove him onto the point of Terminus and then farther, nearly to the hilt.

The shock and bewilderment in his eyes were complete. Not just from pain, or indignation at his colossal mistake or even the surprise of his impending death. It was the shock of dying on Terminus, and Skallagrim could see it in the man's terror-filled eyes. Something more horrible than dying was happening to him, something immense and eternal. He had not sensed it in the others he had slain, but then he had not looked them in the eye. But he witnessed this all in a fraction of a second, and Skallagrim had no time to consider the significance. He twisted his sword and wrenched it free of the man, who was mercifully dead before he hit the ground.

He turned as he heard a muffled scream, then a sickening crunch as Hartbert put his full weight on the head of the man he had pinned to the ground. Then the giant lashed out with his blade at the swordsman facing him, slashing the man's left forearm. It was a vicious cut, and the soldier yelped, then frantically swung his blade at the giant's sword, beating it aside. He lunged with his sword, but Hartbert brought his blade up and over the other man's sword quick enough to parry, then grabbed the man's sword arm and jerked him forward. The struggling man was slammed into the giant's body with enough force to knock the wind out of him. He stood no chance as Hartbert, with the strength of an ox, wrapped his sword arm around the man and pinned him to his chest. The soldier kicked frantically, then used his own head to beat against the giant, but it was a wasted effort. He was being slowly crushed in a suffocating bear hug—eyes streaming, smothered, and helpless to break free. As Hartbert squeezed, the man grunted and dropped his blade. With both tree-like arms wrapped around the man, he tightened his hold, squeezed hard again, and all the remaining air went out of his foe. The man's eyes bulged, and his mouth opened in a silent gasp as he died, his body slowly going limp in Hartbert's arms.

The giant grunted his satisfaction, then, using his tremendous strength, lifted the man's body level with his eyes. Not entirely convinced his foe was fully expired, or just for good measure, Hartbert delivered a bone-cracking head butt to the dead man before dropping his corpse to the ground.

Skallagrim and Hartbert turned toward Erling to see how he

was faring and were just in time to see him swing his sword in a deadly arc, dispatching his opponent as the blade sliced partway through the man's head. The man slumped to the ground, and Erling wrenched his blade free. Leaning on his sword and panting for breath, he returned the gaze of his two companions and laughed.

"Well, I suppose they got more than they bargained for. Are either of you hurt?"

"I'm not cut," Hartbert replied.

"I'm okay too," Skallagrim said, looking around at the slaughter with a strange mix of revulsion and relief.

It seemed the battle glory, the fierce, hate-fueled fury that Terminus granted him, had ebbed, gone like a ghostly whisper on the wind. He was exhausted, and his wounds started to ache again, especially those on his face.

He knelt and wiped the blood and gore from his blade, using the cloak of one of Hartbert's crushed opponents for the task. Sheathing Terminus, he touched the stitches on his face, probing the wound until he was certain it had not reopened.

The lone, remaining horse paced skittishly nearby. It whinnied as Hartbert slowly approached and then began stroking its muzzle while whispering soothing words.

Erling, his eccentric behavior always a puzzle to Skallagrim, was in the process of looting the dead men, rifling through their packs and pockets. He flipped a gold coin in the air and, catching it, gave Skallagrim a quizzical look.

"What?"

"Oh, nothing. It's just that they're not even cold yet." Skallagrim indicated the bodies of their slain foes. "You, sir, are a mystery. I thought you were a rich merchant, and yet you're rooting through the pockets of the dead for spare change."

"Gold earned or gold found, either way, it's still gold! Besides, how do you think I came by this ring?" Erling indicated the glimmering jewel on his left hand, then went back to his ghoulish task, ignoring Skallagrim.

"What is that, anyway?"

"Just a trinket I pilfered from a dead conjuror a few months back," Erling explained as he continued his treasure hunt. "He was a fraud, actually, a flimflam man who claimed to be a sorcerer but who died on the edge of my blade the same as this gent here." He rolled the body over and then moved on to the next. "Somehow in his dealings he came across a few useful, magical things, like this ring. Limited appeal, really. It only worked on the beasts just then and not all that well. I think I shall sell it. Aha!" Erling pulled his fist from deep within the purse of the corpse he was examining and opened his hand to see what he had found. "Bah! Just silver. Still . .." Not bothering to finish his sentence, he pushed himself up and made his way to the rider whom Skallagrim had first slain.

Weary and impatient, Skallagrim walked away to retrieve his pack, shaking his head at Erling's cavalier attitude toward death. Men reacted differently, he supposed. For himself, he was sick about it all—the screams, the cutting, the blood, and the dying.

He could remember so little of his life before the previous night, but he was reasonably sure that killing had not been part of it. Yet somehow things were different now, denatured in some inexplicable, transmundane way. What had just transpired, this flurry of swords and spurting of blood? He had gone at it with precision, with the callousness of a cold-blooded killer. No, that could not be right. He felt, and he felt deeply. He had not gone looking for this confrontation. Rather, it had come to him, and he had faced it with a casual cunning that he had not felt before. Was he cold-blooded? No! Efficient in the heat of battle? That was closer to the truth.

But he knew with uncanny certainty that it was the sword calling the shots. The previous night's alley fight had been desperate. Then the Cold Star had shone. The Black Star had pulsed and fallen from the air. The Terminus sword had screamed in his hand, turning the combat into something ferocious, full of fury and the hair-raising sense that something from beyond Skallagrim's own cursed world had directed his will or imbued it with something deadly and fierce. He looked hard at the thrice-named blade at his side, wondered how many other names it had, who had sent it his way, and why.

Yet now that the fight was over and the sword sheathed and silent, a gloom rose within him like a vast and poisonous vapor, leaching away his confidence and will. It was as if the gloom spoke directly to his heart, making him doubt himself anew while filling his mind with strange revelations.

There had been so much killing in the last few hours, and now the killing itself seemed like a living thing, attached to him like his own shadow, making the task before him seem insurmountable. The killing had saved his life, yes, but it had bloodied his soul and his mind. All he wanted was to save the girl, and so he had left the killing behind, fleeing Archon as one would flee a burning house. But the killing had come again, obstructing his way, drowning the path to what really mattered in a sea of blood, tracking him down in the night to test his sword and his resolve once more. How many more times would it come? Would he get free of the killing and find that beautiful creature whom he had failed?

No, the gloom reminded him. For that was not his only goal. *Find the girl, kill the man.* No, the killing would go with him, and he had to let it if he were to have any hope of success. Several men were dead now, killed by his hand, some before the screaming sword had even fallen from the sky. He could not blame Terminus, and he could not shake free of the killing. It was a taint on his life that he might as well embrace.

And yet there he stood, fighting with himself in a wearying, pointless struggle. Time was passing, and time, he realized, was an enemy too. Forty miles and four nights to find her, and he had barely moved beyond the city walls.

"Look there!" Hartbert shouted, jarring Skallagrim from his dark revery. He was pointing toward the village, where several structures were in flames. As the three watched, remembering the torch-bearing soldiers who had headed that direction, the gut-wrenching screams of women and children reached their ears. "This isn't over yet!"

CHAPTER NINE

A long wail of pain and torment came from the distant flames as the three men stood aghast. They heard angry shouts as dozens of torches flared to life. The flickering tongues spread into uneven lines, bobbing up and down as the shouting grew louder, closer.

"They're coming this way, Mister Hizzard!" Hartbert warned. "We've got to go!"

"Right! We'll have to say goodbye here, Skallagrim," Erling said. An awkward and hurried exchange of handshakes followed. "Take the horse! Go!"

"Give me a leg up." Skallagrim looped the reins over the horse's head, put his foot in the stirrup, and allowed Hartbert to heave him into the saddle.

"You'll never get this animal down from the plateau to the river," Hartbert advised. "Just leave it at the end of the timber road, and it'll find its way to safety."

"Got it!" The horse was skittish, and Skallagrim, no cavalryman, struggled to get the beast under control. Meanwhile, the torchlight and the angry voices loomed ever nearer.

"Forneus is a dangerous opponent," Erling said. He paced nervously, ready to be off. "You can't go barging in the front door. You wouldn't get near it anyway. But you're a thief, Skallagrim. Don't forget it! Find the back door. Everything depends on it! He'll never expect that, but he does know you're coming."

"Got that too!" Skallagrim rested his sword on his right shoulder and kicked the horse into a trot. "In four nights where the two rivers meet beneath the tower; look for me there!" With that, Skallagrim sped away into the night, a phantom-like silhouette in the glow of distant flames.

"Oh, and Skallagrim!" Erling shouted. "Not all that guards the fort will be human!" He turned to the giant. "I say, I don't think he heard that last part, what?"

As Skallagrim raced toward the distant tree line, the torchbearers moved to head him off, forcing him close to the burning village. There was no getting around them and no getting through them unless he wished to ride them down. His horse would have none of it. Already nervous, the beast slowed, then reared as the mob ringed it round.

Another mob! These were neither cultists nor sellswords though; they were farmers and villagers, wielding neither swords nor spears but rakes and pitchforks. Skallagrim's horse trumpeted in terror. In danger of being unseated, he leaned into the animal's neck and struggled to keep his balance. Two men stepped forward, grabbing the reins to steady the beast.

"That's him!" one of them shouted back to the rest. "That's who they were sent to find!"

The mob crowded around Skallagrim, gasping as their eyes took him in. An older man stepped closer to get a better look and was greeted by an apparition of horror. A timber cracked, then fell with a crash in a burning house directly behind Skallagrim. The flames leapt through the roof like living devils, but all eyes were on the stranger. One of the women screamed, and all of the men began muttering in alarm, most backing away from the unwelcome intruder whose sword flashed red in the firelight.

Skallagrim had yet to see the work Old Tuva had wrought upon him, the bruised and bloody zigzag of stitches that held the left side of his face together. But it was on full display for the angry, frightened villagers. They gawked at the baleful visage, which was weirdly aglow in the torchlight. He looked every bit the monster, a demonic rider from a hellish nightmare realm, but the older man was undeterred.

"And you'd be who, stranger?"

"Skallagrim." He sheathed Terminus and dismounted his horse.

"The men who set those homes alight were lookin' fer a man with a scar and a—" He eyed the blade at Skallagrim's hip. "An exotic sword, they called it. We kilt 'em. Hacked three to pieces and hung the rest."

"I suppose they were looking for me." Skallagrim shifted uneasily.

"Well, they said his name was Skallagrim. So I reckon so. Welcome to Dead Corn," he said with a scowl. "My name's Bug."

"So the stories about last night were all true," Bug speculated. The rest of the villagers—cautious of Skallagrim but convinced he posed no threat—had quickly dispersed to deal with the flames.

Skallagrim willingly related all that had happened to him, from the girl's kidnapping and the alley brawl to the fight earlier that evening.

Monday night's commotion in Archon had stirred much of the village, and many of its inhabitants had come out to watch the strange storm swirling over the city. Errant downpours drove most of them back inside, but a few lingered to gaze at the night's upheaval. The old farmer, Bug, was one of them. He had walked close to the city walls, seen with his own eyes the bright star descending from the tempest. He had heard the distant riot of the mob carrying over the fields and the unearthly shriek that could be heard even above the storm.

Rumors had been swirling by daylight, even in the villages that encircled Archon, that a sorcerer and his minions had fought a lone man who wielded the bright star as a sword—fought him and lost. The name "Skallagrim" was whispered by some, though others said he was "Shield Shaker," a demon come in human form, up from the Southern Void. He came to battle the Dark Lords of the North, those black magicians whose blasphemies had brought a curse upon Andorath, committing atrocities unchallenged in their devil-haunted towers.

It was a good sign, said most, but others shook their heads. In fact, that same elder of Archon who had foretold the star was no star at all, that sage whose grandsire had witnessed the War of the

Great Rebellion, he had a dire warning for all.

"This was the sign," he told them, wagging his finger. "When the star falls, Griog'xa will come down out of his tower. He'll walk among men and work a terrible mischief. The doom of Archon is at hand!" How he knew any of this, he would not say.

They had all heard of the depravity of Archon's most dreaded sorcerer, had learned it from childbirth through nursery rhymes and scary tales told on especially dark nights.

No mortal eye hath seen the sage
That inscrutable mystic, the minacious mage
In many a lifetime, in many an age
The Sorcerer Griog'xa

So began one variant of a popular folk epic of the day. Thus, the fear of Griog'xa had burrowed deep into the psyche of Archon's common folk.

They feared his haunted tower, whose very shadows mocked the sun. They worried about the rumblings that emanated from beneath its cyclopean foundations, stared aghast at the terrible lights that flickered from its topmost windows, and covered their ears when the hideous bellowing came forth from its innermost courts and benighted galleries wherein specters were said to roam. They looked away when gargantuan flying beasts soared and circled on rubbery wings about the dizzying heights of its dreaded spire.

They feared the place, yes, but no one in living memory had seen the man. No one had a tale to tell of Griog'xa himself. Would the man whom "no living man hath seen" come down to terrorize them in person? They hoped not.

The stories, rumors, and opinions spilled from Bug's lips like water from a busted dam. He wanted to help Skallagrim, pitied him, and promised to keep his passage through Dead Corn a secret.

"It's not the first time the men of Forneus Druogorim have harassed Dead Corn. They raided ours and several other settlements near here, carrying off children. Children!"

"And the soldiers of Archon did nothing to help?"

The farmer shrugged. "They're afeared of him. Some of us formed a party a few years back when the children were taken. Now you'll hear time and time again that nobody goes into the wilds along the river. I understand why now, but at the time, I felt we had no choice. So, we headed up the Pagarna, but . . ." Bug stumbled on his words, unsure how to proceed.

"But what? What happened?"

"The closer we got to the fort, the . . . well, the weirder it got." Bug shuffled his feet and frowned, uncomfortable with the memory. "One feller broke a leg, and another fell on his knife and nearly bled out. On the second day in, three old boys who farm up the way there," he pointed vaguely north of Dead Corn, "they got stuck in a bog, and it nearly sucked one of them in. The farther we went up the old river road, the worse our luck got. After a big tree limb came crashing down and nearly killed one of the farmer's sons, some o' the boys started getting a might skittish, wanting to head back. I pushed 'em on for a few miles, but when we got within a couple of miles of the fort, I'll have to admit, even I had had enough. We turned back then, and none of us ever tried it again." The farmer shook his head sadly. "We've never forgiven ourselves for it—for leaving those children. But they were either dead or . . ." His voice trailed off into a murmur.

"Or?" Skallagrim urged him to continue.

Bug stared at his feet, unable to meet Skallagrim's gaze. "Worse!" He shrugged, then lifted his eyes. "Don't judge us too harshly for it. Something's bad wrong up there, and I don't think it was your sorcerer."

"What do you think it was?" Skallagrim pressed. He needed to know what he was facing.

"It's hard to say. There was a deep holler just before the final climb to the fort and some old flooded ruins. Somethin' was in there, Skallagrim. I can't say what, but I'd sooner die than go back to that place!" Bug shivered and laughed nervously. "It still gives me the heebie-jeebies, and I'm not ashamed to admit it!"

Skallagrim thought for a moment. "Have you heard of the Old Man o' the River?"

If Bug had been uncomfortable before, he was even more so now. "Of course. For some sadistic reason, the tale is told to every child in every village around Archon. Why?"

"Could it be lurking in those ruins?" Skallagrim asked. "I'm just wondering. Stupid question, I suppose." He shrugged. "But I was warned about it by a man I trust."

The farmer eyed Skallagrim apprehensively. "Of all the terrible things we've heard about the Vales of Pagarna, from nightgaunts to ghouls and all things in between, if I were you, I'd be hoping to hell there ain't no Old Man o' the River. Not if the yarns are true!" He scratched his head. "I wouldn't put too much stock in them though. Let's just hope whatever was in that holler is long gone. It's a pity you have to go to Fort Vigilance at all but especially by the route you're taking. It's not going to be easy, but I wish you the best."

"I've been assured repeatedly that this is the only way for me to go," Skallagrim said. "Whatever lies on the old road between here and the fort, I'll just have to deal with. Sorry to hear about Forneus, especially that he's been a problem for you as well."

"There are others beside Dead Corn who have a crow to pick with him, other towns and settlements spread out near the walls of Archon. They'll not be sorry to hear someone is finally going to stand up to him, even if the man who does it looks like a devil!"

Skallagrim quirked an eyebrow at the comment, still unsure of the misgivings the folk of Dead Corn seemed to have about him. He understood the sword was potentially monstrous, and as long as he carried it, he would be a man to be feared. He was filthy, wounded, and scarred, but he did not—could not—understand the combination of both things, the sword and his appearance.

First, he had not seen himself. Second, the sword, unbeknownst to Skallagrim, greatly magnified the significance of his appearance, lending him an aura of danger. He would learn more about it in time, but for now he thought of himself as a lowly thief who had somehow bound himself to a blade far above his calling. And he had no desire to be the hero of villagers who were loathe to look upon his face. *Find the girl, kill the man.* That was his task, nothing more.

"I guess I need to get moving," Skallagrim said. "Don't want to be the cause of more trouble for you, and there's a young girl out there who needs me."

He handed the reins of his mount to Bug. The horse did little to make up for the violence of the night, but the farmer was happy to take it.

The two shook hands, and Skallagrim, suddenly feeling very much alone, headed out into the night.

CHAPTER TEN

Skallagrim passed through a hedgerow gate. Closing it behind him, he headed to the right, jumped a drainage ditch, and came upon another line of trees and hedges that cut across his path. Finding what appeared to be a thin spot in the barrier, he worked his way through the gap, snagging his pack on a low-hanging branch and stumbling over a hidden root. He came out the other side, panting and cursing, but adjusted his knapsack and made off as quietly as he could, passing like a rustle in the grass.

There was a chill in the air, but Skallagrim was warm from his exertions and did not mind. It was good just to be moving. He stuck as close to the hedgerows as he could to avoid being spotted by any riders who might be hunting him. He was relatively unconcerned about Straker's men now, assuming the rest had all gone by way of the main road toward Ophyr. He might have to deal with them later though, perhaps at the fort, for surely some would head down the Gorge Road to ambush him if he came that way. For now his main concern was the city's soldiers. No doubt they would investigate the village fire, so he quickened his pace and headed toward a dark, distant line that likely marked the country lane that Erling's directions had indicated.

The ground began to slope downwards. Skallagrim came at last to a row of spindly maples and privet hedges that, as expected, lined the lane. Turning back one last time, he gazed at the distant glow of the Dreaming City. Archon brooded like a sentient shadow, the windows of its towers blinking like angry, flickering eyes. The city was watchful, full of disdain, glowering at the lone thief who had made good his escape. Skallagrim was passing beyond its influence. But watching it in the gloom, he knew he would never truly be free of its spell, at least not until he had some answers.

Sadly, Skallagrim wasn't just lacking answers; the right questions also eluded him. Archon was a mystery to him. One day he might return and search out its towers, its crypts, and its labyrinths, find out its secrets and thus untangle the tentacles with which the city had snared his mind.

He turned, pulled his pack high on his shoulders, then forced his way through the scraggly privets to the road, thinking no more of Archon, the Dreaming City.

Ahead of Skallagrim was a wall of black, towering shadow. If there was a timber road that would take him into this fortress of oaks, he would have to search for it in the dark. Certainly, it was not in front of him.

There was no sign of traffic on the road. It was well past midnight, and other than the possibility of riders, Skallagrim did not expect to encounter anyone. Still, which way was best?

He finally decided to head left on the road as it would best match his instructions to stay right of the village. It proved to be a good choice, for he had not gone far when the trees opened up into a small pasture. Just on the other side, he found an overgrown dirt road leading into the trees. Well, "road" was a bit of an overstatement, he mused. It was probably just wide enough for a team of horses or mules to have hauled timber out to be milled, but that must have been long ago. Vine-choked bushes crowded either side of the trail, and small trees grew in the middle of it. Still, it was a way forward, and he would take it as far as he could.

He breathed in the night air, refreshed by the chilly sting of it. The sky had been free of clouds, so he had no worry about bad weather, but the moon, which had thus far watched over him was obscured now by the tall oaks, which leaned over the trail like disapproving, tottering old men.

He liked the night, and he even enjoyed walking in the dark. He thought of the warnings and of the many dangers he might face along the Pagarna River, but that was still some way ahead, so he put those gloomy thoughts out of his mind and continued on, troubled only by his lack of sleep and the straps of his pack, which dug into his shoulders.

He would have to sleep at some point, could not possibly carry on throughout the entire night, but was determined to make it down off the plateau to the river's edge, perhaps crossing the bridge over the Pagarna before making camp.

He shivered as a chilly breeze whistled through the oaks, rattling their branches. However far he made it, there would be no comfortable fire tonight. He had a tinder box but no desire to call attention to himself with a cozy blaze. No one had explicitly warned him of bandits in those woods, but there could be hunters. Worse yet, there could be ghouls. Skallagrim knew little of the nightmarish creatures, but he had been warned. Skulking, foul-fanged beasts they were said to be, feeding on the mouldering dead.

There I go again with the gloomy thinking. He could not help himself. But if he was a thief, he reasoned, then he probably had an alertness for such things.

Ghouls!

Yet, he was not dead. So, what was there to fear from ghouls? If he died along the trail somewhere, he did not relish the idea of being food for such, but then, what would he care if he was dead? And any graves found along the river were supposedly ancient mounds, their occupants having disintegrated into dust and fragments of bone long ago. He began to think an encounter with ghouls highly unlikely, and then he laughed at the grisly notions he had entertained, a little too loudly for his comfort, however. The night had grown very quiet, devoid even of the sound of crickets, which he remembered hearing earlier. No night birds sang. Only the slightest breeze played among the creaking oak branches swaying overhead.

It was still eerily quiet when, after about a thirty-minute walk, the old road played out. Skallagrim had supposed he could pick up a trail that would lead down the plateau, but there was none to be seen, at least not in the dark.

An imposing wall of hickory and oak rose in the darkness to block the ravine, which must lay beyond. Many of last year's leaves were still clinging to their spidery branches, and they crackled like fire as a stiff wind blew up the valley and onto the plateau from the north. This sent volleys of leaves swirling about, creating a noisy carpet on the ground. Skallagrim crunched many underfoot as he searched the end of the roadbed, hoping to spot a path. But the ground at the base of the trees was thick with a tangle of undergrowth that discouraged any ingress or further exploration.

He wondered how high up he was over the valley. Stopping his search for a minute, he listened intently. There was no sound of the Pagarna's rushing water coming from beyond the trees, at least none he could hear, so the river still had to be a good way off. Erling had said there was a path, though, in all fairness, he had also warned it would be hard to find. The slope was said to be steep, and Skallagrim did not relish plowing his way downhill through a thick forest without the benefit of light or a trail, but there was nothing for it. Heading straight downhill from the timber road would dump him out on the trail at some point, and he determined this to be his only course of action. It was that or camp where he was and wait for dawn. But that seemed too much like giving up. He was tired and probably not thinking clearly, but a beautiful girl with eyes as blue as the summer sky needed him. And Skallagrim needed sleep. But he fought it off and shoved his way into the thicket.

It was tough going. Skallagrim's cloak snagged on every branch and every bush as he crashed through the trees and down a slope that was growing steeper by the minute.

Scant moonlight made its silvery way through the treetops to light his way. The farther down the slope he went, the more the canopy overhead seemed to thicken, hiding, at last, the endless vault of space and plunging him into a more terrible night—the night of a forest primeval. The darkness was like the suffocating blackness of a pit, and Skallagrim was its prisoner, slipping deeper down its steep side toward the unknown.

A branch grabbed at his cloak, jerking his head painfully

backward. He cursed, then a rock gave way beneath his right foot, which took both of his feet out from under him. As he fell, his cloak was held in place by the branch, and he was momentarily throttled by the tie and clasp. Mercifully, he heard the snap of the limb, but down he went, landing hard on his behind.

He rolled over, frustrated and angry, but slipped again on the rocks as he tried to stand. He reached out into the darkness, grasping a sapling, steadied himself, and slowly rose to his feet. His thrashing had sent a number of rocks tumbling down the hill, but one rather large stone below him must have gone over an unseen ledge. One second it was sliding through the leaves just a foot or two below where he stood, and then there was silence. A second later it crashed into the canopy far below before finally hitting another rocky surface with a resounding clap that echoed off the face of the ravine.

Skallagrim had come to an impassable bluff or cliff face. He would need to move sideways now, either to find a way around the precipice or to hopefully find the trail he needed.

Grabbing saplings and tree trunks to steady himself, he headed to the right, setting loose more stones that went tumbling down the hill and over the bluff. Anything living within a mile would surely know some great blundering fool was fighting his way down from the plateau, but on he went, panting for breath and cursing each time he slipped.

He had not gone too far when the ground leveled out, and he came to a hard-packed surface. As luck would have it, the canopy opened up, allowing a glimmer of moonlight to fall upon a narrow pathway.

He had found it! Relief washed him over. Even in the dim light, the trail was visible as it wound down from the slope to his right. To go left would take him along the edge of the bluff. Barely visible, the tops of trees far below stretched into the darkness. At the limit of that darkness rose a wall of deeper black that had to be the mountains on the other side of the Pagarna, the rushing sound of which was clearly audible.

His spirits feeling lighter now, he quickened his pace. At times the path veered away from the bluff, but always it led down and down. Skallagrim paused once to drink from a tiny creek that snaked down the slope and plunged through the rocks to the valley floor. He splashed his face with cool water to stave off the desire for sleep, then gasped in pain as it stung his wounds. He would have to clean those wounds often, and he did not relish the agony of touching them again. He shook his head a few times to clear the fog of exhaustion, then continued on his way.

Eventually, the trail turned hard left and took a steep route through the cliffside boulders. He clung to the sides, squeezing his way through and down the rocky way. In the light of day, it would have been no trouble, but as the trail dove deeper into the rocks, the elusive moonlight was doused again, and the descent quickly became perilous.

Skallagrim was struggling on the stair steps now, and surely that is what they were, actual steps that had been cut into the rock or placed with hewn timber for the ease of hunters and trappers. He could not tell how they were made or placed, only that they were there. But the wilderness staircase was steep and uneven, and Skallagrim could not see. He finally opted to sit down and scoot from step to step.

It made for slow progress, but rather that than trip and go headlong down the ravine, breaking bones or busting his head on the rocks below. His scabbard clanked on the hard ground as he drove farther and farther into the inky black of the precipice. Eventually, he reached the bottom, or at least another ledge. He scooted around on his backside for several feet in either direction, feeling like a fool for going about it in that manner, but he was determined to be certain of relative safety before he tried to walk again.

Finally convinced that the ground had indeed flattened out, Skallagrim strained his eyes in the dark, hoping to find any indication of which way to go. If there was a trail there, it was not obvious. He felt his way along the bottom of the cliff, keeping the rocks on his left side, and soon the ground began to slope once more toward the valley. Little did he realize he was walking along the edge of another ledge, and one wrong step to his right would find him sliding to the actual bottom of the plateau.

Skallagrim was growing anxious to reach the river. Hours had gone by since his encounter at the burning village. He began walking faster, hoping to pick up the trail again. Any trail at all would be a relief.

He came to a huge fallen hickory tree too massive to climb over and determined to crawl under it instead. He had to squeeze, sliding as he did through a puddle of mud. When he finally poked out the far side, his clothing was soaked in oozing muck.

He shivered and found he could not stand upright due to the fallen branches and the general clutter of vine-choked saplings and underbrush. So, for a time, he crawled in the dark, feeling like a lowly beast, some primitive dweller of slime and mud.

His brain was full of fog, and he could barely keep his eyes open. He turned once and tried to claw his way back to the tree trunk but never came to it. Instinct told him he was lost, but he thrashed stubbornly about in the undergrowth until his hand hit on nothing, and he realized he had come to another precipice.

"You're lost!"

Skallagrim turned around from the ledge and found himself caught in a tangle of thorny vines that ripped and tore at his clothes. He lunged, trying to force his way through, but snagged on a large vine. It felt as if a large hand had snatched the hood of his cloak, jerking him backward toward the cliff. He scrambled furiously—frantically—to keep from slipping over the edge. Fortunately, his scabbard had snagged, and it anchored him in the snarl of thorns, vines, and branches.

With a great effort, he pulled himself clear of the terror of the cliff but could only go so far. Vicious thorns had cut into his hands, and he was fairly certain he was bleeding in several spots along his arms and legs.

"Damn it! Damn it!"

Skallagrim could do no more, for to go farther in the dark was impossible. Time was not on his side, and he was grimly aware he was already losing the battle.

Four nights until the girl would die, the girl who was as lovely as winter stars and as tragic as a heartache. One of those four nights was only half spent, but it might as well be gone. Skallagrim was finished.

He dropped to the ground, wet, cold, shivering, and completely demoralized. What a fool to think he could make war on a sorcerer when he could not even climb down from these cursed hills. The gloomy thoughts came on and on, slithering into his mind like the slithering thing he had become.

Dark thoughts were always strong when he gave into them, but for now, sleep was stronger, and a true darkness cloaked his mind for a time. Then he fell into a dream of a wonderful blue-eyed girl.

CHAPTER ELEVEN

*H*e watched her dancing in the moonbeams in a clearing beside the silvery waters of a rushing stream. The golden-haired girl, in the glory of her youth, evinced grace and beauty that could only be described in song. She had not seen him, not yet. So, Skallagrim watched quietly from behind the trunk of a great tree, transfixed as she pirouetted, seemingly mesmerized as twinkling lights, which he at first took for fireflies, swirled around her, clothing her naked form in radiance.

She was like living poetry whose verses were woven of shimmering twilight and a faerie dawn, spoken in some long-forgotten age of perilous kings and of glittering spires.

He was entranced, drawn to her by an age-long spell that could not be undone.

Her nearly translucent form spun prettily once more, rippling the air about her like a golden wind across water. Then she curtsied to an unseen partner, and her dance was done. She found something amusing in the action, and it brought forth laughter like the tinkling of elfin bells.

Skallagrim's heart pounded in his chest, and his breath quickened as her spell took hold of him. His feet took unbidden steps into the dusky clearing. She turned then, seeing him at last, and he feared that she might flee. To his great delight, she smiled, and her sapphire-blue eyes were lit with mirth, flashing like twin stars that flared in the dark forest. She laughed again in her magical way, making his heart glad.

The two of them stood only feet apart in the moonlit glade of a forest so wondrous it could only be described in song. They were like youth unspoiled, two spirits from whence no sigh or sin was born, upon whom no troubled thought or pain of burdened mind had yet fallen. He made to move closer to her, but she held up one slender, bejeweled hand and bid him hold his place. Then she sang these words to him with a voice both

SKALLAGRIM — IN THE VALES OF PAGARNA

sweet and sorrowful.

> As I walk tiredly toward the west
> And think of all I've seen and done
> Fortress tall and cavern deep
> Old forest dark, the ocean wide
> And climbing up the mountainside
> My road then led me further on
> So I journeyed westward

> As I walk tiredly toward the west
> My heart cries out for hearth and home
> Familiar faces, friendly smiles
> Now all I know is left behind
> Until at last one day I'll find
> My road will lead me home once more
> To go no more a-questing

As she spun her song, Skallagrim felt the pain of a thousand years of heartache wash over him. As much as it hurt to hear it, he would not have had her cease her singing even if the anguish of her words and her melody were to stop his heart cold.

> Am I to lose my way again?
> Never to see your sweet smile, my friend?
> I'll search to find you and bring you home once more
> My true love, so far away

> As I walk tiredly toward the west
> My heart cries out for hearth and home
> Familiar faces, friendly smiles
> Now all I know is left behind
> Until at last one day I'll find
> My road will lead me home once more
> To go no more a-questing

When the song ended, he realized his eyes had misted. Though he could barely speak, he still tried.

"That's my song?"

"Yes," *she answered in a voice at once full of tenderness and a majesty undreamt of by mortals.* "Your song to me."

"But I have never quested, never been anywhere beyond this forest."

"Not yet," *she replied. A brisk breeze stirred the branches of the mighty trees around them. She glanced at the rushing stream, then looked back wistfully at Skallagrim. Music began to throb the air about them, and the wind began to pick up. A crescendo was building, a climax full of tension, full of threat. The moon dipped behind a cloud, and the twilight glade was plunged into near darkness. The joy of their meeting fled as the air about them became heavy with foreboding.*

The girl's face, once full of light and beauty, was now darkened by some inner struggle. She bit her lower lip as if in thought. "It's nearly too late, my love," *she said.*

Skallagrim spoke loudly now, for the fortissimo of the forest's music was nearing a doom-laden apogee. "What do you mean?"

The wind was whipping the trees now, and thunder rumbled the sky.

"Though I may sleep, the ages will roll by. Do not let them sweep you away, Skallagrim. Find me!"

This filled Skallagrim with woe and gloom, a pain so piercingly sweet that it could only be described in song. "I don't understand!" *he shouted as ominous trumpets blared to join the forest's fearful soundscape. Drums were beating madly now. An end was coming, surely!*

"Time!" *she cried.* "Time is nearly up!" *Then she turned and fled, disappearing in the gloom of the trees. He tried to follow, but his feet were lead and would not move. He called out to her, but the music drowned him out.*

Unnoticed until then, a wizened man dressed in regal white robes emerged from the gloom. With the tempest whipping his snow-white hair and a look of profound sadness flickering like a dull flame in his blue eyes, he held out a hand to Skallagrim, bidding him take it. "Come!" *he commanded.* "It's time to wake!" *Then the roaring of the music swallowed*

Skallagrim at last, and the dream of the beautiful girl fled his mind.

The beams of the rising sun lanced over the towers of the Dreaming City and the tall trees of the Archon Plateau, piercing Skallagrim's eyelids like flaming arrows.

At some point in the night, he had managed, with tremendous effort, to get loose of his pack and turn over onto his back. The sudden searing light in his eyes was unwelcome. He could just reach the hood of his cloak, pinned as he was in a snarl of thorny vines. Grumbling, he pulled it over his eyes. With the Dreaming City behind him, its hold on his mind was obviously slipping, for he could dream again. Hoping for another, he quickly fell back asleep.

Only a few miles to the south in the terrible city from whence he had come, Old Tuva was just lying down in a box of dirt while pulling the creaking lid shut over herself. The sun would not trouble her this day as she habitually nested far below the tower of Griog'xa in a dark chamber, the whereabouts of which were known only to a few. She gnawed contentedly on a leg bone that had once belonged to Gam of the Alibi, sucking the good from each tendon and spitting out the gristle. As she nibbled noisily with her jagged teeth, licking and slopping about with her cancerous tongue, she thought of the mischief she had worked on Skallagrim's mind and face.

She cackled, thinking of new mischief to make upon fresh victims once darkness fell again, then noticed with some alarm that her necklace was missing. Meanwhile, Gam lay legless and stiffening on the damp floor of her sepulcher and thought no thoughts at all.

North, up the Devil's Race Highway in the city of Ophyr, the darkness lingered, the sun merely a glimmer on the southern horizon from whence it rose. Yet, the soldiers of the city were readying for a long march.

Everywhere the hiss and scrape of steel on stone could be heard as blades were sharpened. Spears, pikes, and swords by the thousands were taken from their racks and distributed to waiting battalions.

Nervous men, new to war, fidgeted in their ranks, some telling jokes while others silently cursed their fate.

They would march to a savage realm, north of the Vales, to face the fabled axe-wielding men of Urk in battle. Most had no idea why. Some squabble between the sorcerers of Ophyr and the dreaded Warlock King of Urk, they assumed. No concern of theirs.

At least they would not have to face General Arne Grímsson, better known as the Axeman, for rumor had it that he, the most lethal warrior and commander in all of Andorath, had gone missing some months back. The general was a known terror upon the battlefield, a favorite knight of the Warlock King, and the guardian of many of Urk's most fabulous treasuries, armories, and collections of rare and macabre artifacts. Among those artifacts were reputed to be the very keys to the ancient, deserted fortresses of the Pagarna.

But the Axeman was gone now, and no one knew what had happened to him. Some said he had run off with the Warlock King's favorite concubine. Still others—more reliable voices—claimed he had run afoul of one Forneus Druogorim and died in some hideous fashion—poison, most surmised. So, at least the young, untested soldiers of Ophyr had that to be thankful for.

Still, they were loyal soldiers and would fight who and where they were told to fight. They could not know, though their generals should have, that Archon was sending its army north to lay siege to their city. Or, if they found its walls sparsely guarded, which was the case, Archon's own generals would batter down the gates, assail the walls with ladders, and merely take the place without the need for a protracted siege. Either way, Ophyr would soon find itself between the hammer of Archon and the anvil of Urk. Griog'xa, it seemed, had an arrangement with the Warlock King. War was about to consume Andorath, from the Southern Void to the North of North.

But the thief with the screaming sword knew nothing of these matters.

"Damn it!"

Skallagrim swatted at a biting ant on his forehead, managing to tear his hand on some thorns in the process. He tried to fall asleep again, but his mind was racing, and he could not. The dream of the girl and the white-robed man was still fresh in his mind, causing a stab of heartache as he strove to commit it to memory.

Somewhere up ahead she was waiting for him, depending on him, and he had to extricate himself from the thorns and get moving. If Erling was right, he had three days left to find her before the unimaginable happened.

He found himself imagining the worst, so he shoved his plight to the back of his mind. It was just as well he did, for Skallagrim was also growing hungrier by the minute and was dying to relieve himself. With many an "Ow!", "Ouch!", and more than a few choice swear words, Skallagrim began the tedious process of plucking half-inch-long thorns from his clothing while disentangling the numerous vines that had him bound up and pinned to the ground.

Just thirty miles to his northwest, the blazing glory of the sun tried to pierce the darkness of the Bald River Gorge, tried and failed. The mountains rose sheer on either side of Pagarna's largest tributary. It would be nearly noon before the sun climbed high enough over the peaks to dispel the twilight. These were the Smokestacks, and true to their name, their summits were shrouded in mist and cloud.

On the river road between these heights, Straker, the assassin, waved for his column of horsemen to halt, dismounted from his steed, and searched the damp ground with a torch. Skallagrim could not have come this far without a horse, and there were no fresh tracks to be seen. But he would come. The plans had been laid and the bait set.

He laughed when he thought of it, but the laughter was insincere. Straker feared no man, but this Skallagrim was different. The storm had swirled about him, the star had fallen from the sky, and this man, this thief, fool though he may be, had reached up and claimed the star for his own.

Straker shuddered, issued quick instructions to his men, then remounted and made for the sorcerer's tower.

Meanwhile, the sorcerer Forneus Druogorim stared out of a narrow window near the top of Fort Vigilance and saw the sun, like a torch, rising from a darkness it could not banish. The fort seemed always shrouded in impenetrable mists and fumes that rose from the swampy region just to the south. Forneus shuddered as he considered the source, for he had expended much of his sorcery to protect the southern approach to his tower.

It was an extravagant and unnecessary safeguard—one he regretted. For it turned out that the thing he had summoned there was beyond his control. Its price had been too high. If he could not pay the price, would it not turn on him?

No matter, morning had come, and a dismally bleak morning was better than no morning at all. Night was never pleasant in the cliffside tower, perched over the mist-shrouded Pagarna, even if it was his home. Apart from two sentries watching the bridge, he was alone. Yet for some reason he felt watched, and not by the fell guardian to the south. It was as if his every move was contemplated by an unseen presence within the ancient edifice's cold stone walls. The wind whistled through the cracks like whispers of accusation or scorn. At times when howling gusts swept down the lonely peaks about the solitary fort, through some fault of design in its cyclopean foundations, an obscene moan would rise from the pit wherein the dead thing slept.

The pit! The accursed pit! He had peered into the pit once but would not do so again. Dead though the thing might be, he feared it would peer back. Assuredly, to contemplate the dead thing would be to invite madness. Forneus Druogorim would have to deal with it one day but not yet. Griog'xa knew of it, entertained a sick fascination with its horridness. He was a connoisseur of the monstrous, an aficionado of aberration and of corruption. Forneus would introduce him to the dead thing in his own time. His meddling might just be the death of him, which would be fine by Forneus Druogorim.

He sneered, pushing away the sinister apprehensions that grasped at him like greedy claws. To any sane man, the fort and its surroundings were a place of immeasurable horror. Forneus, however, continued the old lies to himself, that Fort Vigilance was just an old tower, and the wind was just wind. The darkness he had summoned a mile south of the fort would forget about him one day, slinking back to whatever miasmic bog had birthed it, and the dead thing in the pit was simply that—dead.

Still, the place was a mystery, even to the sorcerer. Fort Vigilance was older than anyone knew. Griog'xa had been incensed when Forneus had procured the keys to the place, had demanded his envoys be allowed to inspect it from top to bottom, and was infuriated when they were denied entry. Yes, he very much wanted to meet the dead thing in the pit!

Denying Archon's most notorious sorcerer was ill advised, and Forneus had been flirting with disaster to do so. Yet, there were other things he could do for Griog'xa to appease him and to hold him at bay. *Did I not, at great inconvenience to myself, convey that odd vessel of light north for him?* he reminded himself. *A dangerous affair, I say. It smelled of faerie, the entire business! Yet, I did what was asked. He has no right to complain. Not to mention that I'm doing the both of us a favor with this Skallagrim and his screaming sword—at least up to a point!* Forneus clapped his hands and laughed at the unintended pun.

The sorcerer was, of course, lying to himself, as madmen are wont to do. If Griog'xa wanted inside Fort Vigilance, he would find a way. The faster Forneus could capture Skallagrim and the dreaded sword, the better. He could not wield Terminus himself, but that matter was being addressed.

Otherwise, both he and Griog'xa stood to gain if the Night of Mog Ruith went well. That extraordinary evening was close, of course. Forneus thought intently of the plans he had made for that night and of the experiments that were underway in a vault beneath the fort. First, the rites of Mog Ruith demanded a sacrifice, simple enough if everything went to plan. Once that was done, he could turn his attention to the experiment, the grand act of sorcery underway in the vault. It was a dangerous balancing act, the entire affair. One wrong move, and Forneus would be finished.

He glanced nervously south, shielding his eyes from the blood-red blot of the rising sun. He struggled to reassure himself, but doubts weighed upon his mind like stones upon a liche's cairn. Skallagrim would not come from the south, and if he did, he would die. Even if he survived the myriad horrors in the wilderness between Archon and the fort, Pagarna would claim him at last.

Now that would be a great shame! The thief's body—perhaps even the sword—would be lost for all time, and that was contrary to the plan. No, Skallagrim must arrive either living or freshly dead, but he must arrive.

With some trepidation, Forneus turned from the window and descended a spiral staircase. There was work to do in the stygian vault below; messy, distasteful work. It was a risk to keep these labors secret from Griog'xa, but there was no other way, for the work would not have been permitted. Yet, when it was complete, Forneus mused, either Griog'xa would accept what had been done and assume his new place in the order of things or be the first to die.

Forneus Druogorim would be the master of many sorcerers when everything was complete, and this thought made him snicker in the gloom of his dungeon as he approached the vault's ancient door. But he barely suppressed a shudder when he turned the key. He listened with dread as the door creaked open to reveal an old wooden table and the sallow-skinned, jerking monstrosity that lay upon it. It strove vainly against the mighty chains that held it in place, but it only had the one arm at present and a brain that was, as of yet, incomplete.

Aware its tormentor had entered the shadowy vault, it thrashed madly though ineffectually upon the wooden table where it had lain, lo these many months. Its impotent struggle caused a mixed reaction in the sorcerer, equal parts revulsion and psychopathic glee. But when the creature let forth a scream of rage from the quivering, gaping maw of its face, Forneus Druogorim screamed as well.

This was, of course, the normal routine of the vault: the creature gibbering and bellowing insanely as the sorcerer worked his spells,

Forneus occasionally giving in to the horrors of his labor by commingling his own screaming with that of his experiments. And all the while, unbeknownst to the sorcerer, the dead thing in the pit below was listening.

CHAPTER TWELVE

By now the sun was fully risen upon a roadside inn many miles to the southwest of the sorcerer's mountain fastness. It was there that Erling sat fussing over a poached egg and calling for more toast. He and Hartbert had ridden only twenty miles before Erling called a halt for the night just outside the little town of Deep Creek.

As far as Hartbert knew, Erling had spent the night in a fine bed while he made the best of it in the stable where he could see to the horses. The huge man had already consumed enough eggs, biscuits, and gravy for two normal men. Now he stood brooding by the window, watching the road for signs of danger while worrying for Skallagrim and Erling, who was unusually restless. Vexed by what he saw, the giant shook his head.

Patrols on horseback, presumably Straker's men, were scouring the countryside for Skallagrim. In addition to Straker's sellswords and the bandits, who were known to assail travelers on the Devil's Race Highway, columns of soldiers were moving north as well. War was coming.

The choice to send the thief through the Pagarna wilderness had been correct, though what Skallagrim faced in that wilderness might ultimately be worse than a few dozen horsemen. Either way, Hartbert feared he might never see the likable thief again.

Erling, to his credit, had done more than spend a cozy night in a warm bed. His spies were always hard at work, and several had reported to him only an hour before. Their reconnaissance complete, they were able to confirm that Forneus had indeed taken the Gorge Road and had headed to Fort Vigilance.

Satisfied, Erling sent his spies away again on urgent errands. When Hartbert, his beard littered with biscuit crumbs, expressed his deep concern for Erling's safety on the road as well as Skallagrim's chances in the wilderness with so many mercenaries searching for him, Erling waved a dismissive hand.

"But," Hartbert persisted, "that Straker has dozens of horsemen out there. Even if Skallagrim is coming from the south, they're bound to catch up with him at the fort."

Erling mumbled something incoherent to himself, took a dainty bite of his egg, dabbed at his face with a linen napkin, and stared up at the giant. "One hundred and thirty-three horsemen, to be exact, not counting Straker, and most of them are laying an ambush on the Gorge Road as we speak." He pointed a shaky finger at his huge bodyguard. "I'm dealing with issues other than Skallagrim, my colossal friend. And yet," he said with a flourish of a pale hand, "the matter of the horsemen should trouble you no further."

Erling was flippant about the danger, and Hartbert could make no sense of it. Something else was clearly on his mind that morning, worrying him. He had a haggard, haunted look, and his hands were trembling.

"Yes, and how do you propose we get past them?"

"They are sellswords, my enormous friend. Sellswords!"

"Yes, and what of it?"

"I bought them."

"You what?"

"Well, to be fair, I have bought a good many of them and will shortly buy the rest." Erling absentmindedly twirled the end of his ponytail. "You know the best way to win a horse race? You have to own all the horses, what?"

Hartbert creased his brow. "Would you care to elaborate, or do I have to spend the rest of this day trying to figure it out for myself?"

"Well, it's a simple matter of business, really. I know what Straker paid them, so I paid them more."

Erling seemed to take pleasure in dragging out the exchange while Hartbert, his eyes wide with surprise, cleared his throat and pointed out the window at several horsemen who were riding past at that very moment. "You've done what? How?"

"You forget, Hartbert, I move with ease among the exalted circles of Archon. I have the authority to hire men such as these to be auxiliaries for Archon's army. Those you see out there are already riding to protect the flanks of our brave boys on their long march to Ophyr." Erling stood and joined Hartbert by the window. "The ones already in the gorge will be bought off within the hour. My agents should arrive there shortly, I should say." He undid his ponytail and shook out his hair.

A group of soldiers entered the inn and sat down at a table, demanding breakfast from the innkeeper. They had the appearance of officers, many of them young and, by all appearances, excited to be off to war.

When next Erling spoke, it was with a lowered voice. "Sellswords are a treacherous lot, Hartbert. Gold is the only language they speak, and it's a good thing for Skallagrim I'm fluent in that tongue. Now, clean up your beard, and dab the gravy from your lips. We're to be off shortly!" He retied his hair, tossed a few coins on his table to pay for their breakfast, and was about to leave when he noticed his sorcerous ring was missing.

Skallagrim was unable to sit upright in the tangle of vines and thorny bushes wherein he had spent the night. Though time consuming, he had discovered a method to disentangle himself by carefully pulling each vine free of his clothing. This involved finding a spot between half-inch thorns where he could hold the vine between finger and thumb, push it upwards, sometimes tangling it in other vines or merely forcing it away from his face, then scooting out from under the tangle one inch at a time.

He still managed to snare himself several times, ripping a jagged hole in his pants, and more than once jabbed a thorn into the flesh of his fingers, arms, and legs. By the end of it, he was infuriated, finding it more aggravating than painful. But at last he extricated himself from his prison and, with great relief, managed to stand upright and survey the wilderness around him.

The Pagarna River was a ribbon of mist that wound snakelike

through the valley about one hundred feet below where he stood. Above him ran a line of rocky bluffs, beneath which tall pines and majestic oaks vied for dominion upon a treacherous slope. These were the very bluffs he had scooted down the previous night, and he marveled that he had not killed himself in the process.

He worked his way back toward the fallen hickory, once more worming his way beneath it, then retraced his steps back to the base of the bluff.

He had hoped that with the coming of morning, a trail to the valley would reveal itself. Yet, to his dismay, there was no trail to be seen. Clearly, he had gone the wrong way.

After spending a few dismal minutes searching for an alternative way to the river, he realized there was nothing for it except to go straight down, grasping at rocks, roots, and small trees to steady himself on the descent. This did not prove to be as hard as he thought, however. Though he sent a few stones tumbling down the slope, slid on his backside a few times, and added another half dozen scrapes to his already savaged body, it was with great relief that he stood at last on flat ground, albeit a bog, about one hundred yards from the river.

He sloshed through the shallow morass, stopping once to pick up a stout dogwood branch to use as a walking stick. Its smooth surface, shorn of bark, felt good in his hand. With it, he probed his way through the mud and shallow pools of the bog, coming at last to the riverbank.

Tendrils of mist rose like white wraiths from the calm surface of the water. Some sort of river beast, perhaps an otter disturbed by Skallagrim's approach, splashed into the current and swam away. A large fish jumped near a fallen tree that stretched into the water from the bank near where he stood while overhead a turkey buzzard rode the updraft, circling and presumably testing the air for the hopeful whiff of a fresh carcass.

The Pagarna was farther across than Skallagrim had initially thought, over one hundred yards to the other side, if he was any judge of distance. He could not know it, but he was standing at the widest point in the river. To the north—the direction he would be going—he would soon come upon the narrows and the many rapids that had made it an unfit river for any serious trade. Farther south, only a mile or so away, the Pagarna looped wide around the Archon Plateau, where it emptied into a vast delta and swampland to at last mingle with a great sea.

Skallagrim spied the promised stone bridge a few hundred yards downriver—not where he had thought it to be—and realized he should have gone right at the country lane instead of left to find the actual timber road. No wonder he had not found the trail!

When he finally reached the bridge, he had only to look back at the steep slope of the Archon Plateau to see a perfectly good trail winding down from the bluffs. He chided himself for the mistake, for it was plain to see he could have easily managed that wide path, even in the dark, if only he had taken the time to search for the correct timber road.

Nevertheless, here was the bridge, crumbling in places but certainly intact enough to support his weight. He had lost a few hours for his error, but he would make up for it today. Skallagrim guessed he was still only about five miles from the city, which meant there were thirty-five hard miles to tread before he reached Fort Vigilance. He had three days to do it and reckoned he could.

Though distinct memories continued to elude him, Skallagrim found certain ideas familiar, or at least not as alien as the night before. He knew he had journeyed in the wild before, knew too he had walked many miles with a dogwood staff, much as he held now. Despite having spent much time in the woods, he had never grown accustomed to the sweat and grime associated with trail life. He dreaded cold nights with no fire, the sticky feel of his unwashed body, and the biting insects that, when swarming, would drive a man to madness. Yet, for the sake of the girl, Skallagrim would endure it all.

He paused halfway across the bridge to peer into the dark waters that gurgled past its stone arches. Spitting over the side, he watched it hit the water as a tiny spot of bubbles that was instantly swept away, then continued on his way across the bridge.

For all the terrible tales he had been told about the Vales of Pagarna, it was surprisingly pleasant to look upon. A cool breeze was blowing, and the sound of the river was calming to his senses. If this were a place of ghouls and nightgaunts, it certainly did not look it. Of course, he had not reached the other side of the bridge yet. There, things would soon look differently. His night of killings, of cliffs, and of thorns was merely the opening act in a larger play, a tragedy of several acts that was about to begin.

CHAPTER THIRTEEN

As promised, the old roadbed was easily found after crossing the bridge. Skallagrim's spirits were lifted with the discovery, and he set off at a brisk pace, determined to hike at least half the distance to the fort before sunset. But his cheerfulness was short-lived. As Hartbert had warned, the road was flooded in many places, and in some spots it was completely blocked by large boulders that had slid down the mountainside. And yet, Skallagrim got along fairly well, stopping once to rummage through his pack for food and once more to break off a bit of Blood Vine, which Hartbert had packed for him. He chewed on it as he hiked, hoping it would relieve some of the pain from his many wounds.

He had to watch his step to avoid breaking an ankle on loose stones or roots, but now and then he would stop and gaze out across the river. He had nearly drowned in the ocean of madness that was Archon, but like a strong swimmer, he had, with the help of friends, breached the water's surface to breathe the free air of this lush wilderness. He took in the panorama of the verdant valley, marveled at the bluffs that rose like distant spires or lined the ridges like fortress walls, and stared in wonder at the forest, which swept the whole like a dream-laden flood of green water.

By early afternoon he reckoned he had already come ten miles from the bridge and was mightily pleased with his progress. A straight, clean road would have been better, of course, but Skallagrim was young and fit, even if sleep-deprived and aching from a myriad of cuts, bruises, stab wounds, and stitches. So, he slogged through each swampy patch of ground and climbed over many jagged rocks and boulders without complaint.

After another mile and another hour had passed, the road began to veer away from the river. From there it climbed a bare knoll that brought him out above the treetops. This would be a fine place to stop and eat a few bites from his meager supply, but first he had another look around.

The climbing sun had turned the landscape into a green-hued glory, and all the strangeness of his recent adventures seemed to wash away in the wild beauty of the alien countryside. He could smell the fresh green of early spring all about him, mingling with an earthy loaminess that drifted on a sudden breeze up from the alluvial flats nearer the river.

Below him the road wound back in the general direction of the river, but the forest soon covered any sight of it. Enormous hemlocks, elms, and tulip poplars crowded as thick as thieves in the flats and bogs that lined the river. The sun could barely break through such a thick canopy, so Skallagrim let it shine full upon his face while taking in the sights and smells. There were far-off lines of blue ridges on either side of the river. In the haze of the north, he beheld more ridges, behind which reared the hint of impossibly tall mountains, towering like giant overseers over the mystical, wondrous terrain.

He gazed again at the surrounding forest, and for a fleeting second seemed to recollect a similar place. But just like the song in his dream, the memory fled his mind as quickly as it had arrived. Had there been a spectral woodland such as this, some enchanted forest from which he had come?

He suddenly wished he could climb one of the tall peaks and get a better view, survey this strange world in which he had seemingly awoken only two nights ago. He knew next to nothing about this place, only what he had been shown on Erling's map. None of it was familiar, not just the Pagarna and its wooded valleys and ridges but also the entire world in which he found himself, neither its cities nor its countryside nor wilderness. Nothing! As for the Vales of Pagarna, who among the living knew anything? Few went there. Few dared. Yet there he was, and the feeling of aloneness threatened to swallow him up.

Wanting another ten miles of road behind him before dark, he reckoned he had best get moving. A swig from his waterskin and he was off, staff in hand and the mysterious sword swinging at his hip.

At the bottom of the knoll, the shadow of the trees engulfed him, and the heated air of early spring turned as cool as a tomb. The forest thickened around him, as did the darkness, though a gap in the trees ahead revealed the river running swiftly as its course narrowed. The hemlocks and poplars grew right to the edge where they were joined by ancient willows. They bent far out beyond the bank as if wishing to shroud even the river in shadow.

Skallagrim sensed he was not welcome in that wild, dark place. Even the old road was merely tolerated by the forest, perhaps perceived as a scar perpetrated upon it by the tormented projects of men long dead. Now the wilderness was trying to reclaim it, flooding it with murky, muddy water, hurling boulders at it, and trying to cover the sin of it while washing away the memory of its hurt. The trees appeared to leer. In fact, the entire woodland surrounding Skallagrim seemed thick with watchfulness and judgment.

Foolish man! Foolish children that they should attempt to tame the untamable Pagarna with their ill-conceived projects and their greedy plans. Its secrets are its own! Tamper with them at your peril!

If the forest were alive, thinking in this way, and wished to warn him, Skallagrim was warned indeed. Memory knocked on the door of his mind with a hand as ghostly as the tendrils of mist and fog that lingered upon the river. Tales were told around a fire long ago, tales of wicked forests where the trees had faces. With a horrible will of their own, they would twist the paths that ran between them, leading foolish travelers into dark hollows where they would be swallowed up, never to return to the world of light and men.

He shuddered and plowed on. So far, his path was clear, even if uncomfortably dark. It was not long, however, before the twilight gloom and the silence of the forest began to weigh more heavily on him. On Skallagrim's left the green, swollen river raced unabated, sounding like a mighty, rushing wind stirring the pines on some great height. On his right, however, everything was unnervingly silent and watchful. Once, a crow took note of him from an unseen perch in the canopy and cawed a harsh warning to its clan. Otherwise, another mile passed peacefully and without event.

A small stream bubbled and gurgled over round river stones as it wound its way down from the ridge above him. Skallagrim was able to navigate it with ease. Using his staff to probe each slick stone, he jumped from rock to rock, making his way across and up the muddy bank to continue his journey.

A rumble of thunder from the mountains made him glance up, but he could see nothing of the sky overhead as branches, unnaturally thick with the new leaves of spring, covered him like a roof. It was like walking through a solemn, dark crypt of impossible size, wet and dripping, formed of leaning columns and sagging archways that threatened to collapse at any moment. If not for the scant, dismal light to his left where the river ran some twenty yards or so from the road, Skallagrim would have been walking in complete darkness. He glanced about nervously now and then, mostly toward the sparse light of the river course, if only to remind himself he was not actually within an umbratic, claustrophobic chamber.

The forest was weirdly beautiful in a somber, funereal way, like a colossal mausoleum whose joyless vaults were supported by interwoven columns, their vast, mournful chambers hollowed out by the hands of giants. There was a certain thrill to walking in that place with its cool air and ancient trees whose limbs trailed moss like great sweeping beards of grey. Patches of mist drifted across the road, and there were occasional burbling rivulets to jump across. Skallagrim would stop now and then to drink from them, the water fresh and cold.

A chilling breeze sprang up to rattle the lower branches of the trees, sending their beards of moss waving to and fro and causing the trees to take on the aspect of old men shaking their heads in disapproval. Another rumble of thunder shook a distant hillside across the river, and Skallagrim began to wonder if he would soon be walking in the rain or, more worryingly, dodging lightning strikes while casting about for shelter. He kept walking though, and soon the breeze wound its way on its shivery errand through the endless dark galleries and vaulted hallways of the forest to trouble him no more. The grumbling sky above the mountains grew quiet again as well, which Skallagrim took to be a good sign.

Since the knoll where he had rested earlier in the day, the road had stayed mostly flat. Now, however, it began a routine of climbing away from the river at a steep incline, only to dive again like an errant hawk into dank hollows of hickory or groves of sadly twisted dogwood, their trunks covered in glowing green moss. This up and down of the road went on for another two miles, and Skallagrim, fatigued from the effort, was just beginning to consider taking his second break for the day when the road at last straightened, then curved gently back toward the river. He continued onward, his leg muscles stiff, more from the steep descents than from the climbing.

Another half mile, he told himself, and he would have a quick rest. But he had only gone about half that far when he heard the rushing sound of what could only be a waterfall coming down off the ridge. Not far ahead, he reached a break in the trees where the dim light of a heavily clouded afternoon illuminated the torrent of a substantial stream that cascaded down the hill over giant boulders to join with the swiftly flowing Pagarna. The ruins of a stone bridge were on Skallagrim's side of the stream, but the rocks had crushed the rest long ago. Just below that point was a thirty-foot waterfall that emptied into a narrow pool full of spray and mist. Then the flow continued on its wild way through another series of rocks, boulders, and a tangle of fallen trees before at last joining the river.

There was no safe way across. He would either have to take his chance with the powerful rush of water, clinging to slick boulders and jumping from spot to spot where he could, or go down to the river and brave its savage current to swim around the obstacle. Neither option was to his liking, and after a few minutes of debate, he resolved to cross where he stood.

There was nothing for it except to jump first to one house-sized boulder, then on to another, and so forth. He secured his staff to some straps on his pack, then leapt, none too gracefully, onto the first slick rock face. He clung to it for his life as the maddeningly fierce flow channeled itself around the rock just inches below his perch. With great care, he worked his way up and over the rock and came to another channel of rushing water about four feet across with what appeared to be an excellent landing of flat rock just on the other side. He jumped, but his scabbard tripped him up on the landing, and his feet went out from under him on the slick surface. The next thing he knew, he was sliding into the icy, irresistible embrace of a rushing current that swept him under faster than he could react.

In a flash, Skallagrim was washed downstream, swallowing water and banging into every rock and boulder along the way. He made a futile, desperate attempt to grab onto something, anything at all, that could save his life. In that same flash, he recalled a similar incident from his youth. *This has happened before!*

He knew he must not fight the current and must, whatever else he did, resist the urge to stand up. But he knew he was about to drown in less than three feet of water, and in a panic, he disobeyed the logic of his mind and tried to regain his feet. In one second, Skallagrim came up, blurry eyed and gasping for breath, only to realize his blunder as his right foot snagged between two submerged rocks.

The mindless force of the water could not be resisted, and it shoved him forward. Pain shot through his leg as his foot remained wedged, and for a terrible second, it felt as if the bone would snap. He kicked, just in the nick of time, and his foot came free as the surge pushed him onward.

The last thing he saw before going under was the approach of the waterfall that would funnel him over the edge. A ray of sunlight broke the clouds to form a rainbow on the mist above the cascade. Skallagrim thought it a wonderfully ironic sight to see just before dying.

He gave himself over to the flood, as he should have done the moment the water took him. It washed him, feet first, down the final approach to the fall, and then over he went with all the grace of a log. There was no more banging about, no more scrambling, and no more panic. Whatever was going to happen would be over in a few seconds, which he found to be strangely comforting.

He hit the water at the base of the falls, went under again, then bobbed to the surface at last, sputtering and cursing. He allowed the current to push him past the point of danger, where he was finally able to grab a branch and pull himself onto the rocks that lined the opposite bank. Skallagrim was across, shivering and dazed but across. He dragged himself onto the sandy shore, flipped onto his back, and lay there, panting. His heart was pounding like a drum, but he sat up finally, removing his boots to pour the water out of them.

Skallagrim cursed. This one foolish mistake might have cost him his life and doomed the girl as well. His knapsack was gone, he was drenched, and the wounds on his face were aching again. But he could not just sit there feeling sorry for himself. He needed to keep moving.

In a snarl of fallen trees and branches just a few feet away, he spied his pack, snagged and bobbing in the water. During the fall, he had managed to grab hold of his staff, which he used to fish out the pack. From it he pulled a soggy loaf of bread that he had been looking forward to eating later that day. Glumly, he tossed it into the stream. The rest of the contents, though soaked, could be salvaged later. Skallagrim washed the sand off his feet, put his waterlogged boots back on, hoisted his pack, then climbed the muddy bank back to the roadbed and continued on.

The forest closed in around him once more, shrouding him in a misty twilight. There were willows, hornbeam, and cypress, all wagging their mossy beards in a cool breeze that chilled Skallagrim to the bone. The moss on their bark glowed an eerie green, as did many oddly shaped mushrooms that clustered around their exposed roots like so many luminescent children, clamoring for attention.

Skallagrim stumbled along for another mile, but wet boots and socks made for angry blisters. He was compelled at last to stop as he approached another bridgeless stream. Plopping himself down, he pondered the mistake that had cost him miles and time. He had come fifteen, maybe sixteen miles from the bridge, but he had hoped for much better. Skallagrim needed dry clothes, especially dry boots, and socks if he were to go any farther without doing serious damage to his feet.

The stream blocking his path was relatively calm. If he pushed hard, he could easily cross and forge on for a few more excruciating miles. But Skallagrim knew the ways of the road. Blisters were inevitable if he continued, making tomorrow's road torturously slow and painful. No, he would camp there. Against his better judgment, he would build a fire to dry out his clothes and supplies. It was late afternoon anyway, and there was no telling how fast the sun would fall behind the ridges to plunge the already dark forest into a pitch-black hell where he could easily break an ankle or lose track of the road altogether. He would have to do better tomorrow, a lot better.

He tossed his boots and stripped off his wet, clinging garments, which set him to shivering. His flint was still good though, and in no time at all, he had gathered enough tinder and dry wood to start an impressive campfire. He rigged a short piece of rope from his pack and strung his blanket and clothes over the flickering flames, then ate an exiguous meal of nuts, berries, and salt pork. It was not enough, but it would have to do.

Three hours later, it was growing dark, and the air had cooled considerably. But his things—though reeking of smoke—were dry enough to wear. Skallagrim dressed, threw another log on the fire, then collapsed onto his blanket. He felt in the dark to make sure his sword was handy, then pounded his knapsack into a poor excuse for a pillow. Wrapping his cloak about himself, he shivered once and then fell into a deep sleep where he dreamed of a beautiful serpent that, surprisingly, sang.

CHAPTER FOURTEEN

It was not singing that Skallagrim heard when he woke with a start just a few hours later. A horrific shriek rang out in the night from the direction of the river. It had him sitting bolt upright and grasping for his sword before he had even fully awakened. His heart was pounding like a drum as the terrifying sound reached a crescendo that seemed to combine the worst elements of howling, screaming, and growling. It sounded like the death knell of a hideous beast that was either being roasted alive or torn limb from limb.

He drew his sword and crouched near the remains of his fire. He had not long to wait, however, before the wretched thing let forth another ghastly shriek that rent the night and gripped his heart with primal fear. He was frozen and rattled but focused. Could this be a dreaded ghoul, prowling the flats and river marshes in search of an ancient, flooded grave?

As Skallagrim frantically searched his mind's list of terrors known to haunt the Pagarna wilderness, he realized the beast might pose no threat at all. As it screamed a third time—and it was no less unnerving when it did—Skallagrim had to laugh at himself, for he had heard this thing before. Maybe some of his memories were returning after all?

This creature was not being eaten alive, nor would it come for him. Annoying, yes, but hardly dangerous! It was merely a blue heron, complaining in its horrid, tormented way about some annoyance— some river dispute that concerned Skallagrim not at all.

He searched about for a fist-sized stone, hurled it in the direction of the egregious bird, and was rewarded by the sound of huge, flapping wings as the heron took flight, hopefully, to make its nightly nest on the far side of the river. Skallagrim laughed again, tossed another log on the fire, then bedded down once more.

The dream of the singing serpent did not return, but dreams of the recent violence did. Skallagrim replayed each and every death in his mind, over and over. The desperate faces of his dying foes constricted in pain and fear. Their eyes flickered like sputtering candles, touched by the chilly wind of death. Sputtered and were extinguished, their light fading from the world of men.

Skallagrim knew he was dreaming, tossed from one phantasm to the next, then back again. He willed himself to dream of the blue-eyed girl, but this was denied him. So, he struggled, tossing and turning, eventually falling into a dream of a white shore at dawn.

The bright sun rose like a flame over the horizon, turning a stretch of the ocean into burnished bronze. The older man from the dream of the girl was there. His robes, like his billowing hair, were as white as the powdery sand. Seeing him, Skallagrim felt a sudden and profound sense of sadness. He had failed this man somehow, could read the disappointment in the man's eyes. He felt a great sob well up inside of him and was unable to hold it in. Weeping and overcome, he threw himself at the man's feet.

"Forgive me," Skallagrim sobbed. "What have I done?"

With a strength belying his age, the older man lifted Skallagrim to his feet. "Of course, I forgive you. As to what you have done, I cannot remember it for you. You must do that, and you must find all that you have lost."

"I'm searching for her," Skallagrim replied, "but it feels as if my heart will burst with the burden of it. There's so much sorrow. Too much sorrow."

"Skallagrim, you have set things loose in the darkness, both sorrow and ruin, but do not despair." The old man pointed to the rising sun. "There is no way to the glorious morn lest we first suffer the horrors of the night. Even so, joy must be born of sorrows unfathomable."

"I fear what I'll face. I'm not sure I can do this!"

"When evil looms near, good cannot hide. It must light its way with the lamp of courage or become nothing!"

With that the dream faded, replaced by a series of nonsensical dreams, equally frustrating, for their ludicrous themes were illogical and sometimes outright embarrassing.

Still many hours from dawn, he awoke, felt the pain of a full bladder, and rose wearily to make his way a few yards into the woods where he made use of the trunk of a large, luminescent tree. He had only just finished relieving himself when he heard an odd yet beautiful thing—the sound of a girl singing.

The pleasant sound, unexpected in such a wild place, was carried faintly on the breeze from farther up the ridge. Skallagrim made his way back to his dwindling campfire, retrieved his sword, then crept back to the spot where he first heard the singing. Everything was quiet now, but he waited patiently and was rewarded when, a few minutes later, he heard it again, though it soon stopped.

His eyes searched the oddly glowing forest until he spied a trail. It climbed the ridge, running alongside the stream and the icy cascades that tumbled down the ridge. He made his way along this path and had not gone far when he spotted a tranquil, shimmering pool at the base of a series of rocky outcrops. The stream spilled over them, giving the impression of many waterfalls rather than one. At the base, swimming in the languid pool was a maiden, most fair.

From his observation point high above the pool, Skallagrim found another path leading down to the stony bank. He made his way to the pool's edge, then concealed himself behind an old willow whose branches dipped into the water. He peeked out and beheld the maiden, unclothed and glistening wet, wading to the bank just a few short strides from where he hid. The stream was icy cold, yet the maiden seemed unaffected. She nimbly pulled herself out of the water to stand dripping on the wet, flat stones of the bank. Her hair, but for a streak as green as the glowing moss of the trees, was jet black and long. She knelt, and picking up a garland of blue and yellow flowers that glowed with the same eerie light of the moss, placed it upon her head. She was as beautiful as a faerie's daughter, and Skallagrim's heart leapt within his breast at the sight of her.

Seemingly, she had not spotted his hiding place, though she spun away from him, more of a half pirouette, with the grace and elegance of an elfin dancer, and began her song anew. Skallagrim, embarrassed at having watched her in this vulnerable way, slid down behind the tree where he could not see her and contented himself with listening to her angelic voice.

Wide stretch the grey hills beyond our ken
Where roam the sad, haunted shadows of men
Why do they roam 'neath the leaden sky
Heedless of doom, for they are doomed to die
Searching in vain, yet unceasing, they seek
Ever they look though their chances are bleak
Ever they climb the grey hills, then descend
Down hopeless trails which wind and wend

Her song was full of doom and woe, but the melody was sweetly intoxicating, and it filled Skallagrim with wonder and sudden joy. As he listened, the weariness washed out of him, flowing swiftly away like the silvery flood down the hillside.

'Midst the grey hills
'Neath leaden sky
Wander the weary men
Searching for dreams long flown
Dreams best left forgotten

The ethereal voice ceased, and for a moment, everything was quiet and still. Even the sound of the waterfall seemed subdued, and Skallagrim, feeling as if he was hiding inside a waking dream, remained lost within the spell of her song when the maiden spoke at last.

CHAPTER FIFTEEN

"Surely you are a brave warrior, for do you not carry a sword of great power? Too brave to be hiding from Swanhild, I think." The maiden giggled, a mischievous sound that was as musical as the faerie song she had sung. "Come out from behind your tree, and we will finish the song together!"

Skallagrim—still embarrassed at his predicament—was filled with sudden yearning, a longing that seemed at once perilous and yet perfectly harmless. He thought a poet's thoughts, contemplating lofty ideas and notions that had no place in the mind of a mere thief. Yet when he spoke, he did so shyly.

"I cannot, my lady."

"And why not?"

"For you are naked, and I would not dishonor you in that way."

"Then, sir, kindly hold out my robe. It lies just beside you in your hiding place."

He saw the maiden spoke truly, for a garment as green as the glowing pool lay just beside him. He picked it up and then stood, letting it fall to its full length where it shimmered silvery as if it were made of fish scales. Skallagrim gasped in awe when he spied, glistening upon one breast of the robe, a fish-shaped brooch made of precious garnets.

"Do not be timid, good sir. Step out from behind your willow, and hold up my garment. Look not at my form if you so wish it, though it is wondrous to gaze upon. Look instead at my eyes. Surely, in this no honor would be lost by either of us, though perhaps some might be gained by you?"

Skallagrim brushed stray strands of hair from his face, some of which had stuck to his wound. He felt a sudden tinge of shame at his disfigurement. "I don't wish to frighten you, but my face . . ."

"I care not," the maiden assured him.

"As you wish."

Skallagrim stepped out from behind his tree, holding the garment aloft. His eyes could not help but stray upon her beauty, for she was, though diminutive, perfectly formed and glowing with the loveliness of youth. He caught himself, and blushing, looked up again. She was watching him, her tongue teasing the corners of her lips as she ran her fingers through her silky, shimmering hair. She let her eyes flutter in mock shyness, then pushed her hair behind ears, which curved slightly upward to elfin points.

"My eyes," she said with a sigh. "Look into my eyes. Oh, a bitter thing, for love is blind, but lust is not."

At first he could not, fearing the spell that was already at work on his mind. He struggled to remember his blue-eyed girl, desiring to be faithful to her in every way, but he was just a thief with a mangled face who had put her in harm's way. If she had ever loved him, there was little chance she did now, especially not once she saw him. With a sigh, he gave himself over to the nymph who stood naked before him.

Skallagrim looked into her bright eyes, which shone like the stars of heaven. Yet even the glimmer of starlight in those lovely green orbs could not hide their wildness. They were full of a savagery as untamed as the stream in which she had been playing. They held his gaze, those eyes that were as precious as emeralds, as she strode, nay glided, on delicate feet ever closer to him. Though her face and body radiated a youthful glory unreckoned by mortal man, her eyes spoke of great age. She who locked her gaze with his had seen, with those same eyes, wonders undreamt from days long gone, horrors untold and beauties unsung.

Skallagrim's sword, Terminus, trembled and murmured in its scabbard, but he ignored it, for his mind could dwell on naught but the maiden. Faster than he realized, she stood before him, her pixie face smiling as she looked lustily up at him, her black hair spilling over her body like water over the mossy rocks. She slipped into the robe that he held and then stepped back from him and curtsied. Wet as she was, the garment clung to her and left little to Skallagrim's imagination, but this was his compromise, the concession he had made to her. So, he would sing with her, dance with her if she bade him do so, linger awhile and speak with her of all that had happened and all that plagued his thoughts.

But he would not let his mind take him where it would. There were things he could hold back, though only just. Lust would not conquer him, for Skallagrim's heart belonged to another, no matter what that other might think of him.

The maiden reached with a delicate hand and caressed his wounded face. Her touch was kind and did not hurt. "A lesser lady might spurn the company of one so wounded, but not Swanhild. Now then, sing with me."

To his surprise, Skallagrim's lips formed the words of a song he had no memory of unless it had once strayed into a dream. Yes, that was it, the snatch of a song heard in a dream long ago.

> *Once, they were told of a pool hidden well*
> *'Midst the grey hills by a powerful spell*
> *This is the lure, ever drawing them on*
> *There, they are told, all their dreams have gone*
> *If they could find the insatiate well*
> *Plead with the spirit which in it doth dwell*
> *Then might their dreams come rushing back home*
> *No more 'midst sorrowful hills would they roam*

Here, Skallagrim stopped singing, but the maiden continued, her voice like a gentle sigh upon the breeze.

> *What feeds the pool where their dreams were drowned*
> *The tears of children who, in sorrow, found*
> *The world was broken and by one, betrayed*
> *Their faith in dreams was doomed to fade*

Skallagrim sighed. "Is this the pool? Are you the spirit of which you sing?"

"I am Swanhild."

Fireflies were twinkling on and off, plunging like falling stars, then rising again in sparkling spirals. She watched them with fascination, catching one, then letting it crawl to the end of her forefinger where it took flight once more. She giggled, delighted as she watched it ascend, ignoring Skallagrim for the moment.

"But Swanhild, is there truth to the song? For I search for much that is forgotten, and I long for a dream that I have lost and must find."

She looked his way again, inclining her head. "There's truth in every song, sir. And songs are a key to memory, for they can unlock the vaults wherein memories hide. Songs can hold far more memories than any pool can hold dreams. You have but to find the right one, brave warrior, and much that is forgotten will return." She scrutinized him for a moment. "Though maybe not all."

She giggled again. Though there was something lascivious in the way her gaze lingered upon him and in the silky-soft whisper of her voice, Skallagrim delighted in her every word. He was entranced and did not care.

"You say you are also searching for a dream," she continued. "Of this I would hear more and will gladly answer all that I can, for this is no chance meeting. But first, you have me at a disadvantage, for though you know that I'm Swanhild, I know not who you are."

"My pardon, Swanhild. I'm Skallagrim." He hesitated, then cleared his throat. "Shield Shaker," he mumbled. He felt foolish for adding the moniker that Erling had applied to him. Having said it, he blushed but then recovered his wits enough to set his jaw firm and inflate his chest to show he might be worthy of the bellicose name. To his credit, he wore this mantle of haughtiness well for the better part of a moment. However, that ended the second Swanhild laughed at him in her childlike manner. A thousand such warriors had passed her way, and it took far more than immature posturing to shake her shield.

Skallagrim blushed again as his confidence crumbled. "It's just a name. Two nights ago, it was Skallagrim Quickhands, or so I was told. Of the name Skallagrim, I feel sure. As for the rest . . ." He shook his head.

"It matters not," Swanhild chided him. "What matters is that we have met, that you seek memories locked within the chambers of your heart and mind, and seek a dream that, if I am correct, is not lost but stolen from you and unfairly imprisoned. And lastly, I have keys that might help to unlock all of it, for I am the spirit of the pool. Though the grey hills are far away, and this is not the insatiate well of which we sang, I may still be able to help you."

She smiled at Skallagrim, then brushed a stray lock from his eyes and stroked his wounded face. He stood there breathless, wanting to speak, but Swanhild continued. "And I must say, Sir Skallagrim Shield Shaker, there is little that surprises Swanhild, for though I look like but a maiden, I am very, very old and full of wisdom. Yet, your presence here is unexpected. Until I spied you down by the river yonder, drying out your clothes by your campfire, I thought myself to be all alone in this great wood."

Skallagrim took a step backward, letting her hand fall from his face. Tired as he was, he did not trust himself, let alone this nymph—for surely that is what she was—and he resolved that no matter her beauty, he would remain true to the blue-eyed girl. Still, he was spellbound by Swanhild, intoxicated by the magical sound of her voice, the way she moved, the way she touched him. Blushing red, he turned his face away from her, avoiding the playful gleam of her green eyes.

Sensing Skallagrim's hesitation, Swanhild took his hand in hers. "Fear not, Sir Skallagrim," she soothed, "for I am not some hag clothed in the illusion of youthful flesh. You are not deceived, for I am as you see me, as young as the morning and yet as old as the sea."

"Forgive me, Swanhild. Do not let my uncertainty be mistaken for unfriendliness. I'm weary and have slept little for many days."

Swanhild nodded in understanding while stroking Skallagrim's hand. "I can see you are exhausted and overburdened with much sorrow and turmoil. And you are so terribly wounded. I hope I may help you; that is all."

She tugged at him, coaxing him back up the bank the way he had come. She stopped a short way up. Kneeling beside a young sapling, she gathered some moss and bits of fungi that clung to its exposed roots. "The wounds on your face and head are recent and must pain you a great deal. These will help."

Still, Skallagrim held back. He was bone weary but only half under the spell of this intriguing creature. Only two nights ago, he had awoken in the midst of a fight for his life. Since then he had been at the mercy of others. Had he not allowed himself to be led about by the nose by Erling Hizzard when, in truth, he knew nothing about the man other than a few suspiciously chosen tidbits that Erling had revealed? In addition to being the man on whom Skallagrim pinned all his hopes, he was a smuggler, a connoisseur of abominations, and the associate of a loathsome hag. It was a foolish thing to do, gambling everything on the advice and information of a nervous, condescending man who was, for all practical purposes, a stranger.

What if his blue-eyed lady love was still in Archon, perhaps held in some secretive dungeon or, even now, making her escape and looking for him? Yet there he was in the middle of the wild on his way to a fort he only hoped he could find, about to be led along by the nose again! He shook his head to clear it and nearly stumbled with the effort.

"Will you not take me back to your fire? For the night is chill. I would hear everything, brave Skallagrim, everything you have to tell! Share your burdens with the maiden Swanhild, for I am as sagacious as I am beautiful!"

He had to admit, for all her mystery, Swanhild was charming company. He felt no threat from her, and perhaps she was just lonely and genuine in her desire to help him. So, Skallagrim allowed the maiden to lead him, and again, could not help but admire her sylphlike physique as she climbed the trail ahead of him. *At least she's a prettier benefactor than Erling,* he thought.

Looking back, Swanhild caught him gazing and laughed again. "Come, tell me everything!"

Skallagrim dropped his eyes with unanticipated embarrassment, then awkwardly cleared his throat. "There's much to tell!"

They made their way back to the riverside camp, where, over the next hour, Skallagrim told her all. So caught up in her spell he could barely help himself, he let the entire story spill from his lips. It was a good thing he did, for Swanhild, tiny maiden that she was, had not yet decided whether Skallagrim would survive the night. True, she was no hag, her beauty no illusion designed to fool the unwary, but neither was she a mere winsome lass of the forest. Of all the pitfalls Skallagrim might encounter in the Vales of Pagarna, Swanhild was the most perilous of all. Through the long centuries, many unfortunate souls had run afoul of her. The few who survived called her a witch and for good reason. Yet there was more to it than simple witchery, for Swanhild was a nymph, a nixie, a water spirit who had lived to serve her own ends since the world was young and the moon but a child.

The enchantress listened well to Skallagrim's story, stopping him now and then to ask questions. If, in the end, it seemed that Skallagrim's objectives might line up with her own, she would help him. If not, she would lure him into the water where her power was greatest, and there she would drown him.

Either way, Swanhild had determined to make love to this mysterious, scarred warrior-thief who carried an eldritch sword. Lust emanated from her like a sighing breath. Whatever man she wanted, she took. Only one had ever spurned her advances, but that is another tale.

All was going well in her devious mind when, near the end of his story, she asked Skallagrim to draw the sword that she might look upon its wonder. Perhaps she might be able to tell him something more about it, for her lore in such matters was nearly unrivaled in the lands of the north. Perhaps too she would take it from him.

Skallagrim, under her enchantment and wishing only to please this pretty nymph who gazed at him with the heavy-lidded eyes of a seasoned seductress, stood and drew the blade.

Terminus flashed forth like a bolt of lightning, then pulsed a blackness so complete that Swanhild was blinded. She did not see when the sword nearly leapt from Skallagrim's hand in an effort to pierce her heart. The sword knew who she was and knew her heart for the empty, black thing that it was.

Skallagrim, exerting all of his will, took control of the blade. It was then that Terminus screamed. Swanhild, her beauty intact but her confidence and power shattered, covered her ears with her hands and then screamed as well. Such a thing she had not done in three generations of men.

Then the night, which up until that moment had been one of preternatural wonder and sensual prurience, became a thing of horror.

CHAPTER SIXTEEN

"Put it back! Put it back!" Swanhild, now more a frightened waif than a seducing nymph, pleaded with Skallagrim.

His head was clear now, the phantasmagoria was ended, and Swanhild's spells were blown away like so many dead leaves in a tempest. Still, he had no wish to cause her such distress and strove to regain mastery over the sword, fearing it more than her. The unearthly wail rose so loud and so shrill that it permeated the forest and echoed off the mountainsides, filling every hollow, every canyon, every grove, every cavern, and every pit for many miles around.

Swanhild screamed again. "I know what that is! It comes from beyond the Southern Void! Make it stop! Please!"

Skallagrim slammed Terminus back into its sheath where it hummed and throbbed its disapproval, then grew still and silent as the last remnants of its fury faded away into the distance.

The heart-stopping terror melted into relative calm. Like a breeze of cool, fresh air, something resembling normalcy returned to the campsite.

Skallagrim rushed to Swanhild's side, gently stroking her hair. "It's the nature of the thing. It happened the night it came to me and once afterward. I had no idea . . ."

Swanhild shrank from his touch, still frightened but trying to regain control of herself and the situation. "I . . . I do not blame you," she stammered. "Give me a moment. I need . . . I just need to catch my breath!" She looked up at Skallagrim and smiled in her beguiling way. "You must think me a silly girl."

"Not at all. The sword is terrifying," Skallagrim confessed.

"All swords are terrifying," the maiden observed. "But that—"

"It's a willful blade," Skallagrim interrupted. "That it screams and pulses strange lights, well, it cannot be explained."

"All things may be explained in time, Sir Skallagrim. And with a weapon such as that, it is no wonder you are named Shield Shaker. If the title seems ill-placed at present, I imagine one day you will wear it well. Let us speak no more of it for now." Swanhild sighed and, removing the garland from her hair, scooted closer to Skallagrim. "Sit beside me, please."

He did as he was bidden, and Swanhild, still trembling, laid her head upon his shoulder. "Just hold me for a moment," she pleaded.

Skallagrim could in no wise refuse her, and he wrapped one arm around her small frame, pulling her close. He loved the sensual feel of Swanhild's body as she hugged him tightly, but he could not ignore the suffocating wave of guilt pressing upon his chest, the incessant throb in his heart warning him to get up and walk away from the nymph, his heart's warning of who it was he wronged by inwardly reveling in this intimacy. But Swanhild's spells were strong. The memory of the blue-eyed girl, temporarily at least, joined with the other memories of Skallagrim's life and hid itself away.

The scent of her hair was maddening, combining the fragrances of Moon Flower, Nymphea, Evening Primrose, and all such flowers that bloom nocturnally. Skallagrim caressed her arm, perhaps to comfort her, or more likely because he longed to know the feel of her. Her flesh was cool, still glistening from the waters of the pool, yet as luxuriant as silk to the touch. She sighed, surrendering to his gentle ministrations, then lifted her head from his shoulder so she might look into his eyes. She stroked his face as she had done earlier, and Skallagrim melted at her touch.

"I know you love another," she whispered. "I would not seek to supplant her, and yet there is but one thing I would ask of you, brave warrior. Nay, one thing now and another later. Do this for me, and I will aid you."

"Fair Swanhild, you have but to ask." Unbidden, the words had come too freely.

A thief? Maybe. Though, as the maiden of the pool spoke sweetly to him, a gallant knight awoke within him.

Terminus was humming in its scabbard, rattling against the ground, striving for his attention. The two powers vied for control of Skallagrim, one subtle and seductive, the other forthright and cogent, both beautiful and exotic and promising him visions of himself he could scarce believe. But the powers of a woman, even a woman not supernaturally endowed, will always win out over that of a sword. Terminus was sheathed, disadvantaged, and powerless to protect Skallagrim from Swanhild's wiles.

"Just a kiss," she whispered into his ear. "One kiss to still my heart." She spoke so softly he could barely hear her. "One kiss to bind my fate to yours," she added impishly. Her obvious deception mattered little. Skallagrim, his face reddening, had heard nothing beyond the word "kiss."

Now Swanhild's lips were only an inch from his. Her eyelashes fluttered, and her breath quickened. She did not wait for his answer but drew him toward her with her eyes, drew him into a deep kiss that he could not resist. She flowed into his arms, trembling, pressing her mouth to his, melting in his embrace as the sounds of the forest, the river, and the bubbling stream faded into nothingness.

Of course, there was more than one kiss. In fact, there were many. Kissing her pulled at his stitches, lancing him with pain, but he did not care. Skallagrim wanted her badly, wanted all of her. His hands begin to explore her slender waist, then further.

Like a bolt of lightning, a vision of the blue-eyed girl of his dream pierced his conscience. He pushed it aside. What man could resist this temptress, this wild, magical girl of the Vales? Skallagrim was but twenty-two, impulsive, ready to plunge into the Pagarna wilderness on a mad quest, ready even to plunge into . . . There it was again, the vision of his true love, her face pleading with him. *"Time is nearly up!"* That is what she had said in the dream.

Yet, what he held in his arms was no dream. Swanhild was here, now, his if he wanted her. Though his heart warred with his flesh, the nymph was in complete control.

Mercifully, she had decided both that Skallagrim should live out the night and that she would not make love to him. Later perhaps but not tonight. There was no surer way to snare him in the long run than to bring him close, so very close, and then deny him.

As their hearts raced, and just before the moment could be taken too far, Swanhild pulled away from him and, rising, moved a few tantalizing paces away from Skallagrim. He let her go, watching her while guiltily admiring her beauty as she stood nearer the fire, her robe waving eerily in the glow of the flames and the luminescent vegetation.

She toyed with him, but that knowledge paled with the sudden tidal wave of guilt that crashed upon him. *What have I done? What of the blue-eyed girl?*

Still breathless, Swanhild knelt beside him. "I told you I had no wish to replace the girl you love," she said, though her face remained flushed with passion. It was as if she knew exactly what he was thinking. "You have slain men to find her. What of it? You have allied yourself with a sentient sword and a smuggler to find her. What of that? And now you have kissed Swanhild to find her. Which is worse, my brave warrior?"

Skallagrim made to speak, but she stopped him with a wave of her pretty hand. "Time is fleeting, and there is much to say. Come dawn, I will vanish like the mists upon the river."

They sat opposite each other beside the fire, his legs crossed and hers tucked beneath her chin. Swanhild had made a healing salve from her collection of mosses and fungi, then applied them to Skallagrim's wounds, easing his pain and discomfort a great deal.

"I would tell you more if there were more time. Alas, the hours are slipping away. What do you know of the Southern Void?"

Skallagrim shook his head. "Nary a thing, though I've heard it mentioned."

"Though it pains me to call up these memories, I will tell you more about the Void in a few minutes than most will ever know. Your sorcerer is caught up in the tale, you see?"

He nodded for her to continue.

She spoke next not as the seductress but as a wise sage, full of years and knowledge of the plots, plans, and machinations of men; of sorcerers, wizards, generals, and kings. The unbridled passions shared earlier—only moments before—were forgotten, swept away like so many crumbs from the table.

"There was a wicked king who once ruled all the known lands of the world. The strange lands that exist beyond the swirling mists and fogs of the Void are home to his castle and court. Long before the curtain was drawn separating these lands from those, Andorath was the northernmost realm of his domain. The rest was divided by east, west, and south. To administer the four kingdoms, the king raised up four great and powerful knights. The Knight of the North was named Balor, and he was both the firstborn and the mightiest of the four."

"Balor's Bones," Skallagrim noted.

"Yes, that is he," Swanhild affirmed. "His name is now little more than a curse uttered by the common folk, yet once he was considered potent and wise, especially in matters of war and magic. He had to be, for Andorath was the wildest and most untamed of all the four realms, a land of demons, monsters, fell powers, and defiant principalities."

Something in all this was ringing bells inside Skallagrim's head, and he listened intently.

"One fateful day, the wicked king announced he would name the heir to his entire kingdom. All four realms—east, west, south, and north—would become one, ruled over by his chosen scion. The knights assumed the greatest among them, Balor, would be named the ruler and heir, but it was not to be. For, unexpectedly, the king informed them all he would appoint a fair daughter, a princess, to sit upon the throne and rule over all the lands. All four knights were astounded, for the king had no wife to bear him a daughter.

"He told them more, revealing the magical arts he would employ to bring her forth. As he unveiled his grand scheme, he disclosed that the knights, after all their long labors on his behalf, were to be her thanes, little more than guardians. Balor, thinking more of himself than he should perhaps, offered to wed the daughter."

Swanhild's face darkened as she absentmindedly toyed with a green strand of her hair. "I have always believed Balor did rightly in this, for he who wed the princess would surely become the prince and ultimately, the true king. You see this? You understand?"

Skallagrim nodded, though he was not sure he understood at all. But Swanhild was speaking not as one recounting a history but as one who had witnessed it unfold, perhaps even playing some part in it. So he listened, spellbound.

"The king rejected Balor's offer, even shaming him before his court during a great feast. There would be another knight one day, he claimed, and he, not Balor, would wed the princess. Now the king cursed the Knight of the North for his presumptuousness, cast him out of his court, and named him Mog Ruith."

"Ah!" Skallagrim's eyes grew wide. "The Night of Mog Ruith!"

"Yes! You are beginning to see!" the maiden continued. Her voice, which had begun the tale almost as a whisper, rose with passion. She rocked back and forth excitedly. "Mog Ruith—once Balor—fled to Mag Mor, his tower in the north. Once there he marshaled his forces, strengthened his magic with sorcerous alliances, and, after a time, waged war upon the wicked king. It was called the War of the Great Rebellion, though in truth, Balor only sought the good of all. It was an act of liberation, not rebellion."

She sighed, calmed herself, and then continued. "Sadly, the war was lost. Mog Ruith—Balor—was cast down from his tower into a great crack in the earth. His realm, Andorath, was cursed and remains so to this day. The veil of mists and fog rose like a wall, cutting it off from the other realms. None may pass the Void and live.

"Andorath is alone. For what it has become, a land of corrupt cities, ghoul-haunted, and monster-ridden wildernesses—all of it—I lay the blame squarely at the feet of the wicked king."

"But," Skallagrim interjected, sensing a pause in the tale, "surely Balor, I mean Mog Ruith, would share in the blame?"

Her expression hardened. "Do not speak to me of blame!" Swanhild spat the words at Skallagrim, her eyes boring into him.

"You know nothing of it, no more than I have told you!"

Skallagrim was taken aback. "I suppose not. Still, what has this to do with Forneus, or with me for that matter?"

"These sorcerers, these cults you spoke of, they wish to raise him up."

"Raise him up?"

"Yes, my simple thief. Raise Mog Ruith from the dead!"

"Then they're insane!"

"Irrelevant! It matters not! They can do it!"

"How?"

"A thousand years I could speak to you, and still you would not know. To put it as simply as I can, the knights were brought to life by the king's magic. They did not live, nor did they die as mortal men. By magic they were born, and at least for one of them, by sorcery, he shall be reborn. The Night of Mog Ruith! That is what it's all about! Each year on the anniversary of his downfall, the sorcerers perform their rites, weave their greatest spells, and shout their mightiest curses from the tops of their haunted towers. And do you know what else they do on that night, sweet Skallagrim?"

He grimaced. "I think I'm getting the picture."

"They sacrifice virgins, Skallagrim, both male and female, to Mog Ruith! They believe the males will one day return to be thanes of the risen Knight of the North and the maidens his brides. The blood flows thick upon their altars, dripping down their towers, saturating the ground beneath their lairs, consecrating the very foundations of their power. The bodies of the slain are taken to Mag Mor and dumped into the crack to feed the spirit of Mog Ruith.

"Insane, you say? Yes, they are that! But it does not matter, for they are close to achieving the impossible, nay, the inevitable. It may take them but a few more years, for they are close, Skallagrim. So very, very close!"

Skallagrim was shocked, his mind reeling from these revelations. Yet, he let Swanhild continue her terrible tale.

"They will raise him up and rally Andorath to his banner, marching once more to the south, into the Void and beyond. They will, despite their endless squabbling and petty jealousies, unite behind the risen Knight of the North to kill the king once and for all!"

"You speak as if this is a good thing, yet—"

"I know," Swanhild interrupted. "I have no love for sorcerers and much reason to loathe them. Was it not Griog'xa himself, my own son, who exiled me from Archon? Yet, I would see this fell king cast down, humiliated as he humiliated my Lord Balor. Maybe their combined strength will carry them through the impenetrable wall of fog. Maybe they can break its curse. Who knows?"

She paused, appearing to gather her thoughts before continuing. "My passions are a constant contradiction, Skallagrim. I will help you find Forneus Druogorim, so you can slay him. I would even help you rid Andorath of the rest of his breed if it were within my power to do so. And yet, I would see this king beyond the Void dead and Mog Ruith set upon his throne. The wicked king should be stopped before he can raise up the daughter that he foretold, for if she is permitted to take the throne, I fear her vengeance upon the north will be swift and terrible."

She nibbled her bottom lip, then gave Skallagrim a beseeching look. "You see my quandary? To back this cabal of sorcerers is to ally myself with the depraved, yet to sit idly by is to invite disaster. I am torn." Swanhild grew quiet as if sensing she had said too much, revealed too much about her own motives. Doubt clouded her features, though she waved her hand as if dismissing the thought.

"Forgive me; I ramble. It has been many years since I called forth memories of that time, many years since I told that tale. It troubles me to think of it." Skallagrim's eyes were boring holes into her. She fidgeted and looked away uncomfortably, avoiding his stare. After a tense moment, she laughed and shook her head. "And besides, no one has sought my aid or advice but you! At least not for a very long time. We are a sad pair, are we not? You seek memories while I strive to forget them."

"Griog'xa is your son?" Skallagrim had heard nothing Swanhild had said beyond that. His eyes glinted, full of suspicion. He did not realize it, but he was gripping the hilt of Terminus with his left hand.

Swanhild's smile faded to a frown. She had said too much, yet perhaps because she had allowed herself to be swept away by the thief's plight, or because Terminus had come awake, exerting a power she could not detect, Swanhild said even more. "Yes, and Tuva is his sister. I am mother to them both. My Lord Balor begat me with them long and long ago." She seemed to wither then, and tears glistened at the corners of her eyes.

Skallagrim was stunned by her confession. "If everything you say is true, then these sorcerers . . . they should be . . ." He did not finish his thought, thinking better of it. He did not need to embroil himself in a grander scheme, a murderous rampage against mad sorcerers and necromancers. Let Erling pursue his crusade if he wanted. Skallagrim only needed revenge on one of them, only needed to save the girl from the one, Forneus Druogorim! The rest—their history, motives, means, and objectives—were none of his concern.

"I know what you are thinking, Skallagrim," Swanhild said, brushing away her tears with a trembling hand. "Best to let them be."

"Are they all bent on this insanity?"

"Not all. My son, Griog'xa, secretly stands against the rest. He plays them all like so many fiddles. He only pretends to be the leading player in their plot to raise his father, for unbeknownst to them, Balor had no use for his children—would sacrifice them to his god should he return." She shuddered. "No, what Griog'xa really wants is to sit on the throne himself. Long has he pondered his father's fate, yet even more so, his thoughts run to the mysterious king and to the princess that has yet to be born. His schemes are fixed upon her; I am sure of it though I don't know why. If you should ever meet my son, be wary. Do not underestimate him, for he is cunning and full of guile!"

Swanhild leaned back on her hands and allowed her lissome legs to stretch out in front of her. She had no desire to recall these things, having contented herself with the solitude of the wild for many long years. But now with the unexpected arrival of this Skallagrim, this tragically scarred yet handsome thief with the ghastly sword, the memories rushed back at her. Once, she had harbored secrets and plans of her own. Then had come the twin children, one of them wise but dangerously deceptive, the other hideous to behold and morbidly sadistic, and both of them evil. Like their father, Swanhild hated them both, fearful of one and repulsed by the other.

She glanced at Skallagrim, who was lost in his own thoughts. His sudden appearance was a gift, surely, a boon from the mysterious god she served. The thief's sword, this Terminus, was more than he knew, certainly more than she would tell him.

The wheels of her mind were turning, plots forming. Yet they had both grown so silent that the moment became uncomfortable. Best she should string this Skallagrim along. What she planned might take years, but what were years to Swanhild?

CHAPTER SEVENTEEN

"It is growing windy. Have you noticed?" Swanhild threaded a hand through her hair and watched the thief expectantly.

Skallagrim looked up, his brow knitted, for his thoughts were running deep. *Now, after all of that, she would talk about the weather!* he remarked to himself. But he nodded in agreement, for the chilly wind began to moan through the trees as their mossy branches creaked in complaint.

"Oh!" Swanhild exclaimed.

Their hearts jumped as a loud crash sounded from the darkness south of Skallagrim's camp. They stared toward the noise but could see nothing to cause alarm, just stray boulders that cast eerie shadows and endless, gloomy corridors of glowing tree trunks leading off in every direction except that of the river.

"Probably just a falling branch," Skallagrim assured her.

Still hoping for more than a macabre history lesson about knights and a wicked king, he probed Swanhild with questions. "What of the sword? You said it came from beyond the Void?"

"I believe so," she replied. "It is obviously a powerful blade, and Forneus is right to fear it. Many of Andorath's sorcerers have grown so cunning, so crafty in their spells, that few weapons can kill them." She crossed her ankles in front of her and eyed Skallagrim's sword suspiciously. "You say the blade is named Terminus, and Erling Hizzard told you this?"

Skallagrim nodded.

"Well, Terminus is one of those weapons, one of those rare swords that can kill a powerful conjurer." She looked away and grew quiet again, unwilling to say more about the sword, for, like the sorcerer, Swanhild also feared it.

The wind remained steady, blowing in from the south and carrying with it the forest's complex aromas. The loamy decay of fallen leaves, limbs, and trees mingled with the intoxicating smells of spring verdure. Smoke from Skallagrim's fire wafted on the breeze, blending with the malodorous smell of river water. The sweet scent of Swanhild's garland mingled with the unpleasant odor of his own body. It was a riot of smells.

Skallagrim grimaced, for now and then the wind carried the undeniable stench of putrefaction. Somewhere nearby an animal must have died, reminding him that death was near. Thinking gloomily of death, he recalled that his own life was finite. He had only so much time to live, to find his love, and to exact his revenge— the latter seeming not nearly as palatable as it had the day before. Dawn was only a couple of hours away, and he must be off.

"Is there anything else you can tell me?"

"There are many miles and many dangers before you, but if you survive those, have you given thought to how you will get inside your sorcerer's lair?"

Skallagrim shrugged, unwilling to reveal Erling's vague instructions about a secret back door.

"Of course not!" Swanhild laughed. "You are young, headstrong, and impetuous. You will likely launch yourself at the front door like a battering ram. Am I right?"

"No, but there must be a way in!"

Swanhild rolled her eyes in disdain. "The fort is perched upon a sheer bluff with the river as its moat. There is a bridge, yes, but if you cross it, you will be seen." She toyed with her hair and eyed him incredulously. "The place is impregnable. A legion of Ophyrian soldiers and sappers with ladders would be hard-pressed to gain entry. If Erling truly knew anything about this cliffside fastness, he would have told you as much."

Skallagrim could not bear her derision. "He did! That's why I'm approaching it from the south. I was told to search for a hidden door somewhere along a ridge beyond a ruined city."

She stood, stretching her legs. "Alright then," Swanhild conceded.

"So you were well advised after all. But if you find this door, how will you get past it?"

"It's a door," Skallagrim answered matter-of-factly, "and I'm a thief. If it's locked, I'll pick the lock." He felt none of the confidence he hoped he conveyed.

"As for thievery, you cannot simply pick the locks of the great iron doors of Fort Vigilance," she replied. "Many of the ancient strongholds along the Pagarna are locked by spells that are centuries old. And the keys are either lost or, some say, kept in a vault beneath the city of Urk, far to the north. There is no knowing how Forneus Druogorim came to possess one." She wrapped her arms about herself to ward off the chill. "Your friend Erling should have warned you about all this."

"He did, at least about the front door. Are you telling me the back door is no different?"

"I am! You must have the key to open it. And to think of one man searching that ridge to find it? Impossible! An army could search for days and not find it." She reached out a pretty hand, bidding him take it and rise.

Skallagrim shook his head, perplexed. "Then all is lost. I'm but an army of one."

He allowed her to pull him up and was surprised by the strength of the slender nymph. She led him closer to the stream, where she dipped a toe in the icy water. Skallagrim stood beside her, glumly staring in the vague direction of the fort. Somewhere out there in the dark, many miles away, he would find it, only to be denied entry. He cast about in his mind for an intelligent option to present to Swanhild but could find none. He gave a half shrug in defeat, then sighed.

"Do not be dismayed, Skallagrim. Just be glad that you have found me, for I know precisely where it is." Any reluctance Swanhild had felt about helping this wayward, lovesick warrior was dismissed. She would set him on a course that, if it did not kill him, would likely set in motion a series of events that were much to her liking.

Skallagrim's eyes widened. "Then why did you not say? Please tell me all you can about this fort and how to find its hidden door."

"It is not so much a fort as a prison, though what or whom is imprisoned there, I cannot say. Perhaps you will find out. But over the centuries, dozens of captains and generals have commanded the castle. When each one of these wardens died, they were entombed in a hidden mountainside crypt, it had to be kept secret if for no other reason than to keep its occupants safe from ghouls, but it connects to the fort through a long tunnel.

"The southern approach, the way you have chosen, is hidden from my mind, veiled in a shadow that not even my sight cannot penetrate." She paused, barely suppressing a shudder. "You must pass through the ruined city of Orabas to reach the crypt, and there is an evil there greater even than Forneus. I fear it may be too much for you, even with your sword."

"But you know the way?"

"Of course I do." She laughed, her mood lightening unexpectedly. "And . . ." Her dazzling, emerald-green eyes grew wide as she rocked back on her heels. Flirting now, as before, Swanhild bit her lower lip and raised an eyebrow, refusing to say more until Skallagrim asked her. She had magically transformed from the wise sage back to the precocious lass, all in the time it took to bat her pretty lashes.

Skallagrim crossed his arms. "And what?"

"And . . ." She paused again, drawing out the anticipation, her eyes flickering mischievously.

"Yes?"

"Well, I may not have the key to the front door of your fort, but I *do* have the key to the back door!"

CHAPTER EIGHTEEN

Skallagrim waited impatiently by his fire while Swanhild went to retrieve the key from a hiding place near the pool where he had first spied her. His sword hand was trembling again, but he ignored it.

About thirty minutes had passed when, true to her word, the graceful nymph skipped back into Skallagrim's camp, more like a young lass than the ancient "spirit of the pool" that she claimed to be.

The wind was still blowing cold, whipping through the trees, and causing the eerie glow of the phosphorescent mosses and mushrooms to wax and wane. On the breeze, Skallagrim could still detect the sickly sweet smell of death. Swanhild also seemed to detect it, wrinkling her pretty nose.

"You do remember, there are two things that you have to do in return for my help? One, you have admirably performed and, like the thief you claim to be, stolen my heart in the process." She smiled sweetly at Skallagrim.

Balor's bones! he cursed to himself. *What have I promised?* Outwardly, he merely returned her smile and answered in the affirmative.

She beamed and held up a rusty metal key of ancient design. "What I wish is but a trifling thing, really." Swanhild did not wait for Skallagrim to take the key and instead pressed it into his open hand. "In Fort Vigilance you will find a library, or at least the remains of one. Look for a tiny, red-leather book titled The Droning Book of the Sunrise." She described the book as ancient and wondrously engraved but resisted Skallagrim's questions as to the tome's importance. She grasped his hands in her own, stroking them with her thumbs. "Let us just say there are secrets in that book that would be of no use to you but which are very precious to me. There are spells upon the doors of Fort Vigilance—put there by Forneus and others of his kind, long dead—spells that will keep my kind at bay. Key or no key, I cannot enter the place, but you, brave warrior, will kill the fiend Forneus, rescue your maiden, and retrieve this tiny book for me."

"Assuming I survive and assuming I find the book, I'll get it for you. But how do I get it back to you?"

"Just hold onto it, and one day I will find you," she promised. "We will meet again; I just know it!"

Skallagrim nodded and smiled but inwardly cringed. Swanhild would likely misconstrue any future meeting as a lover's tryst—something he wished to avoid. Then again, was this not guilt that was guiding his emotions? He loved the blue-eyed girl, but once she laid eyes on his ruined face, she was bound to recoil. Even if she forgave him the rest, she still deserved better than him. Meanwhile, the beautiful nymph seemed not to notice his disfigurement or, at least, seemed not to care.

"There is still time left for you to rest before sunrise," Swanhild said while smoothing out the creases of his cloak. "You sleep, and I will stay near and watch over you."

Though exhausted, Skallagrim could never sleep knowing he only had an hour remaining. Why not spend that time awake, enjoying the company of this mysterious creature? Frankly, he admitted to himself, he did not trust her enough to sleep in her presence. Shaking his head, he extended a hand, which she took, and pulled her up. "I should gather my things and prepare to go."

She helped him straighten his blanket and repack the contents of his knapsack—which had mostly dried out—while describing the location of the hidden crypt door that would lead him beneath the sorcerer's lair. She pleaded with him to be wary of the deserted city of Orabas and to make his way through it as swiftly as possible. "I cannot fathom what lurks there, but even the light of the sun is muted in the dead city. Heed my words; there is something black there!"

The packing complete, she spent a moment gazing longingly into the thief's eyes. Then, to his utter frustration and guilt-tinged joy, she stood on her tiptoes and, reaching up with her delicate arms, pulled him down into a farewell kiss. However, just before their lips met, she giggled and turned aside, planting a wet kiss on his cheek instead.

Skallagrim, his face flushed, could not help but laugh. They laughed together, then embraced, more friends than swooning lovers who had missed their chance.

The wind whipped at their hair, chilling them, and for a moment, they held each other tightly, warming each other. The deathly smell that had tainted the air for much of the latter part of the night intensified. Swanhild released her hold on Skallagrim's neck and allowed herself to slip back to the ground. Her brows knitted with concern as she hugged herself to ward off the cold.

"There is something of great importance I need to say about your memory loss, and you need to listen, but ..." Swanhild hesitated, her voice trailing off as she peered into the gloom of the forest.

"But what?"

"Something is wrong!" she warned.

A moan sounded in the night, away to the south but not far from the camp. It began deep and resonant, then rose in doleful intensity, only to transform into a wild croaking, gasping cackle. Skallagrim and Swanhild froze in place.

"Ghoul!" Swanhild yelped.

Skallagrim drew his sword and pushed Swanhild behind him, shielding her from whatever devilry might be approaching. Terminus remained silent, apparently accepting the nymph's presence now that other dangers threatened. "Can you see anything?"

"Not from behind you!" She had both her hands firmly around his waist, fearful and not daring to let go of him. However, frightened or not, she permitted herself to peek around Skallagrim and peer into the depths of the gloomy forest. "I see nothing. But that smell! It must have been nearby, watching us since we first came back to the camp."

They heard the moan again, closer now. It was soon joined by another from the ridge to their left, causing the hair on the back of Skallagrim's neck to stand up. He steadied his sword arm, but with Swanhild clinging to him, there was no way he could fight. "Ghouls," he grunted. "The scream of Terminus must have drawn them to us. But will they attack us? I mean, don't they only pilfer and feed off the dead?"

Swanhild released her hold on the thief and stepped to Skallagrim's side, her chest heaving. "Dead?" she whispered. "You are right in that. So, they will kill us first, then bury us and dig us up later!"

"Oh!"

A third mournful howl came from the south to join with the others in a horrible dirge that ended in the same maniacal cackling as before. Skallagrim and Swanhild strained their eyes, but they could see nothing except the interminable rows of trees and the dark shapes of boulders that littered the roadbed.

"I will be safe nearer the river," Swanhild whispered. "They cannot hurt me there. You should head north; get away from here as fast as possible!"

"I'll not leave you here to face ghouls alone," Skallagrim assured her.

Terminus pulsed white, lighting up the surrounding area, and they both gasped at the grotesque horror that it revealed. The nearest boulder, only feet away from them, was no boulder at all.

The ghoul rose upon scaly legs, swishing a hideous, rotting tail that dangled behind it. Its leering face was a mask of pure hatred, a stiffened rictus with a wide, grinning mouth full of gleaming fangs. The skin of its face was so stretched and tight upon its skull, so rigid and unmoving, that it seemed stitched on. Its body was bulky, covered in matted hair, and swarming with vermin. Its sinewy arms featured huge veiny hands, one of which grasped a long, jagged blade. It growled as it reached its full height, nearly as tall as Hartbert.

Not that it cared, it had once been a man, though a morbidly cruel and soulless man whose name was Nib. In truth, there was little difference between the man Nib of two hundred years past and the ghoul Nib who stood drooling venom now, ready to pounce upon supposedly fear-frozen prey. He had stunk of the grave then, and he stank of it now. Indeed, a foetid stench was rolling off him in sickly waves, causing Skallagrim and Swanhild to gasp for air.

Nib made his first and final mistake in his deadly confrontation with Skallagrim and Terminus. Rather than jumping to the attack, he paused to relish the terror he inspired in his two victims, opening his jaws wide to allow a stream of sickly green saliva to pour forth onto the ground. The ghoul took a deep breath and would have unleashed a terrifying howl and cackle, but Terminus would have none of it. The blade, silent until then, issued its own ghastly call and leapt forth, bringing with it Skallagrim's willing arm. He merely let himself go and allowed the sword to have its way, glad he was not given the opportunity for indecision.

The ghoul's face was a rigid facade, but his yellow eyes widened in alarm as he brought up its blade to counter Skallagrim's. Terminus, like a bolt of hot lightning, struck the serrated edge of the monster's blade with a dull clang, shattering the lesser weapon, then continued through to pierce the creature's sternum. An ichorous discharge bubbled and sizzled up from the wound, and Nib howled in pain. The ghoul threw aside the remains of its sword and lashed out with one huge arm that sent Skallagrim flying backward, landing with a thud at Swanhild's feet.

The monster jumped forward and slammed into Skallagrim with his terrible bulk, hammering him farther into the ground. Skallagrim gasped for breath, the wind knocked out of him. He tried to bring Terminus to bear, but the ghoul was right on top of him, and he could only beat at Nib's side with the sharp edge of the blade. With his free hand, he grasped the creature by the throat, both to choke him and to keep Nib's snapping jaws away from his face.

Fear clutched his heart. Not only the fear of sudden and painful death but also the soul-crushing, heart-gripping fear of the unknown. To face the supernatural was one thing. There had been panic when the sorcerer's eyes glowed red, dread when the screaming sword fell and set him to the slaughter, the terror of the witch Tuva, and even a kind of reverent fear in the company of the beautiful nymph. But this was a monster, a ghoul, a thing of legends, born of horror and death.

The sorcerer's arrogant, leering visage was nothing compared to the malevolent, hateful face that hovered inches from Skallagrim's own, slinging venom in every direction as it strove to deliver a bone-crunching bite to the thief's head. Skallagrim could hear more than see Swanhild beating the ghoul with his staff, which at least had the effect of distracting the fiend from his attack. Nib turned his attention momentarily to the nymph, giving Skallagrim a chance to push himself out from under.

Panting for breath, Skallagrim jumped to his feet and lashed out with his sword, hitting the beast full across the spine with a deadly crunch, breaking the ghoul's back. Nib crashed to the ground, and though his legs were useless, he thrashed about madly with his long arms in a vain effort to grab Swanhild. The nymph merely backed away, allowing Skallagrim to dispatch Nib once and for all, piercing the ghoul's neck and severing his spinal column with the tip of the sentient blade.

Swanhild gaped at Skallagrim, his eyes wide with fear and his face flushed with adrenalin. The howling in the woods about them was intensifying. They heard something huge and lumbering crashing down the ridge nearby. Other sounds came from the south. It was clear more trouble was on the way.

"Skallagrim! You have to go!"

"I won't leave you!" Skallagrim said, clenching and unclenching his empty fist, full of the unreasoning fury of the fight and ready to die in defense of the maiden. Terminus glowed white hot, then pulsed black. He let it have its way now, surrounded as he was by enemies. The sword was at work in his mind, singing the battle song, feeding him with confidence and indomitable will.

"If you let the sword have its way, you will die here!" Swanhild warned. "The ghoul's bites are poison, Skallagrim, and many more will come. Too many!" Her breast rose and fell with rapid breaths. She grabbed his free hand and tugged, urging him to move. "Run with me to the river, and I will be safe. They cannot harm me there. Then fly north toward the fort, and do not stop till the sun is up!"

Skallagrim allowed Swanhild to lead him, slowly at first, then running just behind her as the hideous howling of the ghouls grew closer.

"I have powers of my own," Swanhild called to him over her shoulder, "and I will use them if I must. Do not fear for me!" She was panting, breathless, yet went skipping over rocks and dashing around trees, heading for the bank of the rushing river just yards ahead. Skallagrim did his best to keep up, but Swanhild was lithe of limb and nearly glided through the forest. He slipped once in the mud near the bank but came up fast to follow the nymph the last few feet to the river. Not hesitating, she dove in as soon as her feet touched the water.

Up she came a moment later, glistening and radiant. There in her element, her full beauty was revealed, causing Skallagrim's heart to skip a beat. "Now they will not catch Swanhild, and if they try, I will drown them all, one at a time!" She laughed, and it was not a comforting sound, for there in the river, Swanhild was more than a pretty maiden or a capricious nymph. What she was, Skallagrim could not say, for he was stunned by her beauty and the power that emanated from her. She strode forth from the water, dripping silvery droplets and gleaming with the glory of endless youth, majestic and wild. She made to kiss his cheek, and Skallagrim bent down, permitting himself this last guilty pleasure.

"You said there was something else I needed to know," Skallagrim gasped.

"Yes, and I must tell you quickly!" She reached up and stroked his face, sweeping the brown locks away from his wound. "Your forgetfulness was not caused by the injury to your head or any other traumatic event. Though the strike upon your skull might have killed a lesser man, and I am sure you must have seen something terrible in Archon, something you were not supposed to see, those are not the reasons you cannot remember your past life."

"What?" Aghast, Skallagrim tried to steady his trembling sword hand.

"Someone laid a terrible spell upon your mind, Skallagrim," Swanhild said. "Someone does not want you to remember!"

"Who?" A hammer of fresh pain began to pound in his skull as pressure mounted in his chest.

"It might have been Forneus, or it might be that Tuva played some role in this. Or perhaps another sorcerer, though he would be a mighty one indeed to have done this. I cannot say."

Something howled in the distance, causing them to look fearfully back the way they had come. "I cannot remove the spell, or I would. You will have to kill the one who did this to you, then perhaps the mystery will be laid bare before you."

Skallagrim could say nothing in return, so he simply stood there, his mouth agape. There was the beginning of a fire in his belly, a righteous flame that, once properly ablaze, would not be put out for a long time. However, there was no time to feed it properly now, as danger was close, and the perilous maiden was stepping away, preparing to flee.

"Forget everything else but not this," she called to him. "If you kill Forneus Druogorim and your memory does not return, then it was surely another who ensnared your mind. Go now, Sir Skallagrim. Run fast! Do not forget the maiden Swanhild, for we shall meet again!" Saying this, she turned and dove into the swift current and was gone.

CHAPTER NINETEEN

Imminent death was looming. Skallagrim did not wait pining by the bank, nor did he dwell on his guilt for enjoying the nymph's company—the sweet wetness of her kisses. In his exhausted state, the entire encounter seemed like a dream, as if he had spent the last few hours with one foot in the real world and another in the realm of faerie. He shook his head, hoping to fully wake himself.

A dream? He could nearly believe it, except for the howling and harsh laughter that echoed in the forest behind him.

Swanhild was gone, but she had left him a powerful truth. Someone had put a spell upon his mind, shutting the door to his memory with a lock that not even a thief could pick. He would have to kill that person if he wanted the key, but first he would have to determine who that was.

Swanhild might have told him more, but there had been no time. So, he put her and her staggering revelation out of his head, turned toward the road, and raced like the wind. The farther he ran, the more Swanhild's spell faded until, at last, he could barely recall his attraction for her. He would chide himself later for lowering his guard. He would ponder her tidings too. For the moment though, he had to move.

As if striving to push him north to his goal, the southerly wind blew, sometimes gusting fiercely, causing the glowing fungi to flicker and cast wild shadows in the gloom. Perceived threats played at the corners of his eyes, but he pushed them from his thoughts, thinking only of the blue-eyed girl who would die if he failed.

He jumped over tree roots and rocks, plowed through underbrush, and hurdled bubbling rivulets, finally making his way back to the roadbed. Not stopping to see if the ghouls were close behind, he pointed himself north and fled into the night.

He bolted up the rock-strewn road like a deer, his staff clutched in one hand. After a half mile, the roadbed began to climb away from the river. Then the ridge sloped steeply to his right while to his left the bank plunged precipitously to the water's edge. The road was plenty wide enough, but there was no way to turn off it should he need to hide.

After another half mile, he stopped to catch his breath as the road finally evened out. Higher up the steep ridge were trees that did not glow. Colonies of luminous mushrooms hugged their roots, but even they were fewer in number than those that grew in the river flats. The canopy had thinned over the road as well, and for the first time that night, he saw the glimmer of dim stars overhead.

His breathing had barely calmed when he heard the howling again. There were shouted words of command as well, barked by harsh voices, though unintelligible. He quickened his pace, thinking to save some strength for later, especially should he need to turn and fight. But he had not gone far before he scrapped the plan as the sound of pursuit grew closer. He began to jog, thought better of it, and finally broke into a sprint.

His pack slammed into his back with each stride, and its straps dug into his shoulders, causing his left arm to grow numb. He would have to adjust it soon, or it might drive him mad. The scabbard was banging into his leg, threatening to trip him. The road, with its steep bank, was treacherous. He had no desire to lose his feet and go sprawling down the slope. So, he steadied the scabbard with his right hand as best as he could while gripping his staff in the other. He was a noisy, clattery mess, but what could he do?

His heart hammering, he implored his leaden legs to keep moving as he gulped air. His feet pounded the ground with all the grace of two bags of rocks, the deft strides of a half-mile back nonexistent. He mostly kept his eyes on the ground, hoping to avoid any roots or loose rocks that would trip him up. Finally, sensing a change in the air, he looked up. Was that a faint glow in the sky?

Dawn must surely be near. Swanhild had suggested the danger

would diminish as the sun rose, and he hoped it was true. He had no knowledge of ghouls or their habits, but it seemed to make sense, for they were grave robbers, creatures of the night. He did not know their number nor whether the threat was only from behind, yet on he ran.

Out of the darkness loomed the trunk of a huge pine lying directly across his path. Rather than stop to climb over it, he judged he could jump it.

He launched himself off his right foot and immediately felt his left leg scrape the bark of the fallen tree, realizing he had made a blunder. Time slowed for the heartbeat it took to go somersaulting over the pine and to land with a terrible thud just the other side. He rolled, bruising his right leg on his scabbard.

He would have cursed if he had not, for the second time that night, had the wind knocked out of him. Still, fear drove him to quickly right himself. He came up squarely on both feet, took another giant stride to continue his clumsy sprint, and collided head-on . . . with another ghoul.

Having heard the shouts and calls of its unwholesome brethren, the ghoul had waited in ambush behind the fallen tree, drooling poison from its slack jaw while testing the edge of the adze it carried for a weapon. It was nearly as surprised as Skallagrim when the two collided. Caught off guard, the fiend stumbled backward, teetered on the edge of the roadbed, then went sliding backward down the steep bank.

Thinking fast, Skallagrim, still gasping for air, tossed his staff and drew Terminus, holding it with both hands. The ghoul looked nothing like the one he had faced earlier with the nymph. This one looked oddly human, dressed in ragged pants and a faded coat cut in the style of bygone days, no doubt robbed from the dead.

He could not have known it, but the grave robbers of the Vales were not cut from the same mold as one another. They were as varied as the multitudinous fungi that sprang from the burial mounds near the river. Most had once been human but had succumbed over time to macabre obsessions and abhorrent hungers, which caused them to mutate into multifarious forms, each one a ghastly variation of sepulchral humanity. They were loosely organized, bound to one another by their repulsive appetites, murderous tendencies, and a seething hatred of all who clung to true life.

Those who haunted the Vales, at least the southernmost valleys and ridges of that wild region, were lorded over by Vathek, a particularly loathsome monster who had, in his former life, held the distinction of being Archon's Chief Executioner, an occupation he both loathed and loved. After a long life of killing in an official capacity—and being feared, despised, and rejected by all decent folk—Vathek answered the call of Death, his master. He forsook that fragment of humanness that clung to him still, gathered those wayward souls he could find of like mind, and headed into the wild to scrounge among the forgotten tombs and barrows of the Pagarna Valley, only venturing beyond its tangled forests on occasion to raid the graveyards of Andorath's more civilized areas.

Of late, Vathek had come to fancy himself the King of Ghouls, and there was none of his kind who dared dispute him. Though it was not Vathek himself whom Skallagrim faced now, Vathek had been made aware of the thief's reckless trek through his haunts and was on his way, for he greatly desired to taste once more the flesh of the freshly dead. "Such a rarity in these parts!"

The sallow-faced wretch who had just hooked a tree root with his adze and was scrambling back up the steep slope wished for much the same. His name, not that he used it much, was Abadiah Sedgwick. Long ago he had been an undertaker or had pretended to be as much for several dreary settlements that dotted the bleak countryside around Ophyr. One by one the village chiefs were inclined to dismiss him—most outright banishing him—for he was a suspicious, unlikeable man who seemed to enjoy his job overmuch. He tried his hand as a sellsword for a time, for, at least in this way, he might remain close to death.

To his credit, Abadiah became a fighter to be reckoned with, very handy with war hammers, pickaxes, flails, and the like. But even killers and mercenaries would not abide him long, for he could not well suppress his morbid proclivities. Thus, he was cast out of every cutthroat gang or band of thugs he joined.

Eventually, like the rest of his abhorrent ken, Abadiah stalked the ridges and the flats, digging up old bones and rifling graves where he could find them. It had been slim pickings of late, and the sight of this well-muscled young man had him salivating in a most untidy fashion.

With sickly, venomous slobber spilling from his cursing grave of a mouth, he thrashed and clawed his way back to the roadbed to face the tasty morsel with the gleaming sword. Abadiah would beat him to a pulp with the adze, then bury him in a secluded spot near the river, allowing the corpse to ripen just a bit. He would exhume the body, taking great pleasure in the act, then devour it over the course of a few days. But he would have to move fast, killing him and dragging him off before the others came or before the hated sun rose. He did not hesitate once he was solidly back upon the road and launched himself at Skallagrim, adze held high.

Terminus flashed brightly in Skallagrim's hands. He did not wait for the adze to fall but stepped to the right of the rushing ghoul and swung his sword at the monster's midsection as if he were an axeman chopping at a tree. Abadiah deftly parried with an angled, downward stroke that beat at his opponent's blade, driving it aside and leaving Skallagrim wide open, momentarily defenseless. But the ghoul had closed the distance too quickly and could not bring his own weapon to bear. Instead, he took advantage of his momentum and simply crashed into the thief, knocking him backward. Skallagrim had yet to recover from his initial tumble over the fallen tree and was still gasping for air as he skidded backward, barely avoiding another fall.

Abadiah sought to exploit the situation, but his foe, though visibly exhausted and covered in wounds, had managed to right himself. The ghoul backed up a step, and gripping the adze tightly with both scaly hands, tilted his head back, and laughed. It was a dry, raspy sound, like rocks scraping against one another.

"Most don't put up much fight!" Abadiah's voice was hollow but full of hatred. "Of course, when you think about it, most folks I tangle with are way too stiff to cause much worry." He laughed in his horrible way, taking pleasure in his morbid joke. "But if you want to play swords with me, that's fine. It's going to end the same either way!"

The ghoul reeked of the grave and other miasmic stenches that had clung to his cadaverous hide over the years. Skallagrim had to take a deep breath of tainted air to speak. "I've killed many men," he panted. "Even one of your own kind, though he was much larger than you. You aren't likely to best me! You are nothing but filth, and you smell like a rotting tomb."

Abadiah's eyes flashed. "Oh," he said, laughing. "Can't help the smell. Let's just say I likes to bury myself in my work!" He jumped forward and swung the adze again, but Skallagrim countered and launched his own assault. The two blades met over and over, clanging like a hammer and anvil.

Back and forth they went, man and former man, in a brutal display of hacking, chopping, failed strikes, and counter blows, neither combatant able to land a decisive strike. By then there was little finesse in the fight. Skallagrim flailed wildly with Terminus, biceps bulging. The ghoul parried and pounded away, spewing spittle and curses all the while.

The battle song was screaming in Skallagrim's head, sung no doubt by the sentient sword he wielded. *"Perilous are the days,"* it cried. *"When evil hides in the wicked man and when the good man hides from evil!"* Though there was no need, the sword was calling him to action, throwing him wildly into the fray. It hated! It hated! Oh, it hated the damned with a pitiless, merciless hatred!

But this ghoul would not be beaten as easily as the last. He was also fueled by hatred and wielded a cruel weapon with great skill. Skallagrim had yet to face a foe this desperate—this hungry. Abadiah hammered away at his defenses, trying to split the thief's skull or cleave his torso. It mattered not, for he was in a frenzy, racing the inevitable sunrise that would drain him of potency. His appetite was voracious, driving him into one reckless attack after another, yet he could not make contact with this cursed swordsman, who should have collapsed with exhaustion by now.

Abadiah had to hurry, for the sky was now pink with the approach of dawn. He and the thief could also hear the calls and shouts of Vathek and his band of ghouls coming down the trail behind Skallagrim. He had no desire to share this kill, but he was tiring.

Abadiah took a step backward. Laughing again, he hefted his adze and feinted, throwing a wide swing toward Skallagrim's left side. Skallagrim made to counter, but the ghoul's blade dropped beneath his own as the monster unexpectedly crouched low. Hooking the thief's leg with the adze head, he jerked him off his feet. Skallagrim landed on his back, grunting and wincing. His eyes flashed open to find Abadiah already on top of him, pinning him by the throat with the adze handle. This time there was no Swanhild to distract his opponent. Skallagrim was on his own.

Only a moment before, his mind had been flashing images of the possible ways he might be horribly injured or die by way of the long-handled adze. Split skull, severed limb, or just shattered bones? It was much like an axe, best suited for the attack, not defense. The right blow could split armor, and Skallagrim had none. It could smash a shield to pieces, but Skallagrim had none. It was not a typical melee weapon, but it was a deadly one just the same. Yet, for all the grisly images his brain had concocted, being choked to death by the adze was not one of them. Now it was not only choking him but also threatening to crush his windpipe.

Skallagrim used his left hand to grab the adze's wooden handle, relieving the pressure somewhat, while he beat at the ghoul's back with the hilt of Terminus, hoping to make use of one the sword's unique features. The ricasso, just below the sword's guard, featured twin barbs, as sharp and deadly as two small knives. If he could angle the attack just so, he might get one of those barb's to pierce the monster's flesh.

Yet, he was dizzy from lack of air, and his head was threatening to explode. The icy claws of panic gripped him as he gasped for air, but just before his mind gave way to darkness, one of the barbs connected with flesh. With every ounce of strength he could muster, Skallagrim drove the hook home, twisted the blade, then drove it home again and again.

Abadiah screamed in anguish and rolled off the thief, nearly ripping the sword out of Skallagrim's hand. In a second, they were both on their feet, the ghoul still wielding the adze with one hand while clutching his wounded back with the other. Skallagrim was in no better shape as he wheezed and coughed, struggling to fill his lungs.

The other ghouls were close now, only a few yards away by the sound of their terrible wailing. Skallagrim needed to get past this wretch, but he had no wish to engage him further in useless swordplay.

On the ground just behind the ghoul lay Skallagrim's dogwood staff. It was wedged between the right-hand slope of the ridge and two sizable rocks that lay half buried on the roadbed. Thinking fast, he rushed Abadiah Sedgwick, who was angry and cursing, slamming into him for the second time that day, sending him backward to trip over the wedged staff. The ghoul hit the ground hard on his backside as Skallagrim jumped deftly past. Turning fast, he swung the sentient blade with all his might, aiming for the creature's neck. Terminus connected, and in a split second, Abadiah Sedgwick lost his head.

A geyser of blood erupted from the terrible wound. The body remained sitting, shockingly upright, severed neck smoking from the scorching touch of Terminus. The grisly, severed head arced through the air, landed on the nearby slope and rolled to a stop near Skallagrim's feet. He looked down at the twitching, scowling face, noting with some alarm that the bloodshot eyes, opened wide as if in surprise, were darting back and forth.

Suddenly aware he was not alone, Skallagrim, ripped his gaze from the devastation that was—or had been—Abadiah Sedgwick. The heads of six more ghouls, still unfortunately attached to their bodies, appeared just on the other side of the fallen tree. Brandishing an assortment of odd weapons, from shovels to pickaxes, they shouted, growled, yammered, and cursed—all but one.

King Vathek stood menacingly upon the downed pine where he motioned the others to silence. Though he had long since lost any shred of inward humanity, outwardly, he retained the barest resemblance. He wore what must once have been a suit of fine clothes, stripped from some entombed nobleman in one of Archon's more accessible tombs, perhaps. Now it hung from him in tatters, covered in dirt and grime. The long, lonely years of wandering the wild, of scrounging in the mud for bones, of raiding tombs and digging up mounds, had not been kind to Vathek. By all appearances, he was more than half a monster, while the rest of him looked like a rotting corpse. Worse yet, Vathek hefted a terrible axe whose appearance was so frightful, it must have been forged in hell.

It was said—mostly by the inscrutable librarians of Archon's Eldritch House—that certain ghouls had, in their hunger, torn open the wrong cairns. These were tombs inhabited by fell spirits or dreadful demons imprisoned therein by clever spells. It was further speculated that these demons would, in an effort to walk once more among the living, enter the body of a ravenous ghoul. The unwitting wretch, already emptied of human soul, made an appropriate vessel wherein the fell spirit might abide, working further mischief and evil in the world. King Vathek was one such ghoul.

He was irredeemable, a reprobate, a demon-haunted husk whose eyes glowed like fiery coals and whose mouth was full of fearsome fangs. On the best of days, Vathek was a creature that brimmed with hatred and unbridled rage. This, at least as far as Vathek was concerned, was not the best of days. And right now all that hatred and rage was focused on a lone man holding a bright sword.

CHAPTER TWENTY

"I'm telling you, dark or no dark, there's been no wagon on this road." Looking more like a bear than a man in the faint light of predawn, Hartbert crawled about on all fours, his eyes scanning the hard-packed dirt of the Bald River Gorge Road for any hint of a track that might indicate the sorcerer had come that way with his hostage. "Please, sir! Hold the lantern closer."

Erling did as bidden, holding his lantern over the huge man's shoulder. "Do you think he stole my ring? Skallagrim, I mean?"

"Well, I certainly didn't take it," Hartbert grunted. "You probably just misplaced it at the inn. I wish you'd quit obsessing about it."

"My, but you are in an ogreish mood this morning," Erling quipped. "I suppose that's fitting, you being an ogre and all, what?" He laughed nervously, but the sound fell flat in the pre-dawn gloom, and he cut it short. He put a hand to his aching lower back. "I can't stay bent over like this much longer. The sun will be up in a few minutes, and you'll probably see the wagon tracks then. Let's give it up for now, please!"

Abandoning his search for the moment, Harbert rolled over to sit upon his backside, his enormous legs spread out before him like two logs. "There was much coming and going on horseback, but we knew that. Still, I'd expect some sign of wheels in this dirt." He peered east, where the faint impression of the road faded into the darkness. "You say all of Straker's men were bought off? They're gone, right?"

Erling straightened up, still massaging his stiff back with his free hand. "All but three—apparently, Straker's cousins. They are either guarding the bridge to stop Skallagrim from crossing or holed up inside Fort Vigilance with the sorcerer. Either way, they can watch the approach along this road. You heard what my spies said, and I know no more than that."

"And you still hold they won't expect Skallagrim to come from the south, right?"

"Not in a million years!" Erling was confident on this point, having maintained it from the beginning of their venture.

"How will he get in? Have you thought that through?" In the short time they had spent together, Hartbert had developed feelings of friendship for the heartsick thief, and with every passing hour, he grew increasingly concerned for his welfare. "If he survives the wilderness, that is."

"Oh, have some faith, Hartbert. He'll make it to the fort; you'll see. A trek through the wild was the only way! He would never get through the front door of the fort. It will not open for anyone but Forneus and those he permits, for it's locked by his sorcery. There's a key that will undo the whole thing, mind you. But alas, Forneus has it."

"So, how will Skallagrim get inside?"

"You forget the back door! There are always other ways in, my good giant. Always!" Erling held up his left hand, fretting over the imprint of the missing ring on his fourth finger.

The sun was beginning to rise over the Chimney Tops, and the dark, spectral shapes around them were slowly materializing into trees. To the left of the road, the Bald River churned noisily where it wound along a snaky path toward the Pagarna River, only a few miles ahead. Nearby, Erling and Hartbert's horses waited impatiently, their ears twitching and their hooves pawing shallow trenches in the ground.

"Besides," Erling said. "We're talking about a thief. Skallagrim may not remember it yet, but he's one of the best. He'll find a way. That *is* why I sent him," he added almost absentmindedly.

Hartbert looked up at Erling, his face now visible with the onset of dawn, and pondered this last cryptic remark. He noticed too that his employer appeared nervous, on edge. It was not unusual for Erling to modulate between arrogant confidence and strained, jittery disquietude. He had always been manic in that way. Erling frequently blamed his mood swings on his work, especially the part of his work that included occult research, but something beyond the usual was weighing on him now. Hartbert could read it on his face, especially in his unusually blood-shot eyes, which darted back and forth in the growing light. However, whatever Hartbert thought, he kept to himself. He could not figure out Erling Hizzard. The man had always been a mystery.

Grunting, Hartbert pushed himself to his feet and continued his search for wagon tracks. There were none. He pointed east along the road. "You're certain the sorcerer is there—I mean, at the fort? He didn't go on to Ophyr?"

"Yes! My spies were clear on that."

"And the girl?"

"Oh, who knows, Hartbert? Maybe he threw her onto a horse and took her with him. Yes, that must be it!"

"Must it? What if he handed the wagon off and the girl with it? Maybe he sold her into slavery after all! Then Skallagrim has done all of this for nothing!"

Erling was unmoved. "I told you both, slavery is not his way. It's either a sacrifice he has in mind, or our lovesick thief with the screaming sword has dreamt it all up. He took a nasty hit to the head, remember? No one else saw her but him!"

"But he believes he saw her. He was sure of it!"

"Well, believing does not make a thing so. It's merely believing. Still, I take your point. Skallagrim was adamant about the girl. I hope for his sake he finds her, but the most important thing is that he gets inside Fort Vigilance and kills the fiend, Forneus Druogorim."

Hartbert shook his head in disbelief. "Why, sir? Killing that sorcerer is just an act of revenge, surely."

"What Skallagrim wants and why he wants it's secondary, Hartbert. And you would do well to remember that and remember who pays your wages. I want that sorcerer dead, and I want a look inside Fort Vigilance! Skallagrim is the best way I have of accomplishing that. If we can help the poor fool find this girl of his in the process, then we will!" Hartbert made to speak, but Erling raised his voice, stubbornly refusing to yield ground. "But she is secondary!" He lowered his voice again, striving to regain his composure. "The sorcerer must die." Erling's voice faded to a whisper. "They all must die."

"As you say, Mister Hizzard," Hartbert lied. He would help Skallagrim if he could. Erling's crusade be damned!

"Besides," Erling added as the two remounted their horses. "Look what they did to his face. The sorcerer either wants his arm for some unfathomable reason or wants him dead. Or both! Our Skallagrim needs to see this through. Now, let's be off. We certainly can't help him here!"

There were not many words left to be said as the two made their way along the Gorge Road, knowing that in a few short miles they would see Fort Vigilance for themselves. Maybe Skallagrim would make it and maybe not. Perhaps they would have their own confrontation with the dreaded sorcerer and his hired killers. Doubt and dread began to gnaw at their hearts, but they kept their dreary thoughts to themselves and rode on.

"I'm telling you, this chain is coming loose!"

Forneus Druogorim, sorcerer and keeper of the key to Fort Vigilance, was furious. Worse yet, he was making demands on Straker, expecting things that had not been agreed upon when this mad venture was first presented to him. But, Straker supposed, the conjurer probably had a right to be angry. After all, had Straker not just lost over a hundred men—one hundred men who were needed to apprehend the thief with the freakish sword?

Still, Straker was thought by some—most notably himself—to be one of the best sword fighters in all of Andorath. He did not need one hundred men or even ten to take Skallagrim down. The alley fight in Archon had been botched, though not through any fault of his own. Those unmanageable thugs had been forced on him by the overly cautious Forneus.

If the sorcerer was so fearful of the man, why not allow Straker to simply slay him? Or better yet, why did Forneus not merely blast Skallagrim to death with some infernal spell? So much fuss about an arm and a sacrifice!

Straker might have concerns about the Terminus sword, but he refused to allow an irrational fear of Skallagrim to get the best of him. In fact, he hoped the thief would come, for he wanted another go at him. Arm, face, head, sword—whatever Forneus wanted. But Straker wanted to beat the thief in combat, his skill against Skallagrim's lack of it, his killing blade against the meteoric Terminus—a payback for the embarrassing mess in the alley. For that humiliation he hated Skallagrim and would kill him.

"Hold it down while I adjust this!" Forneus barked.

This was Straker's first visit to the nightmarish vault, the sanctum sanctorum of the sorcerer's maniacal experiments. The subject of those experiments—a pathetic, one-armed creature on a wooden table—was thrashing madly about, threatening to break loose of its chains, clenching its fist and mewling pitifully. This was what Forneus wanted Straker to hold down, but he was loath to touch the thing. Repulsed, he looked away from the creature to reexamine his surroundings.

The vault was a large chamber that lay one floor down from the main hall of Fort Vigilance. It was a frightful place, full of strange, half-observed shadows that bent to and fro at the corners of one's eyes. Alarmingly, these fleeting phantoms of peripheral vision did not seem to correspond to any visible object in the vault. When Straker would try to look directly at one, the thing would immediately blend in with shadows one would expect to find, those of beakers and alembics, censers and aerometers, overly large crystals, and the like.

With the many sputtering lanterns that hung from the supports, these perceivable fixtures of the vault cast perfectly natural shadows. Bizarrely, the one exception—an oddly deformed, man-sized skeleton on display in a well-lit corner of the room—cast no shadow at all.

It was all rather unsettling to Straker, unnerving. The room, with its odd shadows and equally strange occupants, managed to stir an inexplicable feeling of claustrophobia despite its otherwise accommodating size and openness.

Straker knew there were even deeper, more mysterious chambers below the fort. He had had a quick peek through an open door on the opposite wall from which he leaned now. There was a stairway leading down into inky darkness. A chill wind would gust now and then from beyond the door, which refused to stay shut regardless of what was propped against it. More troubling than that, the cold air carried with it the scent of something indescribably old and foul. He imagined that if eldritch evil had a perceivable smell, the odor coming up from beyond that persistently open door must be its apex. That a supremely malefic consciousness was listening to his thoughts did not occur to Straker.

It had not occurred to Forneus either, yet he had lived with the impalpable presence ever since coming to Fort Vigilance. He did not know what Swanhild had guessed, that the ancient fastness was a prison, not a castle lording over villages long abandoned. No, the sorcerer did not know this and had nary a clue what he had awakened when he tentatively peered into the pit. Since that moment, the dead thing, though still very much dead, was alert, interested, and aware.

To Straker, it felt first like the merest itch inside his head, almost a tickle. Then the sensation strengthened, and he became queasy, sickened as the malevolent yet subtle awareness swept aside the cobwebs in the darkest corners of his mind and stealthily probed about, looking for interesting bits.

He stared into the tenebrous maw of the doorway, inhaled the cool, noxious air that channeled upward from unknowable depths, and found he could not tear his gaze away. He was seized by a sudden desire to rush headlong down the beckoning stairway into the chilly depths, down to the source, the only way to satisfy his intense curiosity.

Straker found he could contemplate little else, though was acutely reminded of a funeral he had been forced to attend as a child, the first such sad event of his life.

"You don't have to look," the grown-ups said, though they pushed him toward *it* just the same.

So, he shuffled forward on unwilling feet and stood at last by the dreaded casket. He promised himself he would not look, yet he did. What was there, laid out on lace-trimmed velvet and taffeta, stiff and unbreathing, had transfixed him.

There it lay, a person yet not a person. His child mind could not fathom death, yet there it lay on full display, a helpless, sad mockery of life. Clothed in finery yet for no reason. All made up with no place to go. The uncaring, unfeeling face, its lips tightened and pale, seemed ready to communicate volumes, but what it wished to say was nothing anyone would ever care to hear. It was an empty shell, a husk, full of nothing.

And yet, the thing down below, perhaps it could give voice to the unknowable, the ineffable, the cosmic, soul-crushing truth that had radiated from that casket so many years ago. Straker had but to descend, to walk down the stairs into the darkness . . .

The old memory and the impulsive temptation that followed made Straker shudder. The hold on his mind temporarily broke, and he turned away from the door.

When probed for information, the sorcerer had said very little about what lay beyond the strangely appealing yet singularly horrid door. "Down those stairs are corridors and passages going off in all directions. I believe there's supposed to be a crypt somewhere at the end of one of them. There's a pit also, a very dangerous spot to come across in the dark. I wouldn't venture beyond the door if I were you. One could easily and very quickly lose one's self."

No amount of prying had gotten him to say more.

CHAPTER TWENTY-ONE

Straker looked with disgust at the monster on the table. Weary of watching Forneus struggling with the weakening chain that bound the creature, he stirred himself at last to give aid. "You're right; it's coming loose. You need to bolt the chain to the table better. If he rocks this table over, then he's getting loose!"

"I was hoping you would take it upon yourself to make the necessary adjustments!" Forneus shouted. The monster was sobbing pitifully, perhaps understanding the conversation between its captors, perhaps not. "I certainly pay you enough."

"You aren't paying me for this! I'm here to capture or kill Skallagrim, then I'm hitting the road, see?" He grinned slyly, looking every bit the wolf in man's clothing. He could afford a bit of defiance. Of course, he knew to tread lightly with the sorcerer, but right now Forneus needed him to deal with Skallagrim.

Straker was not the sorcerer's henchman, nor would he play the part of fort custodian or laboratory assistant. And should the sorcerer show any sign of weakness, Straker would pounce. He would love nothing more than to slit the fiend's throat, take his gold, and escape this demon-haunted hellhole. But unless the situation changed, he would have to remain wary, playing his part until the end of the ordeal. Forneus might be mad, but he was not weak—anything but.

With a last tightening of the chain, the monster ceased its thrashing, but even the gag in its mouth could not stifle the loathsome sounds it made.

Forneus showed no concern that this gibbering, wretched thing had once been a man. *Well,* Straker gloomily reminded himself, *that was just the head, legs, and one arm.* Of course, he could not be certain that what was straining against the chain had been one man or many. Whatever it once was, it was now an overly large, haphazardly constructed amalgamation of parts, some fleshy and manlike, others beastly or oddly mechanical. Nothing short of a miracle of science and sorcery, Straker admitted to himself, but it was also the product of an insane imagination. There was no knowing where Forneus had come by it all, what charnel houses he had raided, what ghoul he had trafficked with, nor how many men had been outright killed to achieve this work of madness.

A helpless, bound creature such as this was a temptation to Straker. If left alone with it, he might cut it a time or two and watch it writhe. He preferred to torture and terrify the weaker sex, but one could not be too picky in such lean times.

He glared at it. "So, this is what it was all about?"

Sweating from exertion, Forneus had to speak loudly to be heard above the creature's bellowing. "Yes, aside from the sacrifice that must be performed tomorrow night. I suppose you disapprove?"

"I reckon the Warlock King of Urk would take issue," Straker said, eyeing the battle-axe that leaned upon a nearby wall. "But I neither approve nor disapprove. You've clearly put some thought into it." Straker held strong opinions that the thing on the table, at least part of it, had once been the fabled Axeman, General Arne Grímsson of Urk, but he kept them to himself.

"That I have! There's the matter of the brain's failure to function properly, but there are options to consider. Do not trouble yourself with any of that or with that barbarian upstart in Urk. What I have in mind will work but only if you do your job. There can be no more mistakes. Am I clear on that?"

"My remaining men are hiding near the bridge," Straker reassured him. "If the thief is coming from the Gorge Road, as you say, they'll stop him, sure enough."

Truthfully, Straker was sure of nothing. Skallagrim had already killed many of his men, proving he could more than hold his own in a fight. But those men had been the dregs of Archon's thug society, little more than unskilled butchers who came to the fight unprepared, probably drunk from a night of revelry in the seedy tavern where he had been sent to hire them. His cousins, those who held the bridge, were trained killers, as was Straker. It would be a simple thing to just kill the thief, but it seemed now that Forneus was committed to taking Skallagrim alive after all. A somewhat riskier proposition, but it could be done.

"And you swear you have had no dealings with Griog'xa?" Forneus asked. "None at all?"

"I told you already, I've never dealt with the man," Straker lied. No one had seen Griog'xa face to face in many years, of course, but the dreaded sorcerer of Archon had many ways to make his wishes known.

"He's playing a game with me. I should have known it from the beginning," Forneus said, cringing at a sudden dreadful thought.

"What do you mean?" Straker asked, though he could guess what sort of game was being played, for Griog'xa was the personification of treachery. He was finding that out the hard way now, though too late. Straker could confess his own duplicity, but to do so would be to embroil himself further with the two rivals.

"When the star first appeared over Archon, certain practitioners of the black arts, myself included, had a good idea what it was. Alarmed, I went to Archon and sought out Griog'xa in his tower, for his wisdom in such matters is unrivaled. Of course, no one is allowed to see him. Hearing his voice is another matter entirely, so he spoke with me and confirmed my suspicions." The sorcerer paused, seemingly wondering if he should say more. With a sigh of resignation, he made up his mind and continued. "Griog'xa was rather preoccupied at the time, more concerned about some obscure magical creation he was about to obtain than the threat of the sword."

"And what exactly is the threat of the sword?" Straker inquired.

"The implications of the thing are vast. I cannot—dare not—tell you all. Suffice it to say that if the sword is unleashed upon Andorath, a great many plans will come unraveled, my own included!"

"So, a decision of some sort was reached, I'm guessing?"

"Yes, I suppose we made a sort of, well . . . a bargain, along with a plan about how to proceed. By that point time was of the essence."

"A deal? You made a deal with Griog'xa?"

"Yes, damn it! I made a deal!" Forneus threw his arms wide. "He can be, well . . . very persuasive."

Straker smiled grimly to himself. "I'm sure it seemed that way."

Ignoring the implied insult, Forneus continued. "It seemed easy enough in the moment, and there was no time left for further debate. Griog'xa was certain the sword's fall was imminent, and to prove him out, it fell that very night."

Straker was incredulous. How could Forneus have been so foolish as to have made a pact with the most notoriously treacherous sorcerer in all of Andorath? Of course, he had done as much himself, making his own deal with an emissary of Griog'xa. Like the trap into which Forneus had fallen, it had seemed an easy thing to do in the moment.

All he had to do was drag out the fight in the alley, postponing the capture of Skallagrim by a few minutes. A fistful of gold coins in return for minutes. Precious minutes, he reminded himself, for in those few moments when he could have taken the thief but held himself in check, the Terminus sword had shrieked down from the sky like something out of a nightmare. *Hell's teeth! Griog'xa wanted Skallagrim to have the sword!* He shuddered inwardly and began to wonder if he should confide in Forneus after all. Before he could, however, the sorcerer began to elaborate further.

"He wanted two things," Forneus explained. "His emissary, a creature nearly as terrifying as Griog'xa himself, brought something to the alley that night—the night the sword fell. I was to deliver—" His voice caught, and he looked away as if something profoundly sad had just occurred to him.

"What? What were you to deliver?"

The sorcerer's eyes darted back to Straker. His lips moved as if searching for the right words to describe something, but finding them all inadequate, he said nothing at all.

Straker could not help but notice the red tinge was missing from the sorcerer's eyes. In fact, for a moment it seemed as if he was tearing up. Forneus even bit his lower lip in an effort to suppress its sudden quivering. Unexplainably, the sorcerer now seemed like a frightened child trapped in an old man's body, the last vestige of a bygone innocence peering out through clouded eyes, perhaps seeing some lost glory, a last chance at reconciliation slipping past.

"It was a thing of exquisite beauty," he mumbled. "Indescribable. Perhaps the most wondrous thing I have ever laid hands on." The more Forneus tried to explain what he had seen, the less he appeared as a frightening mage of black magic. He looked frail, bent with age, weary of the world's insanity and still unable to come to grips with his own madness, his own contribution to the darkness that consumed Andorath. He shook his head as if by doing so, he could dislodge the memory. "I'll say no more except to tell you that I did what was required. In the wagon that night, I secured his prize and took it from the city."

Straker gave him a bitter look. "This happened in the alley? Because I saw nothing."

Forneus scrutinized Straker's grave features. "You would not have, Straker. Only eyes accustomed to such enchantments would have seen it—a rare thing of faerie perhaps."

Though the assassin plied him with further questions, Forneus would speak no more of the *thing of exquisite beauty*. Straker changed his tack, seeking to unravel the deal the sorcerers had made. "So then, what was the second thing Griog'xa wanted?"

"Access to this fort. He has always wanted to get a look inside, to seek out its secrets. Of course, I would not agree to that. He eventually relented on that condition, but still . . . I wonder."

"And in return for what you did for him? For carrying his prize out of Archon?"

"I could have the sword and even the thief whose undeserving hands grabbed it from the sky. It was a bargain, or at least I thought so at the time. We were to take him in the alley, preferably before he had the sword. Then, when the sword fell, we would have the weapon and the only man who could wield it. That is why I want his arm, Straker—for what I'm building here in this room." He motioned toward the creature on the table. "But if we failed to take him in the alley, we were to lead him here where there would be no interference or meddling by Archon's Watch."

Something of the old Forneus was returning. Finding his stride, he told the assassin everything he needed to know. "Griog'xa employed certain spells, certain deceptions, to make certain Skallagrim would come, the nature of which even I'm not privy to. Griog'xa conjured a lure, you see, a sure way to get him here. He also made certain an unwitting ally of Skallagrim's, one Erling Hizzard, would be on hand to help the thief, eventually leading him here. You see, there were great deceptions at play. What seemed simple at the time now seems a tad more complicated. The witless thief is not the only one caught up in Griog'xa's schemes, I'm afraid. I should have seen through it."

"He's a known deceiver," Straker stated. "But do you know anything for certain, or are you just guessing?" Straker discerned more than he let on. Now that he was left in the lurch with the hag-haunted sorcerer, he might as well find out all he could.

Forneus laughed bitterly. "In the alley, just when we thought we had things under control, the cultists arrived and ruined it all!" His fists were clenched, and his eyes flared red again. "We had to flee! What else could be done, what with the Watch coming? And who was blamed for that riot? Me! I have it on good account that Griog'xa has all of Archon believing I wield the power in Balor's cult, the so-called *Enlightened*. I tell you, it is not! It's he who pulls their strings!"

"Damn!" Straker had thought he had the gist of it. Now he understood how ignorant he had been to the growing war between the two conjurers. Though not given to doubt, Straker was beginning to feel the gnaw of it in his gut.

The sorcerer glared. "Then your soldiers—your one hundred horsemen—disappear. Hired out to Archon's army! Griog'xa was surely behind this maneuver, for now it has left us open, and that's what he wants!"

"What is he after? The sword?"

"He wants in here! He wants access to Fort Vigilance!" Forneus was frantic now as a terrible realization dawned on him. "Griog'xa never wanted the sword. He doesn't need it. He intends to wield it through this thief. Of all the forms vengeance and treachery could assume, I think you will agree he chose the vilest and most pernicious. Do you see it?"

"Not entirely, no."

"He set it all in motion, Straker. Griog'xa wants to get inside Fort Vigilance; he wants it for himself for all I know. Oh, what have I done?"

Beside himself with dread, the sorcerer took an empty beaker and flung it across the room, causing the monster on the table to jerk about wildly again. "The humiliation of it all! It's like peeling an onion, layer upon layer of deceit and betrayal. He's laughing in his tower now. For all I know, he can see us and hear what we're saying!"

Forneus picked up another vessel and seemed ready to hurl it against a wall when he stopped himself. "Oh no. Oh my!" He wrung his hands, and his eyes grew wide—wild. "Griog'xa's evil knows no bounds! I just realized—"

"What?" Straker asked.

"The prize was not the damned sword nor the arm to wield it. It was the very thing he put into my hands! His emissary literally put it into my hands! And I delivered it to his agents myself!" The arrogance bled from the sorcerer's face. He looked like a hunted man who, finally caught, now faced the gallows. "He wanted me to know, to realize it all before—Oh, I'm to blame. I did it to myself."

"Spit it out, Forneus! Maybe I can help you. What have you done?"

"I conspired with Griog'xa to bring about my own ruin. That thief is coming here, Straker, and he's coming with the only sword in all of Andorath that can kill me!"

CHAPTER TWENTY-TWO

Wraith-haunted Vathek, self-appointed King of Ghouls, opened his maw and let forth a roar to curdle the blood. Skallagrim's hair streamed behind him as if he had been hit with a sustained gust of hell-born wind.

Outnumbered but bravely holding his ground, he watched as the axe-wielding ghoul leapt from the fallen tree to the steep slope on Skallagrim's left, then motioned for the others to follow. They spread out on either side of Skallagrim, effectively flanking him. Not the wisest move, perhaps, for it placed three of the wretched monsters on the downward slope where they had great difficulty finding a footing. However, the three on Skallagrim's left, which included Vathek, were well positioned above him.

With a horrid mental flash of the giant axe cleaving him from stem to stern, Skallagrim leapt upon the fallen tree trunk vacated by Vathek only a second before, the very one that had tripped him up earlier. He spun around to face them, sword held upright before his face, ready to fight whichever one came first, or all of them if need be.

Unable to flank or surround him now, the six ghouls scrambled back to the trail where they bunched up together a few feet in front of Skallagrim, Vathek foremost amongst them. Skallagrim held the high ground, but he was winded. Worse yet, his foes were not. He was panting, still unable to catch his breath after the long run from the river and the fierce combat with the now headless Abadiah Sedgwick. But he was also filled with a sudden and unquenchable anger born of desperation as he realized he was cut off from his ultimate objective.

He was too exhausted to think clearly about the practicality of beating off five half-starved ghouls and the demon-possessed Vathek who led them. Even with its savage hatred of all things evil, Terminus—could it have gotten control of Skallagrim's weary mind—might have preferred him to view the six as a simple, if not challenging, set of combatants—game pieces on a board that could be attacked, countered, and ultimately defeated by tactical prowess. But Skallagrim's mind, though struggling and overwhelmed, was still his own. What he saw, what consumed him most and fueled his anger, were six monstrous obstacles in his path. They stood between him and the wonderful blue-eyed girl of his dream—the frightened captive he had lost in the alley. The clock of her life was ticking, and Skallagrim had finally had enough.

He had been mutilated and abused by Straker at the behest of the arrogant, red-eyed demon Forneus Druogorim. He had been forced to become a killer and then to watch as his love was cruelly torn from him for some insane purpose. After that he had been sent on a mad, desperate mission by a man he hardly knew and barely trusted, though not before being set upon by the ghastly Tuva. *No knowing what she did to me.* Beyond the walls of the Dreaming City, he had been pursued again by Straker's men, forced to kill once more. Then there was the eerie and unforgiving wilderness of Pagarna, with its prison of thorns, the raging mountain river that had nearly drowned him, and last but not least, the temptress—the nymph Swanhild— who though kind in her way was as manipulative as any sorcerer. His memory, all traces of his former life—how he had come to Archon, what he had seen, why he had brought the girl—was hidden, kept from him by sorcery. And now ghouls!

Skallagrim had this day and one more to make it to Fort Vigilance, where he had to kill the sorcerer and save the girl. Time was running out. He had been at it for two nights and a day, barely covering half the distance, and each cursed, blasted mile had been a soul-defeating struggle.

He could not begin to guess what horrors awaited him, but the six fiends who stood before him now, dressed in stolen rags and reeking of the grave, were too much to stand. They would kill him, bury him, then fight over his bones while the heartbreakingly beautiful girl with golden locks and eyes of blue would be strapped to a stone slab and sacrificed to the ghost of a bloodthirsty knight for a cause that Skallagrim cared nothing about. It was too much! Too much!

He might die, but he would mercilessly slay all six of these hideous creatures who had the gall to stand between him and the girl's salvation. He would dive in amongst them with the sky-born sword and hew their evil bodies till every limb was off of them and every head was sent flying down the hill.

As if in response to Skallagrim's desperation and indignant rage, Terminus let forth a tremendous shriek so ghastly that all the ghouls but Vathek either scrambled backward several feet or fell to the ground, cowering. Then Skallagrim added his own fierce battle cry. It was harmonious, this spontaneous duet, this song of unhinged fury.

And there was a new note, an indescribable tonality, in the cry of the sentient blade. If Skallagrim had had the time to ponder it, he might have perceived joy or perhaps triumph in the terrifying sound. For indeed, the blade was victorious at last, having no need to grapple with Skallagrim's mind in order to incite him to violence. He could see the evil at last, know it for what it was, hate it for what it did and was doing, and banish it to hell with the killing stroke. But even as the two prepared to launch themselves into the fray as one inseparable weapon, nature itself had a trick to play.

Bracing to jump, Skallagrim gripped the hilt of Terminus, holding the sword straight before his face. Was that a flicker of light gleaming from its blade? Not the blinding white light Terminus had cast on its own in their previous battles. The red light that glinted now from the deadly steel was but the sun's reflected light as it rose behind Skallagrim. It turned the shining blade into a fiery mirror even as it turned the river valley of Pagarna from a place of darkness and shadows to one of golden tree-clad slopes and bright mists.

There were few places along the old roadbed where the normally thick canopy would permit the direct sunlight of dawn. Fortunately for Skallagrim, he had been forced to make his stand in such a place.

Ghouls could not abide the sun, at least not for long.

He glanced over his shoulder at the red sunrise that at any moment would flare into a glorious dawn and hopefully a tactical advantage. With the first rays of the morning sun shining upon his face, a surge of renewed hope touched the fury of his heart. It did not dull his anger, but there was no longer room for despair. He turned back to face Vathek and his gruesome kindred but instead saw his own face mirrored in his blade.

At first glance, Skallagrim could not absorb what he was seeing. He pried his gaze from the unexpected reflection and looked once more at the monstrous visage of the Ghoul king. Then his eyes retraced their path back to the hideously scarred face that glared red rage back at him from the sword's shining surface. He blinked, squinted, then allowed his gaze to dart back and forth from the monster that was Vathek to the monster in the reflection. In the space of three seconds, a terrible truth—or something perceived as truth—crashed over Skallagrim's soul like a wave upon a storm-wracked shore.

Until then, he had not seen the wreck of his face. Probed it with fingers, yes. Watched the reactions of the villagers of Dead Corn as they turned away from him in horror, certainly. He could not forget their fear of him, though he had not understood the depth of it. Even though suspecting himself changed in some monstrous way, he had secretly—foolishly—hoped that the wound and Tuva's stitches had not wrought an unforgivable destruction upon his face, but nothing had prepared him for the monstrous face that was staring back at him from the blade. And that was the essence of the soul-searing truth that washed over him like a flood. He was no less a monster than Vathek.

Time, precious, merciless time, slowed to a crawl, permitting him a clarity of thought that he had not had since . . . he could not remember. And that fact, in light of the discovery of his ruined face, only solidified his worst fears about himself. He was a thief, a killer, the worst of men. He wielded a weapon that was surely wrought of dark magic, a screaming demon of a sword that had plummeted to earth directly into his hand from a supernatural storm. He had been unfaithful, wasting precious hours with a witch. *Yes! That's what she is!* Nymph or no, Swanhild was a witch. Allowing her to toy with him while the most precious thing in his life was being held captive in a sorcerer's tower, waiting to die, was unforgivable!

The blue-eyed girl, had he not failed her by bringing her to Archon? He did not deserve her, and he was a fool to think he could somehow save her and build a future with her. Now that would never happen. He recalled the terror written on her lovely face. *Fear of my face as much as her kidnapper!* He could not even recall her name, for his mind was enchanted.

He was a lowly thing, driven from the city no less than the ghouls that faced him now. And those monsters saw not a young man with a sword but a scarred and screaming horror with the rising red doom of the sun at his back and a hellishly shrieking, flashing, living sword in his hands.

His worst fears for himself were confirmed at last. Whatever he may have been, Skallagrim was now a monster. As such, he had no fear of what came next.

He dove in amongst them as they cowered, heedless of danger, and scythed a bloody harvest. The heads of two ghouls were immediately hewn from their necks. Two more fell from savage thrusts. Only Vathek and one other escaped his wrath, diving into the woods on the slope.

The sun was rising, and Vathek had no mind to expose himself to its bright, blinding fury and the unexpected savagery of his intended victim. The woods on either side of the road were still shrouded in twilight, so he stood his distance, eyes blazing at Skallagrim while his last remaining ally fled into the gloom.

"I'm Vathek, King of Ghouls!" he roared. "You'll see me again, worm! You are going north, and I'll be shadowing your every move. Whether it be a lonely, dark spot on the road ahead or when the cursed sun slips behind the mountains, I'll find you. This is not over!"

Skallagrim laughed. "On that we're agreed, King Vathek! It's not over. I'm Skallagrim! Shield Shaker and wielder of Terminus!"

Bending low, he wiped the gore from his blade on the rags of one of the headless dead. Sheathing it, he knelt again and retrieved his staff. "I have much to do and so little time left to do it. But when my task is complete, and when it suits me, I'll find you, and you will die. In the meantime, dig yourself a hole to hide in, or slink amongst the trees and follow me if you want. I have bigger fish to fry than you, Lord of Maggots. I'll not be delayed further by the likes of you! Good day." Skallagrim performed a mock bow, then turned and strode north at a rapid pace, for in that direction lay his love and his last hope of salvation, though time for both was running out.

CHAPTER TWENTY-THREE

As a rage-filled Vathek made off into the dark of the forest to gather more ghouls and continue the chase, Skallagrim put many miles behind him. The red sun of morning turned golden, and for a time he enjoyed the feel of it on his tired body. But eventually, the canopy closed overhead, strangling the sunlight and bringing with it the twilight gloom of the deep forest once more.

The road snaked over steep ridges thick with tall trees, down dark gullies where cold streams had to be carefully crossed, and finally back to the muddy flats near the river Pagarna. There were still many miles between Skallagrim and Fort Vigilance, and the wilderness was growing darker and stranger with each painful step.

His ire temporarily spent, Skallagrim's heart filled again with despair and the ever-growing fear that he would run out of time to save the girl, that something else would stop him, and he would fail her once more. He acknowledged that, considering his appearance, the state of his ensorcelled mind, and the unpardonable sin of having put her in harm's way, Skallagrim had no possibility of a future with her. She was too fine a thing for a creature like him. But believing himself to be a monster did not alter his plans to rescue her and slay her captor. He would have to stop and rest and might even permit himself the luxury of a couple of hours of sleep in order to push on through the coming night. After that he would press forward till he found her or until he died.

Skallagrim walked and walked, not stopping for several miles, and then only for a quick bite. He continued on, pacing himself, for a blister was forming on his right foot, causing him worry and nagging pain. He did not care if his boots filled with blood though; he was not stopping for anything or anyone. His resoluteness remained firm for another tough mile, but after that, the sharp, needling pain of the blister began to eat away at his resolve, until at last he could think of nothing else. He stopped at the next stream he came to, acknowledging the smart thing would be to tend to it right away before it got worse.

Beyond the stream, tendrils of mist drifted over the road from the river. However, there was a rare patch of sunlight on Skallagrim's side that might provide safety from any ghouls that were tracking him. Still, he peered about in the gloom of the trees, looking for any sign of Vathek or any of his repulsive breed. Seeing nothing of note, he took off his boots and bathed his aching feet in the icy water.

With the sun nearly overhead, he assumed it to be about noon and guessed he had covered ten miles in his morning rush along the road. That left him another ten or so to the secret crypt entrance that Swanhild had described. There was no knowing how much time he would need to gain entry though, and time was precious.

Should he risk sleep? The thought of it worried him. He could probably wake himself after a couple of hours, his internal clock being fairly accurate and responsive to his instructions on such matters. *Not sure how I remember that,* he thought, but he did. It was not an entirely reassuring thought, however, for in his current state of exhaustion, closing his eyes might well result in him being out for eight hours or more. But if he did not rest soon, he would give way, totally spent. *Better now in the sunlight than to collapse somewhere along the dark road,* he reasoned, not at all comfortable with the idea of waking up with Vathek's axe buried in his skull.

His eyes were closing already. If he did not lie down, he very well might nod off where he sat. *Just two hours,* he told himself. Skallagrim laid his head back in a patch of cool moss by the stream and repeated the mantra to himself over and over, fearful that he would cost himself a great delay by sleeping. *Just two hours. Only two hours. I'll wake in two hours.* The torment of it kept him awake though, so he gave up and let his mind wander, anguishing over every event of the last three days, second-guessing every decision, and attempting to unravel every puzzle that life had presented to him.

As distressed as he was, Skallagrim had yet to reach the low point of his spirit, that final pit of desperation where a man stares into blackness and meets the specter of his own madness. Not quite. He was, however, stumbling around in the darkness of his soul, aware that an ultimate, cataclysmic shaft loomed near. With an arrogant defiance befitting a daredevil, he flirted with doom, dancing along the edge of the pit, pretending that he might, at any moment, take the plunge, giving in to total despair.

Though he placed mental check marks beside each item on an ever-evolving list of woes that had brought him to this place of grief—wounds, guilt, exhaustion, doubt, temptation, the foul taint of the supernatural that had plagued his every step, and the murderous intent of monsters and men—two things were foremost both in feeding his anxiety and altering the way he looked at himself and the world around him.

The first was Swanhild's final revelation. Someone had put a spell upon his mind, robbing him of his memory.

The second was the fateful glance at his reflection in the sword's bright blade. Skallagrim was a monster. It was not simply the view of his scarred and bruised face that brought him to this conclusion. The sight of his wrecked and ruined visage in the blade came unexpectedly, like a guilty verdict handed down at the end of a long trial, one in which he had hoped his innocence might prevail.

The two epiphanies—one accurate and the other perhaps too harsh—were changing Skallagrim, freeing him in some ways, damaging him further in others. He was aware of it, cognizant of the change, but too weary to contemplate the rightness or the wrongness of what was changing.

He yawned, and his eyes grew as heavy as his heart. Turning on his side, he watched the cool crystal-clear water of the stream as it rushed by just a few feet from his aching face and thought of the blue-eyed girl.

It was Thursday afternoon. A lot could happen before Friday night, midnight. What if he arrived too late? What if Erling was wrong, and she was already dead? Well then, he would slay the fiend who killed her, then throw himself from the top of the tower. It was, after all, what a man such as him deserved.

And if he saved her, what then? Something similar, he supposed. Erling was supposed to be waiting near Fort Vigilance. Skallagrim could hand the girl over to him. *No!* He'd rather trust her to Hartbert, for he would surely protect her. Then he could return to the tower and hurl himself off it. Of course, he might die before he was able to confront the sorcerer or his tower. Reluctantly, he reasoned this to be the likely outcome of his mad adventure in the wilds of Pagarna.

Next, Skallagrim pondered the temptress, Swanhild. How fitting it was that she would be so taken with a monster like him. What if she was not truly taken with him but just putting on appearances so that she might manipulate him? Did that mean she was every bit the monster he was?

He had seen his reflection, knew what he was. That she could stomach the nearness of him, even kissing him and stroking his face—not to mention the subtle flirtations, the gentle sighs, and the batting of her emerald eyes—spoke volumes. Pretty or not, she harbored something monstrous within her to abide the likes of him.

His mind returned to the revelation of Swanhild. Much of what she had said to him had the ring of truth, manipulator or no. A man could be controlled just as effectively with truth as with a lie. If she had told him the truth about the spell that was on his mind—and he believed she had—then he had undertaken his great journey, his mission of rescue, under a false assumption. If his mind was under a spell, then perhaps he was more than a mere thief. Why else would a sorcerer or a witch go to such lengths, shutting his mind off from its memories, hiding the truth from him?

Who was he really? Who was the girl? What had he seen? The truth must be dangerous to someone, or maybe a group of someones. He had no way of knowing. Either the guilty conjurer would have to reveal himself—an unlikely occurrence—or Skallagrim might spend a lifetime tracking down and slaying every cursed practitioner of the blasphemous arts before he found the truth.

Fine! Skallagrim had enough anger in him to do that, and he had the sword to help him. But now that he knew his injuries were not the cause of his forgetfulness, he was sickened in a new way. *Invaded, violated, cursed!*

Someone hated him enough to have performed this evil on him. Hopefully, it was Forneus Druogorim, and the coming confrontation with the sorcerer would settle the matter one way or another. If not, maybe the girl could help him. That thought cheered him for a moment, until he remembered she would likely be afraid of him. Even if she could abide his face, he was still responsible for the harm that had been brought to her. However, he loved her with everything in his heart. Whatever punishment life had in store for him next, whatever curse he must bear, if he could just save her, set her free, he could live with it.

Skallagrim's breathing became heavy, and his eyes closed at last. With the sun shining warmly upon his scarred and battered face, he fell into a deep sleep.

The bright morning sun spread a blanket of silver and gold upon a swath of otherwise deep-blue ocean. He was standing on a beach, his toes pleasantly digging into powdery sand of the purest white. It was still cool upon his feet, not yet heated to the blistering oven-like surface it would become later in the day. Someone had drawn a heart in the sand and written their lover's name inside.

A warm breeze was blowing over the gently undulating waves that lapped the shore. It played in Skallagrim's hair, teased his nose with the healing smell of salt, and washed him over with a sense of peace, the likes of which he had never known. Billowing sea oats and long grasses populated the dunes behind him, and from somewhere just beyond came the sound of children playing. Overhead, past the breakers, a flock of pelicans was soaring low in a V formation, one of them splitting off from the rest to dive straight as an arrow into the surf where it hit with a splash, appearing again a second later with a fish in its long bill.

Skallagrim was taking it all in where he stood only a few yards from the water. He slowly became aware of a presence beside him and turned to see the old white-robed man of his previous dream.

"You know, it's not just the smell of this air that brings about the calming of your spirit; it's the sound of the waves as they splash upon the shore," Skallagrim explained. "It's relentless, truly, in the most wonderful of ways. But it's also the sound of those children playing back there. It's the feel of the sand, the hugeness of the ocean. It just swallows me up, all of it." He put his arms behind his head, and the wind wrapped around him. He sighed. "So many things. I find it hard to describe, but it's a peace that transcends any other. I have missed it so." Skallagrim closed his eyes and breathed deeply. He felt his breath catch though, suddenly overwhelmed by a sense of profound joy. He was at peace—at rest.

He did not want the man to see the tears forming in the corners of his eyes, and he suppressed the sob that was welling up inside him. But when he turned to face him again, such was the tenderness on the old man's face, it was clear he understood what Skallagrim was feeling. He smiled at the thief who, at that moment, felt nothing like a thief at all—certainly nothing like a monster. Rather, he felt like a man, caught somewhere between the wonder of a carefree childhood and the soul-weary exhaustion of old age, momentarily freed from cares and burdens, momentarily reprieved from the prison of life . . . momentarily.

Skallagrim let the tears fall down his cheeks, not bothering to wipe them away.

"I know what you're thinking," the old man said with a caring smile. His long hair was as white as the sand, and glossy strands of it were dancing on the breeze. "Ask your question."

"How does one freeze a moment?" Skallagrim inquired. If anyone knew, it was this man. But his words sounded foolish, inadequate. His brow furrowed as he sought the right thing to say, the better question. "How does one freeze a moment in time? Not the things moving through the moment, just the moment. The breeze would still be blowing in from the ocean, the waves would be beating the shore, and the sounds and the smell and taste of the salt would be there, changing, ebbing and flowing as they are now. The pelicans would still dive into the water, children would be playing on the dunes . . . " He struggled to finish his thought, fearing it made no sense. "All of this that's happening right now, could it *just remain as it is, forever? Never ending?"*

"Now," the old man said in a voice both powerful and kindly, "tell me why you would want to do that."

The answer became clear, if only for a moment. "I have a hole in my heart that cannot be filled, not by merely walking here on this beach and standing for a few moments. It makes the ache of my heart all the greater, for I know the moment must pass—will pass—as soon as I trek back through the sand and bid it farewell. I cannot abide it, cannot bear to leave it. I need more!" He paused and looked back at the sea. "The hole can never be filled, can it?"

He noticed the old man had placed a hand upon his shoulder, and he felt himself surrender to a sudden, poignant sorrow. He sobbed, gulped it back into his throat, and managed to continue. "How do I hold onto this moment? Every time I try, it slips away."

"You cannot," the older man proclaimed, his voice tinged with sadness.

"I know," Skallagrim admitted. "I know."

"At least not yet. Not here," the old man added.

Astonished, Skallagrim looked back at the man and saw sunlight reflecting in a single tear that rolled down his wizened cheek.

"Over those waves," the man said, "there's another shore. One day we may come to stand on that beach, you and I. And then I'll have a different answer for you." He laughed, and the sound of it was as music to Skallagrim's ears, for it was filled with joy and something like hope, though far beyond the hopes of mortal men. "But first, Skallagrim. Someone is missing, and someone must be found."

Skallagrim knew of whom he spoke—the blue-eyed girl with hair of gold. Far out to sea, dark clouds were rolling in, threatening to shroud the sun. The children's laughter had ceased, and the formerly pleasant wind began to gust.

"And," the old man added, pointing at the black clouds, "there's that. A storm is coming. You must wake!"

"There's always something—something to keep us from what we want," Skallagrim said, shaking his head. But the old man was gone.

CHAPTER TWENTY-FOUR

In Andorath, evil dwelt in the hearts of men and women. Even for the good folk of that cursed land, darkness had taken root inside them, besieging the fortresses of their souls, ever seeking to gain a foothold beyond the walls that guarded their spirits. Many held out against it, and though beleaguered, remained defiant and undefeated. Some, however—those who had put on the mantle of wickedness—failed to see in it the enduring idea that only the wise had perceived, that the existence of evil was the great clue to a cosmic truth—that goodness also existed. It was a truth that cried out to any who had ears to hear.

A few perceptive souls had heard its call in their dreams, like a joyous trumpet echoing from afar at the rising of the sun, filling their souls with wonder and heartache. The cleverest of these, those whose hearts were filled with longing but not wisdom, sought out its source in the wilds of Andorath, in its cities, atop its mountains, in the depths of its valleys, or within their own drug-induced dreams. As in the song of Swanhild . . .

> *Searching in vain, yet unceasing, they seek*
> *Ever they look though their chances are bleak*
> *Ever they climb the grey hills, then descend*
> *Down hopeless trails which wind and wend*

Some had detected even deeper truths, that if they knew to seek for it at all—this elusive hint of joy unbounded—then it had to exist! It if could not be found in Andorath, then those fleeting sounds of distant, ineffable joy—joy as piercing as heartbreak—surely resounded from a far-off country, blown in upon the zephyr winds of some unguessed shore.

The sorcerers of Andorath mocked such lofty notions as nothing but the musings of poets, idealists, and romanticists. If there was truly anything or anyone that called out to folks in their dreams, filling their heads with the stuff of glory or the promise of peace, then it likely came from beyond the Southern Void. "One day," they brooded, "Balor will rise again." They would join him to burst through the impenetrable fog and the choking smokes of the Void. They would find the Trump of Glory, for that is what the dreamers had named it, smash it to bits, and kill the one who blew it.

Old Tuva, who lay mouldering in her box of dirt, cared nothing for sorcerers, trumpets, or dreamers. She might, on the rare occasion, wonder about the mystery surrounding her father, Balor. But she had never met the man and had no love for him—had no love for anyone. She was Tuva, and she did not love.

What she pondered, however, was the whereabouts of the necklace of talismans that had hung about her neck for one hundred years. Now, after dealing with Erling's thief, it was gone. Something would have to be done about that and soon, for much of her magic was tied up in that length of silver chain and its many charms, those sharp, jagged bits of metal and the strange runes engraved upon them.

She was growing weak without it. Hunting her victims would be hard without it. So she must move soon to hunt down this thief of Erling Hizzard's, and then she would work more mischief upon his once pretty face.

Meanwhile, deep down in the grey silt below the churning waters of the Pagarna, Swanhild lay daydreaming of the scarred thief, Skallagrim. She was as restless as her estranged, hideously evil daughter, Tuva, for she was deeply troubled by Skallagrim's sudden appearance in her life and all that his news of the wider world implied.

Events were unfolding in Andorath, and Swanhild thought

perhaps she had hidden herself away in the Vales of Pagarna for far too long. At one time she had a hand in the great matters of Andorath, working powerful magic, employing her subtle charms, beguiling, and stirring knights to war.

Had she not once strode across the nightmarish, bloody battlefields herself? What would Skallagrim think if he could see her as she had been then, leading a monstrous army, wreathed in the smoke of battle, her dazzling armor shining as red as the sun as it set upon the terror and ruin of the fateful day? Skallagrim only knew one Swanhild, the playful but wise nymph who haunted the forests and bubbling streams of the Vales. What if he knew the other?

She wondered too at her fascination with this man. Swanhild had enchanted his mind easily enough, using her loveliness to distract him for a few hours. Nothing too serious, of course, nothing she had not done to many other men. But had he not done the same to her, charming her as no other man had ever done?

Even if he was unaware of it, something was alluring about Skallagrim, enticing enough that she had spared his life and handed over the key to a secret crypt that might well lead him to the girl he loved. He had, through some indefinable magic, reduced her to a silly, lovesick girl. Now that she could see this clearly, she still did not care. Scars or no scars, Swanhild wanted him.

She had denied herself love for many an age, yet now she fancied it might be possible. For Skallagrim was no ordinary man, thief or no. The sword, the very blade she knew and feared above all others, had fallen from the storm-wracked sky to save him from the jackals that served Forneus Druogorim. Why? And who put the powerful spell upon his mind to keep his memory at bay? What did Skallagrim know or what had he seen that warranted such action? No, Skallagrim was no ordinary man.

As she shifted her slender body in the mire of the river bottom, she placed a hand upon her breast and discovered another question. Where was her brooch? The enchanted, garnet-encrusted breast pin that she had worn for many an age was missing.

Hartbert had no time for daydreaming or plotting. After another flurry of activity from spies and agents making their way along the Gorge Road to report to their master, Erling Hizzard, he and Erling had silently and stealthily tread the remaining miles to the juncture of the Bald River and the Pagarna.

They were hiding now behind a boulder on the other side of the bridge from Fort Vigilance, watching the sentries who patrolled the opposite shore. It was dark there, unnaturally so. Malodorous mists and fogs swirled about the tower, a fortification far more menacing than Hartbert had been led to believe. An oppression was hovering about the place, leaching the will and churning up fresh doubt in the giant man's spirit.

Chief among those doubts was the complete lack of wagon tracks along the Gorge Road. If Skallagrim's lost love had been taken to the fort, she must have been switched to horseback somewhere along the highway. Or maybe she had gotten loose, though Hartbert thought not. For good or ill, there was no sign of her, a fact that did not seem to trouble his employer, who was crouched beside him.

"We shall wait here," Erling whispered, sensing Hartbert's concern. "I have a feeling about our Skallagrim. He'll find the back way in; you'll see."

"And then what?"

"When we see the sentries stirring as some alarm is sounded, then you may charge into the fray and bash some heads, my massive friend. I'll be there at your side, of course. Today you need not worry about protecting me. It will take both our swords to dispatch this lot, what?"

Erling spoke confidently enough, but Hartbert could tell he was nervous. Something was troubling him, haunting him, weighing on him. His restiveness grew worse each time he heard from his agents. Whatever it was, it went beyond their current predicament, which was bad enough.

Hartbert shifted uneasily and turned to face Erling. "Is there anything you'd like to tell me? Something's got you rattled."

"No, no. Well . . ." Erling paused, struggling with some inner doubt. "It's nothing, really."

Hartbert knew otherwise. It was as if his employer had a dire confession to make but not the courage to make it. "Mister Hizzard, you can trust me. Maybe I can help."

Erling shifted so that he could face Hartbert, and for a moment it appeared as if he might tell his trusted bodyguard the secret that was preying on his mind.

"One day maybe, Hartbert. But no, I cannot speak of it. Let's just keep our vigil for Skallagrim and get this business behind us." He seemed to relax then, putting whatever was troubling him aside. "We may have a long wait. Odds are Skallagrim won't make it here until late tonight or sometime tomorrow. Then things should get interesting!"

Hartbert sighed and settled in for the inevitable tedium of a long watch. Yet he had the uneasy feeling that whatever was causing Erling so much distress would inevitably embroil him and Skallagrim too.

He shut his eyes and tried to sleep while Erling kept watch, but worries were buzzing around in his head like so many bees. It did not help when Erling—thinking Hartbert was asleep—was heard muttering, "I have damned my soul."

Thus, the two rode out the day, each nursing their own hidden doubts and fears while overhead loomed the tower of a madman, beneath which brooded the dead thing in the pit.

CHAPTER TWENTY-FIVE

Snap! Crash!

Skallagrim was jolted awake by a disturbance coming from the forest. *Ghouls!* His hand flew to his sword. But after a moment, he rose, listened for a bit, decided there was nothing to fear, and prepared to continue his journey.

Fortunately, he was up at the appointed time and eager to carry on. He stretched, then, making his way to the creek bank, splashed cool water onto his face. He winced from the pain but took it in stride as he stared across the bubbling stream. The tendrils of mist seen earlier wound through the trees like a ghostly procession. Though he was sorry to leave his tiny patch of sunlight, Skallagrim hoisted his pack and set out.

For the first two miles, he barely noticed the creeping soreness from the blister on his right sole. When he finally did, he bore it well and continued into the ever-thickening mist. Though the dim, distant sun rode high in the sky, the farther Skallagrim walked, the more loathe it was to penetrate the fog.

After another mile, the road began to veer away from the river. Skallagrim faced an arduous climb as it gained elevation, taking him farther from the heavily canopied forest where early spring had come and into a stretch of bare, twisted mountain laurels and stunted pines. The mists of the river dissipated, replaced by a thick, chilly fog that clung to the mountaintop and reached down into the dark hollows like skeletal fingers. The scene was bleak, matching his mood.

Rounding a bend, he came to a sudden stop. Strands of sunlight filtered tentatively through the fog, turning the scene bright and golden and lifting Skallagrim's spirits. Either his ears were playing tricks on him, or music was drifting down from the heights.

Mountain folk, he reminded himself, wondering if the stories were true. But the effect was short-lived as the tentative light retreated, giving ground to the cheerless spirit that pervaded the place. The fog rolled in thick again, and the faint strains of music faded and were lost. He put it from his mind and trudged on.

As the road veered back toward the Pagarna, dipping into a shadowy hollow, Skallagrim felt as insubstantial as the wraithlike mists that swirled about him.

For the first two days of his journey, the forest had been nothing if not weird. Yet now there was a palpable change for the worse. Not only had the weather and the vegetation altered as he wound his way back to the river flats, the spirit of the place had transformed as well. An oppression hung over him like a black cloak.

When Skallagrim saw an ancient mausoleum looming through the fog to the right of the road, its bronze door ajar and swinging madly upon rusted hinges, he knew something was wrong, for there was no wind. Skallagrim had the sudden urge to investigate the phenomenon, to take a look inside the granite edifice's dark, compelling interior, but he shook off the temptation with an abrupt shudder. Turning away from the morbidly enticing entryway, he hurried along, not daring to look back.

Not even one of Erling's maps could have told Skallagrim that he had just crossed an invisible boundary where a new spirit held sway, but he knew it just the same. Swanhild had told him much about what to expect on this last leg of his journey, for she had once traversed this same wild countryside. But she would go there no more.

The forests and swamps that stretched below Fort Vigilance were nothing like those south of Lame Deer Creek, where he had rested earlier. Skallagrim hurried along the road beneath the dreaded Craghide Mountain in a rugged country known as the Grimthorn.

An age before the fort was built, it had been the home of an unhappy tribe of swarthy, ill-favored men who scrounged out a meager living either by fishing the swift Pagarna or by farming the steep slopes of the wild ridges. History had long since forgotten their name. They were a sullen people and prone to lunacy—no kin to the folk reputed to live on the mountaintops.

Their priests were said to have consorted with the thing in the pit. What few fish could be harvested from the river were sickly, bony, and bitter to the taste. Their crops were ill suited to the rocky soil and misty slopes where the languorous sun shone weakly, if ever.

Of course, the people themselves were not immune to the strangeness and the bleak oppression of the Grimthorn, its dismal swamps, or its haunted forest. For one hundred years they toiled and sweated in the stinking valley but no more. Their endurance spent, they melted away to die out in less hostile lands.

Stonemasons, craftsmen, and artisans came next with their families. At the instruction of a fierce sect of mysterious knights, they erected Fort Vigilance, setting its cyclopean foundations directly over the pit. For a time the dark oppression over the Grimthorn was lifted, and peace came to the Vales.

A civilization sprang up, its hardy inhabitants flourishing for hundreds of years. It was they who built the stone city of Orabas, which lay now in ruins beneath the northernmost spur of the Craghide. But the darkness came again, subtly at first, then acutely as it leached the will and poisoned the hearts of knights and city dwellers. This tragic upheaval was not isolated to Fort Vigilance and Orabas, for it soon spread to every fort and settlement in the Vales.

After the last of the saturnine, melancholic knights of Fort Vigilance died off, the city died too. It was said that rumblings beneath the old fort triggered an earthquake, and the ground beneath Orabas had sunk in a sudden, violent backwash of the Pagarna.

What few folk survived left. The turbid, nigrescent water did not. So, for ages the ghosts of Orabas had wandered along mud-choked streets amidst broken columns rearing up from the mire like defiant fists. Its liches had slogged and shambled through flooded necropoli whose monuments leaned crazily, half-submerged in the sluggish black water.

In recent years it had only gotten worse. Things had crept out of the mountaintop caves and had slithered into the cold, gripping mud of the Grimthorn, things that had no name and should not be named. Nightgaunts were said to glide down from the top of the Craghide on leathery wings and perch hideously upon its crumbling mausoleums while ghouls scavenged the slimy sarcophagi or crouched in the foeted slurry to suck the marrow of fresher bones, those of trappers or of foolish adventurers who had wandered into the haunted valley only to drown in a flooded pit, their impotent screams dying as the inky, gurgling mud filled their mouths and tortured lungs.

As Skallagrim descended into the Grimthorn, he saw no memory of spring or any lovely thing. Except that it glowed, the leprous, tortured, and half-rotten vegetation that crowded either side of the road was like no other he had ever seen, their abhorrent shapes filling him with loathing. Monstrous, swollen fungi belched clouds of odorous spores beneath ancient, twisted trees whose claw-like branches nodded and scraped in a phantasmic breeze that Skallagrim could not feel. The stench of stagnant decay filled his nostrils as he walked with his head bowed through the ruined and tormented land.

However, he was within a few short miles of his beloved and consoled himself with this alone. No other thought would comfort him. It was her and nothing else.

Despite everything that had gone against him, from his first bloody night in the alley to his recent pre-dawn battle with the ghouls, he had come within striking distance at last. If Erling was correct, Skallagrim was in plenty of time to save the blue-eyed lass. Erling had said that Forneus Druogorim would sacrifice the girl at midnight the following day. Of course, that had been a theory, but Skallagrim had no alternative and no other clues wherein to find hope.

If Erling was right, Skallagrim could save the girl, if not himself or his lost memory. If wrong—if the sorcerer had taken her somewhere else—then Skallagrim would forge out on his own to find her. *Well, no!* He would not be entirely by himself, for he had Terminus.

If need be, the two of them would scythe a path from one end of Andorath to the other. If it took a lifetime to find her, so be it! It was his fault she was in danger. If he could get nothing else right in his life but to find her and set her free, then come what may, he would get it done.

Skallagrim chided himself. It was useless to consider anything beyond the next few hours. He would find the girl in the sorcerer's tower and avenge the great crime that had been done to both of them.

Now and then the fog would part like a curtain, allowing Skallagrim to see the horrid landscape. There were several low-lying hills to be crossed, each one covered with the bloated fungi and the oddly swaying trees. Yet as he traversed each mist-slickened hill, a new horror was revealed, some hellish defect as yet unimagined awaiting Skallagrim on the other side.

Particularly unsettling was a patch of dead dogwood trees, split down the middle from old age. Their roots had risen like sinewy arms from the cursed soil and doubled back on themselves to coil about the disintegrating trunks like choking hands. Blackened ash drifted from the tree's wounds in little puffs with a ghastly sigh, for some dreadful blight lingered within.

More disturbing were the bloated corpse-worms that flopped about in great piles around the base of one ancient burial mound. Why there were maggots and worms in close proximity to such a place was something Skallagrim did not wish to consider. It was centuries old, and its bones should have crumbled to dust ages ago. Perhaps a taint of corruption still lingered within through supernatural means, and on this, the worms had fed and grown fat. When Skallagrim stopped to inspect one of the corpulent insects that had separated itself from the wriggling mass, he promptly turned back to the trail and hurried on. For one torturous second, the thing's face appeared to be that of a screaming man.

Perhaps the knights of centuries past had kept the road in better repair closer to their fort, for now it was more a raised highway than a rocky, stream-crossed roadbed. So far the swamps that stretched to either side had failed to encroach upon it.

Beyond the road's edge, the efforts of man had failed utterly to prevail upon the muddy flats. Crumbling villas lay half sunk in the mire. Multiple cemeteries were in a similar state, speaking not only of the effects of the cataclysmic earthquake and backwash of the river but also of the sheer amount of death that had befallen the folk of the Grimthorn.

Though less grotesque in its manifestation, the next horror to greet Skallagrim was as disconcerting as the last. He came upon it in a swampy dip between two rocky hills—a huge mausoleum in a partially submerged graveyard.

Vine-choked trees, shorn of leaves but still living, had grown around it in great number, their roots tunneling through the compromised foundations. This had caused great cracks to form in the visible foundations, that part not already submerged. The muddy water had no doubt long since infiltrated the structure. Conversely, the rot and corruption housed within had leaked out to create a festering swill that lapped abominably at the trunks of the invasive trees.

The malignant fungi were present in great profusion as well, but it was not these ancillary attributes that caught his attention; it was the writing on the front wall of the edifice. A dour warning, "GO BACK," had been painted in great swaths of black mud, then scratched through. Some other barbaric hand had then scrawled, "KEEP COMING—WE ARE HUNGRY."

The original warning must have been written by the old farmer from Dead Corn, for the graffiti was not old. Maybe this was the point at which his group had turned back, their luck having run out and their fears getting the best of them. There was no knowing what sort of liche came later to obliterate the warning, replacing it with the mocking challenge.

Skallagrim paused to consider the scene, its grim reminder that beyond this point, insanity reigned. People, decent ones, simply did not go farther upon this road.

It did not matter. He would neither heed Bug's warning nor fear the threatening taunt. From now on he would be immune from friendly advice, intimidation, or manipulation of any kind. Skallagrim was going to rescue the girl no matter what horrors he had to endure.

He pondered everything he knew about the Pagarna, especially this final haunted countryside that stretched between him and his destination, for its legends were abominable. After the knights had parted, few had ever gone there again of their own accord. He recalled everything that Bug had told him, everything Swanhild warned him of, and admitted these were not incentives to travel farther. But he would not turn back. The place weighed on him, yes, more and more with each passing mile, but he could bear it. He had to.

"When evil looms near, good cannot hide. It must light its way with the lamp of courage or become nothing!" The words of the old man in the dream surfaced to embolden him. But was Skallagrim good? Was he not a monster himself?

So be it!

There was no time left for pitying himself—no more wasted minutes to be spent in self-reflection or doubt. Just a few hours earlier, he had seen all of himself he would ever require, his true image mirrored in the sun-tinged blade of Terminus. He was a monster, no less hideous than Vathek and in many ways more terrible.

Had a sorcerer not stolen his memory, cloaking his mind with powerful spells? Was Skallagrim not the bearer of a sentient sword, the sky-born, meteoric sword that fell to him from the supernatural storm? Had Skallagrim not been stitched together by a hag's witchcraft, then mended again by the enchantress, Swanhild?

From the outset of this painful, confusing misadventure, he had been the plaything of sorcerers, witches, and nymphs and suspected himself a pawn to the nervous occultist and smuggler Erling Hizzard. Skallagrim was a hunted thing. The sellswords of the sorcerer would capture him and kill him if they could. The soldiers of Archon would chain him up in a dungeon if they found him upon the road. His face was a wreck, a hideous visage that no blue-eyed girl with golden hair would ever love again.

Yes, he was a monster. But having come to grips with that— still having no knowledge that the sword, when wielded, enhanced the savagery of his appearance—he took strength from it, drew determination from it. He gained resolve from it, and he stoked the fires of his wrath, his need to embrace revenge, feeding the embers that this knowledge had kindled within him.

But Skallagrim would not let worries over killing the sorcerer take precedence over the girl's safety. He would kill him if he must, but his priorities were in order. *Find the girl, kill the man.* Once, maybe. Now it was simply, *find the girl.*

Thinking only of her, he slogged on, coming at last within sight of the prison named Fort Vigilance.

As the weak sun gave up its fruitless fight, dipping low in the northern sky, Skallagrim stood wearily upon a great, treeless hill. Its summit was crowned with sagging monoliths and tall obelisks that leaned at odd angles, their sides displaying baleful runes and pictographs.

Before him stretched a vast gulf of darkness, the haunted valley of Orabas, wherein lay the flooded ruins of that doomed city. Even on a rare, bright morning, the sun would not challenge the darkness of that wretched valley. Once maybe but not since the coming of the sorcerer to Fort Vigilance and the evil he had brought with him.

Beyond the valley rose the northernmost spur of the Craghide, rocky and nearly bare of trees. It jutted up from the eternal night that was Orabas, climbing high into the clouds on Skallagrim's right, where it joined the invisible mountain peak. To his left the spur descended sharply, then fell away sheer to the Pagarna River. There upon its bluffs perched the nightmarish tower named Fort Vigilance, far larger and more ominous than he had ever imagined it to be. The lights of its topmost tower shone red through the fog and smoke that swirled around it. For a tortured second, Skallagrim imagined that his love was watching for him just beyond the hellish glow.

He leaned heavily upon his staff, watching as the dying sun framed the silhouette of the fort in burnished gold. For a fleeting moment, the imposing prison seemed a thing of rare beauty.

Just below the fort, about halfway up the spur from the stygian gloom of the valley, the last rays of sunlight revealed two colossal boulders that looked as if they had broken away from the bluffs. The only thing distinguishing them from a dozen others was their location just beneath a beak-like projection on the cliff directly above them. This, according to Swanhild, was the spot where he would find the entrance to the hidden crypt. Skallagrim reached a tentative hand into his pocket, reassuring himself that the nymph's gift to him, the key to the crypt door, was safe.

Gazing out over the valley, a sudden and welcome realization dawned on him. *Nearly there!* His heart leapt within his chest, and his eyes misted. The finish line was right there. The goal was in sight. He choked back a sob but then let it have its way, allowing many to come. Having wept his full, he uttered a great sigh of relief.

Wiping his running nose on his ripped and nasty sleeve, Skallagrim began to laugh, for the terrible journey was nearing its end, and he would soon find his lost love. For the first time since— well, he could not remember—his heart was glad. Though he could feel the darkness and oppression pressing down on him, Skallagrim did not care.

There had been no sound of mirth in that dreadful place for many centuries, and his sudden exultation flared like a torch. For a moment, to any monstrous eye that was watching, Skallagrim became a beacon of light piercing the darkness, striking even into the heart of the valley's oppression.

Until then he had dreaded the moment of ultimate failure, not believing he would ever make it this far. Doubt had been consuming him, but that was over. She was near. *I'll find her! I'm going to find her!*

Relief washed over him in a flood. He threw back his head, hurled caution to the wind, and laughed all the harder. If any liche or nightgaunt had come upon the lone laughing man upon the high hill, they would have turned away, fearing him to be mad—a dangerous lunatic.

Skallagrim's mind raced into the future. *She's safe! She's free!* Now on to a better world, a place where evil held no sway, a place where no hurt might come to rob them of . . . of what?

Then he glimpsed it, like a memory of a memory, snatched away before he could grab it but seen just the same.

Joy!

Whether she would ever love him again or not, she embodied an ideal of perfect happiness to Skallagrim that nothing else on earth could replace. She was to him as an eidolon, a physical and sublime double to a joy that he had forfeited through rashness.

She must be this . . . this joy! Thinking of her always led to the inconsolable pang, the sharp stab of a desire that transcended every other need in his life. Whatever he could do for her, he would, to the point of laying down his life. This admission liberated him, unburdening him of all the pain, terror, and disappointment of his young life. He had become an unfit match for her, a scarred and lowly thief, filthy and undesirable in every way. Yet perhaps by giving all he had, he might repay the debt. To see her sweet face once more, to speak the words to her, "I love you unto my dying breath," and then to throw himself upon the fiend that had imprisoned her. That was all. He would free her and thus be free himself. He would die for her, and thus all his pain and shame would come to an end.

He gazed out into the darkness and pondered. *No. These feelings are not true joy—just a glimpse of it. Likely just the longing for it. I won't live to find the actual thing, though maybe she will.*

Thus, his imperfect interpretation of the desire stabbing at his heart—robbing him of breath, forming tears at the corners of his eyes, filling his heart with a sudden yearning for things his young mind could scarcely explain—might have led him astray. And it might have led him to yet further rash actions, such as the throwing away of his life.

But this was Skallagrim, wielder of Terminus. Fate had other plans for him.

He allowed his mind to drift back to the present. He was still too young to make sense of all he was feeling, so he just allowed it to happen, allowed it to define itself for him in a way he could understand—simple relief. Relief at having neared his goal. Relief at being within sight of the gaunt edifice that imprisoned his love. Relief that all the horror he had passed through thus far had not been endured in vain.

Skallagrim laughed again, but laughter alone could not adequately express what was bubbling inside him. He took a deep breath, and recalling a song from somewhere deep inside his memory, he began to sing.

I see the shadow in your heart
The chains upon your spirit
And all that's kept you far away from me
Yet I have come at last, my love
And I will share your burdens now
That is what was always meant to be
For you and me

It had started as a murmur, a quietly sung stanza from a life he could not remember. But as the words began to flow from him, he took strength from their message and lifted his voice to challenge the darkness, allowing it to ring out over the devastated countryside as a pledge to the girl who waited just ahead.

The memory of love won't die
It is light that cannot fail
It's pierced the darkness that surrounded you
I've found you now, don't be afraid
Just take my hand and walk away
Toward the home you loved and you once knew
That waits for you

When the song ended, everything was quiet. There was no stirring of wind, nor did anything either living or dead rise to challenge him. Even the sound of the distant river seemed silenced.

Yet there was the sense of a brooding watchfulness that radiated from the blackness of Orabas just below him. It was not the same watchfulness as that which emanated from the forest the day before. That sensation bespoke of wariness and judgment, and ultimately, the forest had let him pass. The feeling that rose from the valley had the taint of death about it as if a potent yet mindless killer lay in wait there. Whatever it might be, Skallagrim had a distinct impression that his laughter and his song were not appreciated.

Undaunted, he ignored it and stared out across the sentient void toward his ultimate goal, shocked when yet another presence from the fort—or just beneath it—made itself known. Something there was regarding him too, amusedly. It was not mindless, and it reeked of evil intent. Terminus began to hum within its sheath as Skallagrim's mind reached out to this new spirit, vying with it, attempting to discern its threat. For a tortured second, he wondered if the sorcerer was cognizant of his nearness. But somehow, whether by the power of his sword or by an internal ability he had yet to fathom, he knew that whatever demon was toying with him, barely disguising its malice and villainy, was not that of Forneus Druogorim.

A chill wind sprang up and swept the hillside, whipping Skallagrim's cloak. Its suddenness jarred him free of whatever foulness had been probing his mind.

As the last of the breeze played in his wild locks, he turned his attention to the task at hand. He needed to get down off the exposed hill and get on with the rescue. The barest hint of joy remained in the thought, though it was muted after the strange encounters.

He would have to cross the blackness of Orabas now, but that did not deter his spirit in the least. Skallagrim had done the impossible, for alone he had traversed the southern wilderness of the Vales of Pagarna and had come to stand within sight of the sorcerer's lair and the hidden back door to Fort Vigilance.

The weak light was fading fast. Skallagrim straightened his pack, pulled the straps tight, and took to the road once more to descend into the yawning void where lay the dead city.

He took four steps and then stopped cold in his tracks. From behind him, perhaps no more than a few hundred yards away, came the dreaded sound of howling, screeching, and cackling. Vathek was making good on his threat.

CHAPTER TWENTY-SIX

With his heart in his throat, Skallagrim wheeled around, dreading what he might see, but the fading light and the thickening fog had reduced visibility to a few yards. He heard a sharp command, likely Vathek admonishing his mob to silence, then nothing more.

They were onto him. There was nothing for it but to turn and head down into the darkness.

Skallagrim jogged—rather that than sprint and risk a fall in the dark. Tired as he was, he could maintain the pace for some time. Maybe his enemies would lose him once he reached the bottom of the valley, for there he would finally leave the old roadbed for good.

According to Swanhild, once he entered the ruins of Orabas, he would not have far to go before he encountered a fabulous statue of an ancient knight. Its base might be partially submerged in the black water that lapped at most of the ruined structures, but she was certain the monolithic sculpture would still be standing.

Behind it he would find a narrow alley leading between two colossal mausoleums. He was to follow it until he came to the city's much-feared necropolis. Exiting the alley, he would face the very spot on the ridge where the hidden crypt lay.

At its widest point, the Necropolis of Orabas stretched for two miles, climbing the spur of the Craghide and the far end of the hill that Skallagrim was currently descending. Luckily, he would only have to cross it at its narrowest section, making his way toward the spur and then up an old livestock path to the two boulders that marked the secret way. As the river was running high, the floodwaters would be high as well. He might have to slosh through the vast cemetery, but to find the doorway that would lead him to his beloved, he would swim all the way across the valley if need be.

Skallagrim descended the hill and continued through the fog. There was no more howling nor any sound coming from the ghouls, who were surely following him. In fact, there was no sound at all but the scraping of Skallagrim's boots upon the worn gravel road. The ghouls were behind him though, perhaps even gaining on him. So, he pushed on painfully, noticing with irritation that both feet were blistered now.

The oppression in the valley was as thick as the cold white fog. Something was out there, listening, waiting. Skallagrim could feel it as if a sickly film was coating his mind.

He gripped the hilt of Terminus as he jogged and was rewarded as the sword imparted to him faint impressions of the lurker in the not-too-distant ruins. *Sentient yet mindless, deathless but dead, ravenous though bloated, unfilled though fed.* Even Swanhild could not tell him what the hidden malice of the valley was. He recalled her words with consternation. *"There's an evil there greater even than Forneus, perhaps. I fear it may be too much for you, even with your sword."*

These were not encouraging thoughts. Skallagrim relinquished his hold on the sword, put Swanhild's warning out of his mind, and plunged into the gloom. With trouble both behind and ahead, an unavoidable trap might spring at any moment, but what other choice did he have?

If he could stay ahead of Vathek, he might lose him at the statue of the knight. There the road would bend back toward the river, continuing until it dead-ended at a stone bastion built centuries ago to protect the fort's southern approach. It was undefended now, though anyone attempting to scale its walls would be seen either from the tower or by Straker's henchman, who were in hiding at the nearby bridge.

Skallagrim's path would take him far to the right of the road, away from the bridge, in a direction no one would expect him to go. He would have to rush to the detour now if he were to have any hope of throwing the ghouls off his scent. But the fog was impenetrable, and the detour's location was anyone's guess.

Thick black water flecked with mottled spume encroached upon both sides of the highway. At some point ahead, the road might dip into the suspicious mire. Hopefully, he would not find himself stuck or, worse yet, sinking in it.

More concerning was the unrelenting fog growing colder and damper with each hurried step, chilling Skallagrim to the bone. His hair hung lank about his shoulders, his cloak and clothing soaked and dripping with moisture.

Where was the dreaded city? He should have seen something of it by now.

The oppression of the place beat upon the doors of his heart as if a primordial killer was skulking just ahead in the mist. He ignored the threat and kept his feet moving. Even with the hovering fear and the blinding fog, Skallagrim did not lose heart, having come too far to be deterred now.

He stopped once and turned, certain he had heard the inevitable sound of pursuit behind him, closer now than before. Not waiting for confirmation, he whirled back around and sprinted, striving to put as much distance as possible between himself and Vathek's bloodthirsty ghouls.

It was like running in place. Whether an effect of the mist or the nearness of an unseen demon was to blame, he could not tell. But the fog, the black water, and the road rushed past as if it were they that moved and not him.

A hoarse shout sounded from behind, and other fell voices joined in. Skallagrim converted his fear into speed, hurling himself forward with reckless ferocity. The race must be won, for to fail was to die.

Some sign of Orabas must be dead ahead, for dark patches loomed in the vast sea of white. Before he knew it, Skallagrim had run past two huge, forbidding obelisks that towered out of the fog. The change in the atmosphere was so sudden and so shocking that Skallagrim staggered and nearly fell.

First came a loud crash as if a giant door had slammed shut

behind him. This was followed by a fierce, icy gust that shredded the fog, sending much of it swirling away in tatters to reveal the ruinous dreamscape of Orabas.

The oppression was tangible now, surely directed by a mindless will that had yet to reveal its true form. Having crossed the final threshold into the city, it clamped down on Skallagrim, pressing upon his chest, causing his mind to race with panic. He gripped the hilt of Terminus once more, allowing it to strengthen him, for he could not turn back.

The dead city stretched before him, partially submerged in the foetid swamp of Pagarna's backwash. Its crumbling, slime-covered buildings, beset by aged moss-covered trees, were bizarrely lit by corpse lights and the phosphorescent lichens that clung to their sides.

To have ever called Orabas a city seemed a blasphemous thing, for its sepulchral edifices had been built by no rational mind. Morbidly, they reared from the mire in chaotic array, like rigid dead things risen from tenebrous sleep to challenge the world for the ruin it had wrought upon them.

Marble-pillared villas leaned crazily upon once-opulent manses. The angles of their design were hard to fathom, and their windows stared like lidless eyes. The latter seemed lit from within by viridian-hued luminescent growths. It was that or some hate-filled presence that leered from each charnel house, but to consider that would be to imbue the wretched city with more of a demonic character than Skallagrim's mind could accept.

He was in the black water now, trying to make headway down the city's main street. As it was, he had no time to sightsee and certainly no moment to spare pondering the funereal aspect of each mournful ruin he sloshed past. But of one thing he was sure: Erling Hizzard and Swanhild had both undersold the terror of the place.

Of course, nothing could have prepared him for the true horror of the Pagarna. It was something that had to be seen and felt to be believed.

His quest to save his love had begun as a simple hike down a wilderness road. The farther he went, the more savage the wilderness became until it had nearly claimed his life in the rapids of a waterfall.

What came next was like a faerie forest compared to the landscape of Orabas. The twilight woods where he had first met Swanhild, then battled the ghouls, had been beautiful in their weird way. Since then the sense of danger and oppression had grown exponentially.

Upon entering the region of the Grimthorn, the unpleasant change had been manifest. When looking out upon the void of Orabas, it came again, though his heart had been glad then, for he could see the end of the road—a pathway to the blue-eyed girl. Then he had descended into the sea of white fog as the sun dipped low, coming at last to this region of absolute fear and dread. Orabas!

Maybe the darkness emanated from the land, or perhaps the people who lived here and later built these dolorous structures—daring to call them homes—had brought the darkness with them. Skallagrim could not guess. Either way, the elegiac history written of this land was a lie. Nothing normal had ever lived in such a place.

I just have to cross it!

As he pushed on, the flooded street became more and more choked with leaves and decades of rot, creating a syrupy slush that topped Skallagrim's boots and began to fill them.

"Damn it!"

His squelching boots were slowing him down, as was the suspicious-looking debris that bobbed about in the morass. These were large clumps, oddly shaped, which either floated or protruded obscenely from the slurry. He shoved the objects aside with his staff, alarmed at the unpleasant, jellied consistency of the rag-covered flotsam.

Vathek was shouting at him now, calling him by name.

"Skallagrim! Stop and rest, my friend," he cackled. "Too much runnin' will just toughen up the meat!"

Skallagrim did not stop—did not even look back over his shoulder—for the ghouls were close. With the fog thinning, they could see him too. But had he sensed something strange in Vathek's taunt? An unaccustomed note of fear perhaps? Maybe the Ghoul

King had no liking for Orabas either.

That seemed to make sense, for as Skallagrim waded ever deeper into the mire, he encountered more of the oddly bobbing shapes. Prodding one of them overly hard, he reeled backward in disgust when the thing exploded, releasing noxious fumes and covering him in filth. It gurgled horridly, then rolled over, revealing itself to be the bloated corpse of a ghoul, claimed at last by the death it had once reveled in.

Now it was all too obvious what the grotesque shapes in the black water were. For, upon close scrutiny, they were revealed to be either ghoulish in form or some other monstrous shape, all of them hideously mauled and partially devoured.

There was even the floating corpse of a leathery-winged creature that must be the remains of a dreaded nightgaunt. Its sightless head was missing, and its rib cage was spread wide, allowing the swampy water to fill the cavity. Something had worked it over pretty well, taking huge chunks from its obsidian flesh.

Skallagrim dragged his gaze away from the floating horrors and saw, to his relief, the tall, imposing statue of an armored knight just ahead. Two mausoleums stood on either side of the monument. Crumbling walls flanked the buildings, effectively blocking in the vast necropolis that must lay beyond.

A mound of rubble formed of old masonry, shards of granite, and slick slabs of marble was piled at the base of the statue. Skallagrim would have to climb the obstacle to get up and over, hopefully to continue to the necropolis beyond.

But his hopes of shaking the ghouls off his trail were dashed. He could tell one of them was close now, for he could hear its rasping breath. If he made the top of the pile, he would have to turn and face it. To ignore its proximity any further would be to invite a sword thrust to the back.

Skallagrim tossed his staff to the top of the heap and clambered up as fast as he could, scraping his hands as he struggled for purchase upon the slimy, jagged pieces of debris. He glanced up at the imposing monument, a fully armored knight leaning upon a great sword. The visage was warlike, but the sculptor had conveyed even more, somehow incorporating the idea of brooding malice in the eyes of the terrible face. Nearing the top of the pile, at last he saw with some alarm the engraved words on the monolith's base.

"BALOR, KNIGHT OF THE NORTH"

"Unbelievable!"

His dismay at seeing the cursed name could not be contained. Skallagrim laughed, for it was too much to take—too absurd given everything else he had seen in that devastated valley. He shook his head and kept climbing.

Reaching the top, he drew his sword and turned to face the foe who scrambled up the rubble heap right behind him.

Too easy, he thought, for the monster stood no chance at all. Skallagrim brought Terminus down upon its head, splitting its skull and showering the rubble with brains and blood.

Swarming around Vathek at the base of the statue were six more ghouls, one clad in rusty armor, the rest in everything from a foppish, laced frock coat to a matted wolf-skin cloak. All of them carried either a sword, axe, or war hammer. Vathek leered as he leaned upon his overly large axe.

"You must be on one hell of a mission to come to this place!" The Ghoul King sniffed the air and looked about warily, none too comfortable with his surroundings. It was as clear to him as to Skallagrim that something had killed and eaten many of his kind, leaving their bodies to bob piteously in the murky, death-filled waters.

Skallagrim had no wish to feel the cut of Vathek's murderous axe in his flesh, but he did not fear the ghoul. He had come to view himself as no less a monster than this wretch who challenged him from the bottom of the rubble pile.

"Maybe," Skallagrim replied. "Or maybe I'm thinking of settling down here. Seems to be lots of room. I'd ask you to join me, but it looks as if something here isn't too fond of your kind." He smiled. "Well, that depends on how you look at it, I guess."

"Enough!" Vathek yelled, then looked nervously about, clearly regretting the volume of his outburst.

Skallagrim shrugged. This was not the time and certainly not the place for jibes or sarcasm. He looked out over the weirdly luminescent ruins, the ancient and hoary trees that swayed to and fro, and wished only to be out of that place. He was so close to the fort now, so near to the girl, yet he could not rid himself of these ghouls.

To make matters worse, the spirit of oppression that darkened the air was even stronger now. It was as if a blanket had been lowered over all the ruins, blocking out the starlight and even the moon, which had been near to full.

The air became stifling, suffocating, like being caught in a small, confined space rather than the wide valley Skallagrim knew it to be. Whatever was the source of this strangling oppression, it had to be close by.

Skallagrim glanced behind him. A narrow, water-filled alley ran between the two mausoleums. The way was dark, and he could not see through to the other side.

"Too bad one of you doesn't have a bow," Skallagrim joked and immediately wished he had not, for his voice fell flat in the sepulchral gloom. The tension was as thick as fog and not only due to the obvious confrontation. "Because . . ." He tried to continue, but whatever mindless thing lay hidden in the dead city pressed down upon him with tangible force. His breathing became labored, and he found he could barely raise his voice above a whisper. ". . . then you could just shoot me."

His words were slurred, as if spoken in slow motion, the pitch of his voice dropping until it went below the range of hearing. Some will was at play, some act of sorcery was at work; even Vathek could feel it. He groaned, pressing a clawed and mottled hand against his temple as if in tremendous pain. The lesser ghouls cowered at his feet, their eyes darting about as if unseen foes might suddenly pour from the dark maw of the alley behind Skallagrim, or perhaps the mausoleum doors would burst asunder, releasing a hoard of ravenously vengeful dead.

For the moment though, nothing happened. Everything was still except for the breeze and the trees through which it played. The latter swayed lugubriously, as affected by the grinding deceleration of time as were the stricken combatants.

There was nothing left to say. No pointless taunt or useless threat needed to be, nor could be, spoken. Skallagrim and Vathek locked gazes, acknowledging the dread in each other's eyes. Yet whatever the thing was that sought to dominate them, neither would be deterred. Skallagrim shrugged as if to say, "So be it. Follow if you will." Then he turned and jumped, splashing down into the black water of the mausoleum alleyway. His action seemed, at least to Skallagrim, to break the spell, for the normal passing of time resumed its march toward whatever doom awaited.

Recovering, Vathek motioned to his mob to spread out and flank the giant structures. They would scale the walls and continue the pursuit. As for Vathek, he hefted his axe and climbed the rubble pile, choosing to follow Skallagrim into the darkness.

When Skallagrim landed, his knees nearly buckled at the impact, but he rose and plowed on through the knee-deep water that was, gratefully, free of debris. The mausoleum walls rose on either side of him, and the alley was so narrow he could reach out and touch both sides. The air was stagnant and cold. Using his staff to probe for hidden holes or pits in the paved surface beneath the water, he moved as fast as possible, though he did so in total darkness. It was as if no light of day had ever pierced the thin gap between the twin houses of the dead, which, by their very size, had to hold thousands upon thousands of bodies.

The unwelcome sounds of sloshing and splashing were unavoidable. Anything that might be lying in wait ahead would certainly be alerted to his approach. Another splash came from behind as Vathek landed in the alley.

"I'm comin' for you!" he bellowed, but his voice lacked resolve.

Skallagrim ignored him, plunging ahead toward a faint luminescence looming in the distance. The light gave him renewed hope as if it signified some sort of relief from his pursuers. Of course, it signified nothing of the kind, but he still called upon his final reserves and rushed toward the dim exit.

As Skallagrim raced toward the hopeful glow, he had a sudden, shocking awareness. There was no doubt now. Whatever sorcerous, mindless will had been gnawing at the edge of his conscience since he sang on the hilltop was not far ahead. No matter how absurd or blasphemous its existence might be, no matter how devolved was its form nor how insane was its limited, primordial sentience, in the Dead City of Orabas it reigned supreme.

CHAPTER TWENTY-SEVEN

As Skallagrim hurtled from the claustrophobic darkness of the alley into the eerily lit sprawl of the necropolis, he was torn between the elation of making it past one obstacle and an unsettling sense of dread at what might come next.

But he had only postponed complete disaster, for he saw three ghouls splashing through the black water around the building to his right and another three struggling over a gate just beyond the structure on his left. Cemetery walls, no matter how high, were no match for the ravenous creatures. With Vathek close behind him in the alley, he had no choice but to continue on in the ever-deepening water. It was over his knees now, and he slogged forward, every tortured step sending out wavelets that he feared would serve as an alarm for some imagined horror. *Surely, some fell thing must be hiding just below the surface or deep down in the sludge.* He could feel it. But unseen foes aside, the immediate threat was the ghouls. His only hope was to outdistance his foes and lose them behind a crypt or crumbling monument in the vast graveyard ahead.

Skallagrim could not see his feet through the murky water, but the ground beneath them was strangely yielding. It seemed as if he was walking on huge, rubbery coils that quavered treacherously and were slick with slime.

He heard harsh laughter on either side of him and turned to the right. The three ghouls there seemed to have forgotten him as they beat and smashed their way into a half-sunken crypt. It was no wonder, for to ghouls, the necropoli probably seemed like a ready feast and one they would not have to fight for. However, the three to his left were still in pursuit, angling toward Skallagrim to cut off his escape.

The black oppression, forgotten only for a moment, returned with such intensity that it leached the air of light, blanketing Skallagrim's vision and plunging the nightmare landscape into total gloom. He clutched his stomach as a sudden wave of nausea swept over him. He heard Vathek gasp behind him and the sickly sounds of torment as the other ghouls hacked and vomited into the mire. Then the phosphorescent glow flickered and finally returned as if ten thousand ghostly candles had been lit.

He had just turned to face forward, hoping to forge on, when the ropey whorls beneath his feet twitched madly, then retracted, sending him sprawling face first into the cemetery's miasmic stew. As Skallagrim lurched to his feet, cursing and spewing the filthy water from his mouth, he heard a tremendous thrashing of water to his left, followed by an obscene moan gurgling up from the mire.

It was perhaps the merest of mercies that Skallagrim—so wearied by fatigue and sorcery—could not later recall the full horror of the event that was about to transpire. His ensorcelled conscience simply could not stitch together an adequate picture of that which he saw, something that should not be described nor even remembered by a sane mind. In the moment, however, an abstract part of his psyche was able to grasp what his heart and mind dared not, and he knew what it was that he faced.

Skallagrim was oddly detached from the events unfolding around him. He barely noticed when two ghouls somersaulted through the air, then smashed against the side of a marble crypt. Vathek cried out behind him, but even that sounded distant, as if the Ghoul King was calling through a long tunnel. The ghouls to Skallagrim's right were wailing and sloshing through the mire to take a stand near their lord, but even that seemed unreal.

He gasped, taking a step backward as cold water rose suddenly to his waist. He knew he should bolt, push ahead through the water, and escape, but he had to know—to look! He turned to his left, knowing he would see the inevitable horror that men had carelessly named The Old Man o' the River, the thing that Erling had called an undulate. The monster, whose true name was Pagarna.

What the hell?

From the deep water near the leftmost mausoleum, an impossible evil hove into view. At first glance it looked like one of the ghouls had been snatched up by a beast of enormous size and was being lifted up and driven through the water at breakneck speed. But was it a ghoul or some kind of half-formed, faceless proto-man? The closer it got, the less Skallagrim could be certain. The thing was slick and black, and arms that were far too long and far too many were thrashing madly at the air. Great plumes of water were flung high in its wake as it closed the gap with Vathek. With much cursing, the ghoul urged his three defenders forward to meet the threat.

"Pagarna!" A voice like icy steel screamed in Skallagrim's mind—the voice of Terminus. But no one needed to tell him; he knew now what was meant when men and maps alluded to the Vales of Pagarna. Not a river but this! He had plunged right into its trap.

Too late to back out now!

He waded backward through the water, putting as much distance between himself and the coming confrontation as he could. His blue-eyed girl was close, less than a mile away. He should hurry to her rescue, but to turn his back on the undulate would be to invite peril.

In a black blur of flailing appendages, the creature halted a few yards short of Vathek's ghouls, creating a wave of reeking swill that threatened to engulf all of them, including Skallagrim. Then the full horror was evident as the submerged behemoth exploded from the water to reveal the proto-man was no man at all, merely a vaguely man-shaped thorax or upper section of a much larger and obscenely amorphous creature.

What Skallagrim remembered later was an indistinct impression of gangly, spidery legs, impossibly long and horrifically unfolding from a quivering, bloated body. Four lengthy tentacles uncoiled from random places about the thing's segmented, sagging abdomen, one of which grasped the dying body of the third ghoul that had been to Skallagrim's left.

That accounts for those three, he thought, then realized the absurdity of such observations given the grotesque display that was unfolding before him. It was happening so fast that he could not properly grasp the magnitude of the situation, and yet if he had, he would have screamed.

He watched in a daze as the undulate tightened its hold on its prey, squeezing and constricting until the ghoul's eyes popped from its skull, then its bones audibly snapped. As the monster shoved the limp body beneath its ghastly bulk with a great splash of black water and red blood, it occurred to Skallagrim that he had been walking on top of the hideous tentacles only a moment before.

There must have been a hidden orifice on the underside of the thing's twitching belly, for as the ghoul's carcass disappeared beneath, there came a loathsome smacking sound like blubbery lips closing over slimy meat, then the gruesome sound of biting and watery belching. No sooner had that stopped than the undulate's abdomen began to swell as if to bursting. To the horror of all, both man and ghoul, the belly contracted on itself, releasing jets of black water, gore, and blood from gaping vents that appeared on its flanks.

Sentient yet mindless, deathless but dead, ravenous though bloated, unfilled though fed.

Skallagrim, Vathek, and his underlings cried out in dismay at the sight, recoiling as they were showered with the ichor and muck that the undulate expelled. One of the remaining ghouls cowered, trying to work its way behind Vathek, but the other two rushed in amongst the beast's wriggling legs, hacking uselessly at the shining black carapace. This, Pagarna did not like.

While the visible, corporeal aspect of Pagarna was both blind and mindless, lurking within its beating black heart was a spirit—twisted and bent by insanity—that had guided its reckless malice throughout the long, dark ages of Andorath's torment. It was a spirit forged by the most depraved forms of sorcery. Its father and creator was an Ultimate Evil, the existence of which was mercifully known only to a few. Like the body it inhabited, the black heart's spirit had tentacles of its own, their reach far greater than the slimy appendages that flailed and scythed the air above its attackers, their effects far more terrible and perverse.

As Skallagrim backed through the water, Pagarna sheared away from its attackers in a blur of gangling, spidery legs, each of which must have been twenty feet long. Glistening tentacles rose whip-like in the air, then spiked themselves through the water and mud, plunging deep into the poisoned silt of doomed Orabas. Then the many arms of the shiny thorax stretched high into the air as if in supplication to an unseen demon god above. The spirit of the black heart cried out from within the beast, uttering unspeakable blasphemies in words that erupted like the thunders of hell. Following this the dreadful light of a thousand, thousand glowing lichens began to strobe.

Skallagrim reeled with sudden vertigo, his stomach clenching in another, tormenting wave of nausea. His one thought was still of the girl, though his hopes of living through this terror to find her were dashed. Still, he turned to flee, though the alternating flashes of light and dark left him impossibly disoriented. He was dimly aware of Vathek calling out behind him, though he could barely make out the words.

" . . . not over. I'll yet feast upon your corpse, maggot!"

Flashing images of Vathek revealed him staggering through the flood like a drunkard, clearly affected by the strobing light as he struggled to flee the scene. Skallagrim gave no thought to the empty threat, for it was likely that neither he nor Vathek would survive the night.

But I must live!

Skallagrim was putting distance between himself and the undulate, and that was all that mattered. He would struggle till his dying breath to reach the blue-eyed girl and free her whether she loved him or not. She was so close now, and he could not give in to death or despair. But the horror of the monster, Pagarna, was just beginning.

The spirit in its black heart incanted audibly once more, and geysers of black water shot into the air from a hundred places at once. The plumes sparkled in the weird, flickering light, then seemed to cascade in slow motion in a myriad of diamond-like droplets. From the point at which each geyser had sprung, writhing tentacles sprouted—fiendish bouquets resembling Devil's Fingers fungus. There was no knowing if the tentacles were an extension of the undulate's body or merely some monstrous fungi that obeyed its commands, for the red arms, many of them over six feet long, flailed in the air as if they had minds of their own.

One such arm, slick and smelly with a coating of gleba, whipped the water directly in front of Skallagrim. He did not remember drawing Terminus, but the sentient sword was in his hand. He swept the blade low, severing the tentacle from the submerged, suberumpent egg from which it had burst. An immediate release or explosion of spores caught Skallagrim off guard, and he coughed painfully—his throat inflamed by the toxic particulates he had inhaled.

Several more swollen arms flopped and twisted in the flashing light directly ahead. One plucked at Skallagrim's cloak while another managed to wrap itself around his left leg, causing him to trip. He managed to right himself in the nick of time. The fear of being pulled under the water became foremost in his mind, for if that happened, he would surely drown in the mirk, held down by the hideous arms.

He slashed wildly around him with Terminus, managing to sever another arm while slashing the one around his leg. He heard the undulate respond as if in pain, its bellow calling out over the haunted city like a trumpet of doom as the tentacle released its hold. Another ghoul hurtled like a missile overhead, splashing down just to Skallagrim's left. A swarm of tentacles burst from the water, wrapped around the screaming thing, then choked off its final protests by dragging it beneath the inky-black water.

The strobing phosphorescence stopped as suddenly as it had started, plunging the scene into stygian gloom. There was a great sound like a thousand whips hitting the water, and a dim light returned, revealing the legion of arms retracting beneath the surface. At least that particular threat had passed for the moment.

Behind Skallagrim came the terrifying sounds of flesh tearing and bones breaking, followed by a tremendous thrashing of water that meant another ghoul was being devoured. That left only three foes for Pagarna: Vathek, his lone henchman, and Skallagrim.

Keep moving!

He did not stop to glance back over his shoulder, for as waves of black water lapped at his back, it was clear the undulate was on the move again. He came at last to a long corridor of half-sunken crypts, beyond which a wall of black rose from the gloom. It had to be the ridge. The corridor would lead to its foot and the path to the secret back door of Fort Vigilance.

So close! Just keep moving!

As he slogged on, he recalled Swanhild's warning about the terrors he might face within the necropolis. But the sorrowful ghosts of Orabas did not flit to and fro from their soggy graves as once they had. The wraiths of the Grimthorn did not bang at the doors of their tombs, for they dared not call undue attention to themselves. Even the gaunt, red-eyed liches of the Dead City had long since buried themselves deep in the mud to dream their hell-haunted dreams. A truer terror had come to this domain. All feared Pagarna, the mindless terror of the Vales. Nothing living stirred, nor did anything that was dead. Nothing but two fleeing ghouls—if they yet lived— the monster Pagarna, and a thief named Skallagrim.

Through dark eons, lesser men of the Vales had been reduced to craven, whimpering mendicants that—cowering in the mud— covered their eyes, refusing to look upon the monster's terrifying form. They could no more defend themselves from Pagarna than could they make the river run south to north. Many—forsaking sanity—had worshipped it, though veneration was not what it craved. It acknowledged their piteous, cowardly existence in the same way a glutinous leech acknowledged a blood-swollen vein. Pagarna ate whom it wanted.

Decades might pass between its visits, but inevitably, somewhere along the 500-mile river that was its namesake, Pagarna would emerge, plunging a half-starved colony or town into terrifying darkness while it gorged itself on blood. Momentarily satiated, it would vanish once more to burrow in the deep mud of bog or swamp to wait upon its murderous, ravenous impulse to feed. For centuries, that had been its way.

Then came the War of the Great Rebellion. That had been nearly 150 years ago. The monster Pagarna, scion of the Ultimate Evil, vanished into legend, becoming a mere bogeyman to frighten children. Some unwitting skald or writer of frightful yarns named it the Old Man o' the River. Thus, the true and awesome terror of Pagarna passed out of memory—to all but a few.

Who knows how long the reprieve might have lasted had not the sorcerer, Forneus Druogorim, sought it out in a wild tributary of the river? The people of the Vales were mostly gone, driven elsewhere by other horrors that stalked the vine-choked hills and oddly glowing forests or by their inability to eke out a living among its savage mountains or boggy flatlands. There was simply no prey left to feed upon and no reason to stir itself from deathlike, dreamless slumber. Yet the sorcerer came, perhaps unconsciously prodded by the dead thing in the pit—that nameless, insidious presence that perpetually and evilly toyed with his mind—called out to Pagarna and woke the damned thing up.

Forneus Druogorim employed powerful spells to protect himself from it, exhausting himself and much of his potency in the process. If he had ever had a soul, the sorcerer had lost it then. For he laid before the monster a sacrifice of ten beautiful children, stolen from their homes and drugged into submission. The monster fed well while the sorcerer watched, screaming as his last lingering shreds of sanity fled from him.

When the sacrifice was complete, Forneus promised Pagarna more, much more. Pagarna must come down from the mist-shrouded mountain from whence its tributary flowed savage and cold—come down to Fort Vigilance and there make its home. Its task: to protect the sorcerer from any who might assault his lair, especially Griog'xa of Archon.

So the monster came. In a great torrent of displaced water and a maddening blur of legs and other vile appendages, Pagarna came down to the Dead City of Orabas and waited to feast.

At first the sorcerer fed it plenty. Foolish cultists willingly died alongside kidnapped maidens and strapping male slaves. It became a bloated, disgusting thing, full of blood and ravenous rage. As it grew in size, so did the darkness over Orabas till at last both sun and moon turned their faces from the cursed valley, leaving it lightless but for the horrid, phosphorescent growths that thrived there.

While Pagarna might have guarded the sorcerer's fortress, keeping Griog'xa and his minions at bay, it could not guard his mind. The longer Forneus Druogorim stayed within the walls of the fort, the more his mind was given over to the pernicious thing in the pit. As for that, he did not even guess at its true nature, for it had subtly convinced him not to try. Sadly, if he had taken but a moment to consult the mouldering records in the fort's dusty library, he would have known that the strong walls behind which he hid were erected not to keep foes at bay but to keep the thing in the pit from escaping. Fort Vigilance was, as Swanhild knew, a prison.

As the months crept by, he became increasingly obsessed with his mad experiments and less and less able to grapple with reality. He stopped feeding the monster in the valley, though inwardly, he dreaded its retribution. Of course, the mindless Pagarna cared nothing for retribution. It only wanted to be fed. Of late it had to content itself upon poorer fare, ghouls, and the rare nightgaunt that strayed into the necropolis or the old ruins of the city. They were bitter meat and not to its liking.

It could smell the thief's blood though, even if it could not see him. Man flesh was more to its liking. The monster would gorge on his bones and shower itself in his blood. With no thought except to that of its own gluttony, it veered away from its pursuit of Vathek and turned to pursue Skallagrim, to hunt him down amongst the crypts and devour him.

CHAPTER TWENTY-EIGHT

Several hours had passed since Skallagrim last saw Vathek. Forced from one hiding place to the next, he had made little progress toward the far side of the necropolis. He had crawled on his belly through muck and mire, often thinking he had rid himself of the monster, only to hear the lash of its tentacles or the gurgling of its bloated stomach each time he emerged from the water to check. It had kept itself cloaked in inky darkness whenever he spotted it, so he was spared having to relive the sight of the undulate's twitching black tangle of appendages or the bizarre and faceless proto-man that projected like a masthead from the thing's carapace-armored body.

Now and then, cornered against a broken monument or scrambling through a tangle of fallen tree trunks and broken limbs, Skallagrim, shivering from wet and cold, was forced to turn and fight. The undulate seemed wary of Terminus and would lash forth tentatively with a tentacle, only to retract it before the blade could connect. Inevitably, the thief would break contact, slipping away in a flooded ditch or diving behind a row of crowded tombstones. Thus, the two combatants played cat and mouse throughout the weary night. Dawn would be upon them soon, though likely without a sunrise, for natural light was an unwelcome guest in the Dead City.

At present, the undulate was searching for Skallagrim in a distant part of the necropolis, so he proceeded in the gloom toward what he hoped was his primary goal—the ridge and the fort's secret entrance. As soon as Skallagrim splashed back into the murky water, he heard the monster react. The interminable hunt was on again.

The water was shallower there, but his feet were sticking in mud. He lifted his staff from the water to find it dripping with reeking black scum that glistened in the eerie light like boiling tar. Skallagrim struggled through the clinging filth, knowing any second he must turn to fight.

He paused, contemplating. Were there other eyes on him? Friendlier eyes?

There was no way to know, so he pushed on, trying to keep his wits as stinking gasses bubbled up from the mire, threatening to overwhelm him. His facial wounds were throbbing with fresh agony while a fever raged inside him.

He was drowsy and not just from lack of sleep. He had inhaled a cloud of spores from the red tentacles, and they were having a horrible effect. He was sickened in body and soul. But if he did not make a final push toward the hidden door, soon he might collapse and drown in the flood.

The monster could not be far behind. It grunted and hissed as it splashed through the nightmarish streets of the necropolis. Skallagrim dared to look behind him and saw it heaving its bulk over a large crypt, its ghastly tangle of legs thrashing madly with the effort. It was only fifty yards back and would be on him soon.

The limit of the river's filthy backwash was close, for the ground was rising quickly as it sloped toward the dark line of the ridge. It gave him much-needed hope, driving him onward till, at last, he came near to a final row of crypts and the crumbling wall that marked the end of the necropolis.

With Pagarna speeding through the shallow water just behind him, he quickly surveyed the fifteen-foot-high wall he would need to cross. To his left a crumbling columbarium, its weirdly carved urns spilling from their niches, leaned upon the wall like a mourner in despair. It looked climbable—just. If so, he would be free of the cemetery, and more importantly, of Orabas.

His boots were full of muck, his pack was soaked, and his cloak was so drenched it dragged him down, but there was no time to shed them. *Up and over the wall! Up the ridge! Through the hidden crypt!* Dawn was surely close, leaving him one more day before Forneus murdered the girl.

He cursed, for everything seemed to be going against him now. If only the Old Man o' the River was not hell bent upon eating him, there might be time to pull off the impossible.

Skallagrim risked one more look behind him. Pagarna was racing to his left, seeking to cut off his escape. In the blink of an eye, it jumped, coming to rest upon the ruins of the columbarium. There it crouched, waiting.

The creature's details were mercifully hard to comprehend, for a sickly darkness continued to radiate from it, hiding all but the horrid legs. It was not a natural darkness—nothing like shadow nor even the desolate black of a starless night. This was a spiritual blackness that slimed over reality, hiding truth and blotting out sanity.

Skallagrim was near to collapse for a hundred reasons, not least of which was the sorcerous spores that he had inhaled. They were at work within him, coating his consciousness with despair even as they worked to paralyze his body. But he was not done yet, far from it. His escape from Orabas was in sight; it was now or never.

In defiance, he climbed upon a cracked ossuary and, staggering, raised Terminus high in the air, willing it to action.

"Light!"

And light shone forth from the blade.

"Scream now, Terminus! Sing your song!"

And scream it did—as if the world was ending.

In Fort Vigilance the sorcerer and the assassin bolted to the nearest window looking south. They peered fearfully into the void of Orabas as if some evidence of phantasmic combat might suddenly emerge from within the darkness that shrouded the valley. They saw only the flash of searing light from Terminus as it pierced the tenebrous veil. That and nothing more.

Two miles to the south, Vathek stopped in his tracks. He had heard that scream before and knew what it meant. Knew and was grateful it was not he who faced the thief. That would come another day. With his rotten heart in his throat, he turned and slunk away into the hills.

Just over the Pagarna River, Erling and Hartbert were both startled by the distant scream.

"That'll be our boy, what?" Erling whispered. "Told you he'd make it!"

"He's close, that's for sure, Mister Hizzard." Hartbert fingered his sword hilt and noticed his hands were shaking. A preternatural scream like that of Terminus was enough to unnerve even the sturdiest of men. As evidenced by the sudden, distant shriek and the threat of bad weather that was beginning to boil in the clouds overhead, great and terrible things were afoot. "Is there nothing we can do to help him?"

"I fear we're but witnesses to the better part of these events." Erling patted the giant on his great shoulders. "Still, if he makes it into the tower, we will see what can be done about those guards by the bridge. For now, we wait."

For a moment the veil of darkness surrounding the undulate parted, revealing a shuddering, twitching horror.

How it hated the bright light that pierced its blindness and the horrid scream that set its limbs to spasming. The spirit of its black heart was suddenly dismayed, reminded of an ancient dread it had nearly forgotten—that of a different man who strode triumphantly over bloody battlefields in ages past, a king who slew the wicked, full of power and terrible majesty. A king who blinded Pagarna and banished it to cursed Andorath, there to live out its days in abject misery and hunger whilst it waited upon final judgment. But this was no king who defied it now, just a filthy man with a tiny blade— blood and food, nothing more.

As the light of Terminus lanced the valley's perpetual night, shredding the evil cloak of darkness that surrounded Pagarna, Skallagrim saw anew his reflection in the metal of the blade. He swept his gaze back to the horror that thrashed and flailed upon the rubble—looked and learned the real truth about himself. Skallagrim was no monster!

A thousand images flashed in his mind, searing his conscience with sudden clarity. The murderous faces of those who had scarred him in the alley, those who had hunted him beyond the walls of Archon—monsters all. The unknown entity that had bespelled his mind, robbing him of memory and hope—a monster. The witch who glided from the darkness beneath the city, smelling of death, full of rot, and cackling with sadistic glee at the sight of his terrible wounds—a monster. The ghouls in the forest, those reprobates and fiends who had willingly given themselves over to evil—monsters, every one. And this twitching, swollen demon perched on the detritus between him and the wall? A monster, cursed and damned.

Oh my!

Realization hit him with the force of a war hammer. He knew then what he should have known all along and would have known but for the thousand and one distractions that had kept him from seeing it. The spell that hid him from his past, the pain, the fighting, the fear of his disfigurement, the need for revenge upon the sorcerer and Straker, Erling's devious plots, and the temptations of Swanhild—all were laid bare before him. They were but trickery and beguilements to keep him from the actual soul-cleansing truth.

I'm no monster!

It was not the outward things that damned a man or even evil his deeds, for deeds could be forgiven. Rather, it was that which filled his heart.

I don't even need revenge!

Skallagrim knew his own heart, for he had heard it in the song upon the high hill over the Dead City. He had seen it in the dreams of the old man and the blue-eyed girl whose hair was golden. He could even feel it now as he faced Pagarna in the festering desolation of the necropolis. Whatever it was, be it goodness, hope, bravery, or all those things and many others besides, his heart was full of it. It brimmed with something ineffable, a transcendent emotion or spiritual quality that moved him to great deeds and to the forsaking of despair.

He suspected that, given time, this sudden supernal epiphany might lead to further revelation, but time was a luxury he did not have.

Even if I'm dying, it does not matter.

He cared not for his own well-being in that moment, only for the hope of freeing the girl. And there was something else he dared not admit to himself before—she would love him still! The girl to whom he had given his heart would see past his scars. He had been a fool to think otherwise.

Thus, the thief who was no monster faced a true monster—a veritable demon of antiquity—with a profoundly new view of himself and the girl he wished to save. If he had been able to recall her name, it would have been his battle cry. As it was, he merely screamed like a savage as he jumped from the ossuary and charged the slope of the leaning columbarium.

Pagarna waited till he got close, then uncoiled a whip-like tentacle that scythed the air toward the approaching thief. Skallagrim saw it in time and, dropping his staff, grasped Terminus with both hands, swinging the blade at the oncoming appendage. With a sickening slap, the blade made contact, severing the arm.

Not since the ancient wars beyond the Southern Void had Pagarna been attacked with such ferocity or with such devastating results. Others had cowered as its shadow loomed over them, unable to defend themselves or even to die manifesting some final surge of bravery in defense of hearth and home. So, as they whimpered in the dark, their bowels emptying from abject fear, they died to the sounds of wailing wives and screaming children. Pagarna devoured them all. The men of the Vale had been weak, but not this man! He fought for love, and his weapon was hope, hope in the form of a sword whose edge was honed for the killing of such as Pagarna.

The monster tried to maneuver away from the wild warrior with the bright blade but found itself with its back to the wall. It could turn and scuttle over, yes, but not without inviting more vicious cuts. It had fed too well on the sorcerer's ghoulish tidbits over the last year and had grown too fat to move as it once had. Now it must stand and fight, though it shuddered and seethed with pain from the lost tentacle. It retracted the gushing stump and, bellowing from an unseen mouth, reared on its back legs, swatting viciously at Skallagrim.

What the . . .

An arrow streaked overhead from out of the gloom, then another. Both hit the undulate's body and ricocheted, useless. Someone else was nearby, hidden in darkness, but it was no comfort. In a flash, the matter was forgotten.

Skallagrim leapt forward, thrusting his blade into the hideous man-shaped thorax. Green ichor spouted in a plume from the terrible wound, and the monster recoiled, nearly ripping Terminus from his hands. A spindly leg struck a savage blow, knocking him sideways off the columbarium. He landed with a thud amongst a clutter of broken urns, tried to stand, lost his footing, then managed to rise just before a second tentacle whipped in and coiled about his middle. There was no time to wait. The arm was unimaginably strong and would squeeze the life out of him in seconds if he did not act. He hacked at the slimy appendage for all he was worth.

He only managed to partially sever it, however, and was lifted high in its crushing embrace, then flung through the air. He came down hard, hitting a tombstone and cracking it upon impact. He stood, felt his knees buckle, and went down again. Pain shot through his left leg and side. Fearing a broken limb, he tried once more to stand and found he could just barely. He had probably broken a rib in the fall, but what choice did he have? For good or ill, the fight must continue to its conclusion.

Skallagrim was abruptly overcome with the conviction that he had forgotten something—something important that could help him. But there was no time to waste wondering about it, so he brushed the thought aside. Grunting with pain, he squared his jaw, then limped, rather than charged, back into the fray.

A fierce gust began to stir his sodden cape and hair. Looking up, he saw the pale circle of the moon. There were storm clouds, too, carried fast on the wind and the hopeful hint of pinkening sky to the south. The darkness of Pagarna was failing.

Skallagrim was not driven by a desire to kill the thing, merely to get past it. Yet there it waited, an obscene obstacle to everything that mattered to him. He closed the distance slowly and painfully, but as he staggered to within mere feet of the monster, his world went spinning. He was burning up, exhausted from days of battle and toil and sickened by the red arm's eructation of spores. Bruised and battered, wincing with pain and brutalized by sorcery, Skallagrim sank to his knees before Pagarna.

He looked up in time to see the faceless form of the proto-man lowering over him. With its many arms, shiny and black, it grasped him and pushed him to the ground. He had just managed to keep his sword arm free, but the arachnidian legs were tugging at him, forcing him beneath the monster's bulk, presumably toward its waiting mouth. He wept then, not from fear but from the certainty of failure. His vision blurred, and he cried out, railing against the inevitable. Surely it would not end this way, not after he had come so far.

He was losing consciousness, and the fight had gone out of him. But before everything went black, he recalled his desperate fight in the alleyway. He had lived through it, yes, but the strength he needed to prevail had not come from within. Someone had sent it. He had called to them, though he could not remember who they were, only that they loved him and would help him. Miraculously, the help had been right there above him throughout the entire horrible episode. He just had to ask for it. Then it had come as if from heaven, descending from the storm like an angel of wrath, full of glory.

Through a haze, he took a final glance at the sword's indistinct shape.

I don't know what you are nor why you were sent to me, but you're mine now.

Nothing. He cursed inwardly, knowing he had all the help he needed within his grasp, just not the understanding required to use it.

He was turned over and around by the hideous legs. Horrid

slurping sounds came from the dreadful mouth that was trembling to devour him. But there were also other sounds—the muffled sounds of thunder overhead.

Lightning!

In the alley, the sorcerer had cast an ineffectual spell at the descending sword, and Terminus had responded with a thunderbolt. Could the same not happen now? Skallagrim had no idea how to communicate with the sentient sword, and he had neither the wind nor the will to shout any command, so he whispered it once more.

"Lightning."

Terminus flashed, nearly blinding him.

BOOM!

Thunder banged the air as if the end of time had come! Recoiling from the shock, the monster's many arms released him. There was a ghastly smell of burning fat and a horrid gurgling sound as the undulate's flesh cracked open, releasing the vile fluids of its age-long engorgement. It mewled in agony, backing away from man and sword in a frenzy of legs and writhing tentacles. It stumbled off the wreckage of the columbarium and crashed to the ground. Shuddering, the wounded monster released a vaporous cloud of spores, causing Skallagrim to gasp for air.

Terminus had dealt Pagarna a terrible wound. Its hide had never been pierced, and it had never known such pain. The sword also granted the gore-covered thief enough strength to stand—to walk. Retrieving his staff, he leaned upon it, then watched in awe the terrible anguish of Pagarna.

He would only ever remember a part of what he saw, for human eyes were not meant to see such, nor was the human mind made to grasp the entirety of terror in this form or given the words by which such a thing can be described. Even so, he knew that if he survived, the vision would haunt his nightmares forever.

Mindless it may have been, but he could feel very well that its malice was bent upon him. Pagarna, the Old Man o' the River, had had enough of the thief with the bright sword, but one spell remained in its dreadful black heart, and this it cast.

Falling upon the last bastion of its sorcery, the spirit of the black heart cried out to the Ultimate Evil that had spawned it, stirring it from deathlike sleep in an icy, subterranean hell far to the north. The Evil heard, and sending forth its potent thought, lent to Pagarna the hideous strength it would need to escape. Blackness boiled around it once more. Then the air seemed to explode in plumes of spores and foul ichor as the valley's phosphorescent light strobed madly again.

Skallagrim reeled, drenched in the reeking suppuration of his wounded foe. He wiped the filth from his eyes with a muddy sleeve and watched as the monster sped away in a blur of legs and flailing tentacles. It churned the toxic waters of the flooded necropolis, then lurched over the walls that guarded the entrance. Its shadow receded in the distance as it fled through the Dead City of Orabas, setting its course for the river beyond, then on, Skallagrim assumed, to whatever lightless hole or swampy bog it could find. There it would hide in woe and anguish, nursing its wounds on an elixir of spite and malevolence.

As the darkness of its spirit ebbed and the storm subsided, the sun rose as red as a clot of blood. Its light, though dismal and weak, was still light.

Skallagrim turned back to the wall. Summoning his waning strength, he staggered to the top of the leaning columbarium and pitched himself over the side. He thought his knees would break with the impact of landing, but they did not. Sharp pain lanced both legs, however. Still, he gritted his teeth and rose. Looking up at the impossible slope before him, rock strewn and wild with wide swathes of thorns and twisted trees, he set his sights on the only spot upon the ridge that mattered and began the long climb.

CHAPTER TWENTY-NINE

So loud was the noise of Pagarna's torment that Straker's kinsmen stepped out of their hiding places to gawk, one of them even walking out onto the bridge to get a better view south.

"Look at those fools, Hartbert," Erling mocked. "What are they up to?"

"Something's coming," Hartbert warned. "Something bad. Can't you hear it?"

"Of course I can!" Erling rose from behind his hiding place, urging the giant to join him. "They can see it, whatever it is."

"Balor's bones, Mister Hizzard. What is that?"

A swirling mass of black churned the waters to the south, even as the sun rose red behind the hills. It was moving fast, making a beeline for the river. As it plunged into the swift current, steam exploded into the air, and the waters around it began to boil. It turned and headed north directly toward the bridge.

Upon the span, the lone guard was pointing toward the strange phenomenon and shouting to his cousins, completely unaware of the peril it posed. By the time he fully understood the danger he had exposed himself to, it was too late. The undulate's black fury reached the bridge in a flash, a V-shaped wake trailing behind it. In a flurry of wild arms, tentacles, and arachnidian legs, it climbed the bridge and fell upon the screaming guard.

"Oh my!" Hartbert gaped, transfixed by the scene.

"I . . ." Even Erling seemed unable to wrap his mind around it and stumbled for words. "Son of a troll! Can it be?"

For a moment the black cloud parted, revealing the true horror that lurked within. Erling and Hartbert, though in no immediate danger, took an irresistible step backward as the wayward guard was shoveled beneath Pagarna's bulk and devoured. A moment later the vents upon its monstrous flanks opened, and plumes of blood and black water ejected from its swollen stomach, splashing obscenely upon the bridge.

"Can it be what?" Hartbert murmured. His shoulders slumped, and his arms dangled uselessly at his sides. Over the last several years, the giant had lived through famine and battle, had seen his share of brutality and dark magic, but none of it had prepared him for this.

"I think you were right to warn of the Old Man o' the River," Erling confessed. "Unless I'm mistaken, there it is."

"Well, I never!"

The remaining guards were fleeing back up the riverbank toward the shelter of the fort as Pagarna shuddered, remembering the terrible wounds inflicted upon it by Skallagrim. It bellowed once, a brash, braying sound that echoed off the walls of the fort and the surrounding ridges. The impenetrable blackness swirled around it once more, hiding its form as it leapt from the bridge to tear upriver. Flocks of waterfowl took to the air in alarm, and a solitary crow called out in warning to its unseen ken. Then all was quiet.

It would be a long time before Pagarna, the primordial terror of the Vales, was seen again by mortal eyes.

"Now what?" Hartbert queried as he and Erling ducked behind the rocks.

"Either our Skallagrim was eaten by the thing, or, more likely, he wounded it badly with Terminus. We shall hope for the latter and continue our vigil." Having said this, Erling laid down, shutting his eyes to sleep as if nothing of any consequence had happened. Dismayed, Hartbert shook his head and turned a wary eye upon the fort.

The weak sunlight was working around the edges of Fort Vigilance and Orabas farther to the south, though for the most part, the darkness held sway. Either repulsed by the madness of Forneus Druogorim or leery of the dead thing that skulked and plotted beneath the fort, daylight remained loath to shine upon the sorcerer's lair.

Skallagrim stumbled up the ridge, leaning heavily upon his staff, thankful he had kept it, for now he truly needed it. Above him, a steep, rocky slope terminated at a point that projected from the ridge. Upon its shelf sat the two boulders that, according to Swanhild, hid the secret crypt and tunnel by which Skallagrim could gain entrance to the fort. Everything depended upon her information. If she was wrong, Skallagrim's mission was doomed.

Most of Fort Vigilance was hidden from view just over the ridge, though the topmost turret was visible about 200 yards away. The thought of crawling that distance in a tight tunnel was dreadful. Of course, the mission was likely doomed whether he could navigate the passage or not, for even if he were able to enter the sorcerer's lair from beneath, what then? By stealth he might find the beautiful captive, free her, and lead her to safety. He might but probably not.

More likely he would be caught by guards and dragged before the sorcerer. He had given much thought to killing the fiend, and he would if he must. But the desire for revenge had dulled considerably since setting out from Archon. The sentiment simply did not suit him.

He shrugged, fretting over his predicament. In his current state, could he take on several fighters at once? Would his luck hold? Could Terminus aid him in a fight against black magic? He did not know.

If Erling was correct, the girl would be sacrificed, or more to the point, *murdered* at midnight that very night. Skallagrim could not bear to think of it anymore. He had to save her.

He coughed painfully, then wiped the sweat from his brow with a dirty sleeve. He was burning up and not just from exertion. A fever burned inside him like a torch, either from infection or a reaction to the undulate's spores; he could not tell which. Tragically, he was suffering from both.

Open wounds could kill a man in the wilderness as easily as a ghoul's axe. Meanwhile, an insidious colony of spores spread fine filaments throughout his lungs that would kill him soon if not treated. Worse yet, the spores were occultic by nature. Only a handful of alchemists and wizards knew the ghastly significance of such an infestation—of how it might ripen in the organs, taking shape in unspeakable ways even months after the victim had breathed his last. No, death was not the worst thing that could happen to a man in the Vales.

Of course, there were cures, potions one might take to stave off the effects or even completely eradicate the contagion from one's body. But Skallagrim had no way of knowing precisely what his ailments were, nor did he know a wizard capable of making such magic. He just knew he was sick and had resigned himself that he might die trying to rescue the girl. Shivering, he dragged his eyes back to the task at hand.

A thought crossed his mind but was gone in a flash. There was something he was supposed to remember, something that might help. Yet for the life of him, he could not recall it.

He ran his staff along the top of his pack just beneath the shoulder straps, for he could not carry it otherwise and climb. He made a few adjustments to his baldric, then began a precarious ascent. He reached the top easily enough, only slipping once. Quickly crossing the distance to the twin boulders, he was rewarded with the sight of an ancient door hidden just within the shadows between the two.

On either side of the door, carved figures stared impassively— knights from the look of them, clad in chainmail, swords drawn. The door itself was imprisoned beneath ropes of thorny vines, pallid and sickly from lack of light, making it clear that no one had opened the crypt in ages. Using his cloak to protect his hands, Skallagrim ripped the vines from the door, exposing its rusty surface. Even such a minuscule effort left him breathless. Then came the fresh agony of renewed coughing, his blighted lungs threatening to collapse with the pressure.

With a trembling hand, he took Swanhild's key from his pocket and placed it in the keyhole. His first attempt was thwarted, for the key refused to turn. Fearing it might break off inside the lock, he took a deep breath and tried again, jiggling it carefully until it caught. It clicked! Without a thought for the horror that might lay on the other side of the door, he tugged upon its ornate handle. He heard a ghostly sigh of stale air as the seal of lichens and rust was broken, then the ancient door creaked open.

Steps led down into inky darkness. Unable to think clearly, Skallagrim lurched across the threshold, closed the door behind him, and headed down. The darkness was complete. *This will not do,* he thought. Unless the tunnel led straight ahead with no pitfalls, he would not make it far without a light. He turned back, prepared to exit. There must be the makings of a torch somewhere outside. Yet his heart was in his throat as he pushed upon the door, for it refused to budge. He felt around for a keyhole, but there was none to be found.

Fool!

He slouched in the darkness, cursing his stupidity. There was nothing for it but to plunge into the tenebrous depths of the ancient sepulcher.

The fearful descent was mercifully short, only a few steps bringing him quickly to a tight corridor. He stopped, listening, eyes wide but seeing nothing. Had the flicker of a light abruptly extinguished just ahead?

He waited, breathless. But when no sound came forth from the darkness, and the phantom light failed to return, he took a few tentative steps forward.

Perhaps Terminus might deign to light his way? But Terminus was a weapon of war, its light serving a higher purpose than mere luminescence. After a few attempts at willing the blade to become a torch, Skallagrim slammed it back into its sheath, feeling foolish for making the attempt.

Perhaps he could fashion a torch with his staff? He would rummage through his pack for any scrap of dry material. And if there was nothing dry enough to light, then he would just work the flint until he could set the end of the staff ablaze. A few minutes of light were better than none. Yes! That was the answer.

No sooner did he think of setting fire to the staff than the end of it came alight with a radiance all its own.

"Balor's bones!" he exclaimed. Given his surroundings, he instantly regretted the outburst.

"I knew there was something about you," he whispered. There had to be a story behind the dogwood staff, for surely it had been the magically endowed stave of some wizard. Well, it did not matter. He had a light, though what it illuminated was not reassuring.

The corridor was short, just an entryway into the actual tomb. Holding the staff aloft, Skallagrim crept forward to where the passage emptied into a larger chamber. He gaped at what he saw.

Coffins were heaped upon coffins, their wooden pieces crumbling and strewn throughout the crypt, their bony contents scattered across the floor. He tiptoed over the detritus of centuries, past piles of leering skulls, unavoidably crunching bits of bone underfoot.

He made his way to a dank portal on the far side of the room, peered within, and was greeted by a sigh of air, pungent with the odors of ancient decay. It caused another painful coughing spell, but he braced himself and stepped beneath the forbidding arch and into the next vault.

Its walls were lined with recessed shelves of niter-encrusted marble, each bearing a darkly stained oak casket. Despite their age, most appeared in fair condition, though two lay alarmingly open, their seals broken. Their stout lids were propped against the far wall where another arched doorway loomed as black as night. A wrought-iron gate had once barred further egress, but it had been torn from its mangled hinges and lay twisted upon the wet stone floor. Skallagrim had the sudden, gnawing feeling that going beyond that threshold would invite utter destruction upon himself. Something was waiting there in the dark, something that made his skin crawl.

He hesitated, for he could feel himself growing weaker by the minute. His breathing was noticeably hampered, and his head was swimming. Taking a long drink from his waterskin, he cleared his throat to ward off further coughing, but he could tell his lungs needed relief. Any moment he might give in to another fit, one that would surely be unbearable. But he thought of the girl who was waiting just ahead, beyond the terror of that place, and knew he would crawl to her if necessary.

Fortunately, it had not come to that yet. He moved past the open caskets, not daring to peak at their contents, and made his way to the ominous doorway. Beyond lay damp, dripping steps that would deposit him onto a flooded floor that shimmered luridly in the light of his staff. Ducking his head to clear the short entryway, Skallagrim stepped inside and began the brief descent. When he raised his head again, he realized too late that he was not alone.

First came the memory of the terrible presence he had felt upon the hillside over the Dead City of Orabas. Not the murderous, mindless spirit of the undulate that emanated from the flooded valley but the brooding, intelligent force that had contemplated him from beyond the void. Some instinct had warned him then that it was not the sorcerer but some subterraneous evil beneath the fort. It had taken note of his hopeful song, then sought to perceive his thoughts and intentions. He strove with it then, only for a moment, and had prevailed. After that it was driven from his mind by more immediate threats: ghouls and the horrid beast that haunted the flooded ruins.

Now he had stepped from one haunted domain into another. A different spirit held sway there, even as Pagarna had once held the dark valley.

Its presence wound through his mind like a twisted, seething vine that might squeeze the very life from him. He had felt Pagarna's awareness upon him during their battle, but that awareness was primitive compared to the sentience considering him now. There was nothing mindless about it. This was a super intelligence: curious and full of a giddy malice barely held in check.

That was not all.

Even as Skallagrim, wracked by the pain of his lungs' rebellion, sank to the wet floor, gasping for air, he became cognizant of two figures contemplating him from the vault's shadowy interior.

Moaning hideously, they sloshed forward, chainmail glimmering in the pallid light, skeletal faces leering, eye sockets glowing red with inner evil. Liches! Fell guardians of the tomb, the very pair of knightly warriors whose likenesses were carven upon its hidden entrance. They had been brought back to a grey, wretched existence, deprived of deathly sleep, forced to endure a horrid un-life by means of necromancy and black magic, all while serving the very thing they had once imprisoned.

Losing consciousness but still dimly aware, Skallagrim cringed as they hoisted him up with rough hands and winced as his staff was ripped from his grasp. He had no strength left to fight them.

There's something—something I'm supposed to remember! For a second, he had it, but the glimpse was fleeting, unraveling like a wraith upon a midnight gale.

Before the blackness closed in completely, bony fingers gripped him beneath each useless arm, then dragged him through the water in the same direction he had been going, toward whatever fresh horror life would subject him to next.

With the ghostly rattle of chainmail and the harsh steps of iron-clad feet echoing upon the dripping walls of the ancient charnel house, the liches hauled their helpless prisoner into the darkness, toward his fate . . . and his doom.

CHAPTER THIRTY

They were playing in the garden, a place so pristine that to breathe its air was to breathe poetry; to bask in its sunlight was to become a song. She was there, the blue-eyed girl whose locks were like spun gold. They were holding hands, running barefoot through the long grass, wet with the dew of a perfect morning. Past beds of purple phlox, irises, lilies, and aster they sped, around splashing fountains whose waters were like shimmering silver they danced. Beneath tall oaks with laden limbs of wisteria, they spun around and around till, dizzy, they fell at last into each other's embrace to go rolling down a gentle slope, their laughter as melodious as the songbirds who sang to them from the low branches.

Coming to rest at last by a glassy pool, he plucked stray blades of grass from her hair. She smiled like an angel might, for she was translucent, the light of the sun filling her and spilling out in golden beams.

His sweet garden nymph, so vivid and yet as ethereal as faerie dust.

"I saw you sleeping in a bed of flowers," he said. "I had to know if you were real."

"I am not yet born," she replied, her voice like rippling silver. "But I am real."

"And we're in love, yes?"

"Oh, yes." She giggled and, blushing, lowered her eyes. "You were to guard me, to watch over me."

"For him?"

"Yes, but we need not stay. You could take me away, to where he will not follow."

"And then we can be together?" He cupped her chin in his hand and lifted her face so that he might bask in the wonder of her eyes. But as his gaze met hers, he saw the crystal tear that had slipped down one rosy cheek and felt the piercing sweetness of a heartache that only star-crossed

lovers might share.

Skallagrim was standing deep in the dark forest once more, the music blaring, the wind so fierce it bent the tall trees, sending showers of leaves and flying branches in every direction. "Time is nearly up!" he heard her shout as before. Then the girl fled, and he could not follow, for his feet were like lead. Not so now, so find her he must. From behind him came a voice.

"They say you are a thief, but they truly have no idea."

It was the voice of the wizened old man. Though he spoke quietly, his words were easily heard over the tempest, laden with irony and sorrow.

Skallagrim did not stop to hear him out but plunged into the forest to find his true love. He raced north, coming at last to a wall of white, a barrier of mist and cloud, just in time to see the beautiful girl pass within. He took a deep breath and followed her in.

The beach again, absent the serenity, for an angry storm front moved on high. The persistent wind that swept the ocean sent out countless white horses that crested and then boomed upon the shore. The old man was there, his white robes and hair billowing in the salty gusts that raced ahead of the front.

"I thought she was to be mine." Skallagrim was weeping, overcome with guilt and sadness. At his feet was the heart drawn in the sand, the lover's name inside. Would it survive the coming storm or be washed away forever by the tide?

"You had but to wait," the old man said kindly. Reaching out, he brushed the tears from Skallagrim's face. "What is done is done, and it cannot be undone."

"It's what I do next that matters. There must be a way to make it right again."

"Then you have hope, and therein lies the answer."

"But surely hope alone will not suffice unless hope itself can become a weapon." Skallagrim looked deeply into the old man's eyes. They were blue and bright. Old though he may be, he was eternally young as well, like a morning that dawned bright and fair at the beginning of all things—a

morning upon which the sun would never set.

*"And who says that hope cannot be a bright sword?" The old man
spoke with great authority, speaking not so much to Skallagrim but to
the storm that raced overhead, his voice brimming with mystery and
majesty. "Until the breaking of the world, upon such weapons we must
rely."*

*He placed his arm around Skallagrim, then turned so they faced the
stormy sea together. "The years will not be kind, Skallagrim. But forget
not the other shore of which I spoke."*

*"I have not," Skallagrim replied. "There's peace there and an end to
suffering."*

*"And there is joy, Skallagrim, a joy untouched by evil. But first, the
storm."*

Lightning flashed, and the dream was gone.

Sorcery might have locked the door to Skallagrim's memory, but
dreams were slowly picking the lock. But the past did not matter
now. Now mattered now.

It was dark, terribly dark. He lay on his back upon slick, hard
stone, his right arm dangling in space. The damp surface beneath
him was sloping toward an unknown void, like the edge of a drain,
but he was not slipping toward it, not yet. He felt around with
his left hand, his fingers coming into contact with wet stone and
something more—his staff.

He heard unsettling sounds, the plop, plop, plop of dripping
water, the low rumble of wind channeling through unseen shafts
and corridors of blackness, the faint metallic clink of chains from
somewhere below.

He remembered his encounter in the vault, knew he had passed
out, and cringed at a sudden onrush of panic. The girl! How much
time had passed? The liches! Where were they? His head was a
knotted fist of agony. He was drifting away again, but he managed to
hover on the grey border between delirium and painful wakefulness.

Terminus was at his side, rattling in its sheath, humming with
life. Only a moment before, something else had stirred him to

consciousness. It was a voice, a fell voice in the dark. He heard it again, like a sickly gasp from hell.

"Who are you?"

He could neither move nor answer. Then he realized the question had not been directed at him, for another voice answered, strong, unwavering, and defiant.

"I am the Angel of the Sword. You shall not prevail!"

"Who are you?" Again the challenge from a raspy voice, full of arrogance yet tempered by a fierce curiosity. It was accompanied by a fresh blast of chilling air that blew from the empty space beneath Skallagrim's sword arm.

"Who are you?"

"I am the Angel of War. You shall not prevail!" Was that the voice of Terminus, speaking aloud? The sword was pulsing in its scabbard, throbbing with awareness. It had to be.

Skallagrim could not tell if he had overheard an actual conversation or passed again into strange dreams. He could not wake himself entirely, but he could fully sense his own body, his damp clothing, the uncomfortableness of the knapsack upon which he lay.

The voice of the fell spirit was coming from somewhere deep below him. When it spoke, reality teetered on the edge of a waking nightmare. He felt vertigo and the terrifying sensation that his soul was being dragged into the pit by unseen hands.

A pit!

Yes, he was lying next to a pit. Terminus was warning him, connecting with his mind on a level he could not understand. He lay on the brink of a terrible shaft, a deep cavity in the tortured earth, a prison wherein lay a spirit of death. It was shackled there deep, deep below, its chains forged by dwarven smiths of a bygone age. Spells were upon it too, this monstrous prisoner of the pit, crafted by mighty wizards who had served the king beyond the Southern Void.

Terminus showed him more, though there was no comfort in the visions that flooded his mind. This abominable thing that spoke from below was the very reason Fort Vigilance had been built. Terminus, the sentient sword that fell from the sky, knew the tale and comprehended the tragedy.

Words formed in Skallagrim's mind, words intended only for him, spoken by a voice both savage and fair. *"Vigilance be damned! Foolish knights to think they could sit upon death's emissary, to keep watch upon the incarnation of cosmic terror. They kept its body in the pit, but its thought could reach beyond. It listened to their plans, and it crawled into their dreams. It leached their will and robbed them of sanity. This is no wraith, no liche, and no sorcerer. This is a demon—a son of perdition! Beware!"*

"Who are you?" the demon asked again. Skallagrim heard the sound of great chains dragging across rocks far below. This time the question had been put forth with force.

"I am the Angel of His Wrath! You shall not prevail!" Terminus remained recalcitrant.

From the pit came silence, contemplation, subtle regard. Skallagrim could feel the thing's mood changing. It had sensed tremendous power from the sword and knew not what to make of it. There would be a change of tack when next it spoke.

"Who are you?" A gentle sigh, nothing more.

"I am the Angel of the Sword. You shall not prevail!"

Silence, a moment only.

"Angel?" The demoniac voice was conciliatory now, conveying no sense of death or strife, just the kindly voice of a lonely thing, longing for companionship. *"I could have said as much of myself once. Now I'm but this lowly thing consigned to darkness."*

Silence from Terminus.

"We are both prisoners, are we not?"

"I am the Sharp Edge of the High King's Wrath. You shall not prevail!"

"High King?" The voice was amused though still calm and kindly.

Skallagrim felt an itch in his head, followed by a willingness to sympathize with the voice. There was guilt too, as if he had been caught eavesdropping, for it knew he was listening now.

"High King, you say?"

Nothing from the sword.

"I suppose you have answered my question. For now I know who you

are."

Terminus said nothing in return, and Skallagrim wondered if it had revealed some vast secret when it spoke of the High King.

"It is such an angry thing, is it not?" This was addressed to Skallagrim. *"Am I due no respect in my own house, no deference from this Angel of the Sword, as it calls itself? Evil are the days indeed that such threats—such malice—should be poured out upon the weak by a thing so mighty."*

The speaker from the depths was much aggrieved. Such a poor and pitiable thing down below left to rot, entitled to little else than the dismal protection of dank stone walls and the peaceful oblivion of unending darkness. If nothing else, it could spend its time in rest and quiet contemplation whilst it waited for the doom at the end of the world. But now even its rest had been disturbed. Yes, the unjustly imprisoned captive had been deprived of even that.

"I am nothing." A whisper, barely heard. *"An insubstantial shadow . . . meaningless . . . no threat."* The voice faded like vapor, the final sigh of the dying.

Skallagrim's heart softened, filled with compassion for the mysterious prisoner whom he regarded now as something of a kinsman. Surely a voice this kind, this amiable, could not belong to a monster. No! What lay below was a victim, a creature wronged and maltreated. It deserved far better than half answers and impudence from Terminus.

It was impossible to tell how much time passed. Thirty minutes? An hour? All was silence, interminable silence.

Then a sigh from below, as tenuous as gossamer. *"Weak. No threat."*

Silence once more, but for the quiet lapping of water in some dark pool, the muted rumble of wind as it wound its way through lightless burrows, and the incessant dripping. Skallagrim strove to move his legs, but they would not respond. He reached out to touch his staff for reassurance, but his fingers were growing numb from the cold and wet.

There was movement below. He could sense the spirit's mind, alert, thinking, calculating.

"Great sword, hear me out, for I am but a prisoner in a hole, undeserving

of wrath while you are, after all, a prisoner of iron, sentenced to serve out your term by the same twisted mind that put me here. Poor us, to be treated thus." Chilling air was rising from the pit, and with it, the smell of rotting meat.

"*Poor us, to be treated thus,*" it sang whimsically. "*That rhymes!*" It laughed, and it was not a pleasant sound, more like a death rattle, the snickering of a demented mind. "*But I speak a truth. Do you not see it? For I can, and clearly. Some might say . . .*" It hesitated as if searching for words. When they came, they seemed full of understanding, of empathy. "*Some would say you suffer a fate worse than I.*"

Silence. Waiting.

"*Here is truth. You shall not prevail!*" The voice of Terminus was like the whisper of finely honed steel sliding into a scabbard. Having said its peace, it would lend power to its wounded wielder now, wasting no further speech upon this demon.

For several moments there was silence, though Skallagrim could hear his heart pounding in his ears. He was helpless, unable to move, his breathing labored.

A flash of memory—gone as quickly as it came. There was something he was supposed to remember but could not. The consciousness in the pit took notice of this abrupt mental effort and turned its attention toward him.

"*You are a thief, are you not?*" The voice was gentle, nearly purring with inquisitiveness. "*I have sensed it in your thoughts, though why have you come here?*"

Skallagrim would not answer, dare not. He was not even sure he could speak without triggering an agonizing coughing spell.

"*Was it the girl of whom you dreamed? The merry lass with the golden curls? Does Forneus have her? Is she why you came?*"

A fresh wave of vertigo sent Skallagrim's head drumming, painful enough to block out all other hurts. Though he would not answer, he could not suppress the pain at hearing the insidious voice speak lightly of the innocent girl. He pitied it no more, was spellbound no more, for the resolve of Terminus had broken the thing's brief hold over his mind. Still, two wills were striving within his thoughts, one that would probe his dreams to seek out a weakness and another more noble, more savage, that would save him if it could.

He tried hard to block thoughts of the blue-eyed girl but could not.

"So that's it! You think he has the girl!" Again, the sound of chains far below, the shifting of a hideous bulk that slithered about in sunless waters. *"I'm certain I could help you if you would speak with me. I cannot hurt you; they made sure of that."* The voice was insistent, full of care. *"Let me help, friend, for I feel a great affinity for you. We have both shared such hardships, have we not?"*

When Skallagrim refused to answer, the thing below became restless. There was furtive movement, the purposeful rattling of chains, and the obscene splashing of foetid waters in the dark.

Then it was quiet.

"I have just looked into the mind of your sorcerer, and I can tell you about the girl if you want. You just need to ask me."

Not a word from Skallagrim, though he could not hide his panic—or his intense interest in what the demon was saying.

"Forneus is mine, you know? I slept for many years until he came. But he unlocked the fort, you see, intruded upon my dreams, and woke me up." A pause, then a wicked snicker. *"Such horrid, exquisite dreams I dreamt in the long years, immemorial. Dreams of blood, of chaos, of rending, and of slashing. But Forneus came."* Another pause as if waiting for a response from Skallagrim that would not come. *"I have been at him for a long, long time. He is quite mad, so it's no wonder he has led you on this merry chase. And all for . . ."* The demon left the sentence hanging in space, torturing Skallagrim with silence.

"What? All for what?" Skallagrim's words rasped from his throat, but he had to know, for he loved her.

"There you are!" Laughter now, like the tittering of an amused little girl, a precocious brat who had just scored a point in a silly game. *"Well, friend . . ."* It tried to speak, but demented laughter overcame the attempt, for the demon had indeed scored a point. The game being played, however, was like that of a cat toying with a frightened mouse. *"I am sorry. Please forgive me. It's just that you have*

come so far, and when you think about it, it's just . . . well, you must see my point."

"What about the girl?" Skallagrim was sobbing now, begging. He placed an image of the girl in his mind and focused. He needed her above all else. His eyes were tearing as he tried to rouse his body to action, but he could not manage it. He was impotent, helpless, and ashamed. But she was somewhere just above him, waiting to be rescued. "Tell me what you know!" He tried again to move, to rise from the floor, but the best he could do was flail his arms feebly.

"You're asking the right question. It is all about that girl, is it not?" He heard a straining of chains down below, a tumultuous commotion of effort. *"I will tell you all I know."* Skallagrim heard water lapping against the pit's slimy walls *"But I need to come closer to tell you. I am coming up now."*

Skallagrim got his fingers moving, stretched out his left hand, and grabbed his staff, willing it to give light. It obliged, but like before, its radiance only revealed horror. He was lying next to a gaping wound in the earth about fifty feet in diameter. Ancient people had lined its edge with flat stones, damp and glistening, but the pit itself had been gnawed and hollowed out by the nameless things of the dark in eons past.

An arm was coming up out of the pit, long and sinewy. It looked vaguely human but was too long to be that, and the skin was ashen grey. Up it came, slick with slime, as straight as a fleshy lance. Then it flopped down, mercifully, on the other side of the pit from where Skallagrim lay. The livid fingers began to creep along the edge of the pit, searching.

"I know you're here somewhere," the voice teased. *"They left me just enough slack so I could come up and have a look now and then. Though, as you must have noticed, there is little to see."*

Skallagrim watched the horrid hand, dreading its touch. It would drag him into the pit if it found him.

"Poor Forneus. He knew I was here, right here beneath him. Can you imagine that? But he never bothered to check on me. Never inquired as to my well-being. Couldn't be bothered, I suppose." The demon's voice

was a mocking wind from the deep, a voice from the grave, from beyond realms of sanity.

"*So I ate his mind!*"

A surge of fresh horror came at Skallagrim—wave upon wave of relentless panic. He strove clumsily, desperately, to drag Terminus from its scabbard, but he did not have the strength.

"*I have been dancing down the dark halls of Straker's head too, searching out his secrets, peering into every shadowy corner. There are some juicy morsels there, I can tell you. Absolutely obsessed with torture and killing. It was shocking, and coming from me, that's saying a lot! So much blood on that one's hands!*" Skallagrim recoiled inwardly at the mention of the wolfish man who had shredded his face. The demon picked up on the acknowledgment. "*Yes, you know him. I will eat his mind next. You, however, you I will not eat!*"

The pallid, waxen hand was closer now, the cadaverous fingers probing every inch of the ledge. Their long, yellow nails clicked upon the wet stone like a bizarre spider, dancing a lunatic *pas seul*.

"*I'll just bring you down here with me, and then we will have a long talk about all those missing memories of yours. And about that girl too. I will tell you all about her, oh yes!*"

Skallagrim tried to roll over but only succeeded in sliding closer to the pit. Now his head was hanging over, and he could see fully, the dead thing in the pit.

"*I told you, I just want to help you. I insist!*"

He could see far below, too far for mortal eyes but not too far for the bearer of Terminus. Archon! He had seen its like beneath Archon, the Dreaming City. He could remember it now. It ate minds. It had told him as much! That thing had been dead too, most assuredly. But Skallagrim had just learned an awful but valuable truth. *The dead can hurt you! They can crawl back from hell and wound you over and over and over and over . . .*

He shut his eyes tight, refusing to look. To see it again would be to sear his soul. He conjured an image of the blue-eyed girl and held to it.

"*Oh, that lovely girl,*" it taunted. "*Such pretty eyes! Eyes of blue!*"

Pretty blue eyes! Eyes of blue! Blue, blue, blue . . ." It gibbered on and on as the spidery fingers poked and prodded the damp stone only inches from Skallagrim's face. They would find him in a second. *"Blue moon shining in the dark, dark night. She danced in the twilight, blue eyes bright. Along came a thief, and before he knew, she'd stolen his heart with those eyes of blue."* The fingers, having danced in time to the rhyme, paused in their searching. *"You like my little poem? I swear that girl is all you think about. Those blue eyes just pulled you in, didn't they?"*

"Blue!" Skallagrim shouted, the word leaping from his tongue, for the demon's insane, singsong prattle about the girl's eyes had jogged his memory at last. *"Blue!"* He remembered the words: *"Should you find yourself terribly injured again or up against some foe you feel is beyond you or your terrifying sword there, drink this potion—all of it."* Erling's vial of Caeruleum was in the pocket of his baldric, full of the glowing blue potion that might just save him.

He fumbled at the pocket and managed to get the vial. In desperation, he opened it and drank the contents in one gulp. He rolled himself away from the pit, trying to get free of the hand before it could locate him.

Almost immediately, Skallagrim felt the potion working, rousing him, filling him with vitality. He tried to stand, but the hand had found him, the grey fingers wrapping around his ankle with hideous strength.

"Oh, didn't you have somewhere to be before midnight?" It laughed wildly, the harsh braying echoing throughout the dungeon. *"It must be nine o'clock by now. Ticktock! Ticktock!"*

CHAPTER THIRTY-ONE

"My cousin is dead, Forneus, devoured by your freakish watchdog!" Straker was furious, having witnessed the grisly death of his kin only moments before. His eyes, dark rimmed from lack of sleep, bored holes into the sorcerer's as they faced off on either side of the great slab table. The poor wide-eyed creature between the two, Forneus's experiment, thrashed and tugged at its bonds. It mewled, its swollen tongue trying pitifully to form words. "Can you not just give it some water so it will shut the hell up? I can't think with this racket, and you need me thinking!"

"You dare to speak to me thus? In my own hall?"

Straker looked behind him at the gaping door, dreading the blackness that yawned behind it, feeling the threat of the unknown that called to him from somewhere just beyond. He was not so sure it was the sorcerer's hall after all. Something else ruled there.

"Would it hurt to just give it a drink of something?" Straker had to shout to be heard over the creature's pleas. "Or can we take our conversation elsewhere?" He looked with disgust upon the monster. Was it, at least the better parts of it, not General Arne Grímsson, the dreaded Axeman of Urk? Though horribly mangled, the face bore a faint resemblance. The battle-axe leaning near the door was so like the one he had carried to fame and glory in a hundred battles. So, yes, it had to be him. Of course, the wretch seemed to have been assembled from a number of components, some human, some animal, and others mechanical. He shuddered to think of the bloody chaos that would ensue if the creature somehow freed itself.

The sorcerer slapped the creature. "Shut up, damn you!" He turned to Straker. "No, I will not. It does not require water; it requires a right arm! And that is something you promised me and have failed to deliver!"

The monster was whimpering now, its face slick with tears.

"I've been over this with you." Straker fought to calm his voice, but the gaping door was beckoning, and he struggled to think of anything else. "The storm, the sword, the mob. You were there! You know!" He failed to mention he had been paid to delay the thief's capture, paid by Griog'xa, the dangerous sorcerer of Archon, chief rival of Forneus Druogorim. He cursed himself inwardly. *This is what I get for riding the fence between two madmen. A fistful of coins, yes, but I'm trapped in hell with a lunatic!"*

"Griog'xa!" Forneus spit the name as if it were poison on his tongue, causing Straker to flinch. Had the sorcerer just read his thoughts? He was only mildly relieved when Forneus continued, clearly unaware of his duplicity.

"I had assurances from Griog'xa that the thief would follow us down the Gorge Road, but that had to be him down in Orabas, right? You heard the sword, that scream! What else could it be?"

"I wish I could forget it. But yes, that was the sword."

"But is it possible? I mean, no one should have been able to come up from the south. No one should have gotten past Pagarna!" The sorcerer was pacing now. In a dramatic show of frustration, he swept his arm through a row of beakers, sending them smashing to the floor, causing a fresh bout of wailing from the creature. "The wilderness should have killed him. The ghouls should have torn him to bits. And Pagarna? Damn that thief, the undulate cannot be defeated."

"But it was," Straker said darkly.

"You think he's still alive, this thief? This Skallagrim?"

"We shall have to wait and see." The words came in a throaty rasp, like the low snarl of a wolf seeking dominance over another.

"Do you think he can get in here?" The sorcerer was incredulous, his plans coming to ruins before his eyes. "If so, then double the guard."

Straker dealt the sorcerer a withering stare. "What guard? My men have been bought out from under me. I have two cousins left of the three, and they are wasted on the front door where Skallagrim cannot enter anyway." His eyes darted suspiciously to the dungeon door, which was ajar—full of threat. "It's likely he will search for another way in. Something you've missed." He looked back at the sorcerer and crossed his arms, determined that his point would get through. "There is no guard, Forneus! Just you, me, and the two out front."

"Then what's left? You can't let him get near me with that blade." Forneus shuddered. Terminus, he believed, was the only sword in all of Andorath that could slay him. He had paid the heavy price of his miserable soul for such might, such invulnerability, but it would all be for nothing if Skallagrim was not stopped. It had taken all of his necromantic power to call the creature upon the table back from death. Even sorcery might not save him, for he had expended much of his power in bringing forth the undulate and keeping his horrible experiment alive on the slab. Even Straker did not know how weak he was becoming.

"I'll keep him off you; have no fear. But you have to accept it; we're on our own, Forneus." Straker was doing his best to explain, but the sorcerer's glaring eyes were full of accusation, of disappointment.

Straker slammed a fist on the table, barely missing one of the monster's fearfully muscular legs, causing it to flinch. "Don't look at me that way! There's nothing else we can do, Forneus. It is what it is."

"Why do people say that? Of course it is what it is! What else could *it* be?" The sorcerer shot Straker a warning glance. The wolfish assassin made to speak, but Forneus cut him off. "Never mind. It's just something Griog'xa once said in a letter." He took a deep breath to calm himself. "Anyway, there is a contingency in place. Just follow my instructions."

Let the thief come! Without him, his experiment was useless, the sacrifice to Balor impossible. *So yes, let him come!* For the sorcerer had one final weapon in mind, possibly the greatest in his depleted arsenal, one lingering hope, one last dart to fling at his naïve, young foe. Guile!

Nightfall in Archon, the Dreaming City. No one dreamed though, no one but the dead thing far below the tower of Griog'xa. Even Old Tuva could get nothing past him.

Dreams had eluded her for over a hundred years. Of course, no dream worth dreaming would dare cross the threshold of her corrupt and deviant mind.

No, she did not dream. Instead, Tuva—the hag daughter of Swanhild and the twin sister of Griog'xa—sulked. And she plotted. The thief had stolen her necklace of talismans and charms, so she pouted with a putrid, cankered lip and schemed with a brain twisted by a life of evil and the blackest witchcraft.

As the sun set red in the north, Tuva came out of her box of dirt to creep through the vast labyrinth of tunnels beneath the city. She was out and about now, stalking the shadows in the back alleys of Archon's warren of decrepit dwellings and leaning towers.

Vampiric, ravenous—she must feast on blood before all else. Then she would do something she had not done in ages. Old Tuva would slip out of Archon, take to the fields and forests of Andorath, always careful to avoid the larger towns and major thoroughfares, and she would find Skallagrim. And finding him, she would do such things to him, things only a mind debased and eternally broken could conceive.

Her charms and talismans were everything to her, the sharp, jagged bits of metal, the runes, the silver chain—all of it magical, granting her unholy power and demoniac, vital force. Without it, she would wither. It was already happening. She could feel it.

For the first time in an age, Tuva was worried. Short of finding the damned thief and retrieving what was stolen from her, she would likely perish. She had nowhere to turn.

Old Tuva's brother, Griog'xa, would not help her. He allowed her free reign of the dank tunnels beneath his tower, for he pitied her. But she had never laid eyes on him. His instructions to her came through mysterious means, his assistance, never.

Her mother, curse her! No help there! The nymph, repulsed by Tuva's frightful countenance, had abandoned her at birth. To think of her was to be reminded of beauty denied, of revenge unsatisfied. Mayhap she would seek her out as well one day. Then there would be a reckoning.

The hag's father, the once-powerful Knight of the North, Balor, was long dead and burning in hell. True, the sorcerers of Andorath planned to raise him up, but that would not happen soon. Old Tuva, the conniving hag, was on her own.

"Erling Hizzard," she hissed. He would know where Skallagrim was, and he owed her many favors—at least that is how she saw it. Find the smuggler, and the thief would be close. That should not be too hard. And it best not be, for her power was ebbing. For that reason, she must be quick. Find the thief, take back her charms, and make him pay!

Woe to the unlucky villages she would come across on her journey. Oh, there would be weeping and gnashing of teeth, to be sure. Farmers would wake to find their beasts slaughtered and mothers to find empty cribs, their shrieks piercing the dawn skies like sweet music. They would learn fast to lock their doors and bar their windows come nightfall, for Old Tuva was coming. And Old Tuva was always hungry.

A rare moonbeam found its way through the thick canopy of a strangely glowing forest to fall upon a comely lass. Her hair, but for a stray strand of green, was as black as night, glistening wet where it fell upon her slender shoulders. Her skin was as white as porcelain, her eyes as green as an emerald sea. To peer too deeply into them would be to drown in splendor.

She danced upon a mossy sward, her feet skipping over slick stones. She splashed in the cold waters of a mountain stream, then went gliding among the trees, ghostlike, her toes barely touching the ground.

Swanhild cared not for a missing brooch, for she fancied herself in love. She had fallen under the spell of the unwitting thief and could think of little else but him. Skallagrim had not stolen the garnet brooch, merely taken it as a memento of their magical night together. It was the act of an infatuated, star-crossed lover, not a petty thief. Either way, she cared not.

And the girl Skallagrim sought? Why, he did not even know her name! It was unlikely he would find her in Fort Vigilance. Even if he did find and somehow rescue her, they were both young. The fire of their love might smolder for a while, but time would invariably snuff out the blaze. If not, then Swanhild would kill her.

As the object of her misplaced affection slid precariously toward the brink of a lightless pit, subjected to the taunts of the demonic prisoner of Fort Vigilance, unable to move and struggling to breathe, Swanhild sang a fair song. She swayed back and forth to the rhythm of music that played only in her pretty head.

In faerie forest 'neath the moon
As silver stars hung, shimmering
There danced the lovely Endereth
As light in shadows glimmering
A nightingale did sing its song
From a lofty oaken tower
Her gown the moon made milky white
As starlight seemed to shower
To make a helm of diamond light
Fit for an elven princess
The night did weave a starry crown
To grace her golden tresses
On that night fair Elrenn strode
With armor made of sunlight
The shadows fled before his feet
To make the very air bright
The elven blade Anoniel
Was hung upon his side
His shield was forged by dwarven hands
And made of dragonhide

She sang of an actual tryst, of two lovers who had met many

years ago, a tale called forth from the dark recesses of her mind. As the song unfolded, she imagined herself to be the fair elven princess and Skallagrim the noble knight in armor, as bright as the sun. She wrapped her slender arms about herself as if he was holding her. Then she danced with her imaginary partner, twirling about the moonlit glade, reveling in prurient fantasies.

That the tale was true was a thing known only to her. Rather than think of how she knew it to be genuine—of how she had spied on the two lovers, of how she would later thwart their passions, haunting Endereth until her dying day—she thought only of the joy of romance newly discovered and of lust as savage as war—as greedy as hunger.

> *Elrenn was a warrior proud*
> *Who'd wandered long and weary*
> *Into the elven glade, he crept*
> *To see a vision eerie*
> *He beheld fair Endereth*
> *And heard the nightbird calling*
> *Her beauty snared him as with chains*
> *His heart for her was falling*
> *Endereth did make a spell*
> *To draw proud Elrenn to her*
> *He caught her up in mighty arms*
> *To hold her fast and woo her*
> *Then dancing there in elven wood*
> *Twain, for a time, were one*
> *Both night and day, the moon and sun*
> *As spells about them spun*

She was obsessed. It had happened before, countless times to countless unfortunates. From stray wanderers like Skallagrim to proud knights and gentle poets. There had been warriors aplenty, painters, sculptors, and even a wretched tavern keep who had given her the shelter of a room one stormy night. But she pushed these men from her thoughts, for most were long dead, and all had been shallow affairs. Skallagrim was different.

She sighed, conjuring a memory of the thief. How he had looked at her, the hunger in his eyes. The sword was a problem, of course, but she cast it from her mind. There was nothing but the feel of Skallagrim against her body, the touch of his lips upon hers.

The nymph was so glad she had not made love to him there by his campfire, for now the expectation of their eventual pairing was exquisite—maddeningly so. And that, she decided, would happen at a time of her choosing.

She paused in her dancing to look upon the rushing river where she had made her home for many years.

Too long have I dallied in the forest whilst the great events of the world unfolded without me. Too long have men known the peace of existence without Swanhild to direct their warring. Andorath has grown complacent while I have danced beside the cold pools. The sorcerers have grown haughty while I have run like a deer beneath the trees. Too many years. Too much time. I shall go now into the world and shake it by its roots, devouring the unwary like a beast, drowning the vainglorious in a sea of blood and sorrow.

And then I shall find Skallagrim, and he will love me until my grief is quelled, and the horrors of time are washed away.

While some, for reasons of lust or revenge, had set out to find Skallagrim, and others waited in dread for Skallagrim to come to them, others simply waited.

For Erling and Hartbert, the day was nothing if not utter tedium. Though bored, the long hours spent in hiding had been fraught with apprehension, for the pair had seen no sign of Skallagrim. Two days they had waited, with little excitement except for the undulate's dawn retreat. But that had been hours ago, and the shocking terror of that bloody event had faded like a mist.

They hoped Skallagrim had survived the encounter, but they did not know. In the hours immediately following the monster's passage upriver, Erling had seemed optimistic. "He'll find a way in, mark my words. Skallagrim lives!"

But the weary hours had passed with no sight of the thief or any alarm from the fort that might indicate he had gained access. The two remaining guards, Straker's cousins, had forsaken their hiding places and merely stood watching upon the bridge, apparently as bored with their vigil as Erling and Hartbert were with theirs. At least the guards could stretch their legs. There was no such comfort for Skallagrim's stalwart allies, however. They dared not show themselves yet and so remained hiding in the same cramped space behind the rocks as they had the day before.

Erling had quietly though persistently complained about a pain in his back throughout the day, his grumbling wearing on Hartbert's nerves. The giant, still nursing the burn on his hand from touching Terminus, kept his troubles to himself, mostly.

As the dismal sun dropped behind the Chimney Tops, he finally voiced his concerns. "Mister Hizzard, if you're right, the girl dies at midnight. We're about six hours away."

"There's not a thing we can do, Hartbert." Erling motioned toward the bridge. "If we rush in prematurely, one of those guards will alert Straker, what? Wait for some sign that he's in."

"Such as?"

Erling shrugged. "How should I know? Just keep an eye on those two. If they make a rush for the front door, we'll know something has happened. In the meantime, we must be patient and stay put."

Despite his warning, as the hour grew late, Erling and Hartbert stealthily made their way closer to the bridge, hiding in the shadows just beside a stone abutment. They were close enough to hear the guards talking, bemoaning the loss of their brother to the monster.

Hartbert kept a wary eye on the pair but also took note of his partner's jittery behavior. Erling was no coward, so it was not their current predicament that had him perturbed. Of course, if he asked him about it, Erling would only allude to his vague, scholarly pursuits in matters pertaining to sorcery and black magic. Dwelling on such things would fray the nerves of any man, Hartbert admitted. Still, something else was going on. Hartbert could tell.

For one, he knew his employer desperately wanted inside Fort Vigilance. Erling had never spoken of what exactly he expected to find, but Hartbert assumed he cared more for that than for Skallagrim's well-being or the captive inside. It was not a comforting thought.

For another thing, two days ago, Erling's spies and agents had brought news that obviously troubled him. War was brewing in the north, and Erling wanted to be in the thick of it. There must be some profitable venture in the offing, but who knew what other pots he had his hands in. Nothing of much import was ever conveyed to the giant, so he had to content himself with guesses and keep his ears open. Hartbert's job was to keep Erling alive and well, so he would do just that, even if Erling had "damned" his own soul.

As the hour grew late, Erling's optimism vanished like a ghost at daybreak. He tugged at a gold chain dangling from the pocket of his traveling frock, revealing a bejeweled pocket watch that had been a gift of an unsuspecting aristo's wife back in Archon. "Nine o'clock," he whispered. "Our boy is pushing his luck, what?"

"Shhhh! Listen!" Hartbert's eyes grew wide. "Do you hear that?"

"It's muffled, like it comes from far away," Erling replied. "But I believe it's coming from beneath the fort there, eh? That's the scream of Terminus, no mistaking it."

"Look!"

From the fort's tower, a window was flung open, and a bright light flared from within, silhouetting Straker's wolfish form.

"Get in here now!" he shouted down to his cousins. "The two had heard the eldritch shriek of the sword and stood gaping at Straker, their backs to the bridge. "The fox is in the henhouse, boys. Now we earn our money!"

Hartbert was beside himself, ready to jump. "We attack now, surely?"

"One second more, you restless ogre." Erling placed a hand of warning upon Hartbert's shoulder as he watched the window, waiting for Straker to leave. He obliged, slamming the shutters and vanishing within, heeding the frantic call of the sorcerer from somewhere within.

"Now?" Hartbert pleaded.

"Yes, yes! By all means!" Drawing his sword, Erling leapt from behind the abutment to lead a bloodthirsty charge across the bridge. His own blade scraping from its scabbard, Harbert was right behind him.

CHAPTER THIRTY-TWO

"Hell's teeth!" Having heard the otherworldly scream coming up from the tenebrous depths below the fort, Straker wheeled to face the dungeon door.

"The thief is here!" Forneus stepped away from the door as if any second Skallagrim might come bounding through with Terminus held high.

Straker stared into the darkness that radiated from just beyond the hated door, which resisted any attempt to keep it shut. He knew that behind its stubborn frame was a wooden stair leading down into a lightless dungeon, a maze of tunnels, corridors, and a crypt. He knew there was a pit there as well, and in it, a prisoner. Now, beyond belief, a thief with a grudge and a screaming sword was down there as well. He should have ignored Griog'xa's instructions and killed the man when he had the chance. The paranoid theories of Forneus Druogorim had proven correct.

"You don't say?" Straker snapped.

All the long, maddening hours spent placating, reassuring, and reasoning with the nervous sorcerer had worn him down. He wanted out of this mess. But every time he considered walking out on Forneus, his mind was inevitably drawn back to the door and to the whisperer in the darkness beyond. Such promises it had made. He dreaded the sound of it but was fascinated by it as well. Those whispers, like the last exhalation of a dying man, had thrilled him, filling his mind with visions both ghastly and grotesque. Of late he had taken to the bottle, drinking more and more, pretending that wine would dull the horror as his confidence waned and his thoughts turned morbid.

Straker was a killer with a killer's heart, but the whisperer in the dark was death itself. *"Come down and dream with me, my son,"* it had said. *"Cast aside your doubts and fears. Come down, confess all to me, and I shall make you whole, for I am the Father of Death."*

He had let it prowl about the darkest corners of his mind, and Straker's mind had plenty of those. Like long-buried coffins, one by one the vaults of his innermost secrets were ripped open. Now all the skeletons were out and about, running down the corridors of his conscience, dancing mad spirals in the ballroom of his murderous heart. Phantoms all! Grim reminders of each and every man, woman, and child he had robbed of life.

Staring at the door earlier that afternoon, Straker had experienced a rare moment of clarity, the faintest glimmer of self-awareness, and shuddered. A terrifying realization had reached out with clawed fingers, threatening to choke the life from him. For as the skeletons wheeled in macabre circles around his imaginings, each one leering accusingly as it passed by, he knew there was a price to pay for a life of sadism. Straker grasped with perfect, soul-searing certainty that when the candle of his life flickered its last, and the haunted house of his spirit grew dark, what was left of him was bound for hell.

"Ignore them," the voice soothed. *"Just come to me. I shall open the door to your mind, and we will let those nasty dead things dance right out. They shall trouble you no more!"* It snickered, and Straker knew what he was dealing with, knew but did not care. *"They'll have to go! You see, we simply must make room for more!"*

The thing in the pit could not be ignored. It had the answers, all of them. It could very well be a god. If eternal hellfire awaited Straker, then he had damned well better make the most of his remaining years upon the earth. He was still on the right side of the grass, as he liked to say. With a god on his side, he could do holy work, bloody work. He could return to cold and distant Yod, claim its cities and wield its armies. Hell, he could carve his mark upon a thousand faces, a thousand Skallagrims.

"Yes!" the voice urged. *"With an army, you can do much!"*

Indeed! It will be so! Then he would rape, pillage, plunder, and murder till the lamentations of Archon's wretched people rose to a deafening crescendo, till the streets of Ophyr and Urk ran red with blood.

"Everyone has the power to kill," the dead voice had explained with a nonchalance that shocked even Straker. *"But most are afraid to do it. The fearless, like you, control life itself, and he who controls life is a god!"*

A god? Straker liked the sound of that. So, he would not be leaving Fort Vigilance anytime soon. Even if the fiasco of Forneus and this cursed thief could be dealt with, Straker would face his fear and open wide the black door, descend the horrid stairs into unfathomable darkness, and acquaint himself with the god of death, the whisperer in the dark. The thought both excited him and filled him with terror. He drained a glass of red wine, his fourth so far that night.

"Straker? Are you listening?"

"What?" Straker was jarred from his vile musings. "Oh, yes. I'll attend to it immediately." Forneus had been shouting, demanding he fetch the two remaining cousins, adding their swords to his. All the while, the poor monster upon the table had thrashed about, pleading for water in its pathetic way.

As the two rushed from the laboratory vault, taking the steps to the main hall two at a time, Straker gasped a question. "You're certain of your plan? He'll fall for it?"

The sorcerer laughed, resolved at last. "Yes, I am, and yes, he will."

CHAPTER THIRTY-THREE

Not long after, the thief in question was making his way up a flight of wooden stairs toward a door that, unbeknownst to him, had refused every attempt made to keep it shut. The sight of it had inspired hope in Skallagrim, for blessed light spilled from beyond its threshold. At last he was leaving the dark dungeons beneath Fort Vigilance and entering the castle proper, albeit the lower level.

It had been a fight, to be sure. The battle with the undulate was unexpected, its spores a poison to his constitution. It had thrown him hard onto the ground, bruising him badly. By all rights, he should be dead from the encounter.

The eerie confrontation with the demonic prisoner in the pit had been a close call as well. Without Erling's blue potion, he would surely be dead by now, or worse. The Caeruleum had been a last-minute gift given to Skallagrim in the heated moments after the bloody skirmish outside the walls of Archon three weary days ago. He had nearly forgotten it—had only remembered in the nick of time as the demon's spidery fingers had laid hold of him.

He recalled those last frantic minutes beside the pit and cringed. Vertigo, the grey arm, the spindly, dancing fingers that had grabbed his ankle, pulling him toward the gaping hole—he tried to cast it all from his thoughts but found he could not.

It had seemed like a waking nightmare, but Erling's elixir had acted quickly, coursing like fire through his veins as it burned off the fog that had risen in his brain, igniting his limbs with ensorcelled strength. Then, without a thought, he had drawn Terminus from its beautiful sheath. The savage blade had pulsed with bright light as Skallagrim brought it down, severing the demon's hand from its insanely long arm. It screamed, but the shriek of Terminus was louder, weirder, and more terrifying than even that.

Skallagrim had jumped back from the pit, beyond the reach of the wildly swinging arm. It was already sprouting a new hand, as ghastly as the first. As the scream of the sentient sword faded, echoing off the dungeon's damp walls, reaching even the ears of Erling and Hartbert on the other side of the Pagarna, Skallagrim had heard an evil cackle coming up from the pit.

"You cannot kill me, even with that sword! I'm already dead, you see!"

Skallagrim, who had wisely said little to the demon up until that point, answered. "I have the distinct feeling that there's a second death waiting for you somewhere down the road. And then something worse will follow." The thief moved back several yards from the hole where he was certain the arm could not reach him. Either way, he had no plans to stay and chat. Time was of the essence if he wished to save the girl.

"I'm the Lord of Death, you fool!" The pronouncement was full of threat, but the voice was raspy, thin, and tinged with uncertainty. Skallagrim's words had hit home, slicing through the demon's arrogance like a sword.

Skallagrim was searching his surroundings, illuminating the horrid chamber with his staff. A brick-lined corridor led off in one direction that looked like a way out. "You are lord of nothing. Nothing beyond your pit."

The demon's arm went limp, then withdrew into the darkness of its prison. There was a rattling of chains and what might have been a whimper, a last attempt to keep Skallagrim near. *"Do not leave. I can help you find your memory. I can tell you about the girl."*

"Goodbye," Skallagrim replied. "I don't want your help."

His knapsack was in tatters, soaked, and falling apart. He shrugged it off, spending a moment rummaging through its contents, moving certain smaller items into the pockets of his baldric: a ring, a brooch, a silver necklace hung with jagged charms. *Why did I take these?* Some instinct must have woken inside him with each theft, though he barely recalled the deeds. *Quickhands, indeed! Well, it doesn't matter now.* What little food he could scrounge from the pack was damp and unappealing, but he wolfed all of it down, then kicked the pack aside and made off toward the corridor.

It led him straight to a central hub of sorts, from which ran other passageways, some appearing cavernous by nature while others were lined with brick or stone blocks. A stout ladder hung from an open trapdoor in the chamber's ceiling, and Skallagrim recognized he was in the oubliette of the fort. He bolted up the ladder, stuck his head through the opening, and was rewarded by the sight of the wooden staircase and the lighted doorway. A chilling wind had rushed up and around him from the dungeon below, so he had wasted no time climbing, glad to leave the terror of the demon's prison behind him.

He was in! Despite everything and everyone that had conspired to stop him—raging streams, the temptations of Swanhild, Vathek and his ghouls, the Old Man o' the River, and the dead thing in the pit—he was inside Fort Vigilance, still fit enough to finish what he started. His own inner struggles had been as real as the monsters he had faced—fear as chilling as the winds of the pit, doubt as dark as the endless night of Orabas, self-loathing and guilt that had cut him like the blades in the alley—yet there he was.

Others had helped, to be sure. Erling and Hartbert, even Swanhild. And without Terminus, he would be dead. Determination and stubbornness had played their part as well. But over and above every other consideration—love! The love of a blue-eyed girl. Love had brought him there to that nightmare fort upon the spur of the Craghide, and love would see him through whatever came next.

He had allowed himself the briefest pause to embrace triumph— he deserved that much. But true victory would only come when the girl was safe. To congratulate himself at that moment would have been supremely premature, and Skallagrim knew it. *Onward!*

There was no reason to believe the fell spirit of perdition, but its warning about the late hour could not be ignored. The girl would be sacrificed at midnight, the light fading from those beautiful blue eyes forever. That could be hours or mere minutes away. Unable to bear the thought, Skallagrim pushed it to the back of his mind. *One thing at a time. Stay focused. Keep moving.*

He did keep moving, except for one terrifying moment when a sudden, sickening tightness around his ankle stopped him in his tracks. He looked down in shock. The demon's severed hand was there—still gripping his ankle, grasping at his lower leg with wriggling, flexing fingers, climbing his leg!

Skallagrim knelt and pried the repulsive, spidery hand from his leg, tossing it back the way he had come. It landed with a thump, then scrabbled away, clicking and clacking upon its sharp fingernails. All the while, evil snickering resounded from below.

Ignoring the demon, Skallagrim climbed to the top of the stairs and peeked through the doorway. He was in a hurry, but there was no reason to plunge headlong into another horror or into some devious trap.

But by entering the large vault of Fort Vigilance, the sorcerer's own special chamber of horrors, his sanctum sanctorum, Skallagrim found both—horror and a trap. The latter was not obvious at first. The former, however, thrashed and tugged against its chains on a wooden table in the middle of the large room.

Unaccustomed to the light, Skallagrim blinked rapidly as his eyes tried to adjust. Lanterns sputtered, and mad shadows danced at the corners of his vision like living things. Bubbling alembics and beakers throbbed with eerie luminescence. He tried to take it all in: the huge, deformed skeleton in one corner, the large axe leaning upon the opposite wall, the shadows that fled each time he looked directly at them, blending deceptively with the ordinary objects of the chamber. But his eyes were inexorably drawn to the struggling figure in the center of the vault.

It strained at its chains, trying to get a glimpse of the unknown threat that had entered the room behind it. That it was a monster was not in question. That it was some sort of sorcerous experiment gone wrong was clear as well.

As Skallagrim approached silently, he discerned its basic humanoid form was composed of many disparate parts. Some made sense: a head, an arm, two legs, and so on. Other elements of the creature's design were clearly conceived by a mind bereft of sanity. What had at first glance appeared to be the shredded remains of a rough tunic turned out to be the hide of some diseased beast, cruelly stitched to the creature's torso. The leering, dead skull of some monstrous animal had been crudely attached to one shoulder while a great lump of unidentifiable flesh, ridged with spikes and throbbing with bulging red protuberances, stretched hideously from the creature's left flank and around its back.

It lay piteously upon this ungainly lump, its human head unable to rest upon the table. To Skallagrim, it appeared as if the creature was in great pain. He wondered who or what it had once been and how long it had lain thus.

As the creature was chained and posed no threat, Skallagrim approached for a closer look. Parts of it appeared mechanical in nature, including an assortment of metal gears and greased cogs, all bolted to the monster's frame in various locations. The rest was human. Though it was missing a right arm, its other limbs were powerfully muscled, appearing to have been removed, then reattached and resewn to the trunk.

The creature looked at him fearfully, and by all appearances, was weeping. Skallagrim stared down at it with a troubled brow. The same man responsible for his own face being carved into bloody ruin—Forneus Druogorim—was also behind the living tragedy strapped to the table, and Skallagrim hated him for it.

As he continued to watch the creature, their eyes made meaningful contact, and the thief's heart was wrenched by a sudden, profound pity. For the creature, like him, was a broken thing. Unlike Skallagrim though, it had no hope. Whatever mad scheme Forneus had dreamed up for it would inevitably fail—had already failed. The creature would not survive or, if it did, it would live in excruciating pain for the duration of its miserable life.

Though he wore a brave face, Skallagrim was overcome with sorrow for the creature. *It's still a man*, he thought, *though a man robbed of dignity*. He had been foolish to reckon it a monster. He had thought as much of himself just a day ago, only realizing the truth after confronting the undulate, that grotesque evil that had haunted Orabas. It was evil that made the undulate a true monster, not its appearance, no matter how terrifying.

Maybe that had been Forneus's intent, to cobble together a monstrous aberration and then unleash it upon Andorath. *Likely!* And there was no knowing what this man had done in the life he had known before running afoul of the sorcerer, for something about him bespoke violence. Yet there were no innocent men, so his deeds, whatever they had been, were not enough to convict him, to label him a monster.

The eyes are, indeed, the windows to the soul, for there was something else, an ineffable gleam in this man's eyes that Skallagrim had caught. Imperceptible at first, but the deeper and longer he looked into those sad orbs, the more he saw. There was good inside him. He had known compassion, love, charity, all of those things and more. He might be the victim of a monster, for Forneus Druogorim certainly was that, but the tragic, shattered figure on the table was nothing of the sort.

Skallagrim broke off the glance, his eyes straying to the right side of the man's body. He pondered the missing right arm and then understood the insanity he had fallen prey to. "I think part of me was to be attached to you," he said. The man seemed to comprehend. "Can you speak?"

The creature tried, opening his mouth weakly, revealing a swollen, parched tongue. Nothing came out but a dry, mournful whimper, but he kept his mouth open, his eyes darting to a water bucket and ladle that sat upon a table and then back to Skallagrim.

Precious time was slipping away, but the thief filled the ladle and brought it back to the man without hesitation. He reached a tentative hand beneath the man's head. "This may hurt, but I'm going to try to lift your head a bit, so you can drink." The act of mercy was made difficult due to the hideous lump of flesh that wrapped tumor-like behind the victim, but somehow they managed. He drank all that was offered until, at last, the bucket was empty. He sighed then, his huge eyes filling with a mixture of relief and gratitude.

Skallagrim nodded toward the door on the opposite wall. "Is the sorcerer nearby? Through that door?"

The man nodded, his eyes wide with warning.

"There's someone else in this fort who needs my help. But I promise, if I live, I'll come back." He meant it.

This is it! Through the door and on until he found the girl and freed her. There was no need for a plan beyond that. He would try stealth if time and the situation permitted it. If not, he would carve a bloody path to her with the screaming sword. Forneus and Straker had best not try to stop him!

As Skallagrim made for the door, he took a parting glance at the man and hesitated, for something had caught his eye. Running back to the table, he dropped to one knee.

Sure enough! Rising again, he kicked at one of the bolts that secured the man's chains to the table. It came loose. He kicked again and sent it rattling across the floor. "If you can take that one good arm of yours and work at the chain, I think you can get loose. Just keep working at it, and don't give up."

He headed back toward the door, not realizing he had just freed General Arne Grímsson, the dreaded Axeman of Urk.

CHAPTER THIRTY-FOUR

Skallagrim had only halved the distance to the door when it creaked ominously on its hinges and burst open. In leapt Straker, sword drawn. Behind him loomed Forneus Druogorim, eyes tinged red with the same inner heat that Skallagrim had seen in Archon's Rum Alley. His right hand was outstretched, two fingers pointing ominously at the thief. All the strange, half-seen shadows in the room converged on the doorway like living spirits flocking to their master's defense. But in the chamber behind Forneus were other shadows, those of men. Skallagrim heard their shouts of anger as they cried out for his blood.

His heart in his throat, Skallagrim let his staff fall from his fingers, so he could grab for his sword's hilt. That was as far as he got.

A thick, swirling smoke issued from the sorcerer's hand, and from it shot a black bolt of energy that hit Skallagrim in the chest, knocking him off his feet and robbing him of breath.

He landed with a thud several feet away, skidding into a table full of burbling beakers and sending them crashing to the floor. He tried to rise, stumbled, then gasped for air, finally standing up. He went for his sword again.

"Wait!" Forneus shouted over the unseen mob. The lupine assassin had been circling the wooden slab table, not rushing but carefully closing the distance between himself and Skallagrim. Upon the sorcerer's command, he stopped in his tracks.

"You came for something, I believe?" Forneus asked Skallagrim, eyeing him with disdain.

The sorcerer's spell had left the thief stunned, hammer struck, but he nodded and stayed his hand. The girl's safety superseded every other concern. He kept his hand on his sword's hilt, just the same.

"I understand how you must feel." The sorcerer smiled wickedly, taking a haughty stride into the vault. The bizarre shadows swirled around him, lending him a menacing countenance that even Straker had not anticipated.

"Do you?" Skallagrim's eyes bored holes into the sorcerer's.

The chained man upon the table remained silent but kept a fearful eye on Straker, who loomed over him. Skallagrim could see Straker in his peripheral vision and stayed alert and ready to defend himself should the assassin come closer.

"Of course I do." Forneus took another step into the room. "You want to kill me, and I'm certain you would like to kill Straker too, am I right?"

Skallagrim held his tongue at first, refusing to engage in senseless banter with the fiend, but he finally relented. "I came for the girl."

The sorcerer clapped his hands. "Ah! See there, Straker? He came for *the girl!*"

Straker chuckled. "So that was the lure."

Forneus gave a knowing wink to Straker. "A stroke of genius by Griog'xa that has played into our hands. Observe."

"I won't let you kill her," Skallagrim warned. The vague exchange between his two enemies seemed loaded with meaning, but he could make no sense of it. He needed to get control of the situation fast. "If you have something to say, say it. Otherwise, I'll draw my sword and take my chances."

Forneus waved a dismissive hand. "Humor me, thief. You were told I would sacrifice her tonight at midnight, correct?"

"Yes."

"Too rich," Forneus said to Straker. The two obviously shared an inside joke. Forneus turned back to Skallagrim. "The hour grows late, thief. If you wish for her to live, you will stay your hand."

"I have done just that." But Skallagrim's hand never left the hilt of Terminus, and he was crouched, ready to attack or defend. The sound of the mob had reached a crescendo, but as of yet, none of them had entered the vault.

"You'll not like what I have to say next, but I suggest you listen if you really care about the *girl*."

Skallagrim nodded, then glanced at Straker. The assassin had not budged, but upon making eye contact with Skallagrim, he blanched and looked away. The thief stank from his encounter with the undulate, for he had been showered with the ichor of its wounds. He looked savage, his clothes in tatters, his face, arms, and hands covered in dried blood and filth. Master swordsman or not, there was much about Skallagrim that inspired caution—nay fear—in Straker.

The sorcerer took another ominous step into the vault. "She's just upstairs—still safe, mind you. But thirty elders of Balor's cult are keeping her company. You remember the cult, do you not?"

Skallagrim nodded. "Of course."

"Good. Because thirty more of them are armed to the teeth and crowd the hallway just beyond the door there. I can hold them back for a while, but they expect a sacrifice to take place two hours from now. Frankly, I don't intend to disappoint them. It is the Night of Mog Ruith!"

Scowling, his eyes wide, Skallagrim gripped the hilt of Terminus, his knuckles turning white with the effort.

Forneus took note. "You'll never get past Straker, thief. You'll not get past me either, nor those bloodthirsty demons outside the door there. Certainly, you will not get past the thirty madmen standing guard over that lovely girl." Forneus sneered, taking another step toward Skallagrim. "Get that through your ugly head!"

The odds were impossible, but Skallagrim would not give in—could not give in! Forneus and Straker feared his sword. He would use that fear to his advantage. "Terminus might have something to say about that," he challenged, sliding the blade an inch out of its scabbard. The sentient sword had begun to rattle against his side.

"Have it your way, but I don't fear your sword," Forneus lied. "If by some fluke you manage to dispatch the two of us, you will not get past the cultists, not all of them. Then you and the girl will both die." His tone softened. "But I have an offer for you."

"I'm waiting." A gust of cool air blew past Skallagrim from the open dungeon door, causing him to shiver. The shadows that had swirled around the sorcerer seemed affected too. They withdrew from him, fleeing back to their respective corners, deceptively taking their places as proper shadows of proper objects. Even the noise from the hall seemed to subside, the wrathful cries of the mob growing distant and muffled.

Straker was not immune either. He cowered as the gust chilled him, whipping his long black hair into his eyes. Skallagrim remembered the demon's words, its threat to eat the assassin's mind—its claim to have already eaten the mind of the sorcerer. He knew from where the sudden wind had blown, for it carried with it the scent of death.

The moment passed, but Forneus seemed smaller somehow, less forbidding. The sorcerer had been listening intently to the breeze as if it had carried words—words unheard by the room's three other occupants.

Skallagrim could not know that Forneus had nearly exhausted his sorcery. Still, the fiend held all the cards. Skallagrim must either hear him out or fight. He had already held his peace far longer than he wished.

Forneus straightened, holding his arms out wide. "I promise you the girl will live. But you, thief—you will be the sacrifice!"

Skallagrim slumped, knowing the sorcerer had won the exchange. He cursed himself, for he had not maintained even the pretense of defiance. His body had admitted defeat as easily as his mind.

He had not foreseen this outcome, believing until then that he would somehow find a way to free the blue-eyed girl and escape with her or that he might die bravely in the attempt. Surrendering to Forneus, accepting an offer to trade his life for the girl's, had never occurred to him. If he took the offer, he would be dead shortly, his body later dumped in a pit near Balor's old fortress—Mag Mor, far to the south. Lifeless, dead, cold, stiff, rotting . . .

Of course, he could still fight. Maybe Terminus had powers as yet unrevealed. He might win through with the screaming sword, might save the day.

No. Sixty crazed men, a sorcerer, and an assassin? *Impossible!* If a show of bravery resulted in the girl's death, then everything he had been through would be for nothing. His life would be wasted, and hers along with it.

"How can I trust you'll set her free?"

"You only have my word. I only need one of you. But time is running out, Skallagrim." The noise in the outer chamber grew again. Forneus glanced behind him at the open door, then turned back to Skallagrim, glaring. "Either take my offer, remove your sword, and lean it by the table there, or refuse and draw your blade, taking your chances." Forneus saw the hesitation in Skallagrim's eyes. "We dare not leave her alone with those terrible men for long. No telling what sort of lurid things they're dreaming up for her." He shook his head with feigned disgust. "I saw how they were eyeing her. Did you notice, Straker?"

The assassin nodded. "It was shameful."

Forneus wagged a finger at Terminus. "Now remove your sword, thief."

"I think you'll find the blade is of no use to any but me," Skallagrim boasted. He did not know this for sure, of course, but it would not hurt to mention it. If the sword was all that Forneus really wanted, the rest was show—manipulation.

Forneus seemed to sense Skallagrim's thoughts. "I care nothing for the blade, but you will not need it any longer. Do you accept my offer or not?"

Skallagrim's spirit was caving into the inevitable. Forneus knew his weakness, had nailed him to it by making the offer. The girl could not die, not this way. He would not allow it. Still, he would not give in to death so easily. If Forneus was lying, he would fight to save them both, sword or no sword. "Can I see her?"

"If you hurry. There's time enough to let you watch her ride across the bridge to safety, but you best accept now. Otherwise . . ."

"I accept," Skallagrim said coldly. "Just take me to her."

The deformed victim upon the table began to struggle at his bonds once more, whimpering in protest. Straker, following the sorcerer's example, slapped the man mercilessly, again and again.

"No!" It howled in defiance—the first actual word it had spoken since its necromantic rebirth. Forneus, Straker, and Skallagrim all looked at the poor wretch in disbelief. Straker slapped him again, causing his head to roll toward the thief. The two locked gazes again, and Skallagrim could not help but see the man's eyes were full of warning. His own were dimmed by resignation.

Forneus returned his attention to Skallagrim. "Your sword, remove it."

Skallagrim allowed Terminus to slip back into its sheath. This time there was no eldritch scream, no pulsing of light, no song of battle to pierce his thoughts and lift him on high to glory. His short time with the sentient blade, that meteoric gift from the storm—Cold Star, Black Star, Terminus—had come to an end.

They could not touch Terminus—dare not touch the blade—for it would burn them, and they knew it. Still, Skallagrim had surrendered it and left it leaning against the wooden table. Straker pounced on him immediately, tying his hands behind his back with a short stretch of rope.

The shouting in the hall ceased, and the shadows of the mob faded to nothingness.

Turning with a whirl of his black robes, Forneus strode from the terrible vault. Straker pushed Skallagrim from behind, forcing him to follow.

"So, freak. I told you I'd see your ugly face again, remember?" With Skallagrim's hands tied and the sword well beyond his reach, Straker felt emboldened.

How could Skallagrim forget that awful night of blood, slaying, and death? How could he forget what Straker had done to him, marking his face for life—albeit a short life. "I never said you wouldn't. You think for a second I wasn't going to track you down if only to find the girl?" Skallagrim spat the words at Straker.

Straker laughed. The sound was as cold as winter, as cruel as thorns. "Well, that's the problem." Straker had hold of Skallagrim's bound hands, shoved them painfully up his back, and jerked him to a halt as they topped the stairs leading to the fort's main hall. He leaned over the thief's shoulder, speaking directly into his ear, his breath reeking of stale wine. "There is no girl, you idiot." Straker's voice was venomous. He pushed Skallagrim hard, sending the thief sprawling into the vast hall.

"What do you mean?" Skallagrim could not believe his ears, but the words had the ring of truth, for there was not an ounce of deception in the assassin's voice. And where were the cultists? Had they simply vanished into thin air?

His heart pounded like a drum. Blood rushed to his head, ringing his ears with crippling pressure. "I saw her! Forneus took her in the wagon! I saw the girl!"

Straker, ever the wolf, howled with laughter. "After I carved you up, I thought I'd made a monster of you, a regular devil. But you're neither. You're just a fool!"

"But I saw her!"

"An illusion, just like the cultists you heard back there." Straker had a foot on Skallagrim's back now, pressing him down upon the hard, stone floor.

"What do you mean?" Skallagrim tried to turn his body over, resisting Straker. "I know the girl is real. I know it!"

"You have pitted yourself against sorcerers, fool." Straker kicked Skallagrim, rolling him back over. "I thought we might get to test swords, you and I, but you just handed yourself over, delivered yourself right to his door. Don't you see what you've done? None of it was real!" He laughed then with the cruelty of a demon.

"Get him up, Straker." The sorcerer stood on the far side of a massive oak table in the center of the main hall. Behind him rose a wide stone stairway leading to another level of the fort. An enormous fireplace blazed on the far side of the room. Upon its hearth, shields from a forgotten era leaned one upon the other. Knightly banners from a bygone day thronged the rafters. They were in tatters and blew sadly in the chilly draft that seemed always to blow from the lower levels. Torches sputtered from a dozen sconces on either side of the room, creating shadows that writhed like tormented souls. Painted on the walls and floor in great, black-and-red swaths were arcane runes and glyphs, symbols of black magic, sorcery, and necromancy.

There was a small, arched alcove on the left wall with rusted iron bars for a door. Straker forced Skallagrim toward it, shoved him inside, and slammed the door.

The sorcerer began climbing the stairway, then turned and called out to Skallagrim. "There's no girl, thief. Never was. She was just an illusion meant to bring you here. Get that through your head." He motioned for Straker to come to him. "The Night of Mog Ruith is upon us, and there are final preparations to see to. When I return, you and I shall speak, thief." With that he whirled around, black robes billowing behind him, and climbed the remaining stairs. Straker followed like an obedient dog. "And after that . . ." The sound of lunatic laughter trailed away in the distance.

As they disappeared from view, Skallagrim slammed himself into the iron bars of his cage, hoping they might give. They did not.

Despondent, he crumpled to the floor, listening as the suspicious breeze whistled through the nooks and crannies of the great hall like the hissing of a serpent. A thousand questions assailed him at once. *Were they lying? Where was she? Was she dead already? Was she even real?* On and on it went, mingling with self-accusations as he tortured himself for his failure. *I must be a fool. I did all of this for nothing. My life has been for nothing!* Then, bubbling up like poison from a mire of guilt, came fear, and with it a double portion of grief. Fear, for short of a miracle, he would be killed. Grief for the loss of the blue-eyed girl. She was either dead, lost somewhere else in the bleak and terror-ravaged realm of Andorath, or she had never existed.

He shook his head violently, dismissing the latter. She had to be real no matter what they said or how convinced they were of it themselves. The girl was real. And he . . . he had lost her.

But Skallagrim was a rudderless ship, tossed from one wave to the next as a storm raged in his mind. No sooner had he convinced himself of her realness than the hope was torn from him by his old foe, doubt. He was, after all, the only one who claimed to have seen the girl. Erling had been in the alleyway with him and had not seen her, and his spies had brought no word of her. Had he imagined it all?

Maybe he should have just given himself up in the alley. He could have spared himself the horrors of the Vales. Instead, had he fought, killed, and suffered for a mere illusion. Four days of living hell, and for what? He had delivered himself right to the sorcerer's door, as Straker had said. All that devil had ever wanted was him—probably the sword as well.

No! It cannot be! Love is no illusion!

Or was it?

Confusion assailed his mind, firing arrows of dread, apprehension, and sorrow into his last remaining hopes. He was alone—lost and alone. He would die not even knowing who he truly was, for his past had been stolen from him. The only memorable joy of his life that might bring him comfort was the dream of the girl in the garden. And truly, that was merely joy hoped for—not joy itself—a thing unreal, out of reach. Now even that was being stolen.

Am I even real?

He was drowning in a sea of sunken hopes. He considered giving in to it, allowing himself to plunge into its interminable depths, knowing he would never hit bottom. For Skallagrim there could be no pain greater than to see his one memory of joy—indistinct as it was—torn from him in the dark hour before his death. It had been a lifeline, as frail as gossamer. Now he would drown without it.

He sensed tears forming at the corners of his eyes. "What have I done, what . . ." There was a catch in his throat that he suppressed for all of three seconds before succumbing.

He wept long and hard then, great, mournful sobs pouring out of him, reverberating throughout the dark hall.

The chilly breeze ceased, pausing perhaps in awe of the unfamiliar sounds of a profound lament, born of the sorrow of love lost. The ragged banners stopped their flapping, the torchlight dimmed, and the darkness grew. Down below in the vault, a sentient sword trembled in its scabbard as the resurrected man who lay next to it, chained, debased, and for the moment, forgotten, stirred with purpose.

Skallagrim fought hard through the tears, conjuring a vision of the girl. Perhaps just another illusion—this one of his own making—but he did not care. He remembered the words she had spoken in his first dream of her. *"Though I may sleep, the ages will roll by. Do not let them sweep you away, Skallagrim. Find me!"*

"How?" he cried as if she would somehow materialize and answer him. "How can I find you?" Skallagrim replayed the vision over and over in his mind, filling himself with unbearable heartache. He struggled to make sense of it all but was too overcome with grief—grief as bitter as poison—to unravel the riddle of her plight.

Then a moment of clarity, as searing as the sun. *"Though I may sleep, the ages will roll by."* If she was real—and for the moment, he would cling to that hope—it was more than just a problem of finding her. "Ages will roll by." He said it aloud into the darkness, then repeated it. "Ages will roll by."

His sobs subsided as he pondered his fate—their fate. "I have doomed us."

Death was coming for him soon. Death would swallow his dreams of her as well. He had to find a way to face what was coming next, a way to fight it, to deny death its prize. But he had been stripped of everything that might help him: his staff, his sword, his hope, and the sublime vision of the blue-eyed girl. *No!* For that brief glimpse of her, of joy, was everything. Everything he needed, whether he lived or died. He could face nothing without it.

Whether or not she existed, the love he felt for her could not be denied. He would grasp that, embracing the illusion of her, holding fast to his dreams even if they were delusions. He could face death at the sorcerer's hands if he could hold true to her just a little longer. Hell, he could even face living! Fighting! He just needed to believe in her. *"Though the ages roll by!"*

Skallagrim spoke now as if the girl could hear him. Whether she was a dream or not, he willed her to hear him. "Whatever I did to bring us to this cannot be undone for ages. Is that what you were saying?" For a moment, he could see her, a tragic phantom, ravishing in the glory of her youth. He caught the scent of her, like a floral-laden breeze from the garden of his dream.

To be in her presence with the ethereal light of faerie shining upon and through her was to live inside a song. To look into her eyes was to be lost in a sea of innocence. There was sorrow in those eyes too, inconsolable and impossibly deep. *"Ages will roll by,"* she whispered sadly.

The apparition was vivid, stark, and full of glowing life. Skallagrim looked upon a face that was fairer than the dawn at the world's beginning, shining with the hope of youth yet full of peril. Wars would be fought for such a lass. Kingdoms would be overthrown to find her. Andorath's great and terrible powers would be shaken to their very core for the want of her. Even a desperate, hopeless, wretched thief—his face carved to a bloody ruin—could be taught to live for the love of her.

One glimpse of her in a back-alley hell, two dreams, and the ethereal, light-filled vision that hovered before his eyes in the cell would have to be enough. It was enough!

Skallagrim had been transfixed, his heart promising everything to the vision of the girl, yet he willed himself to move, reaching a trembling hand toward the phantom. *Just to touch your cheek. Or that my hand might linger upon your hair, for just a moment.*

Harsh laughter came from the stairway. The sorcerer and Straker were returning, breaking the spell entirely, the vision dissipating like a misty rain.

Skallagrim was jarred to his senses, still reeling with sorrow but growing hot now with a more useful emotion: anger. If it was going to take ages to find her, if his dreams held any truth that corresponded to the hellish reality of the Vales of Pagarna—and he believed they did—he must survive.

Fortunately for him, he remembered something that might help.

CHAPTER THIRTY-FIVE

Skallagrim was hauled to his feet, then shoved toward the table in the center of the hall, his wrists still bound. Forneus had seated himself in a grand chair with a high back. A plain wooden chair sat opposite the sorcerer.

"Be seated." Forneus motioned to Straker, who pushed Skallagrim into the chair. "We shall go up those stairs in a bit and attend to business, you and I. For the time being, I thought we might have a chat. You may have questions, and there are certain things—facts I don't mind sharing with you." He smiled then, a smile that stretched unnaturally wide across the skin of his gaunt face.

It seemed that proximity to this diabolist had a way of dampening the will, for Skallagrim felt as if he had come to the end of a long road. *It was all for nothing!* All his hopes had been but leaking vessels cast adrift in a storm, shattering to ruin at last upon the rocky shores of reality.

No! I must live! He stared down at the table, refusing to lock eyes with his conqueror.

The sorcerer's voice jarred him back from despair. It was deep, like Straker's, but hollow as an empty grave. "You must have questions. If so, you'd best ask them now."

"While you chat with lover boy," Straker chimed in, "I'll go check on our guards. They never came, damn them."

"You do that. Skallagrim and I will be just fine. Return in half an hour." Forneus's eyes turned back to Skallagrim as Straker loped up the huge stairway and vanished in the gloom. "I can see you are in deep despair."

Skallagrim allowed himself to look at the sorcerer, his eyes full of accusation, but he held his tongue.

"I'm not a cruel man, though you think it. There are spells at my disposal that can remove your grief from you. Allow me to do that."

"You'd take even that from me?" Skallagrim shook his head. "It's all I have left. I think I'll keep it."

"Is that your wish? To grieve the loss of a love that never happened?"

"I saw you with the girl," Skallagrim stated matter-of-factly. He might burst into tears again at any moment, but he resisted, unwilling to give the red-eyed sorcerer any satisfaction.

"Of course, you did. You were under a spell." Forneus leaned across the table, noting the anger in Skallagrim's eyes. "I'm not to blame for your deception. That was Griog'xa."

"But why? I don't know the man!"

"No one does, not really." Forneus's fingers began to tap a rhythm on the table as he recited the rhyme of Griog'xa in a mocking, singsong voice.

No mortal eye hath seen the sage
That inscrutable mystic, the minacious mage
In many a lifetime, in many an age
The Sorcerer Griog'xa

Forneus cocked a brow and snapped his fingers, pleased with his performance. "He's the one you should point your finger at, though at present, I don't suppose you can."

"Did he take my memory as well?"

"Perhaps. Perhaps not. I know nothing about that. But the illusion of the girl, that was him." He paused, thinking. "There was a peculiar item of faerie magic—at least that's what I call it—in the wagon with me that night. I had agreed to carry it north for him, for Griog'xa." Forneus hesitated again, stuck upon the memory. "Quite a lovely thing, really. Ethereal and brimming with a wondrous light. Perhaps you saw it?"

"I did." Skallagrim's curiosity was piqued, mystified by the sorcerer's sudden hesitancy. "A man in dark robes brought it to you.

What was it?"

"I cannot explain it. It was . . ." He stumbled, truly unable to describe it.

An awkward moment passed as the sorcerer lost himself within a memory of loveliness. His lower lip quivered, and there was a hint of a tear forming in one eye. "I tried to perceive it, but . . ."

"Yes? Can you say what it was?" Something was off about this, for even the red flame of the sorcerer's eyes was doused. He looked frail, his face awash with confusion.

The moment passed, and the evil gleam returned to Forneus's eyes. "An inconvenience. A distraction. I don't know! I did as I was asked and was rewarded badly. Used! Maybe he manipulated it to cause an image of a girl that only you could see. Maybe not. Either way, it was Griog'xa, not me."

Skallagrim did not wish to press the issue. He had the man talking, wasting time. But something had just transpired that he could not explain. And for the possible rescue of the girl, he would grasp at any straw. "Where did you deliver it?"

Forneus glared. "It was handed over to agents of Griog'xa on the Devil's Race Highway, if you must know. There was no good reason he could not have had his own men take it to begin with." He paused, calming himself. "It's good we're talking, you and I."

"Why?"

"For I understand more clearly now. That bit of magic in the wagon was nothing more than legerdemain. Subterfuge! Just a lure for you and a distraction for me. And I admit I was more than intrigued by that wondrous light, for it was like something from another world." The sorcerer's face softened for a moment only. "I was gullible to fall for it. He essentially told me what he was doing, and I helped him do it! He'll pay for that, damn him!" His eyes flared red again. "He gambled a lot to get you here."

"So, then why?"

A powerful gust channeled up from the dungeon, causing the torchlight to sputter and stirring the ragged banners to billow like wraiths. A deep moan, as if from a great beast in torment, came rumbling up from the floor. As the eerie wind subsided, it carried with it a thousand fell whispers that went swirling about the room, fading at last to a single, delirious tittering.

Skallagrim shuddered. He glanced over his shoulder to the doorway that led down to the vault and beyond.

"Ignore that. 'Tis naught but a flaw in the design of this place. It happens often." The sorcerer's voice conveyed a confidence he did not feel, and his eyes betrayed doubts he strove to master.

Skallagrim was wriggling in his seat, as if trembling from the insidious chill permeating the vast hall. "I think you may have ignored that flaw to your own undoing, Forneus," he spoke with contempt. He tried to sound confident, though inwardly, his emotions were going back and forth like a pendulum. *What was the mysterious light? Could it have something to do with the girl?* Where only moments before he had come to grips with her loss, now he was questioning that loss all over again, despair threatening to overwhelm him like a monstrous tide. Despite that and the certain knowledge that if he did not get free of his bonds, he would shortly die an untimely death, he kept his composure. "So, why would Griog'xa do this to me?"

"Nothing personal, I'm sure." Forneus tapped his temple with a long finger. "I have figured out most of it. He simply wanted you to come here and kill me with—" Forneus hesitated, struggling to acknowledge Skallagrim's sword. "With Terminus!" He slammed his fist on the table. "Griog'xa wants this place for his own." He waved a hand in the air, indicating the fort. "I dared refuse him. So, of course, the fiend wants me dead." He reached into his robes and brought forth a metal loop upon which dangled several oddly shaped keys. "It riles him that I have the only key. Spells have sealed the door, barring entrance to anyone I choose. Though, of course, you found your way in."

Skallagrim feigned indifference as the sorcerer returned the keys to their hiding place deep within his robes.

"I suppose he knew you would follow me here if you were convinced there was a girl's life at stake. If you thought I had taken her, you would seek revenge. I would be dead, and no one would point the finger at him."

"But that plan would leave me alive, with the sword. What if I sorted it all out for myself and then went after him?"

"Trust me, Griog'xa is a master manipulator. He would turn even your need for vengeance into something useful for himself. Why, the act of sending you through the wilderness, even that was used to his advantage."

"How so?"

"Well, there is no knowing what you stirred up along the way. Unless you want to tell me?"

"I think not." Skallagrim had no intention of recounting his battles with Vathek and the ghouls, nor would he reveal his encounter with Swanhild.

"Right!" Forneus slapped the table again. "But it's stirred up just the same! He put a hook in your nose with this nonsense about a girl and virtually dragged you up the river." He tore his gaze from Skallagrim, and his voice quavered with anger. "My undulate is gone, at least for now. You have clumsily and unwittingly cleared the way up the old road for him."

"But you wanted me here too. You sent Straker to take my arm. To kill me! Why?"

"I preferred you alive, of course, for my grand ceremony at midnight." Forneus hesitated, sensing Skallagrim's lack of understanding. "Griog'xa played us both for fools. He arranged for you to be in the alley, and Straker was to take you captive there. If we failed—and he made sure of it by stirring up the cultists—then he promised to create a sorcerous lure to bring you to the fort. It was an illusion, nothing more. Powerful stuff, I must admit. I can conjure sounds—such as the mob you heard in the vault—but nothing so complex as the living, breathing girl you must have imagined. He even deceived your friend, Erling Hizzard."

Skallagrim looked up questioningly. "Erling? How?"

"Apparently, he has it in for me too. Griog'xa knew he would suspect your imaginary girl would be used as a sacrifice tonight. And

Erling would tell you where to find me, though I cannot imagine what the excuse was for sending you through the wilderness. To avoid the soldiers, perhaps?"

Skallagrim nodded. "Supposedly, the road was closed. There was talk of a war, of soldiers on the move."

"Well, there you are!" The sorcerer clapped his hands. "And who do you suppose is instigating that war?"

"Let me guess—Griog'xa?"

Forneus nodded. "He's an evil genius. Can you see it now?"

"It's like a game to him, moving us around like pieces on a board."

"Oh, but it goes deeper. That clever bastard has several games going at once, many pieces being moved from square to square, then from one board to the next. And all of it working toward some ultimate aim of his, something inconceivable to us." The sorcerer stared into the darkness over Skallagrim's head. He was calculating, his brows knitted, his eyes scanning the empty air as if to see the unseeable. He seemed to be on the verge of a colossal epiphany but could not quite grasp it. "I knew he was brilliant—twisted and brilliant. But I confess, I underestimated him." He shook his head to free his mind of doubt, then scowled at Skallagrim.

"And somehow, you got past my guard dog—the Old Man o' the River, as you may know him. Pagarna!" Forneus scowled, his eyes glaring like hot coals. "He was meant to deter greater foes than you. However did you manage it?"

Skallagrim glowered. "Let's just say I'm highly motivated."

"As am I. It took the lives of many innocents to coax that creature down to Orabas. But you are alive and well, as I had hoped."

"For my arm? Am I to assume it has something to do with your sadistic experiments in the vault? The man with the missing arm?" Skallagrim had judged Forneus rightly, that the truth to all might be pulled from him if he could just keep him talking.

"Sadistic? What I do, I do for a greater good! Andorath will thank me one day."

Forneus was arrogant, and even in his weakened state, had the power to back it up. But he was also mad, his mind devoured by years of sorcery just as Erling had warned. Of course, he had fallen prey to the dead thing in the pit as well, and Skallagrim suspected all of the sorcerer's blasphemous experiments and plans were the design of that chained demon. Forneus might once have been a man, but now he was a husk, an avatar to the evil prisoner below who had eaten his mind.

"As for your arm . . ." The sorcerer's mouth twisted into a devilish smile, wide and disturbing. "Your arm will be joined to his body. Need I explain why?"

"So that he can wield Terminus for you?" Skallagrim shifted in his chair, his shoulders flexing as his hands sought relief from the ropes that bound them. Shouting came from upstairs. Straker yelling at his guards from a window, he supposed.

The sorcerer, oblivious to the noise, kept his gaze firmly upon the thief. "Exactly. Minus the additions I have made to him, he is—or was—a great general from the north, from Urk. He's left-handed and wields an axe like no other. Imagine the terror he shall strike in my foes. The fearful countenance swinging the mighty axe with one hand and Terminus in the other. Can you see it?"

Skallagrim needed to buy time. The best way to achieve that was to keep the lunatic sorcerer talking. "I can see it. You'll unleash a monster upon the land, assuming you can control it."

"The general's resurrected mind is a disappointment, I'll admit. But that will soon be remedied. There's a surgeon of great skill from Ophyr, familiar with the sorcerous arts—a genius with the scalpel." He leaned over the table menacingly, his body seeming to stretch closer to Skallagrim than possible. "He'll transfer my brain into the creature's skull," he whispered conspiratorially as if someone or something might be listening. "Imagine that. You will join with the general and me to form one awesome, death-dealing body!"

Skallagrim's mouth hung ajar.

"Do not think me mad, Skallagrim. There is a reason this must be."

Skallagrim remained quiet, willing Forneus to say more.

"My body is dying." Forneus sat back in his grand chair, shoulders slumping. "Yes. Now you know a secret. Even Straker is unaware."

Skallagrim took a deep breath. "We all die, Forneus."

"Need we? This way, even a part of you will live on." The sorcerer's gaze searched Skallagrim's, imploring him for understanding. Not finding it, he continued. "This body," he declared, indicating his own, "is over two centuries old. It's give out, Skallagrim." He became animated, waving his hands about. "But my mind is alive, like a flame that will endure forever. There are plans, such plans! My mind, my being, they must endure. So I shall place it in a stronger vessel—"

"You fear death," Skallagrim interrupted, voicing the truth. "You're a liar and a murderer. Your life has been a monument to blasphemy, and now you fear the end of it."

"Blasphemy? Against what? Whom?" Forneus was indignant.

"If my memory were not robbed from me, I could tell you. But I think there is a higher power that will demand an accounting of you, and I think you know it."

Forneus cringed and seemed to grow smaller.

"That's it then. You're afraid."

"Higher power? You know nothing!" He slammed his fist on the table again. "It was a higher power that brought Andorath low. The wicked king beyond the Southern Void cursed us and cut us off. I, Forneus Druogorim, would see him toppled from his high place!"

"And you would replace him with the Knight of the North? Balor? Dead Balor?"

"I and others will resurrect him. So, yes, I would do that."

"Really? Or maybe you have higher expectations?"

"What do you mean?" Forneus inclined his head.

"I think you are an ambitious man, Forneus. I think you intend to set yourself upon a throne one day. I speak truth, do I not?"

"Silence!" The shadows grew large in the hall, and the whispering wind began to seep up from the dungeon with renewed malice. The sorcerer's eyes darted around the room, betraying a deep paranoia. He leaned once more across the table. "There are things that can hear you, thief," he whispered. "But yes, once I—or I suppose I should say *we*—are resurrected, then why not?"

"You sorcerers!" Skallagrim spat the words in disgust. "You're obsessed with death and resurrection. Why not turn your attention to those already living? You could do something to help people. What you propose is a sacrilege, an offense to all that is good and natural. People die. They are not meant to be brought back against their will."

"Birth and rebirth. Death and resurrection." Forneus rose from his chair, his hands clasped behind his back. He spoke with the authority of a noble sage, but his eyes radiated madness. "You may think of it as blasphemy, but does not nature itself reveal the act of resurrection in myriad ways?"

"How so?"

"Why, each dawning of the sun is a resurrection of the day."

"Yes, but no one has to murder the sun for that to happen!" Skallagrim tried to calm himself. He was hurling truths at Forneus like javelins. Too much of that and the sorcerer might end the debate. "Besides, the sun hides its face from you, Forneus," he muttered, barely audible. Skallagrim shivered from the cold but sat tall in his seat. Though the fireplace burned with a lively flame, it was not enough to tame the perpetual chill of the fort. "Fort Vigilance is wrapped in mist and shadow, haunted by perpetual gloom."

The sorcerer threw his hands into the air. "The undulate brought the darkness here, not me!"

"But you brought the undulate!"

Forneus grew sullen, for Skallagrim had scored yet another point. "To protect my work, yes. To protect my home."

"Home? You have made yourself a home in a house of horrors."

"Horrors?" Forneus cocked his head.

"Liches are roaming the catacombs beneath you!" Skallagrim jerked his head toward the vault door. "There's a demonic prisoner chained in a pit down there!"

"Do not speak of them!" Forneus growled through clenched teeth.

"Then what of the poor man on the table in your vault? A piece of this and a piece of that, all stitched together to accomplish what?

He's an amalgamation, without hope. You took a living man and made him the epitome of sorrow."

"The epitome of sorrow?" The sorcerer raised his eyebrows in surprise. "What is life if not a merging of sorrows? My creation may represent that notion on some level I had not considered. He is poetry, perhaps, a metaphor for life."

"He doesn't represent life. You've killed him. And you're killing him again!"

"Then the metaphor holds," the sorcerer said, speaking as if to a wayward pupil who had failed to see some obvious truth. "For the apex of all sorrows is death."

Skallagrim eyed Forneus coldly. "You can't see it, can you?"

"It is you who cannot see, thief! There, in my creation, it's all on display. There, on that table, lies the immutable truth. Certainly, he is crude and mindless, and that was not my original intent. But once I stood back from him, really saw him for what he is, then I understood completely."

"Understood what?"

"It's death from which we all strive to escape. He's my escape, and to a lesser extent, yours."

"My escape is simpler. Just untie me!"

Forneus laughed darkly, acknowledging the sarcasm. "But now you and the general will be joined with me. We shall all escape it and to a grand purpose, for there will be no greater power in all of Andorath. The strength and cunning of a warrior, the mind of a master sorcerer, and the arm that can wield Terminus, all working to save Andorath!"

"I'm not convinced it's worth saving, Forneus. You have driven yourself mad in this place. It would be easier on you—and frankly, the rest of Andorath—if you would simply give in to the inevitable, like all of us must, and just die."

"But I'm not ready!" The sorcerer made a fist in the air. "You cannot possibly understand, for you are young, and the fire still burns strong within you!"

"Then let me grow old so that I may face death with dignity one day as a free man." It had to be nearing midnight. Skallagrim was in no frame of mind to beg, but for now, he had as much reason to postpone death, as did Forneus.

"No." Forneus took a deep breath to calm himself. "You will die at midnight and thus be spared the ravages of old age."

"Were you never young? Did you never love? You would deny me a future? The possibility of happiness?" Skallagrim shook his head in disbelief. *Just keep talking, you bastard!*

"Happiness? It's a fleeting thing." The sorcerer began to pace back and forth, speaking not so much to Skallagrim as to his own fears. "It will betray you in the end. There will be no happiness as your aged body dies before your eyes. Life becomes a curse."

A burning log popped in the fireplace, causing them both to start.

"Life is a flame, not a curse." The sorcerer was bereft of reason, but Skallagrim would not yield the debate. "You should spend the time you have left rekindling it."

"Impossible! Toil but fifty years upon this wretched earth, and you would know what all the aged know. When the flame of youth is spent, it's spent, Skallagrim. It will never come back, that happy fire that burned in our untarnished hearts. It's out. Drenched by the soul-crushing storms of age, its last hopeless, flickering embers are trampled into ashes by the uncaring boot of time. The last sad sparks of joy go spiraling. The flame of youth is extinguished; its last choking smoke rises black and wraithlike, swirling into nothingness. The inner fire gone, we devolve into shadows and haunt the halls of memory, where we hear but echoes of laughter, remnants of the passions that we might have lived, the exquisite temptations that we dreamt of but had not the courage to live out."

So caught up was Forneus in his discourse that he failed to notice the racket going on up the stairs behind him. Straker was calling out desperately to his cousins. The eerie wind had risen from the dungeon once more and played at the wavy strands of Skallagrim's hair.

"Echoes of laughter?" Skallagrim had to keep him talking, if only for a few more moments. "Are you that bitter?"

"Yes, echoes." Forneus clenched his fists. "They taunt me—torture me." He looked down at his body, smoothing the folds of his robes. "I'm old and in a bad state," he said, his voice quiet, feeble. "Life has become lonely and sad, like a dance you can only watch from the corner. You would not understand."

"You have a bleak outlook on the world, Forneus Druogorim." It was Skallagrim who was lecturing now. "If I could only watch the dance, appreciating its beauty rather than participating, I'd be content with that. But at some point, the music has to stop—even for the watchers."

"Well, there we disagree, Skallagrim." The sorcerer's face grew grim, his jaw set. "For me the band must play on." He smirked and whirled away from Skallagrim to face the stairway. "Straker! Get down here!"

Good! As the sorcerer turned, Skallagrim made use of the time.

A moment later, Forneus turned back toward his prisoner. "I have enjoyed our talk, but your time is just about up, thief. Any last questions?"

"A couple, yes."

The sorcerer nodded impatiently, indicating he should proceed.

"There's nothing I can say to convince you to let me live? Nothing?"

"No, nothing." Forneus was growing irritable, ready for the conversation to end. "Anything else?"

Skallagrim sighed. The course was set—no way around it now. "Yes. I was told there was a library here in the fort."

"A small one, yes. What of it?" Forneus eyed Skallagrim curiously.

"How do I find it?"

"Turn left at the top of the stairway, then down a long corridor on the left." The sorcerer drew closer to the table, looming over it, his crimson eyes full of suspicion. A crash and an angry shout resounded from the vault below. Forneus ignored it, accustomed now to the many disturbing sounds that came up from below. "Why do you ask?"

"I promised a friend I'd have a look. There's a book she mentioned. I thought it sounded interesting." Skallagrim had scooted to the edge of his seat.

"You're mad!" Forneus shouted. "I don't pretend to know what game you're playing, but time is up. Straker! Come now!" Doubt creased his brow as he leaned impossibly far over the table toward Skallagrim, sinister and watchful. He had seen something he did not like. "What do you have behind your back, thief?"

Skallagrim's hands moved faster than lightning. With his right hand, he grabbed Forneus behind the head and slammed it onto the table, gripping it tightly by the hair. In his left hand, he wielded a jagged piece of metal—one of Old Tuva's talismans. With it, he slashed the sorcerer's neck, severing the jugular vein. That done, he flung the sorcerer backward and watched as he stumbled to the floor, his eyes registering shock, his nose broken, and his neck spouting a fountain of blood.

The sorcerer rose weakly, his hands clenching his throat as he tried in vain to stem the red tide that surged from his body. "You cannot kill me with that, thief!" he raged. "Only the sword—" The sorcerer's words were cut short as he strangled on blood, coughing a scarlet mist.

From below came a scream so ghastly, it sounded as if a banshee were loose in the vault. There was more crashing, banging, and bellowing as it became apparent that someone or something was coming up the stairs.

Skallagrim jumped to his feet, not sure whether to run or to continue his assault. "Your body was dying. Time was killing you as surely as any sword!" He looked at the hag's razor-sharp talisman in his bloodstained hand, thankful he had removed it from his abandoned knapsack, packing it into the belt pocket of his baldric. His hands had been busy the entire time he debated the sorcerer, slicing through his bonds. He put the bloody thing away and rounded the table on Forneus.

The sorcerer's face was going white from loss of blood. He took a step toward Skallagrim but slipped in the dark pool that was growing at his feet. "Only the sword!" He choked out the words with a spray of blood. Removing one hand from his throat, he described a symbol in the air with his finger. The figure hovered in the air as if drawn in oily black smoke. "Behold," he sputtered. "The spirit of Mog Ruith has come to save his servant! Balor has come!"

CHAPTER THIRTY-SIX

He has summoned the Knight of the North! Skallagrim blanched as his sense of space and time distorted. *Is there no end of horrors in this place?*

Many things happened nearly at once, none of them good. First, the sorcerous rune that hung in the air expanded, filling the room with menace as it took on the shape of a colossal knight—a demonic phantom—born of smoke and blood. This would not be Balor in the flesh, for no sorcerer had the power to call up his physical form, not yet. No matter, the specter of Balor was enough as fear rolled off it in waves. Wraiths appeared, fearsome, screeching and whirling about the chamber as if they rode upon a blast of wind from the North of North. Accordingly, the room's temperature plummeted.

The sorcerer's eyes flared red, full of malevolent triumph. He lifted both arms, reveling in the madness—not caring that blood pumped from his neck in bright ribbons. The wraiths swirled around him, whipping his black cloak into a flurry while the phantom knight grew in form and height.

Forneus Druogorim was not going to die. Terminus must land the fatal blow. The horror was not over.

Next came the wolf, Straker, leaping down into the chaos with his saber drawn. There was fear in his eyes, for he had no idea what had happened, but he charged forward, ready to defend Forneus— or, more likely, himself.

A heartbeat later, the door that led to the vault burst asunder. The thing that charged into the room was huge, hideous to behold, and on fire! The sight of it caused Straker to stop in his tracks and Forneus to lose his concentration. The shape of the ghostly knight wavered, and the wraiths shrieked and dissipated. Skallagrim could not tell what he was looking at, but he got clear of its path.

The blazing behemoth sent the sorcerer into a spasm of fear, his eyes wide with realization. "No!" he cried as it headed straight for him.

His creation—the abomination—General Arne Grímsson would battle one final time. The Axeman was loose, hurtling through the room like a blazing meteor, his body a living torch. With his one mighty arm, he brandished what no man but one could wield without burning, without catching fire. Terminus!

Flames wreathed about him, and black smoke boiled. He came fast, and he came screaming his war cry, a sound that had once caused entire battalions to turn and flee. The form of Mog Ruith, Balor, Knight of the North—if that is what it was—faded, turned to shadow, and disappeared. The wraiths were but a memory, their terror receding as their tattered forms vanished from sight. The sorcery of Forneus Druogorim had abandoned him.

Skallagrim's nostrils were filled with the smell of burning flesh, but he watched in silent awe as a terrible judgment fell upon his foe. One act of mercy on the part of the thief had brought it about.

Terminus let loose its fear-inducing battle scream as its burning bearer closed the distance with Forneus. The sorcerer stood paralyzed as the Axeman's arm swept down from on high, screamed as the blade's keen edge sliced through his shoulder, crumpling him to the ground.

Despite the mortal wound, Forneus managed to cry out one last denial. "It was not my fault! None of this!"

Skallagrim stepped back from the sorcerer's wilting form, flinging his arm up to shield his face from the fire. The Axeman, flames leaping from his body, kicked the sorcerer the rest of the way to the ground. With a grunt, he plunged Terminus into the heart of Forneus Druogorim, then crumpled to the floor beside him, a flaming ruin. Now, as before in the vault, both sorcerer and victim screamed as one.

Skallagrim stood there transfixed. "Nothing was ever your fault, was it? Not the spells, not my face." The thief winced as the heat grew in intensity and glanced at the Axeman. "Not even him." He watched, wide-eyed, as the red light of the sorcerer's eyes flickered with abject terror, then dimmed. "For my part, I'd forgive you if only you'd ask." But the eyes of Forneus were fixed and devoid of understanding.

No sudden rush of memory flooded back to Skallagrim's wounded mind. There was nothing. He did not know where he had come from or even the name of the girl for whom he searched. Nothing! Swanhild had warned him. Only by killing the sorcerer responsible for the spell would his memory return. If her words were to be believed, then Forneus had spoken truly. He had not done it. Then who? Tuva? Griog'xa?

Skallagrim flung the question aside as he looked upon the ruin of the sorcerer. The corpse's jaw went slack, emitting a last, long exhalation of air. A thin wisp of greasy smoke rose from the gaping mouth and then quickly dissipated—the final vestige of the demon that had possessed him. With that, the sorcerer, Forneus Druogorim, was dead.

Straker stood rigid, jaw agape, in shock. That all the sorcerer's plans had come to ruin in the blink of an eye was more than he could process.

Keeping a wary eye on the unmoving assassin, Skallagrim knelt beside the sorcerer's still form to search his robes. *The keys!* Now they were his.

He rose, wrenching Terminus free of the corpse, jumping back as flames from the Axeman's body took hold of the sorcerer's cloak. Soon, both bodies were roaring like a bonfire. The madman had truly been joined with his victim, though not in a way he could have foreseen. Skallagrim turned from the sight to retch, the smell of burning flesh too much to bear.

Despite this, as Skallagrim's bruised and battered body finally ceased its convulsing, he took note of the keys clutched in his left hand, barely suppressing a smile. *Manipulators!* He had instinctively taken a prize from each of them, even the slightest offender. A necklace of talismans from the hag, a brooch from Swanhild, and from Forneus Druogorim, he had taken a fort.

Well, he had almost taken a fort. The prisoner in the pit was chained. Skallagrim would take great precautions to keep it from his thoughts, knowing that to let down his guard would be to lose his mind, becoming a twisted instrument of the dead thing's will. But there was still the matter of the assassin, Straker.

Since the Axeman's fiery arrival, Straker had remained still as a statue, frozen with doubt. The sorcerer was dead. So was Straker's mission. He could escape now—get past the thief and leave that wretched place. But the demon set loose in his head was quick to remind him of his need for revenge.

Skallagrim had humiliated him in the alley four nights back, besting his hired swords in combat. Straker had lost dozens of riders under his command to some treachery on the part of Griog'xa. But he lay the blame for this upon the thief as well. Skallagrim had defeated the undulate, causing it to flee up the river, devouring his cousin along the way. Skallagrim's allies were out front now and had killed his two remaining kinsmen. He had seen their bodies lying in the courtyard before the door. Their unseeing eyes stared up at him, seeming full of condemnation.

Yes! There was a need for revenge.

Straker lunged through the smoke as Skallagrim brought Terminus up just in time to parry a savage thrust.

"Now, thief! Now you will die!"

But Skallagrim struck next, bringing Terminus down in a sweeping arc toward Straker's head. The assassin parried, then bounded backward several steps.

"You had your chance in the alley!" Skallagrim said as he circled his opponent. "But you didn't take it."

"Griog'xa, fool!" Straker attacked with a sharp blow upon Terminus, testing Skallagrim's reflexes. "We have all been dancing to his tune from the beginning." Straker lunged again, but his blade glanced off a buckle on Skallagrim's baldric.

"You were working for them both?" Skallagrim smirked. "Then

you are just the plaything of sorcerers—a dull dagger in the hands of madmen."

"There's nothing dull about my sword, freak!"

Straker stepped in as if to deliver a powerful overhead blow, which Skallagrim was quick to parry. He came in again, seemingly with the same attack, but at the last second, sidestepped. Skallagrim was caught off guard as Straker feinted, dropping his saber to strike at the thief's exposed leg. The blade sliced through flesh just above Skallagrim's left knee, causing him to stumble backward. He was winded though undeterred.

"You know what?"

"What, thief?"

"I sicken of hearing the name 'Griog'xa.'" Skallagrim stood solid, his right foot in front. He readied himself, lifting his sword so the hilt ran perpendicular to his face, the blade pointed at Straker. "Though I don't desire it, I believe I'll kill him one day."

"Then you'll do it as a liche!" Straker feinted again, then lunged.

Skallagrim swept the saber aside and, turning his hand, thrust Terminus hard at Straker's undefended right side. There was no finesse in the attack. It was not the move of a skilled fighter, but he tagged his opponent just the same.

Straker winced with pain and threw himself back to avoid another strike. He looked down at his side, his eyes registering shock as his shirt darkened with blood.

Skallagrim realized he was facing a real swordsman this time, not a mere thug or hired sword. But he knew that Straker's mind, having fallen prey to the thing in the pit, would not be as sharp as it once had been. Even so, he remained alert, calling upon all the power that Terminus would grant him, giving himself over entirely to the sentient sword.

Terminus flashed and throbbed with an otherworldly light. Skallagrim could feel it humming with life in his grip, and he let its battle song fill his mind. Time slowed to a crawl, granting him a reprieve before the inevitable, final flurry of swords that would finish the fight—one way or another.

It was a marvel to him, his determination and readiness to face the assassin. But it was no wonder after all he had faced over the last four days. The slain had piled around him in the alleyway, fallen to his sword. He had faced down the hideous brotherhood of ghouls that haunted the old forest road, killing several. Then had come the terror of the undulate and the demon of the pit—both a threat to his mind, spirit, and body. They were not erased from the earth, but he had faced the threat of them with courage. The undulate had fled into the wilderness, wounded and defeated. The demon had tried to snare his mind but failed—held at bay by the defiance of Terminus and Skallagrim's own burgeoning wisdom. He had even faced the dreaded sorcerer. Skallagrim had fenced him not with swords but with words—keeping him mired in a rambling, circular debate until he could cut free of his bonds. The thief had fooled him, then cut his throat and sealed his doom.

A change had come over him, and it felt right. There was no fear. It had been vanquished like a defeated foe. If he died fighting Straker, so be it. There were questions, yes, but doubts evaporated like mist from his mind. Despair? Gone like a wraith at dawn. He had even ground the worm of self-loathing beneath his heel. Skallagrim was no monster—no freak. He had learned this in the tenebrous void of flooded Orabas. Sorrow remained, but what of it? Men were not promised a life without it. He was reminded of Swanhild's alluring voice, of the words she had sung by the stream.

What feeds the pool where their dreams were drowned
The tears of children who, in sorrow, found
The world was broken and by one, betrayed
Their faith in dreams was doomed to fade

Well, to hell with that! He would hold fast to his sorrows and his dreams, for sorrows made dreams all the sweeter. He would guard them fiercely until he found the girl or until that far-flung day when all the sorrows of the world would die.

Heartache cloaked his soul like a choking smoke, but it would not break him. What soul had not felt the suffocating effects of a broken heart when spurned by a love? Or, in his case, when robbed of one? No, he would cling to that as well. For to banish it would be to annihilate a sacred truth, that only love could mend his brokenness.

Of course, love would not mend a sword thrust to his heart.

Terminus flashed black into his hand, and time resumed its normal course. He tried to lock gazes with Straker, but the assassin seemed dazzled by the preternatural flashing of Terminus, his eyes darting back and forth between his foe and the blade he carried. It was dawning on Straker that he faced two opponents rather than one.

Straker flinched when the blade flashed again, plunging the great hall into total blackness for a heartbeat. He feared it would scream at any moment and knew his heart might freeze if it did.

Terminus did not scream, but its bearer stamped forward on his right foot and lunged. The assassin beat the blade aside, then pressed forward with his own sword, missing Skallagrim's left arm by a hair's breadth.

What followed was a series of rapid blade strokes by each combatant. Nothing connected but steel upon steel, ringing like the mighty hammers of dwarves in a fabled, subterranean forge. As the longsword and the saber clashed and parried, the thief and the assassin circled round and round to claim an advantage.

Skallagrim was growing tired, his endurance waning. Unable to get past Straker's defenses, he feinted, then disengaged. Straker's sword had only managed a shallow cut upon his left leg. So far it was holding his weight with no problem.

The blades darted close again, touched, and veered away.

Skallagrim's chest rose and fell with rapid breaths. "I'm told you like killing, that you like hurting people."

"I do, very much so." Straker was circling his foe but stopped when the door to the vault was at his back.

"You called me a freak, a monster, but it's you who is the monster!"

Straker laughed, the sound like a bloody blade scraping against bone. "You seem to have a conscience, and I seem to be absent one. So, yes! I am the monster!"

"And a soulless bastard!" Skallagrim lunged but was deftly parried.

"Monsters have souls!" The laugh again, the terrible laugh. "Then again, maybe not!"

"You're as insane as Forneus."

Straker's eyes were merciless and unblinking. "I would argue—" He swept his saber through the air with a flourish. "That the borderlands between sanity and insanity are at best, grey and indiscernible. Where one begins and the other ends, we must decide for ourselves."

Skallagrim stepped forward, letting his blade caress the edge of Straker's saber. "You sound just like him. You've lost your mind."

The assassin beat Terminus aside and made a half-hearted lunge at Skallagrim's face, more taunt than attack. "I think we might be possessed by the same demon," he answered with a sneer. His face was contorted by bitterness, and lunacy played at the corners of his eyes. "They say I was dropped on my head when I was a baby, you know. Maybe that's the problem."

Straker launched a desperate attack. They went back and forth, the wolf and the thief, at one point coming face to face with blades locked. Caught in the spell of Terminus, Straker stared into the eyes of a bloody angel of wrath and blanched. His own eyes went wide as he flung himself away from Skallagrim, realizing at last that he might have met his match.

Regret hit him like a hammer. Why had he taken this job? Why had he involved himself with the two sorcerers? Why had he not killed this thief before the alien sword fell from the sky? But there was a god who waited below, whispering in his ear, tantalizing him with the life he might have if he survived this encounter.

He was sweating profusely. Slinging his dank hair from his face with a snap of his neck, he flayed Skallagrim with his eyes. "I've killed a hundred men in combat. Outright murdered twice that number.

You don't stand a chance!" Straker aimed a cut at Skallagrim's neck, but it was deflected. He flicked his wrist, bringing his blade over that of his foe's, and lunged, his point coming to within a half-inch from Skallagrim's left eye. Close but not close enough.

The assassin stepped back, gasping for air—growing weaker and weaker as the stain on his shirt spread ominous and large. His breath came in ragged gasps, but he managed to hurl a taunt at the thief. "After I kill you," he panted. "I think I'll hunt down that girl of yours—see if she really exists."

"Yeah?" A dagger's point teased Skallagrim's heart at the mention of her.

Straker reached behind him with his free hand and brought forth a wicked knife from his belt, the same knife he had used to carve Skallagrim's face to bloody ruin. "If she does, I'll mark her face with this, just like I did yours. And then—"

Straker did not finish his thought. If he imagined that by goading Skallagrim he would unbalance him, causing him to make a mistake, he was dead wrong. He felt the slash to his upper right arm before he saw it coming. An expert swordsman, Skallagrim was not, but fast with his hands—Quickhands, Erling had called him—he certainly was.

For Skallagrim, wariness had given way to a kind of wild, savage joy. It was like charging into battle with a thousand men at his back. Madness gripped him by one arm while the oddest sort of bliss pulled at the other—both forces combining to sling him toward his enemy like an arrow from the bow.

For her! his mind shouted. But he gave voice to a barbaric battle cry that sliced the air like an axe, ferocious and overflowing with wrath. Terminus joined him, shrieking like an eagle plunging toward the kill, the sound of it blasting through the fort with the force of a sudden squall.

It was too much for Straker. Miraculously, he parried twice while retreating. Skallagrim's third stroke arced through the air with a flash, taking Straker's left ear before it sank deep into his shoulder, barely missing his neck. Skallagrim yanked Terminus free of the ghastly wound, setting loose a spray of bright red blood.

Straker cried out with pain and fright, stamped forward as if he were about to attack, then turned at the last second and fled the room, disappearing into the gloom beyond the shattered vault door.

Skallagrim paused to catch his breath, then headed for the doorway that would lead him down to the vault and, if need be, beyond and below to the oubliette.

Had he just defeated Straker? Maybe? Nearly?

It was a relief that he had not been the one to kill the sorcerer, for no matter how deserving the man was of justice, Skallagrim wanted no part of revenge. Revenge could eat a man alive, and there would have been little or no satisfaction in a murderous act. Certainly, he had cut the man's throat without a second thought but only in self-defense.

He stopped in his tracks, literally and figuratively, for he did not want to lie to himself. Had it felt good? Driving that jagged talisman into the sorcerer's neck? He ran his hand through his long locks, pushing them out of his eyes. No, it had not felt good. It felt like . . . like panic!

Skallagrim could live with what he had done. He would have finished Forneus off if it had come to that, assuming it could have been done without Terminus. But he did not have to. Unwittingly, Skallagrim had delivered the death-dealing weapon to another. It was the Axeman who dealt the killing strokes with Terminus. As much to save Skallagrim as to wreak vengeance upon his torturer? Who could say?

He smiled grimly at his foolishness. *Get out of your head.* For a moment only, he had been conflicted. Now was not the time to explore his or anyone else's motives, for, with Straker alive, the battle was only half won. Whatever the motive and whichever hand struck the blow, the deed was done, and Forneus was gone.

He headed down the stairs to find Straker. After that, he would need to search Fort Vigilance from top to bottom to ensure the girl was truly not there. His mind told him she was not. His heart? That was another matter.

In his ramblings, Forneus had cast a lifeline to Skallagrim's despairing mind, a clue as precious as gold. *"Ethereal and brimming with a wondrous light."* Skallagrim had seen the otherworldly light, too, just before the appearance of the blue-eyed girl. Might that not have been her, concealed by enchantment? Because of his connection to her—the love they shared—perhaps Skallagrim could see through that enchantment when others could not.

Forneus, in his blindness to Griog'xa's machinations, had loaded the *item* into the wagon that terrible night in the alley, had delivered it north along the same road that Erling and Hartbert had taken. Maybe his allies had knowledge of it already. Maybe the girl was already safe.

Those were the thoughts he placated himself with. It would allow him to push on until all the horrid business of Fort Vigilance was done. To disbelieve in the girl's existence, to admit the possibility she was only an illusion, would have been to suffer the most profound grief, the death of his beloved. But if his heart held even a sliver of hope for her nearness, he would honor it. The fort must be searched, but he could not do that with Straker loose somewhere below him. He must hunt him down and face him again.

He made his way through the wreck of the vault laboratory, its floors strewn with broken glass and shards of wood from the table and other furnishings. Not a beaker or an alembic had been left intact. The huge, misshapen skeleton was crushed, and even the weird shadows that had inhabited the space were gone—fled with the demon that departed Forneus, perhaps.

The battle-axe was embedded in the open door that led to the dungeon. Even a mighty stroke from the Axeman had failed to shut the damned thing.

Skallagrim retrieved his staff and scabbard, both thankfully undamaged, and passed through the dreadful doorway, then crept down the stairs, coming at last to the trapdoor of the oubliette.

Where to find Straker? He did not need to think much about it. There was no riddle here. The blood trail had led right to the trapdoor.

Straker would be waiting by the abominable pit, for the dead thing within it would be calling to him. He might think himself safe down there in the dark, with his demon god so close. He might think to avoid retribution for what he had done to Skallagrim's face—for what he had done to a hundred others.

Why not pull the ladder up and just block the hole? Skallagrim wondered as he stared down into the blackness. *No, I have to finish this.*

Skallagrim willed his staff to light the way, then descended the ladder into the dungeon, ready to finish off the wounded wolf. It would help to think of him that way, as a beast, not a man. He would find Straker and kill him because that is what brave men did to wolves.

Revenge? It was impossible to eliminate it from the equation. Skallagrim was a flawed man, not an angel. Justice? Certainly. Straker deserved it, but justice was far beyond the scope of Skallagrim's needs. Need? Yes, that was it. The deed needed to be done for the sake of the girl—expeditiously.

Skallagrim slid Terminus from its scabbard, set his jaw, and headed down the corridor, the light from his staff creating fantastical shadows upon the damp walls. He did not see Straker at first, for his eyes were drawn irresistibly toward the black maw of the pit. Might the horrid hand be crawling around the perimeter on its spidery fingers, nails scratching and clicking hideously?

Straker stepped out of a hidden alcove on Skallagrim's left and placed himself between the thief and the pit, saber in one hand, torch in the other. His face was bloodless, and the look in his eyes bespoke madness. "There was no hope for me," he said, staring down at his bloody shirt, "so I serve a new master now. I'm told you have met?"

A lonely wind began to howl and moan through the lightless corridors, carrying with it the taint of a sulfurous vapor. The steady drip of water could be heard down in the pit along with a faint, repellent sloshing sound.

"First a sorcerer, now a demon? Where does it end, Straker?"

"When I'm a god!" The assassin's booming voice blared, sending echoes chasing one another around the chamber and out through the tangle of dank passages.

Skallagrim was taken aback by the intensity of Straker's proclamation. This was beyond madness. He stepped closer to his foe, sword at the ready, yet hesitated to close with him.

"Straker, you must know that isn't going to happen. He's lying to you." Skallagrim pointed his blade at the yawning void of the pit. "He's just a dead thing, unwanted and lacking any power unless you grant it to him." His enemy had let it go too far and was to be pitied for it. "Get him out of your head, and die a free man. There's still hope for that at least!"

The sound of rattling chains drifted up from the pit. With it came the stench of death. As before, vertigo threatened to overwhelm Skallagrim. Was his soul being dragged from his body to be hurled into the void?

"*No! Stand firm! He will not prevail!*" Terminus, ready to counter any spell from the demon, hummed with life.

Straker's eyes were vacant as he walked backward a few steps to the edge of the pit and fell to his knees. "Then end my life and get it over with. I won't stop you!" His voice was quivering with desperation. "I could have killed a dozen men while you were standing there. Do it! Hell is preferable to what he has in mind for me!" Somewhere down below, the dead thing was laughing hideously. "I thought I wanted this, but I don't!" Wind blasted from the pit. "Hell's teeth! He's telling me to jump!"

Straker tore his eyes from Skallagrim's to look behind him into the pit, then back again, his face a mask of dread. "It's too late," he whimpered. "He's got me!"

Still holding the torch and saber, Straker threw his arms wide.

"No!" Skallagrim darted forward, his sword arcing toward Straker's neck. He had to kill Straker, not in an act of revenge or expediency but of mercy.

Before the thief could close the distance, Straker took one final, pleading glance at him, then flung himself backward into the abyss.

He howled piteously as he fell, the sound sending shivers up the thief's spine.

Skallagrim just managed to stop himself from falling in after Straker and teetered on the brink of the pit. The light from the falling torch grew fainter and fainter until it finally blinked out at some abysmal depth. If there was a splash, Skallagrim did not hear it.

Damn! Well, that's that.

As he turned to leave, a spectral voice drifted up from below like a gasp of poisoned air. *"It could have been you! It should have been you!"*

CHAPTER THIRTY-SEVEN

Skallagrim stood upon the topmost turret of Fort Vigilance and waited upon the sunrise. He hoped—though acknowledging to himself that it was a fool's hope—that there might be a sign, some indication that all he had been through might mean something.

The air was chill but calm. Dawn was at least two hours away, and the silver disc of the moon rode high in the sky, unwilling to yield up the heavens. Like Skallagrim, it seemed a lonely thing—for it rode the firmament in solitude, its light drowning even the brightest of stars. Mist rose from the river to swirl about the tower upon an imperceptible current. Even the Dead City of Orabas was blanketed by clouds, the ancient blackness that oozed from its flooded ruins held in check.

To the silent sentinel—weary and burdened—it seemed as if he was standing upon the quarterdeck of a warship, sailing to an unknown shore on a sea of unending white. Would that he might drown his sorrows in it.

Terminus was sheathed at his side, quiet and unmoving, while his staff leaned upon the battlement. In his right hand, he held *The Droning Book of the Sunrise*. It was very ancient, so he had used great care when thumbing through it in the fort's moldy library. Much of it had seemed incomprehensible, but then Skallagrim was too fatigued to dig deeply. *Another day.* He placed it back inside a leather satchel he had acquired in his search, along with other books he had been drawn to—books that might shed light on the horror of Andorath and, hopefully, his current predicament.

Beside the satchel lay a small chest filled with gold coins. Next to that a bag of silver coins and several small rubies. Wherever he landed, wherever his road took him next, this small trove would help.

"I stole the rubies but lost the diamond," he lamented to the moon. The moon, steadfast and cratered with flaws like himself, looked on and said nothing in return.

He hung his head in deep thought. *The girl.* He had searched, but she was not to be found. Of course, he could search more, but he knew the truth of it. She was not there. *Why did I put myself through all of this?* Because there had been no other choice. At least now he had a clue; the ethereal light that was sent north. Not much, but it was something—a place to start.

Even in his dream, the girl had appeared translucent, sunbeams seeming to shine through her. A latent memory? Surely. His heart ached at the remembrance, but he wrapped himself in the hurt as if it were a blanket. It was easy enough to believe her to be a creature of light, as transcendent as that rare sort of sunshine that unexpectedly breaks through a storm-wracked sky.

The words of the old man from his dream replayed in his mind. *"There's no way to the glorious morn lest we first suffer the horrors of night."* Well, the night was passing at last, and with it, hopefully, the horror.

He would not miss this sunrise for the world. It had to mean something—to have made it through the long, deep dark of the forest, of Orabas, of the stygian dungeons and chambers of the fort— to welcome the coming of the sun and the banishing of shadows. If the jewel of the dawn, the shield of the heavens, could somehow light this world—this terrible world—then perhaps it could even chase away the shadows of his heart.

Skallagrim stared south as if the mere thought of the sun would launch it skyward. There was still time. Soon, he would leave Fort Vigilance, find his friends, and tell them of his intentions to journey north. But he had promised himself this much—to wait upon the dawn at the tower top. The search would continue no matter what they thought of it.

They knew where he was—Erling and Hartbert. He had shouted down to them hours ago, his voice echoing off the surrounding ridges. Hartbert had immediately called back, asking about the girl. Erling had urged him to come down right away. He wanted to know everything that had happened and probably wanted to enter the fort for his promised "look inside." Erling wanted the sorcerer dead, and that had come to pass. Now he wanted in.

But Skallagrim had put them both off, telling them only what was necessary—the girl was not there; the sorcerer and Straker were dead. He assured them he would come out shortly after sunrise and left it at that. What use was it yelling back and forth all night anyway? They would know everything—or most of it—soon enough.

After Straker's plunge, Skallagrim had climbed the trapdoor ladder, pulled it through behind him, and sealed off the oubliette with debris from the vault. The liches would not gain entry to the fort, and the dead thing in the pit remained chained. He could search the rest of the fort in relative peace, though even his heart—once convinced of the girl's nearness—knew she would not be found.

He had bandaged the fresh sword cut to his leg, then raced to the topmost room of the tower, where he was to be sacrificed to Balor, the Knight of The North. Sure enough, there was a primitive, bloodstained altar but no girl. The room reeked of incense, but other odors asserted themselves, suspicious and cloying. Arcane symbols and drawings were scrawled in charcoal upon the floor and walls, many suggesting rites both blasphemous and revolting. One narrow window looked south and another north. A stone staircase led up to the battlement. Some fresh air would be nice, but Skallagrim would save that for later.

He found a shrine upon a table behind the altar, upon which stood a basalt statue of a knight, its face cracked and leering, its eye sockets set with black onyx gemstones. The thing was nearly three feet tall and heavy, but he heaved it off the table, and it crashed to the floor, breaking into myriad pieces. The gemstones came loose from the crumbling face to spin enticingly at Skallagrim's feet, but he left them where they lay.

Too much insanity revolved around this Balor—renamed Mog

Ruith by a supposed wicked king who ruled far to the south. Too much sorcery and too many plots. Skallagrim had been caught up in it, and so had the girl. Maybe Erling was right to wage war upon all sorcerers if their endgame was to resurrect a dead knight who required the blood of innocents. How many young lives had been sacrificed last night in Andorath? In years past, how many had died in this very room, wounded, drugged, and terrified?

He had fled the room, pale and disgusted. *Let the sorcerers have Andorath. Let them go mad trying to raise a dead knight.* He cared not. Erling could wage a crusade against them if he wanted. Skallagrim just wanted to touch the golden curls and stare into the blue eyes once more. He wanted the girl safe at his side. Then maybe the two of them could figure the rest out together, undoing the damage done to them both. Maybe they could find their way back to wherever they had come from—back to safety and an end to terror. Maybe.

He halfheartedly searched several rooms throughout the fort. It seemed Forneus had not made much use of the place, though one bedroom had clearly been occupied. In it, Skallagrim found articles of clothing, all of which were flamboyant and garish. Most of it was black, embroidered with red and gold thread that outlined threatening symbols of dark sorcery. It looked more like the garb of an actor playing the role of a wizard than it did the genuine article.

He had found the small trove of coins and rubies there as well. There had to be more loot hidden in the fort, some of it hoarded by the knights of old. For now though he had enough. He had smiled upon the tiny pile of treasure, allowing himself to feel rich for a moment. For a twenty-two-year-old with rags for clothes and nowhere to call home, it was a small fortune.

It took another hour to fling open all the doors, search the guard room, and loot the pantry. He had no wish to endure a protracted search, for he knew she was not there. Of paramount importance to Skallagrim was to leave Fort Vigilance and prevail upon Erling and Hartbert to take him somewhere where he could rest and heal. Not back to Archon for certain! Somewhere north. Maybe he would return one day and search the fort thoroughly, root out its horrors and its secrets, follow every dungeon corridor, and map out every last passage. Or maybe he would just come back one day with help and tear the whole place down to its foundations. *One day.*

He stood tall upon the battlement, looking south as his thoughts turned to Archon, the Dreaming City. Skallagrim was master of one fort, one tower of madness. In Archon, a hundred such towers stood, each one brimming with evil. *What of it?* He would never return there, not unless his search for the girl led him back.

There was a dead thing in the terrible city, down deep in a pit. And just like that insidious demon that sulked somewhere below him now, it ate minds. That much he could remember.

Maybe it was beneath the Spire of Griog'xa. Had he been so foolish as to go there? Was that what started all of this? So many questions, but one thing was certain. He had seen something forbidden there—learned things he was not meant to know—and had paid for it with the loss of his memory.

Of course, he remembered all that came after the horrid cut to his face. He had committed it all to memory, every word spoken. Something the ghastly witch Tuva had first said to him resurfaced like a drowned corpse, floating back to the surface of an otherwise idyllic lake.

"Old Tuva is a coming fer ye, again!" she had shrieked. There it was, that one vital word: "again." She had seen Skallagrim before. Had she done something to him then? She was, after all, Griog'xa's sister. Erling might not know that, but Skallagrim did. Swanhild had admitted it to him.

The more he dwelled on it, the more he came to believe that it was indeed in the abode of Archon's dreaded sorcerer where all his troubles had begun. It had to be. If so, he must one day kill Griog'xa to end the spell put upon his mind.

One day.

Just four nights ago, he had stood within sight of Archon and had cursed it, promising to return one day and cut the evil out of its heart. His need for vengeance had waned since then. *No, it's vanished completely.* But if he trekked north and still could not find the girl or any clue of her, then his return to Archon and a confrontation with its chief necromancer was inevitable. It might be anyway. Then need would trump the thirst for revenge, should it resurface. He would not even have to fool himself with notions of justice—not with need guiding his sword hand.

He could feel that hand trembling again, that bloody right hand by which so many had been slain. He clenched it tight to make it stop, but the tremor reached his right shoulder in the form of a single, unintentional twitch. Not a painful one but troubling nonetheless.

He rested his other hand upon the hilt of Terminus, and it responded with a knowing tremor of its own. He relaxed, letting it speak to him in its weird way. It came first in the form of sound traveling to his ears as if from a long distance.

Drums of war! Trumpets blaring! The defiant screams of a forlorn hope as they threw themselves at the wall's breach and the sad, demented choirs of the wailing wounded trampled beneath their feet!

Unafraid, Skallagrim closed his eyes, allowing the sword to bring forth another vision of war.

An invading army from the north was marching down the Devil's Race Highway to lay siege to Archon. Of course, they were using the highway, for it was the only viable approach to the plateau with siege craft, cavalry, and columns of infantry. And of course, Archon had sent out its regiments to meet them before the city gates, throwing all its available force at the one visible foe. The northern force's assault would end in disaster, as had every other attempt to take the city through long ages of battle and bloodshed.

Except that this time a new general had taken to the field, but he was not marching at the head of the northern force. Instead, he stood exactly where Skallagrim stood now—upon the tower of Fort Vigilance, the forgotten key to Archon. And like Skallagrim, he was staring south—south at the open wilderness road, the road no sane man would take. The same road Skallagrim had conquered.

The general raised his sword high in the air and then brought it down decisively, a signal to his captains to begin their covert march through forty miles of bogs and ghoul-haunted forest. Infantry only and only one regiment. One thousand men. They would make for the village of Dead Corn, arriving in the pre-dawn hours two days later. Then on to the secret smugglers' tunnel, which would take them beyond the walls of Archon and into the city's midst.

The general turned to head down the stairs where he would join his men. Skallagrim saw a terrible scar zigzagging across his left cheek, and the sword he carried was Terminus!

Skallagrim was jolted and released his grip upon the sentient blade. "What nonsense!" he said and then laughed. "You would get me into a world of trouble if I let you have your way." He looked upon the beautiful sword that hung at his side. "I should throw you into the river and walk away," he scolded and then instantly regretted it. He would never abandon the sword. He had tried to let it go once in Archon, and it had stuck to his hand like glue. He only had himself to blame. It was he who had reached up and grabbed Terminus from the air. But then again, it was that or die.

Doom and destiny. He was tied to Terminus for life, or at least until whoever had sent it to him asked for it back.

"I'm sorry," he whispered. "I owe you a lot."

He had to admit, his journey from Archon up the wilderness road, his taking of the fort and its keys—it might just have greater implications than he had imagined. *Whatever!* He was no general. Just a thief, wounded and tired. A heartsick lover who longed for an angel gone missing.

"One day," a fair voice whispered into his head, like the whisper of steel drawn from a scabbard.

"If you say so," he replied.

He turned his face from the sword and resumed his watch upon the south, barely suppressing a yawn. Should he sleep for a while? He did not want to miss the sunrise, but he could wake himself in plenty of time. *Maybe.* Who was he kidding? If he laid down and closed his eyes, he might well sleep for a month, and there was still much to think through.

So, Erling had been used and misled. He had been right about many things but wrong about so many others. The girl had not been in the fort, though, of course, the sorcerer had been. Forneus was not in complete control of the Enlightened of Balor, the cult of madmen who, along with the Watch of Archon, had been used to thwart the sorcerer's plans.

Somehow both Forneus and Griog'xa knew that Terminus would fall from the clouds and into Skallagrim's hands. But Griog'xa wanted it to happen, whereas Forneus feared the event—and rightly so. Terminus had meant the death of him.

Erling did not know or had not admitted that Skallagrim's memory loss was due to sorcery—not a wound and not mental trauma. He had also misjudged the situation at Orabas, mocking the idea that the Old Man o' the River might well be hiding there.

Of course, there were many things Erling had done right and had rightly guessed. He had kept Skallagrim alive, and for that Skallagrim must be thankful. He knew about the back door into Fort Vigilance and that Forneus was mad. He had bravely fought the sellswords in the moonlit melee near the walls of Archon. There was also a burgeoning friendship between Skallagrim and Hartbert that would not have happened without Erling.

He shrugged. Who could he turn to in all of Andorath but Erling Hizzard? Resigned, he committed himself to a continued alliance with the smuggler and "connoisseur of abominations."

Skallagrim laughed grimly. Once not long ago, he had considered throwing himself from that very tower, convinced he was a monster, undeserving of love, a failure. Now he only wanted to stand there and watch the sunrise. He would never kill himself. For one, that was not his right. For another, there was so much to do. His quest had only begun.

Suicide! How had he even considered such a thing? That had been what, one day ago? Or was it two? The days and nights had blended like the mud, silt, and slush that filled the flooded streets of Orabas. As far as Skallagrim was concerned, the entire affair since the fight in Rum Alley had been one long, unending, torturous night. And it was not over.

He looked over the side of the battlement and imagined himself plummeting from such a height into the swirling mist. How long before he hit the rocks at the base? Three seconds? Four? Would that not be easier than to face the interminable fight that lay ahead of him?

A sick oppression began to sap his strength, a feeling of darkness and death. Finality. An end to suffering and pain. The peace of oblivion, of unending sleep and rest. Like a whisper on the wind, morbid thoughts began to crowd his mind like mourners gathering beside a grave.

He shook his head to break himself free of the gloom. Were these his thoughts or those of the insidious creature in the pit far below?

His wounds were aching again as the effects of the Caeruleum wore off. The pain was the only thing keeping him awake. At least the coughing fits had not returned. He leaned heavily upon the battlement to steady himself, for he could barely keep his eyes open.

Would the coming of dawn bring meaning, at least to that part of Skallagrim's heart where poetry and song had found a haven? Maybe it would be enough to just watch the sunrise, to see the end of this terrible night.

Curious. Just two mornings ago, the sun had risen as an ally, turning the tide in the battle with Vathek and his ghouls. But the price of that had been the revealing of his own reflection in the sunlit blade of Terminus. Skallagrim had thought himself a monster then, no different than his foe. But he had learned better since. Despite the sun's transgression—perhaps only a trick played upon him by his weary mind—he welcomed its return.

The pre-dawn air was crisp, but it was not enough to keep his eyes from closing. He had defeated hired swords, ghouls, a monster, a demon, a sorcerer, and an assassin. But he would not win the battle to stay awake—not a minute longer.

"A quick nap. One hour," he proclaimed, setting his internal clock. "One hour," he repeated as he slumped down, placing his back against the wall and closing his eyes, surrendering to exhaustion. "One hour," he murmured as sleep took hold.

CHAPTER THIRTY-EIGHT

*S*kallagrim raced north, coming at last to a wall of white, a barrier of mist and cloud, just in time to see the beautiful girl pass within. But to enter the mist was forbidden. One could never return, never find home again. Not unless . . .

But to leave her to her fate was unthinkable, for she was more precious to him than gold, silver, or all the fair jewels of the earth. He took a deep breath and followed her in.

A sudden booming noise struck his ears, as if a door of unimaginable size had been slammed behind him. The storm calmed, the wind ceased, and the ominous music that had rippled the air was no more.

There she was, just ahead—his faerie princess, his garden nymph— robed in the whiteness of the Void, so beautiful, her loveliness might only be described in a song. The mist glistened in her golden locks like diamond dust, and her eyes were as bright as stars. She smiled upon him with such radiance that it filled him with desire and wonder, dimming his mind to danger. He gazed upon her like one bespelled, but a hot fire awoke within him, and he shook himself loose of her magic.

Racing to her side, he took her by the hand. "We cannot be here."

"And we cannot return," she answered. "But we can be together."

Because he was young, he imagined he could still undo the damage. "We should go back," Skallagrim urged. His mind could not grasp the unavoidable consequence of his actions—their actions. It had only been a moment ago. It could still be undone!

Clutching her hand, he turned and prepared to flee with her back the way they had come. To his dismay, there was only a crushing wall of black—no barrier of white, just black. The unforgiving black of regret, the unfathomable darkness of what might have been. There would be no escaping this. An immutable law had been broken.

The maiden saw the fear in his eyes, and now she too felt the weight of her transgression. "We can only go forward."

"I have heard of a city," he said, "where we might find help."

"Just never leave me, and I will go where you lead."

They turned back toward the misty white of the Void and, holding hands, walked into it, allowing it to swallow them.

The ocean had calmed as the violence of the storm raced farther down the coast. Skallagrim stood a little way into the surf, allowing the incoming waves to splash about his knees while the receding water slowly buried his feet in the wet sand. It felt good. And though his heart was burdened, he was glad his dream had brought him back to this place of paradisiac beauty.

In his peripheral vision, he was dimly aware of the lover's heart drawn in the sand just off to his right—the true love's name etched within. Like him, it had survived the tempest.

The pleasant sounds of playing children came to his ears from just over the dunes, as sweet as music. Pelicans were cruising the skies once more, some breaking formation to dive into the water as their keen eyes caught the silver gleam of scales just beneath the surface.

The morning sun had broken free in the east again, and the air was heating fast. Funny. In Andorath, dawn broke to the south, but not here. Skallagrim could feel the warmth of it, but he looked away, choosing to face the receding storm, his eyes locked upon black curtains of rain that beat upon the distant sea to the south. In their midst a waterspout emerged like a writhing snake, churning the water in a tumultuous path. As turbulent as the life of one devoted to sorcery, he reminded himself, a disruptive, pointless existence.

He tried to look away but could only think of how terrible it would be to face the storm's wrath in a ship. And so he watched, wondering if he might see a stray vessel floundering in the waves.

"He wearies of peace, the man who loves the storm." The voice of the wizened man came to his right, just near the sandy heart.

"I don't love it, but it's magnificent to behold. I much prefer the calm," Skallagrim replied. He turned to face the old man, letting the sun warm *his back.*

The old man's hair was as white as the sand, and his white robes billowed in the sunshine. He watched Skallagrim with ageless eyes that sparkled like blue sapphires, full of power and wonder. "Do you still wish to freeze the moment?"

The question pierced Skallagrim's heart with an arrow of guilt. "No." He hung his head, not daring to meet the old man's gaze. "Not yet. I haven't found her. I've failed."

"Failed? That's not true, and I think you know it."

"Well, I don't have her. I don't know where she is or if she's safe." Skallagrim winced at the thought. "No, I know she isn't safe. Not safe at all."

"Then you must find her," the old man said sternly. "And unless you have given up, you have not failed."

Skallagrim shook his head as he walked from the surf to stand close to the man. "I'll never give up—" He hesitated, then added in a quiet voice that was full of pain and worry, "though the ages roll by."

"And they will, Skallagrim, they will."

"I know." Skallagrim felt tears forming at the corners of his eyes and feared he would choke as he spoke next. But he raised his head, daring a glance at the glorious figure who stood before him on the beach. "I just have so little to go on."

"What are you?"

Skallagrim was taken aback by the strangeness of the question but hazarded an answer. "They say I'm a thief."

"Some folk say I am a wicked king, but that does not make it so. So, I ask again, what are you?"

"But I have stolen, and more than once." Skallagrim's brow furrowed at the admission.

The old man was undeterred. "So, that is it? Those acts define you?"

"No!"

"Then what are you?"

"I don't know how to answer!"

"Try!" The old man said forcefully, though he placed a kind hand upon Skallagrim's shoulder.

A brisk breeze, warm and full of the scent of the ocean, began to blow, pushing gently at Skallagrim's back while rippling the serried ranks of sea oats lining the dunes. Palm trees towered just beyond, their fronds blowing gracefully in response.

"Try."

Skallagrim took a deep breath. "I'm a man with a purpose—and a sword!"

"There it is! Simply stated." The old man stroked Skallagrim's hair in a fatherly manner, brushing it from his eyes where it was always wont to stray. "And now that you have said it, never again forget what you are!"

"And the sword? What is it?" Skallagrim's voice grew tense, fearing an end to the dream and needing so much more from it before it did.

The old man laughed. "We have already established that! It is hope. But I will add that it is hope found in the midst of despair. It is hope with an edge!"

"It fell from the storm. It came to me. How?"

"I threw it high in the air!" The old man pointed toward the northern horizon. "It sped like a comet above and beyond the wall of mist. Then it hung in the sky and waited on you." He looked back at Skallagrim, his eyes full of tenderness. "There is no greater weapon I can give to you. Hope with an edge!"

"Terminus!"

"Yes, Terminus. A final point in time and space. It will stay with you till the end."

Skallagrim absorbed every word, storing it in the vault of his mind, but he plowed on with his questions.

"Till the breaking of the world?" Skallagrim repeated the words he had heard before, though he did not understand their meaning.

"Yes, until then."

"I have heard its voice. It said it was an angel of wrath. What does it mean?"

"You will learn in time."

Suddenly, the old man was standing several yards away. The air was turning golden—all haze, mystery, and sunshine. It was as if the old man was standing upon the last refrain of a wondrous song that was fading away, its melody at once unforgettable and unknowable.

"You can tell me no more?" Skallagrim, his voice edged with frustration, looked back to the sea. Wave after wave turned silver and bright, rolling toward him like the years of a glorious age. The dream was fading. He looked back to see the old man already farther back upon the gleaming sand, already halfway to the dunes.

"Thus far I have only told you what you already know." Despite the distance between them, the wizened man did not need to shout to be heard. His voice was as close as a whisper. "You just forgot it."

Though he guessed at the answer, Skallagrim voiced the question. "Then this is all a dream?"

"It is time for you to go, Skallagrim. You have a long road ahead of you. There will be trials and sorrows aplenty, but I think you will manage to find joy in the midst of them."

"But she's real! The girl is real! You can tell me that, right? I don't even know her name."

"Of course she is real! You know that! Just remember, there is nothing lost that cannot be found if sought."

"Who is she?"

"You can read, can you not?" The vision of the old man was fading. Everything was gold—bright gold and glorious sunshine. "Now go forth and find my daughter!"

With that he was gone, leaving Skallagrim standing alone upon the shore. Taking one last look at the sea, knowing he might never behold it again, knowing he might never feel its peace again, he turned his back upon it. With tears welling in his eyes and lonely thoughts wandering through his mind, he headed toward the dunes. He stopped only to look down at his feet, down at the sand, down at the heart drawn there and the lover's name written within.

"LIRAZEL"

"Lirazel!" Skallagrim woke, his eyes suddenly aware of the brightening sky. He stood and peered over the battlement at the rising of the glorious, triumphant sun. "Lirazel!" He knew her name! That creature of heartbreak and light, that living song with eyes of blue and hair of gold. Their past was hidden from him, but her name no longer! "Lirazel!"

A rare day had dawned, for the sun came not as a weak and dismal light that cowered and quailed, unable to pierce the defiant darkness of the Dead City. Nor did it come as a blot of red blood over a cursed land, just another horrid fixture of Andorath's undying torment. It came as a wheel of fire—golden, powerful, and mighty. It came as a sudden, joyous revelation. A realization! A remembrance! For once it came as it should.

"Lirazel!"

It came like a spell-breaker, lighting the darkest corner of his ensorcelled mind, feeding it hope, granting it a name—a name that had been lost but was lost no more.

With the swift sunrise came a sound, faint at first, then swelling as if a thousand, thousand trumpets were joining to create one rapturous clarion call. A drumming throbbed the air as if giants were beating upon the tympani of heaven. It roared out over the mountains and marshes, stirring the limbs of trees long haunted and waters savage and deep, then filled the Vales with echoing thunder, shaking the long, dark night from the tenebrous void of Orabas.

The golden glory of the mountaintops and the joy of poets long dead—the sun was rising upon a choir of brass, a symphony made of one chord, sublime and full of majesty.

Though many heard it—those of Andorath who had kept watch over their hearts—they did not hear what Skallagrim, alone, heard next. For over it all, to his ears came a great shout from afar, as if an archangel had given voice to a word of command. Now the night was banished, and with it all the shadows were scattered. Then, to his utter amazement, the voice began to sing, joining in with the symphony of brass. One solitary note did it wield, this full-voiced herald of daybreak. And so the sound grew to a great crescendo, filling Skallagrim's heart with wonder and visions.

As if bidden by the unknown singer, Skallagrim drew Terminus from its sheath and held it aloft, letting the golden light fire the sentient blade even as the tremendous sound set the sword to quivering in its own response.

Then Skallagrim's voice rose over the fleeing mists to join with that cherubic herald, giving voice to words from a song half-remembered.

> *Awake at last from winter's deathly sleep*
> *Roused by horns and drumming deep*
> *My king, he sang to usher in the spring*
> *And such my joy to hear my sovereign sing!*
> *I've heard the sound*
> *Of one enthroned and crowned*
> *That song of songs still echoes in my heart!*

He perceived then the beauty of a distant world, a world beyond the curse, beyond the misty veil, and for now, beyond his reach. He perceived and remembered much—not all but enough.

He knew his heart belonged in the south, in that land of swift sunrises and golden haze, of enchanted forests where perpetual twilight held no terror, of sun-drenched beaches where children played free, and lovers drew hearts in the sand. And in the midst of that realm was a fair garden, born of a song, wrought by the deep, deep spells of faerie—where it was always morning.

But he also knew, for now, he was cut off from that realm by his own doing and that his path lay north. If he were ever to journey south, to somehow find his way back to that enchanted realm, first, he must go north. He must find her. He must find his Lirazel.

The triumphant sound was fading in his ears. Perhaps, Skallagrim hoped, it had been heard even by that gentle soul of gossamer and light, she who, though not yet born, had stolen a thief's heart. If so, she would find courage, his garden nymph with eyes of dazzling blue and hair of golden curls. She would know he was coming. Lirazel!

The voice and the sound were gone, the spell broken. Once more, the sun was just a sun, and the morning—though brighter than most in this fell place—was just morning. The aches and pains of wounds—of life—resumed their merciless siege upon Skallagrim's body and mind. The joy, the glimmer of hope, that brief glimpse of a glorious realm—whatever it was—spilled from his heart like sweet, golden honey from a broken pot. Something indescribable had just happened to him, but his smile sagged, and his shoulders slumped.

He needed to get off the tower and out of that place, find somewhere to rest and heal, to plan his next move.

Hearing again the river that ran savage and strong down below, Skallagrim glanced over the parapet. He saw Erling near the bridge, tending a blaze to ward off the morning chill while Hartbert stood transfixed, watching the southern sky. Maybe he had heard what Skallagrim had—the trumps of glory, if that is what they were.

It was time to head down, face his friends, and begin the next part of his journey. Sheathing Terminus, he gathered his treasures, grabbed his staff, and bid farewell to Fort Vigilance.

EPILOGUE

"What's this?" Erling shouted as he drew his sword, causing several sturdy horses tethered nearby to stamp nervously.

"Balor's bones, Mister Erling! It's our Skallagrim!"

"Good morning." If Skallagrim had looked bad at their parting, he looked far worse now. He was covered with the filth of his journey, fresh wounds, and the foul blood and gore of the undulate, Pagarna. His clothes were but shredded rags, and he walked with a limp.

Erling sighed, then relaxed and let his sword slip back into its scabbard. "Dear me," he said, laughing. "You look as if you crawled from the grave!"

Hartbert frowned, then stuck out a meaty hand to shake Skallagrim's. "You're alive, and that's all that matters! We sure were worried about you, weren't we, Mister Hizzard?"

Erling stepped forward and made a move to slap Skallagrim on the back, thought better of it, and settled for patting him gently on one shoulder. "That big ogre fretted the entire time. Thought I'd never hear the end of it! I knew you'd get through, though. I'd not have sent you otherwise."

"It was—" Skallagrim stopped himself, unsure of how to finish his thought. "Well, it was epic. But not in a good way." His smile, when it came, was forced. "Still, I'm glad you're both okay."

"We're fine, Mister Skallagrim," Hartbert said. "Got rid of a couple of guards for you. That's about it."

"My giant friend forgets that I—" Erling performed a mock bow. "Rid you of an army of horsemen!"

Hartbert grunted. "One hundred horsemen, Mister Hizzard. Hardly an army!"

"Still." Erling winked at the haggard thief. "A grand gesture on my part, if I must say so myself!"

"Admittedly," Skallagrim confessed. "And I thank you very much. I'll want to hear all about it."

"And we want to hear about your every move, my friend. Each worthy foe, each monster faced, each trial met with courage and overcome!" Erling motioned for Skallagrim and Hartbert to follow him toward the fort. "We should head in. Get out of this chill and hear all about it!"

"Wait," Skallagrim bid him. "Not yet." Sweat was beading on his brow as a wave of exhaustion pressed down upon him. He waited till it passed, started to say more, but was interrupted by Hartbert.

"The girl? What news of her? Any clue? Anything?"

"I know her name."

Hartbert grinned from ear to ear, clearly overjoyed.

Erling, however, was aghast. "Her name? Impossible! Forneus could not have—" He stopped himself from saying more. His eyes narrowed, then twitched nervously. "It's just that—"

"Forneus didn't tell me her name. I remembered it."

"Well, that's something, isn't it, Mister Hizzard?" Hartbert gave Erling a nod, willing him to show some enthusiasm for Skallagrim's minor yet meaningful victory.

Erling caught the hint and made a half-hearted effort to correct his awkwardness. "Excellent news, dear boy! I'll lay odds you learned even more. Am I correct?"

"Yes, much more. I don't have much to go on, but I won't be giving up." Skallagrim leaned heavily on his staff and nodded toward the horses. "These belong to the guards?"

"All but two," Hartbert answered, noticing the staff for the first time. There was something familiar about it, but he put it out of his mind. "You take one, of course, and the rest will fetch a pretty penny." He frowned. "But there was no wagon."

"No, well, actually, there was a wagon. But it would have gone north." Skallagrim paused. "No sign of it on the road, I suppose?"

Hartbert shook his head and frowned. "There were many wagons on the road—too many. I shouldn't have bragged about my tracking skills!"

"There's war brewing in the north," Erling added. "Not long after we parted ways, the highway became jammed with cavalry, infantry, and the supply train, of course. Hartbert is not to blame."

"Of course not," Skallagrim said. "Listen—Erling, Hartbert—I need you to do something for me."

Erling fidgeted nervously but nodded, "Certainly. Just name it."

Skallagrim took a deep breath. "That town you mentioned the night we left Archon, Stiff Knee Gap—about fifty miles from here, right?"

Erling nodded. "Yes, I mentioned the tavern—the Down And Out."

Skallagrim swayed on his feet but quickly steadied himself. "You said the folk there owed you favors, right?"

"Indeed," Erling replied, smoothing out his long ponytail. "As a matter of fact, I intend to take you there after our business here is settled. It will be a good place for you to recuperate. You know, rest up, gather your thoughts, get those stitches out after a couple of weeks."

"Do you need to sit down a bit, Mister Skallagrim?" Hartbert eyed the thief with growing concern. "You look a might peaked."

Skallagrim waved away Hartbert's concern and directed his attention back to Erling. "Stiff Knee Gap. You can get me there, no problems? What about the soldiers?"

"We'll just scoot across the Devil's Race in the dark," Hartbert blurted. "If need be, we'll tie your hands till we cross; tell them you're our prisoner."

"We have thought it through, Skallagrim," Erling interjected. "And let's just say that Stiff Knee Gap is the sort of town the authorities—and soldiers, for that matter—will steer clear of."

"I see," Skallagrim answered uneasily. Wiping the sweat from his brow, he scrutinized Erling. "But we'll be safe there?"

"Completely, dear boy!"

"And Mister Skallagrim," Hartbert said, smiling, "they've got an inn there called the Winking Pig! Best damned smoked pork and brisket between here and Ophyr!" He inhaled deeply as if he was picking up the scent of the inn's smokehouse from where he stood. "The rooms aren't half bad either!"

Erling was growing impatient. "As I said, as soon as we're done at the fort—say in a week or so—we shall head straight there."

"Well, that's the thing, Erling." Any remnant of the blue potion seemed to have drained from Skallagrim, and his face tightened with pain. Still, he stood straight and locked eyes with Erling. "Our business at the fort is done, at least for now."

"What do you mean?" Erling's jaw clenched. "You got the keys, right? Surely you didn't just close that door and walk away without the keys. If so, we'll never get in. This will all have been pointless!"

Skallagrim pulled back his ragged cape to reveal the metal keyring that hung there. "The keys are safe. But as I said, we're done here. We're leaving now."

Erling's mouth fell open. "But you promised!"

"And I'll keep my promise," Skallagrim replied. "In my own time." He glared at the smuggler while reminding himself of the man's crusade and his unhealthy fixation on matters of the occult. "And never suggest to me again that this was for nothing."

Adamant, Erling stamped his foot. "You need to think this through, boy!" He jabbed a finger toward Skallagrim. "You seem to forget the nature of our relationship! You work for me, and we had a deal!"

Hartbert shifted nervously on his feet, unsure whether he should intervene. But Skallagrim shot him a ferocious look that stunned him, and he took a step back. Skallagrim returned his gaze to Erling. "We're friends. That's what you said. Friends. And I'll keep my promise. Maybe in a month or so, we'll make our way back here, and you can have at this place for a week if you want. But I'm going to tell you something, both of you." He paused to make sure he had their attention. "Are you listening?"

"Of course we are, Mister Skallagrim," Hartbert replied apprehensively.

Erling was seething, but he nodded for Skallagrim to proceed.

There was something different about the thief. He was not the same scared boy from the alley fight. Twenty-two years old maybe, but his eyes radiated fierce confidence—demanded attention. He would not be backing down.

"There's nothing in that place that's going to help anybody, Erling."

Erling looked away from Skallagrim and shook his head. "You simply don't understand what's at stake."

"Oh, I think I do. Now let me finish."

Erling sighed and nodded.

"Hartbert, if you want to protect your employer, you'd do well to talk him out of ever going in there."

The giant shuffled his feet and said nothing, unsure of his place in the exchange.

"I care about you both," Skallagrim continued. "To spend any time in the fort is to invite the same madness that befell the sorcerer. I'll tell you more after I've had time to think it all through."

He pushed the brown locks away from his eyes, wincing as his hand brushed the painful wound on his cheek. "You have no idea what I've just been through. I'm tired and sick. It's been a living hell!" He pulled up the shredded remains of his tunic to reveal a dark bruise on his left side. "Hell, I'm pretty sure I've broken a rib." As Erling and Hartbert grimaced at the sight, he let his tunic fall back into place. "My lungs are filled with poison, and I'm more cut up than the last time you saw me. I'm likely to die of infection if you can't get me some help." He swayed on his feet. "The Caeruleum—I've used it all."

Erling looked him up and down. "Living hell, you say?"

"That pretty much sums it up."

Cowed, his two friends nodded. "I suppose it does," Erling admitted. "And, of course, we're friends. I should not have suggested otherwise."

"And?"

"And this adventure of yours was not for nothing. I just, well—never mind. I should not have said it."

"Right! You shouldn't have said it. The world is rid of Forneus Druogorim and minus a few ghouls." Skallagrim pointed vaguely downriver. "The stories about the Old Man o' the River have been settled once and for all—they're true! It's wounded badly. That was no small feat, I can tell you."

"I'm sure it wasn't," Hartbert said. "We heard the racket all the way back here!"

"And most importantly, I have a few clues about the girl. That is why I came here, after all." Skallagrim walked wearily toward the horses, waving for his companions to follow him. "It's going to take time to find her—far more than I would have ever thought."

He turned to see Erling and Hartbert standing stock still, crestfallen. "It's alright. Come on now. We're going to this Stiff Knee Gap of yours and have some barbecue. I'm going to get a bath and sleep for a week. After that, I'll tell you what's next."

Hartbert looked questioningly at his employer, who merely shook his head, resigned that his inspection of the fort would have to wait until Skallagrim was ready, or at least in a more approachable mood. "Let us do as he says, my enormous friend. It is what it is."

"Oh, and Erling?" Skallagrim said, turning back while fishing something out of a pocket on his baldric.

"Yes?"

"Here ya go!" Skallagrim tossed a shiny object through the air, which Erling snatched with a surprised look on his face. It was a jeweled ring—Erling's jeweled ring. "It must have slipped off your finger in the fight the other night. Thought you might want it back!" Smiling, he picked the best of the horses for his own and mounted up.

With several miles behind them, Hartbert slowed his horse to allow Skallagrim to catch up to him. The thief had mostly stayed in the back, silent and somber.

"Probably a dumb question, but how are you doing?"

"To tell the truth, I'm in a deep gloom. There was a moment this morning when I stood on the tower, and everything seemed to make sense. But now a sick feeling has settled over me." He rubbed his eyes with a grimy hand, for sleep seemed intent upon shutting him down—even while on horseback. An immitigable melancholy filled his heart like the ashes of a dying fire. "If I had to put a name to it, I'd say that death has gotten into me, like a knot in my gut." Skallagrim poked himself hard in the stomach to drive home the point. "And frankly, I'd rather give into it than face another day of this."

"Now, Skallagrim, you mustn't go on like this," Hartbert admonished him "She's out there somewhere, counting on you. Talk like that isn't going to help her."

"I know, I know," Skallagrim said glumly. An image of Lirazel flashed in his mind's eye, followed by a sledgehammer of guilt to his gut. There would be no giving in to anything, not with her life on the line. "It's just how I feel right now. I need a bath, some clean clothes, and—and sleep, that's what!"

"That you do." Hartbert took a deep puff on his pipe, then exhaled a satisfying cloud of fragrant smoke into the crisp morning air of the gorge. The sound of the Bald River rapids was constant to their right, wild yet somehow calming—reassuring.

"Ultimately, I won't give in to death, and I won't give up the search for the girl. Knowing that, knowing that after everything I went through, the hardship has only just begun, well, it's got me down."

"Of course it has. But you've got hope and a strong sword. That puts you ahead of most."

"But I have enemies too, Hartbert. I can't even say who they are, but this thing with my memory, it was done to me on purpose."

"I have no doubt of that."

"And I have no idea why she was taken from me or where to search for her."

"It's true. But you love her, right?"

"Oh, yes." Skallagrim smiled for perhaps the first time since he had sung on the hill over Orabas. His smile, so wide and so genuine, gave away everything to Hartbert. Skallagrim's love for the girl ran deep, and the sudden reminder of it—the acknowledgment of that love—caused even him to blush. He even managed to laugh.

"Yes, Hartbert. I haven't got it all figured out, not even a fraction of it. But the girl is as real as you or I, and I love her. Finding her is, well, it's everything."

"She's worth the trouble then?" Glad to see the flicker of joy in his friend's eyes, Hartbert gave Skallagrim a knowing wink.

"Yep! That and then some." Skallagrim rode through a wispy cloud of Hartbert's tobacco smoke. He waved it from his face but had to admit it smelled enticingly good.

"Mister Skallagrim," Hartbert said, growing serious again. "If I'm any judge of things, there's a long, dangerous road ahead of you. But I'll help you in any way I can. You'll meet others too. It may feel like you're alone, but I promise, you're not."

"That's good to know, and I thank you for saying it."

"Hope and a strong sword, Mister Skallagrim. Remember that."

Skallagrim grinned, considering his enormous friend. It was hard to remain pessimistic in his company. "And a large friend with yet another sword, right?"

"That too!"

Hartbert laughed, causing Erling to scowl disapprovingly over his shoulder at the pair. The smuggler remained in a foul mood, for Skallagrim was calling the shots now, a disagreeable reversal of fortunes and one to be tolerated only temporarily.

"What are you two going on about?"

"Just letting Skallagrim know that we aren't done looking for his girl. We'll continue to help him, right?"

"Assuredly," Erling grunted.

Skallagrim laughed to himself, amused by Erling's grouchiness. "Hartbert? Do you still have that extra pipe? And enough tobacco to share?"

"I sure do, Mister Skallagrim. But I thought you didn't smoke."

"Well, Hartbert, I'm starting today!"

A few minutes later, Skallagrim was puffing away, suppressing the occasional cough but enjoying himself nonetheless. "Hartbert?"

"Yes?"

"Just wondering," Skallagrim said quietly. He nodded toward Erling, who had ridden some way ahead. "How long have you been working for him?"

"Oh, off and on for about five years."

Skallagrim knew so little about his new friend and was compelled to learn more. "And before that?"

Hartbert's brow creased, and he let out a big sigh. "Well ..." He scratched at his beard and looked off at the hillside as if an answer could be found hiding somewhere in the trees. "To be honest, now that you mention it, I don't really remember."

"Nothing?" Skallagrim gave his friend a quizzical look.

"It's the oddest thing!" The giant stared straight ahead, clearly bewildered. After a moment he shook his head and stretched. "Well, I haven't slept much these last few days. I must be getting slap happy!" He laughed at himself and turned to Skallagrim. "How's the pipe?"

He remembers nothing? That's odd. Skallagrim—alarmed but not wishing to embarrass his friend with further questions—looked over and smiled. "Well enough. It'll take some getting used to." He took an awkward pull on his pipe and blew out a cloud of smoke. "Say, can you teach me how to blow smoke rings? I mean, when we get to where we're going?"

"Oh, yes, Mister Skallagrim." Hartbert laughed. "That and a lot besides!"

THE END OF BOOK ONE

ACKNOWLEDGEMENTS

Supporters:

Foe Breaker: David Murphy

Shield Shaker: Kevin Patterson, Boris Stalf, Todd Lewicki, Olivier Malvaut-Saintespes-Lapale, David W. Lang, Danny L. Blake, Arthur Ziemann Jr., and Jason Kai Petersen

Swordsman Of The Vales: Michael Benz, Hans Vought, Tracy C. Bailey, Rick Rosinski, Brad Birzer, Joseph Costa, Thaddeus Wert, Scott Blondin, Jason Limbaugh, Mike Rumpza, and James Hutcheson

And...

Kevin Miller (editing), Jason Limbaugh (Beta Reader), Brad Birzer (advance reviewer), Thaddeus Wert (advance reviewer), Brian Murphy (author of Flame and Crimson – A History Of Sword-And-Sorcery), Adrian Collins (Grimdark Magazine), Jason Carney (Whetstone Magazine), and Dieter Zimmerman (Goodman Games)

ABOUT THE AUTHOR

First off, he prefers "Steve" to "Stephen." Now that that's out of the way...

He's best known as the bassist and co-writer for the prog-rock group Glass Hammer. A professional musician for most of his life, he started at the age of twelve as a church pianist. Since then, he has traveled the US and a handful of other countries in various bands.

He has a million stories of life on the road as a musician throughout the 80s, most of them downright hilarious, some of them utterly shocking. "It was the best of times; it was the worst of times," he will tell you. Don't get him started.

Fortunately for him, in 1990, he had the good sense to marry the right girl, come home, settle down and start a business. Since then, he has busied himself in the production of numerous albums for songwriters, the recording of audiobooks, and in the day-to-day tasks required to operate a recording studio while maintaining the persona of prog-rock star, prolific songwriter, and lyricist. This last bit, he enjoys to the fullest.

In 2005 he penned the epic poem, The Lay Of Lirazel, which was published in 2014. For that effort he was honored with The Imperishable Flame Award by The North East Tolkien Society.

Steve makes his home in Chattanooga, Tennessee, with his wife Julie and son Jon-Michael.